Woodbourne Libr
Washington-Centerville P
Centerville, Ohio

W9-AFT-290

DISCARD

THE SIXTH GUN

BOOK 7: NOT THE BULLET, BUT THE FALL

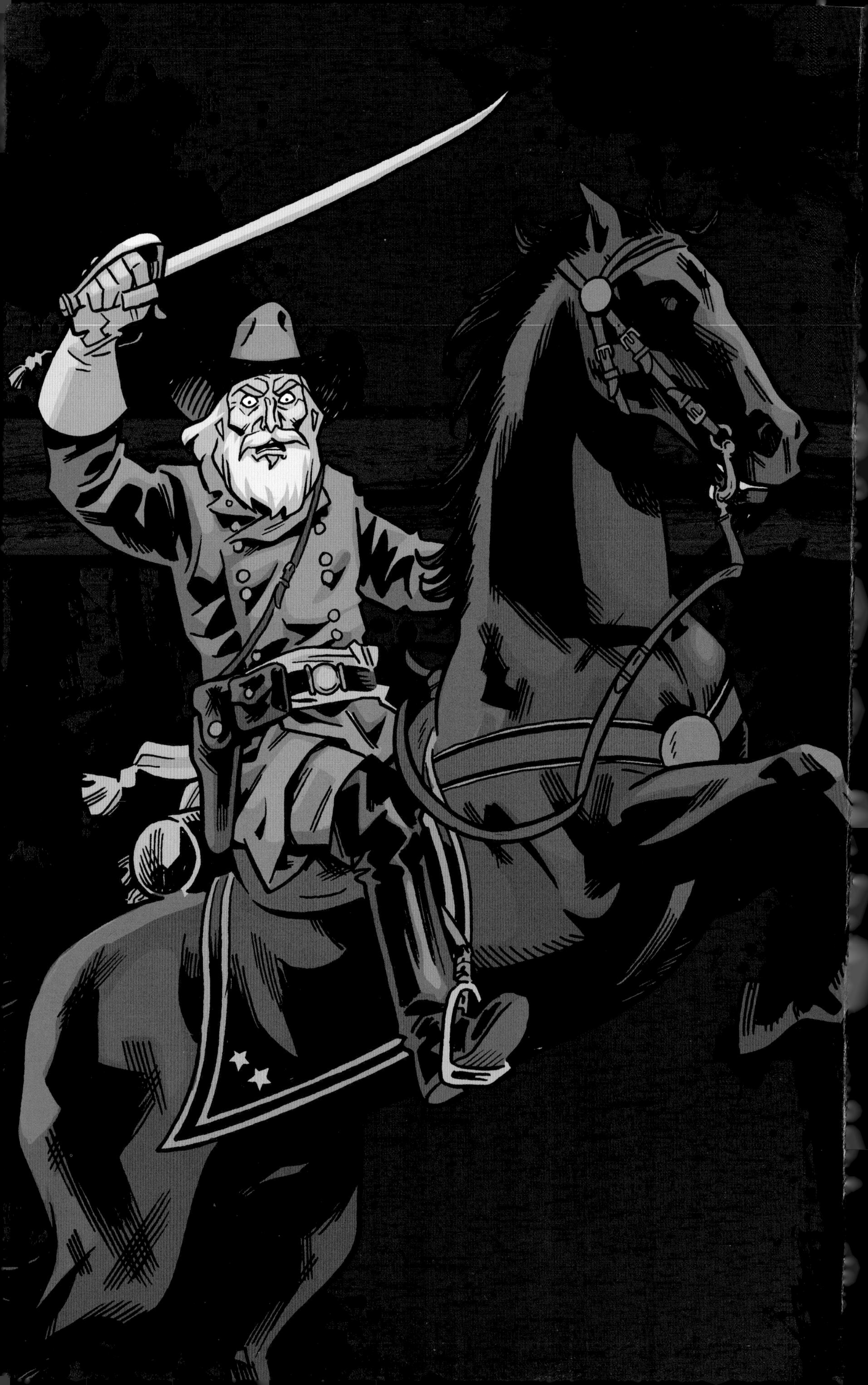

THE SIXTH GUN

Book 7: Not The Bullet, But The Fall

WRITTEN BY

CULLEN BUNN

ILLUSTRATED BY

BRIAN HURTT

CHAPTER 6 ILLUSTRATED BY

TYLER CROOK

COLORED BY

BILL CRABTREE

LETTERED BY

CRANK!

EDITED BY

CHARLIE CHU

DESIGNED BY

KEITH WOOD

WITH

JASON STOREY

AN ONI PRESS PUBLICATION

THE SIXTH GUN™
BY CULLEN BUNN & BRIAN HURTT

PUBLISHED BY ONI PRESS, INC.

JOE NOZEMACK *publisher*

JAMES LUCAS JONES *editor in chief*

CHEYENNE ALLOTT *director of sales*

JOHN SCHORK *director of publicity*

CHARLIE CHU *editor*

ROBIN HERRERA *associate editor*

TROY LOOK *production manager*

JASON STOREY *senior graphic designer*

BRAD ROOKS *inventory coordinator*

ARI YARWOOD *administrative assistant*

JUNG LEE *office assistant*

JARED JONES *production assistant*

THE SIXTH GUN: NOT THE BULLET, BUT THE FALL, September 2014. Published by Oni Press, Inc. 1305 SE Martin Luther King Jr. Blvd., Suite A, Portland, OR 97214. THE SIXTH GUN is ™ & © 2014 Cullen Bunn & Brian Hurtt. Oni Press logo and icon are ™ & © 2014 Oni Press, Inc. All rights reserved. Oni Press logo and icon artwork created by Keith A. Wood. The events, institutions, and characters presented in this book are fictional. Any resemblance to actual persons, living or dead, is purely coincidental. No portion of this publication may be reproduced, by any means, without the express written permission of the copyright holders.

This volume collects issues #36-41 of the Oni Press series *The Sixth Gun*.

ONI PRESS, INC.
1305 SE MARTIN LUTHER KING JR. BLVD.
SUITE A
PORTLAND, OR 97214
USA

onipress.com
facebook.com/onipress
twitter.com/onipress
onipress.tumblr.com

cullenbunn.com • @cullenbunn
brihurtt.com • @brihurtt
mrcrook.com • @mrtylercrook
@onibree_bill

First edition: September 2014
ISBN: 978-1-62010-141-4 • eISBN: 978-1-62010-142-1

Library of Congress Control Number: 2014903881

10 9 8 7 6 5 4 3 2 1

Printed in China

BECKY MONTCRIEF - A brave young woman who holds the Sixth Gun, a weapon that can divine the future.

DRAKE SINCLAIR - A treasure hunter with a bleak past. He now holds four of the Six.

GORD CANTRELL - Drake and Becky's ally. He knows some small measure of the dark arts, and he's uncovered a set of books that detail the terrible history of the Six.

NIDAWI - The host of Screaming Crow, the shaman who once tamed the Thunderbirds.

NAHUEL - A hunter and warrior sworn to protect Nidawi.

ASHER COBB - A nine-foot mystery mummy with prophetic powers.

CHAPTER
ONE

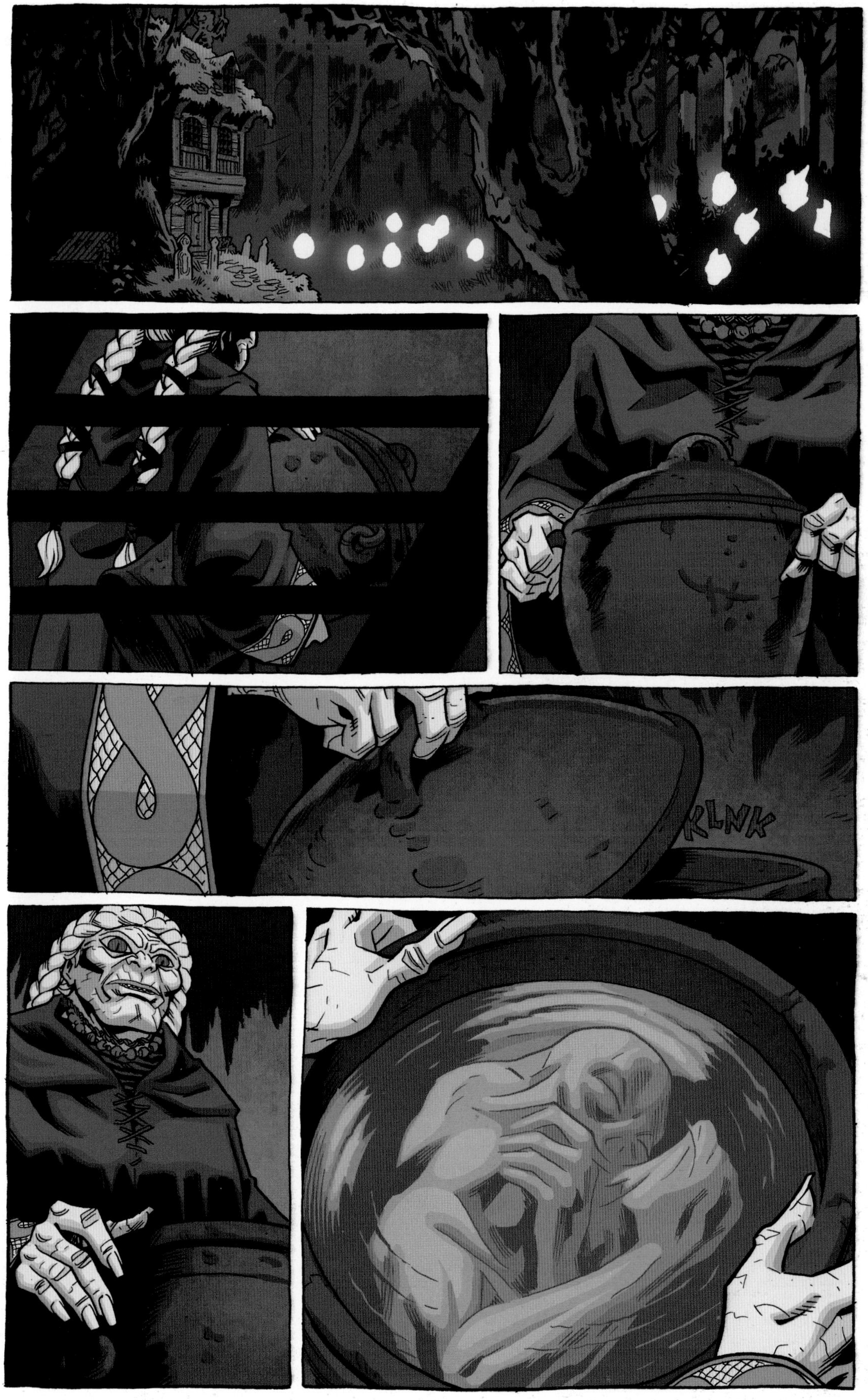
KLNK

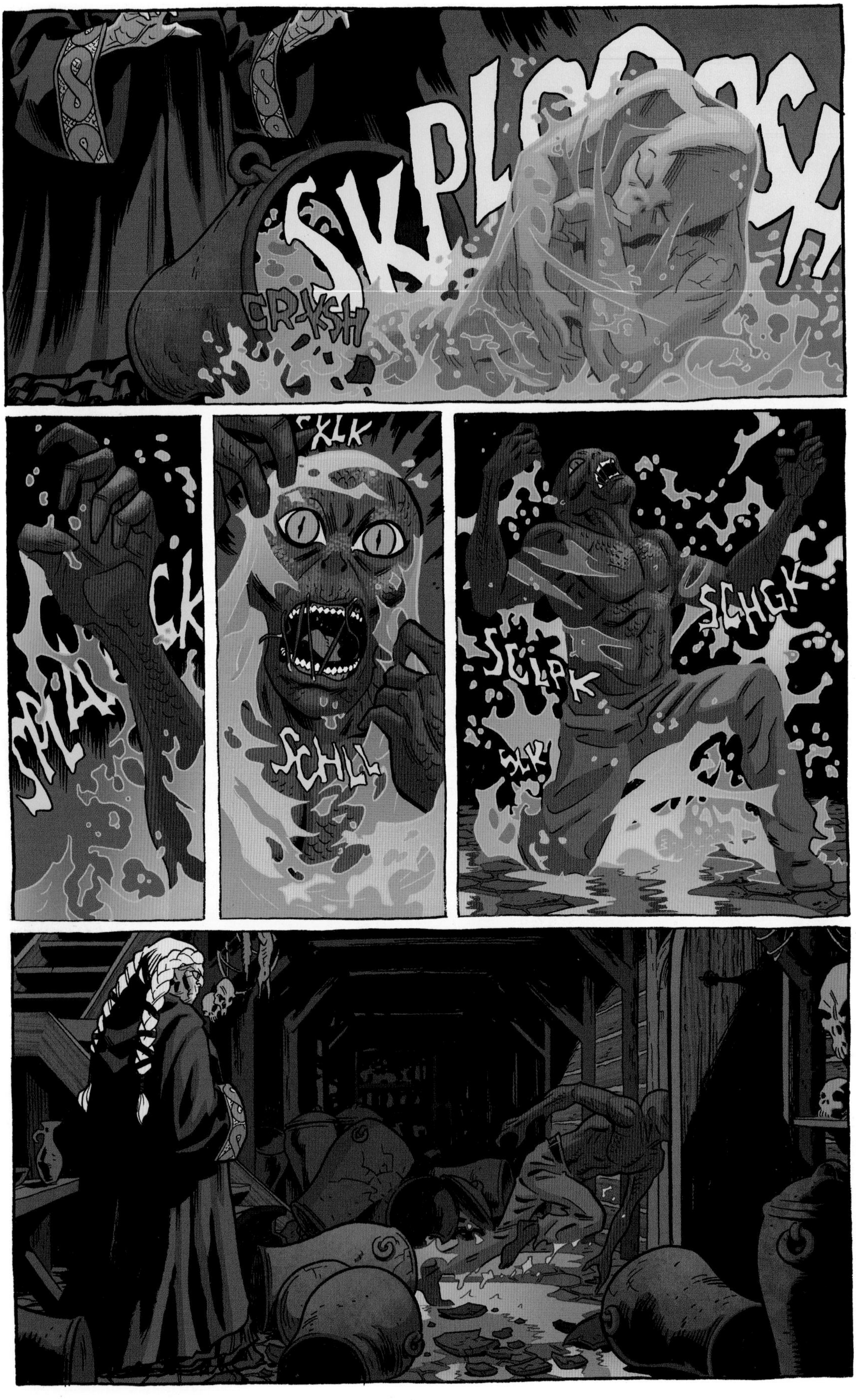
CRKSH
SKLK
SCHILL
SCLAK
SCHGK
SLK

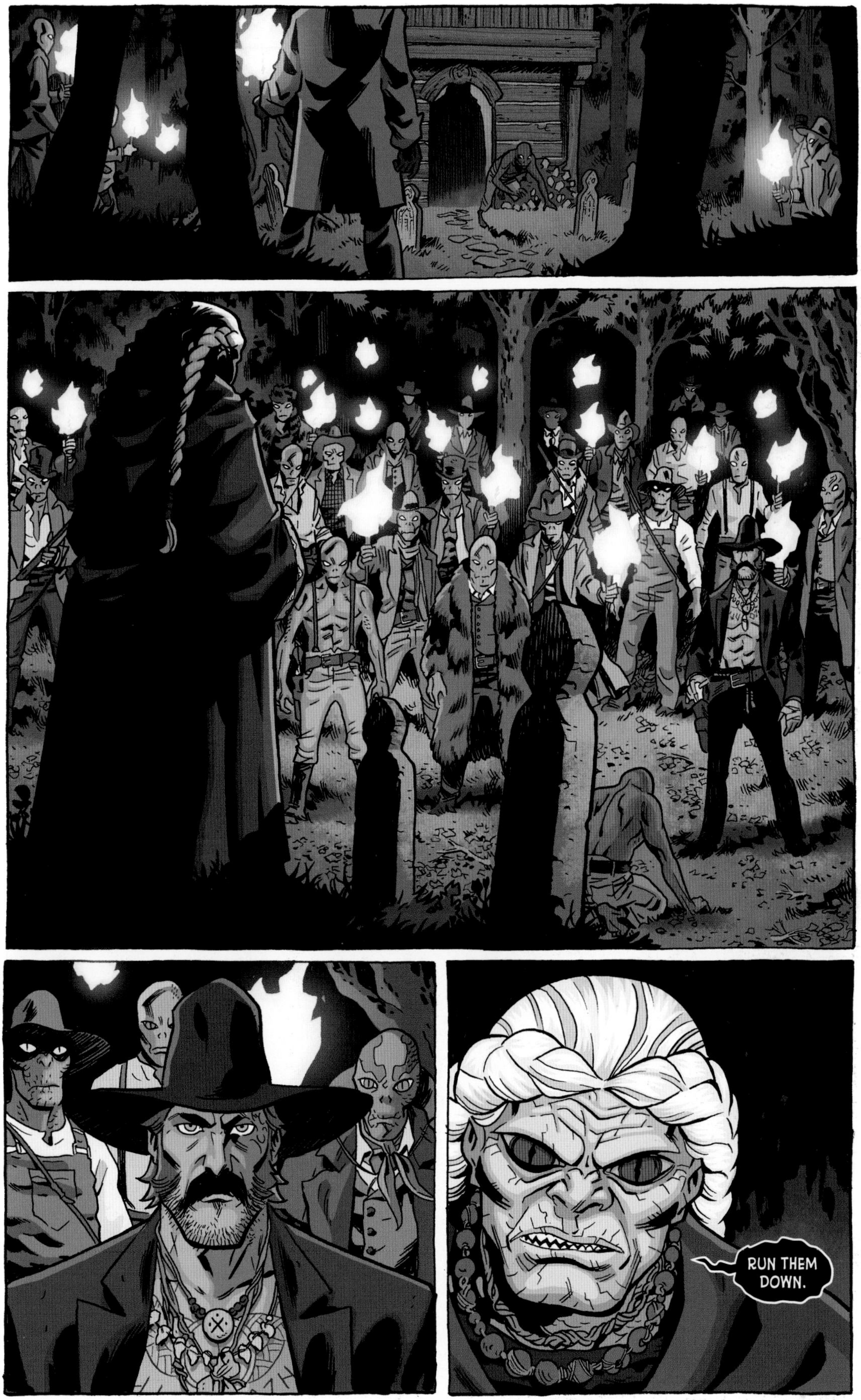
RUN THEM DOWN.

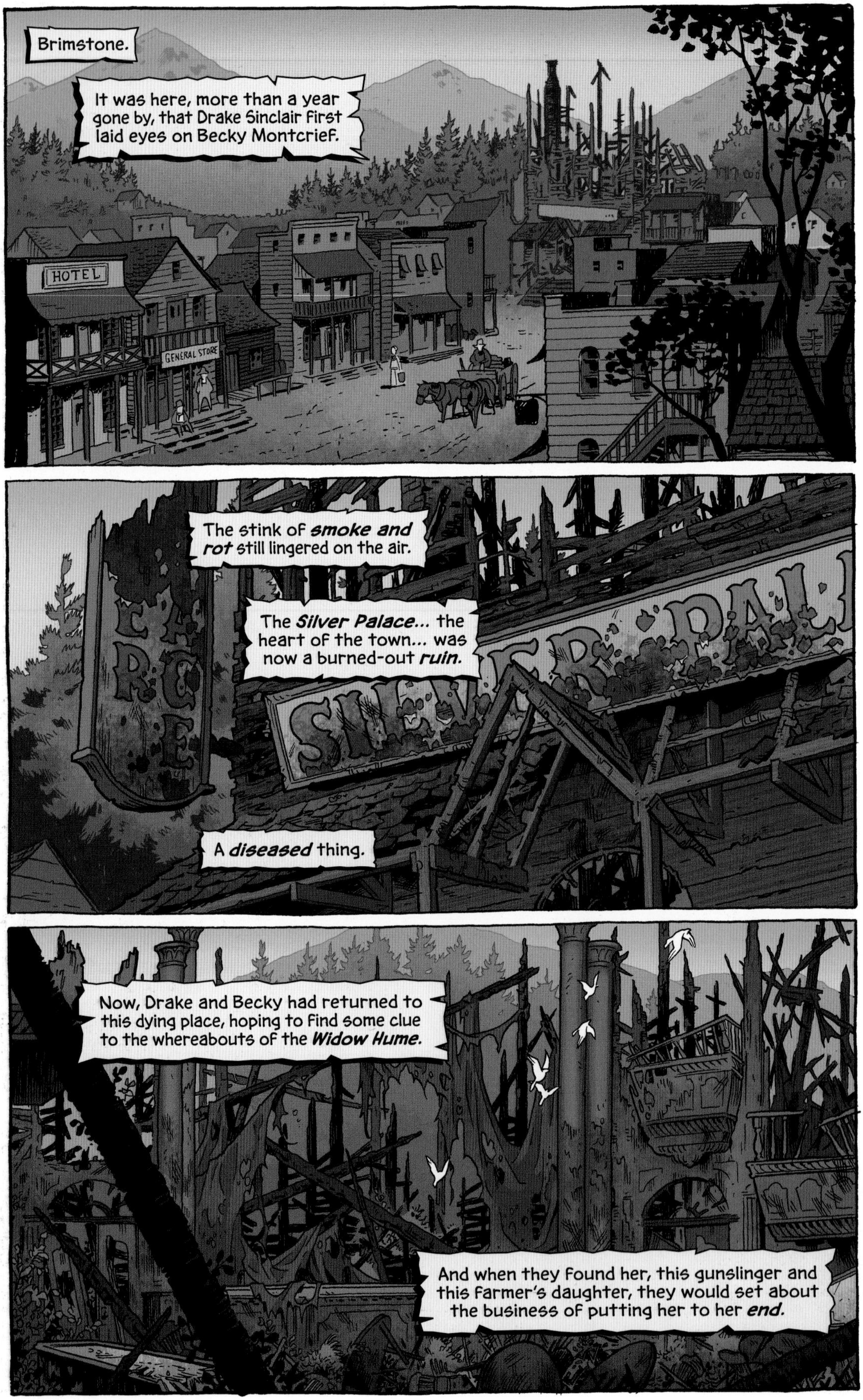
Brimstone.
It was here, more than a year gone by, that Drake Sinclair first laid eyes on Becky Montcrief.
HOTEL
GENERAL STORE
The stink of *smoke and rot* still lingered on the air.
The *Silver Palace*... the heart of the town... was now a burned-out *ruin*.
A *diseased* thing.
Now, Drake and Becky had returned to this dying place, hoping to find some clue to the whereabouts of the *Widow Hume*.
And when they found her, this gunslinger and this farmer's daughter, they would set about the business of putting her to her *end*.

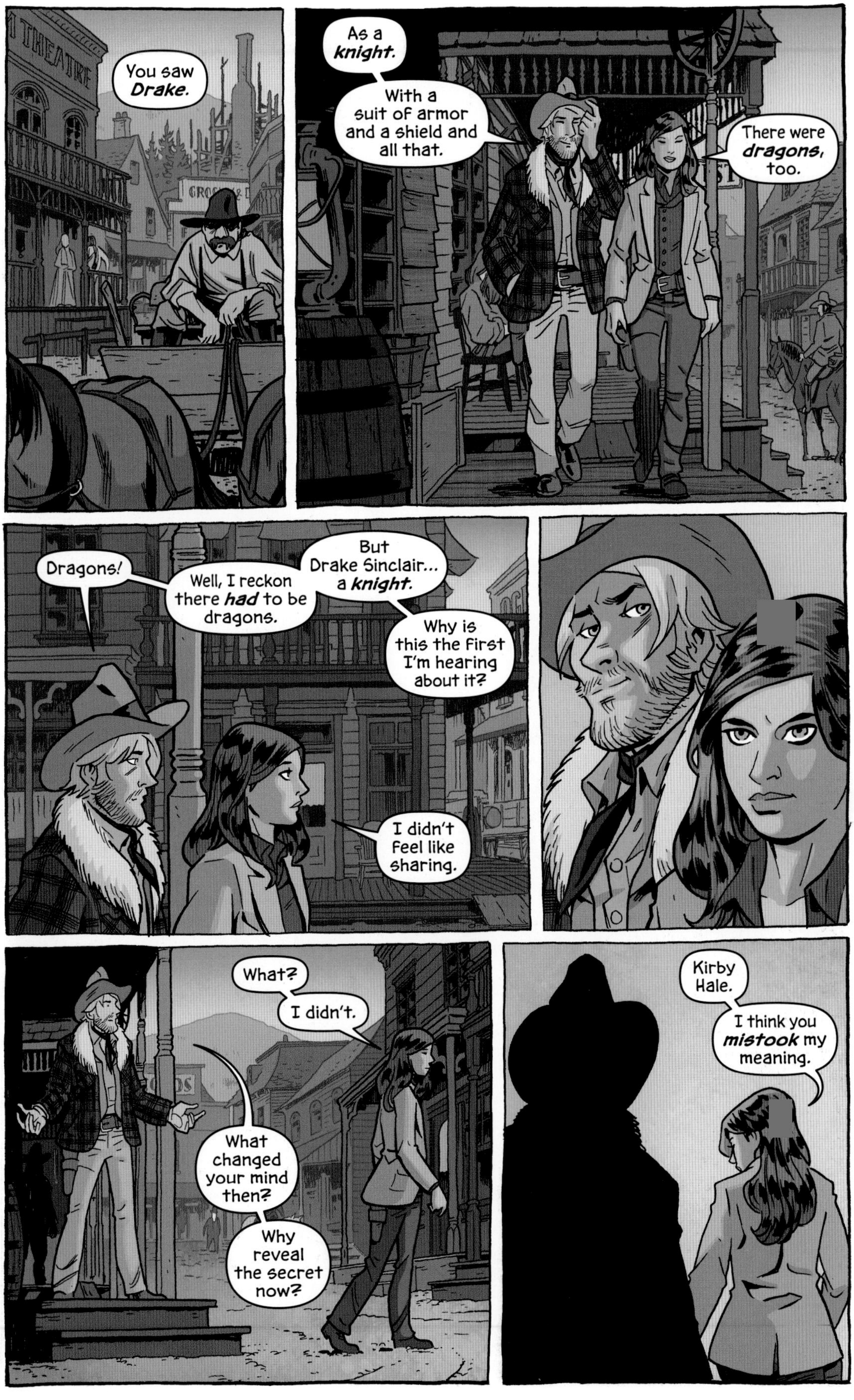
You saw *Drake.*
As a *knight.*
With a suit of armor and a shield and all that.
There were *dragons,* too.
Dragons!
Well, I reckon there *had* to be dragons.
But Drake Sinclair... a *knight.*
Why is this the first I'm hearing about it?
I didn't feel like sharing.
What?
I didn't.
What changed your mind then?
Why reveal the secret now?
Kirby Hale.
I think you *mistook* my meaning.

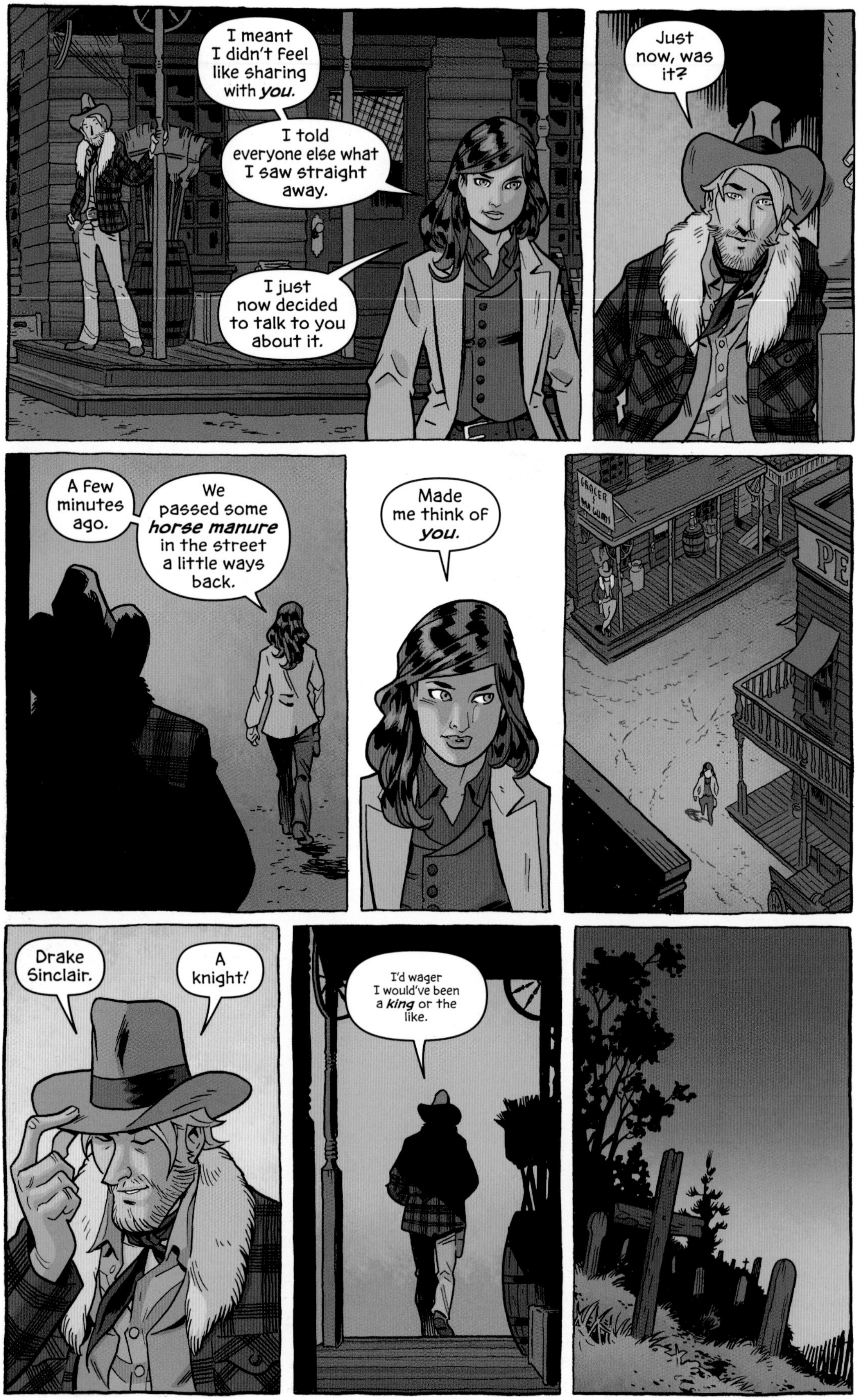
I meant
I didn't feel
like sharing
with *you.*
I told
everyone else what
I saw straight
away.
I just
now decided
to talk to you
about it.
Just
now, was
it?
A few
minutes
ago.
We
passed some
horse manure
in the street
a little ways
back.
Made
me think of
you.
Drake
Sinclair.
A
knight!
I'd wager
I would've been
a *king* or the
like.

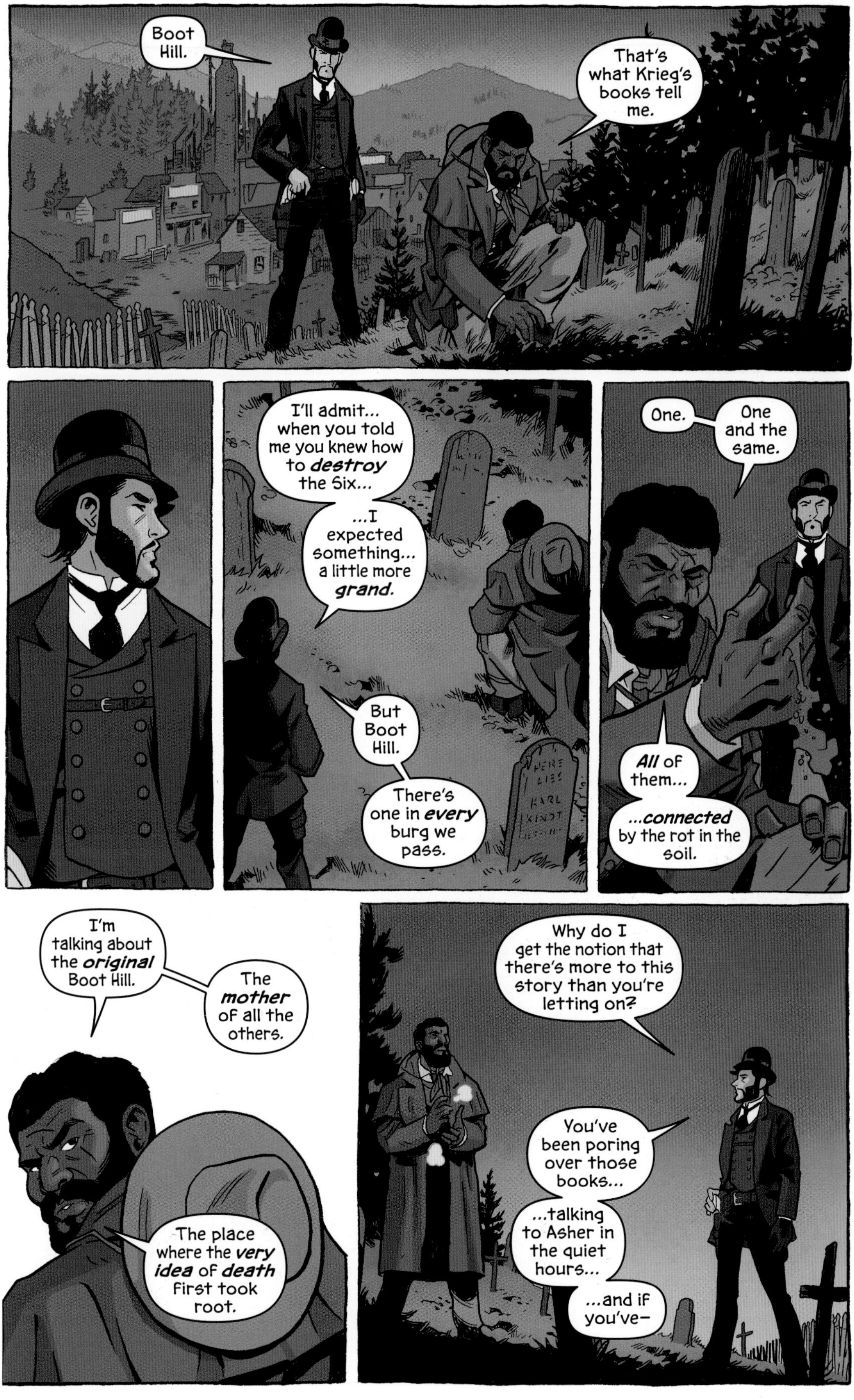
Boot Hill.
That's what Krieg's books tell me.
I'll admit... when you told me you knew how to *destroy* the Six...
...I expected something... a little more *grand.*
But Boot Hill.
There's one in *every* burg we pass.
HERE LIES KARL KINDT
One.
One and the same.
All of them...
...connected by the rot in the soil.
I'm talking about the *original* Boot Hill.
The *mother* of all the others.
The place where the *very idea* of *death* first took root.
Why do I get the notion that there's more to this story than you're letting on?
You've been poring over those books...
...talking to Asher in the quiet hours...
...and if you've–

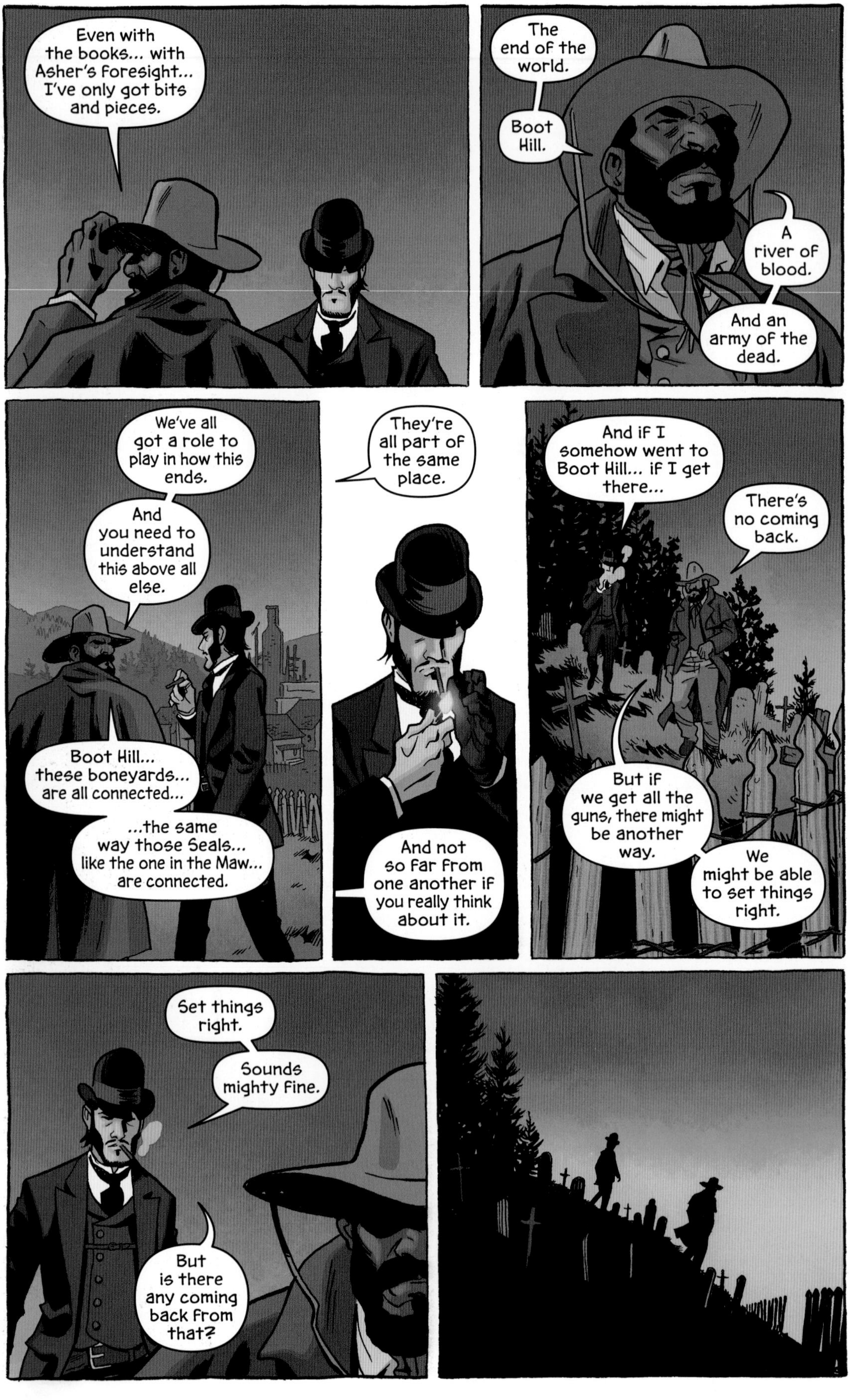

Even with the books... with Asher's foresight... I've only got bits and pieces.
The end of the world.
Boot Hill.
A river of blood.
And an army of the dead.
We've all got a role to play in how this ends.
And you need to understand this above all else.
Boot Hill... these boneyards... are all connected...
...the same way those Seals... like the one in the Maw... are connected.
They're all part of the same place.
And not so far from one another if you really think about it.
And if I somehow went to Boot Hill... if I get there...
There's no coming back.
But if we get all the guns, there might be another way.
We might be able to set things right.
Set things right.
Sounds mighty fine.
But is there any coming back from that?

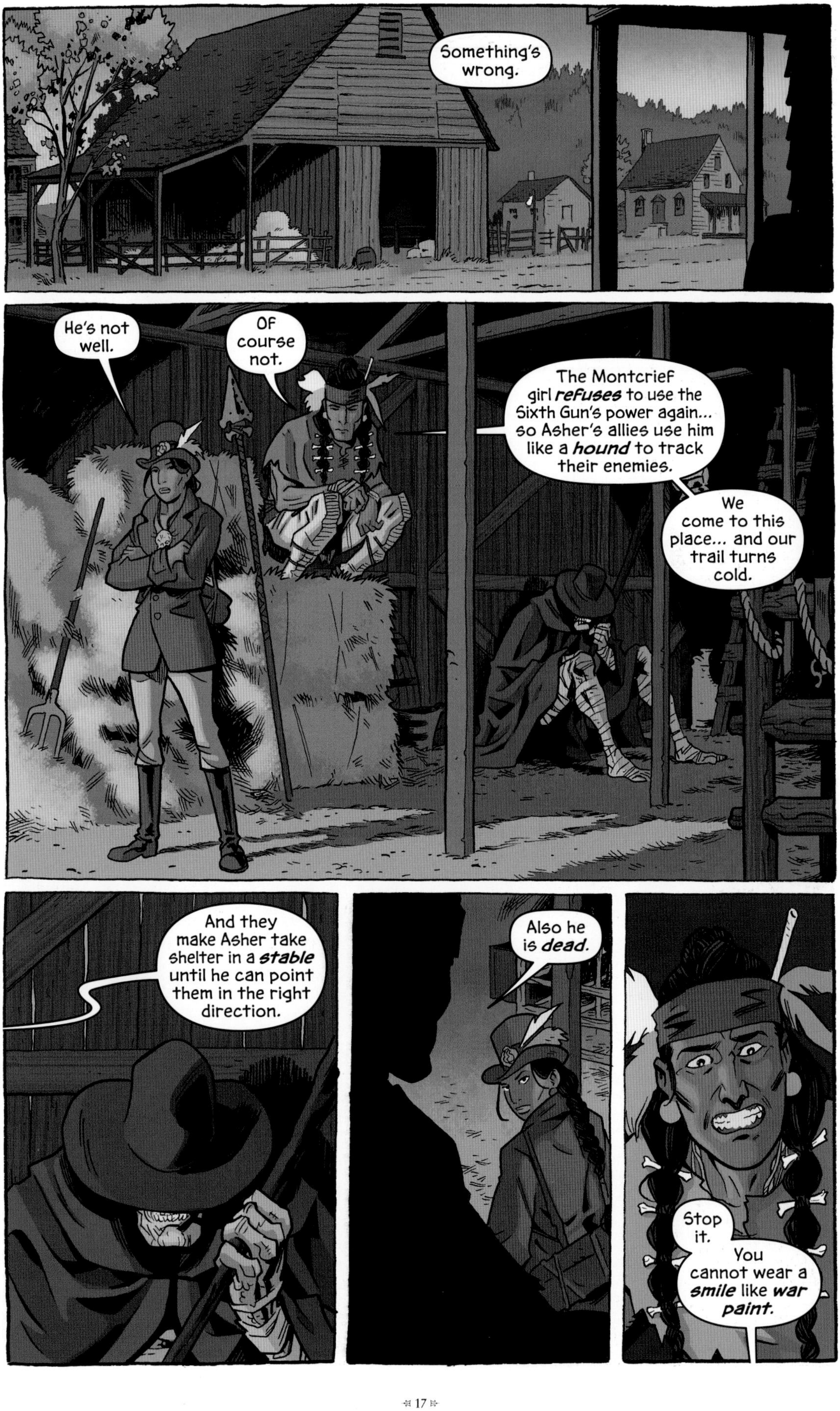
Something's wrong.
He's not well.
Of course not.
The Montcrief girl *refuses* to use the Sixth Gun's power again... so Asher's allies use him like a *hound* to track their enemies.
We come to this place... and our trail turns cold.
And they make Asher take shelter in a *stable* until he can point them in the right direction.
Also he is *dead*.
Stop it.
You cannot wear a *smile* like *war paint*.

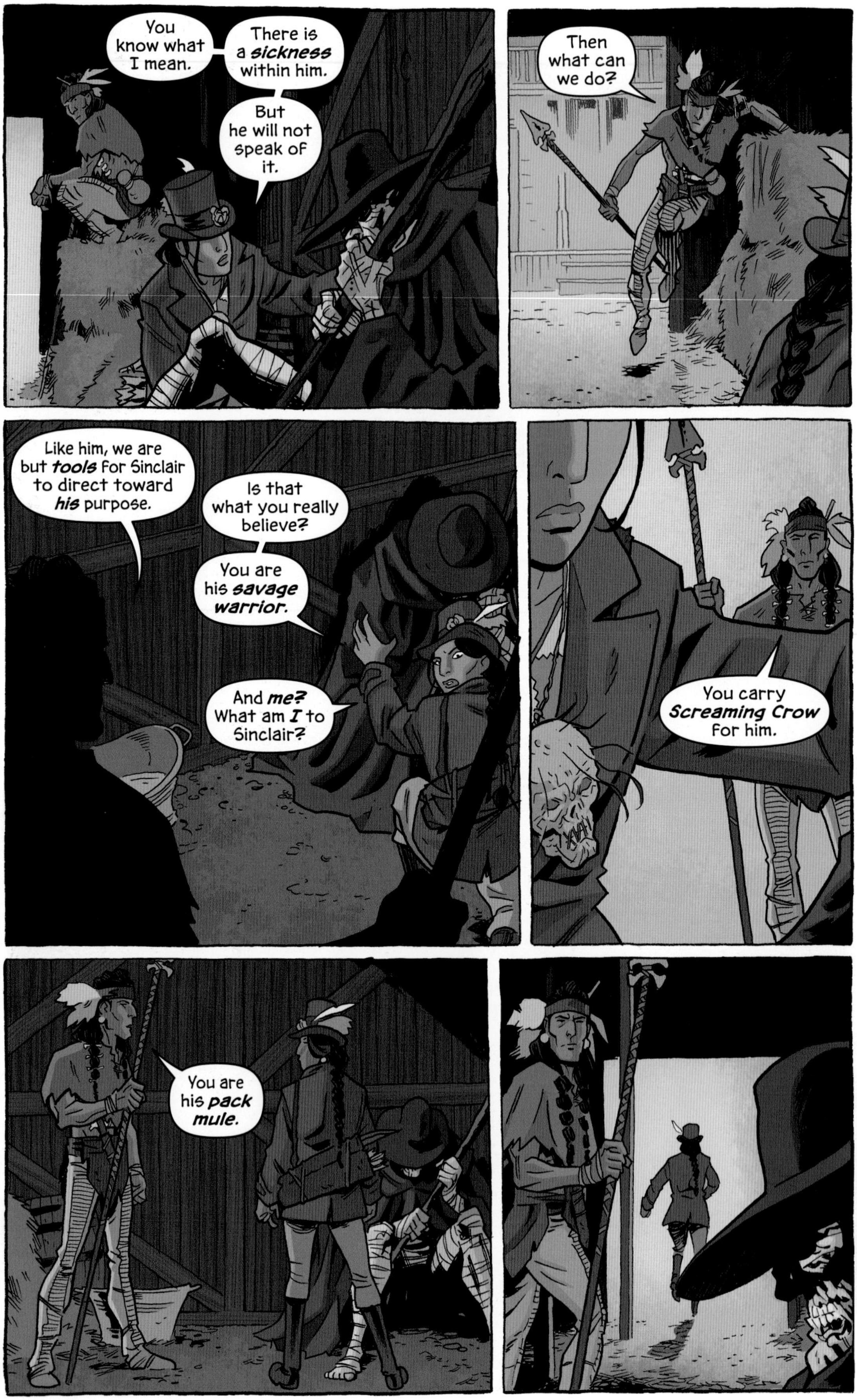

You know what I mean.
There is a *sickness* within him.
But he will not speak of it.
Then what can we do?
Like him, we are but *tools* for Sinclair to direct toward *his* purpose.
Is that what you really believe?
You are his *savage warrior*.
And *me?* What am *I* to Sinclair?
You carry *Screaming Crow* for him.
You are his *pack mule.*

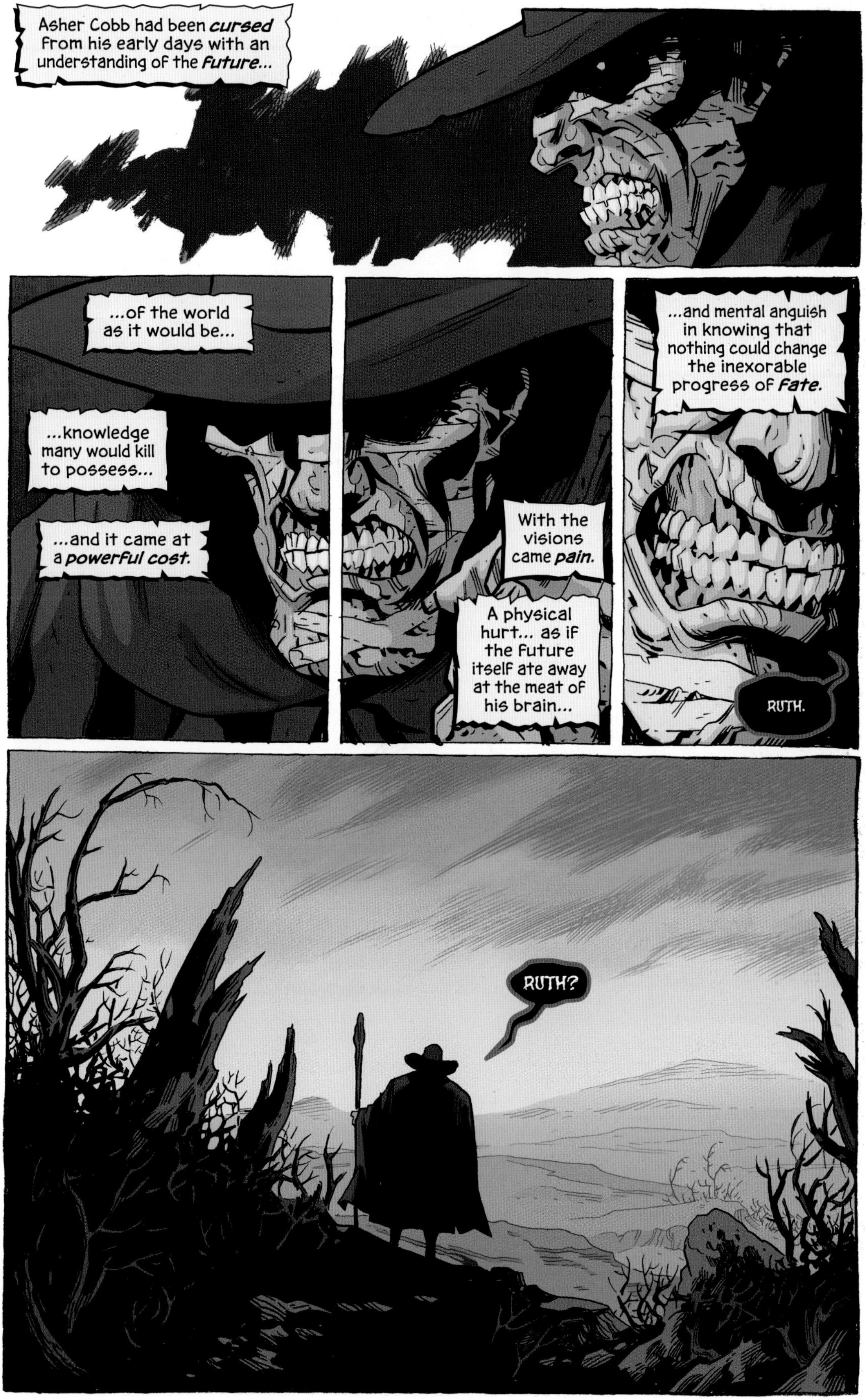
Asher Cobb had been *cursed* from his early days with an understanding of the *future*...
...of the world as it would be...
...knowledge many would kill to possess...
...and it came at a *powerful cost*.
With the visions came *pain*.
A physical hurt... as if the future itself ate away at the meat of his brain...
...and mental anguish in knowing that nothing could change the inexorable progress of *Fate*.
RUTH.
RUTH?

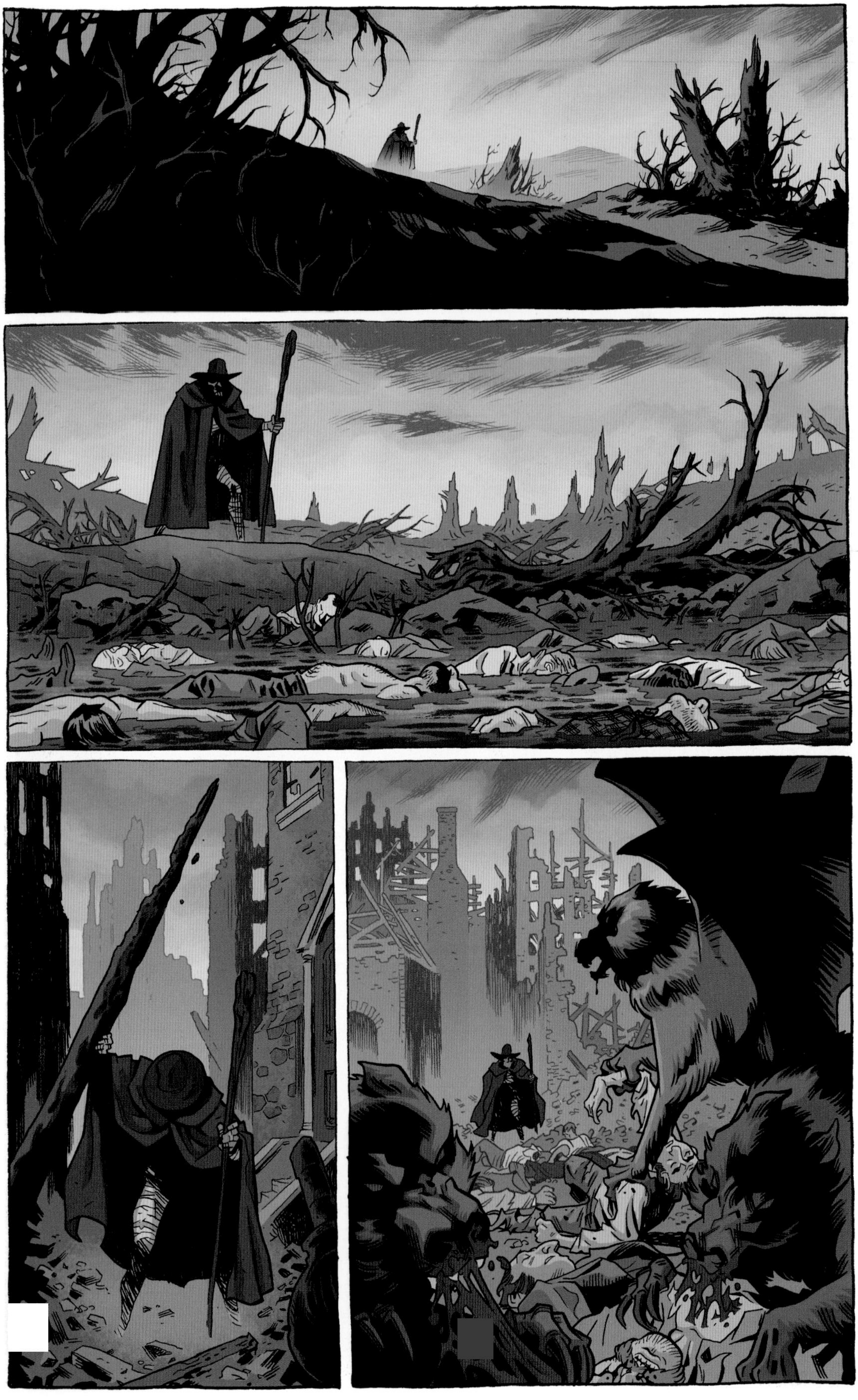

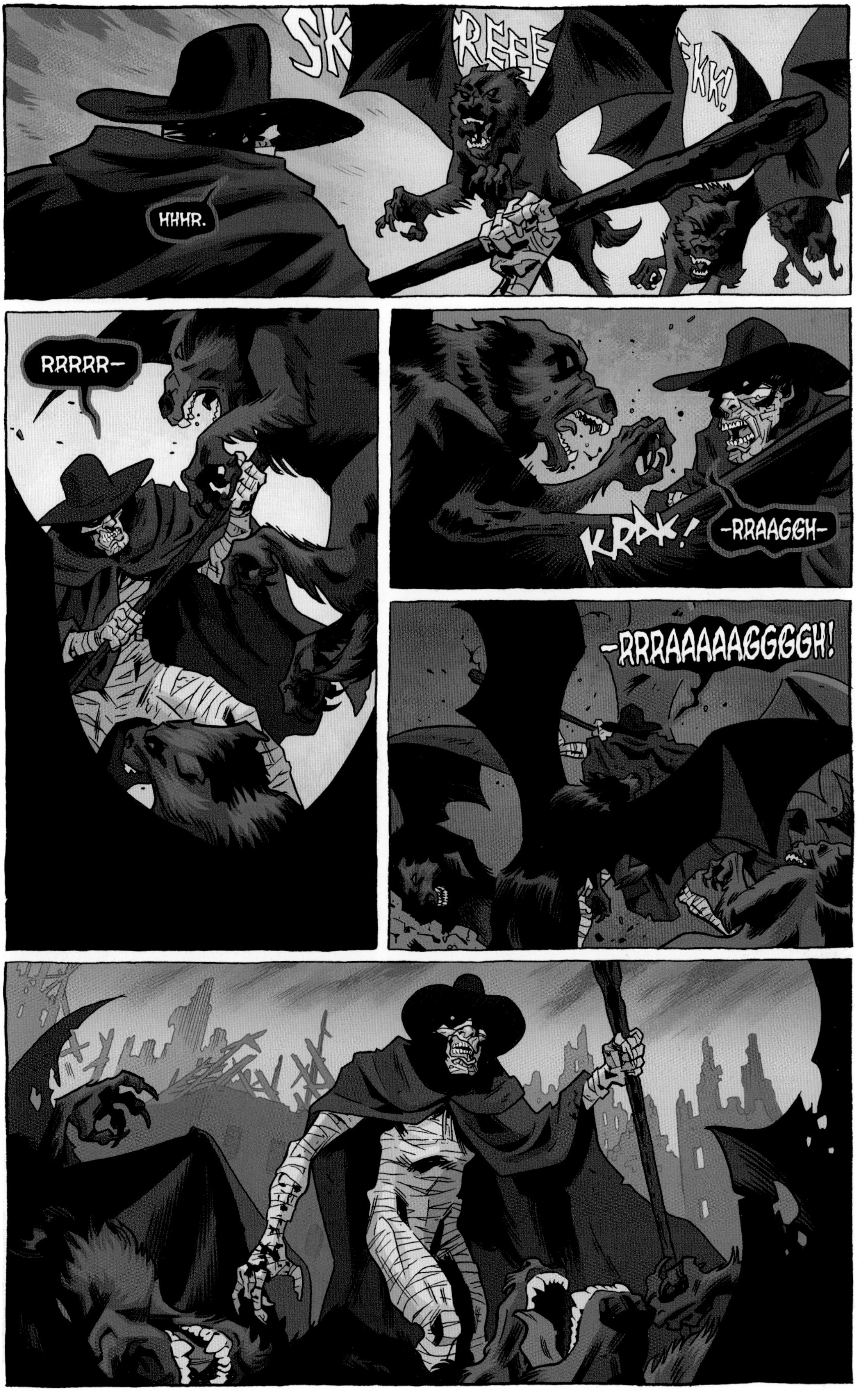
SKREEEEKK!
HHHR.
RRRRR-
KRAK!
-RRAAGGH-
-RRRAAAAAGGGGH!

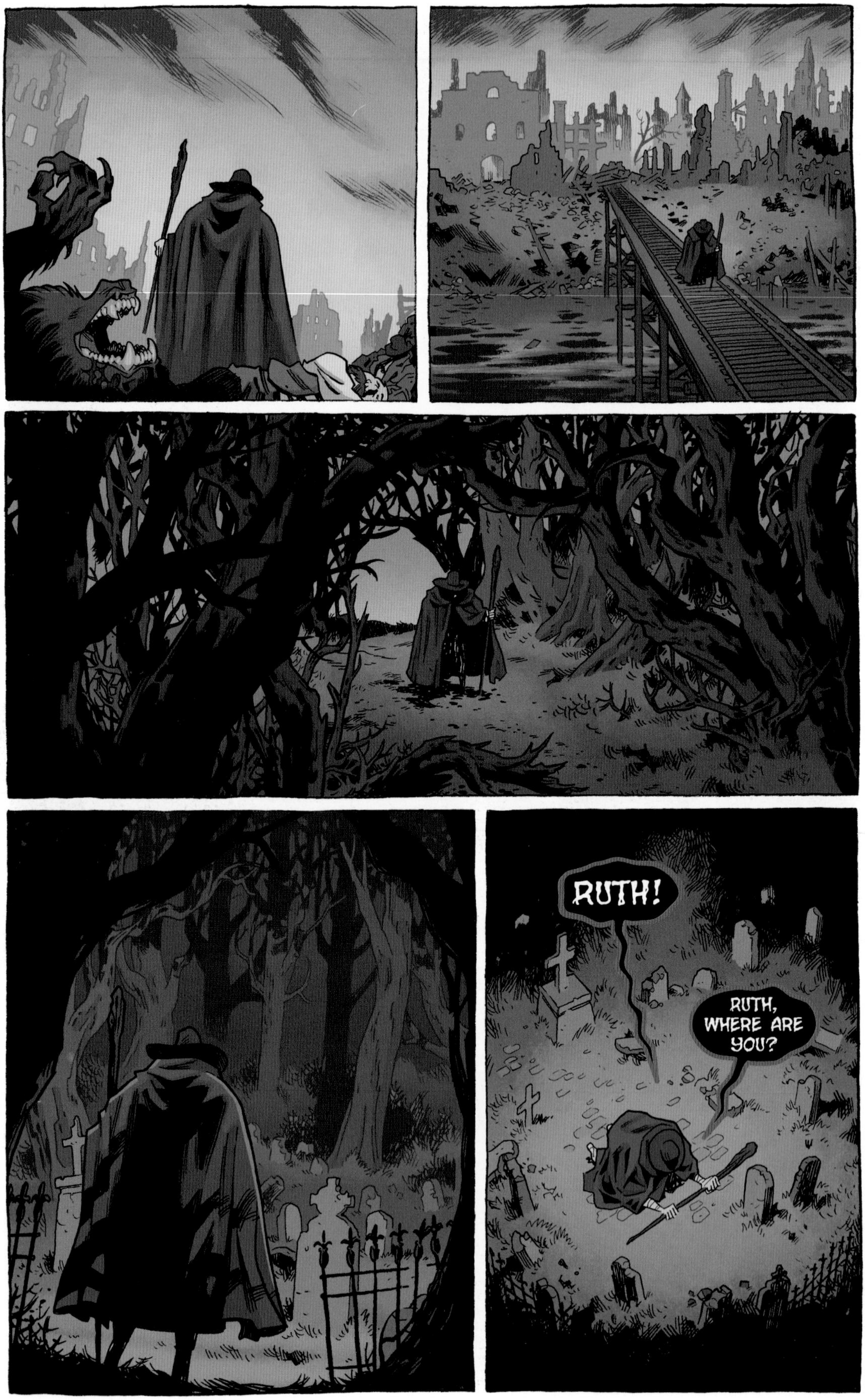
RUTH!
RUTH, WHERE ARE YOU?

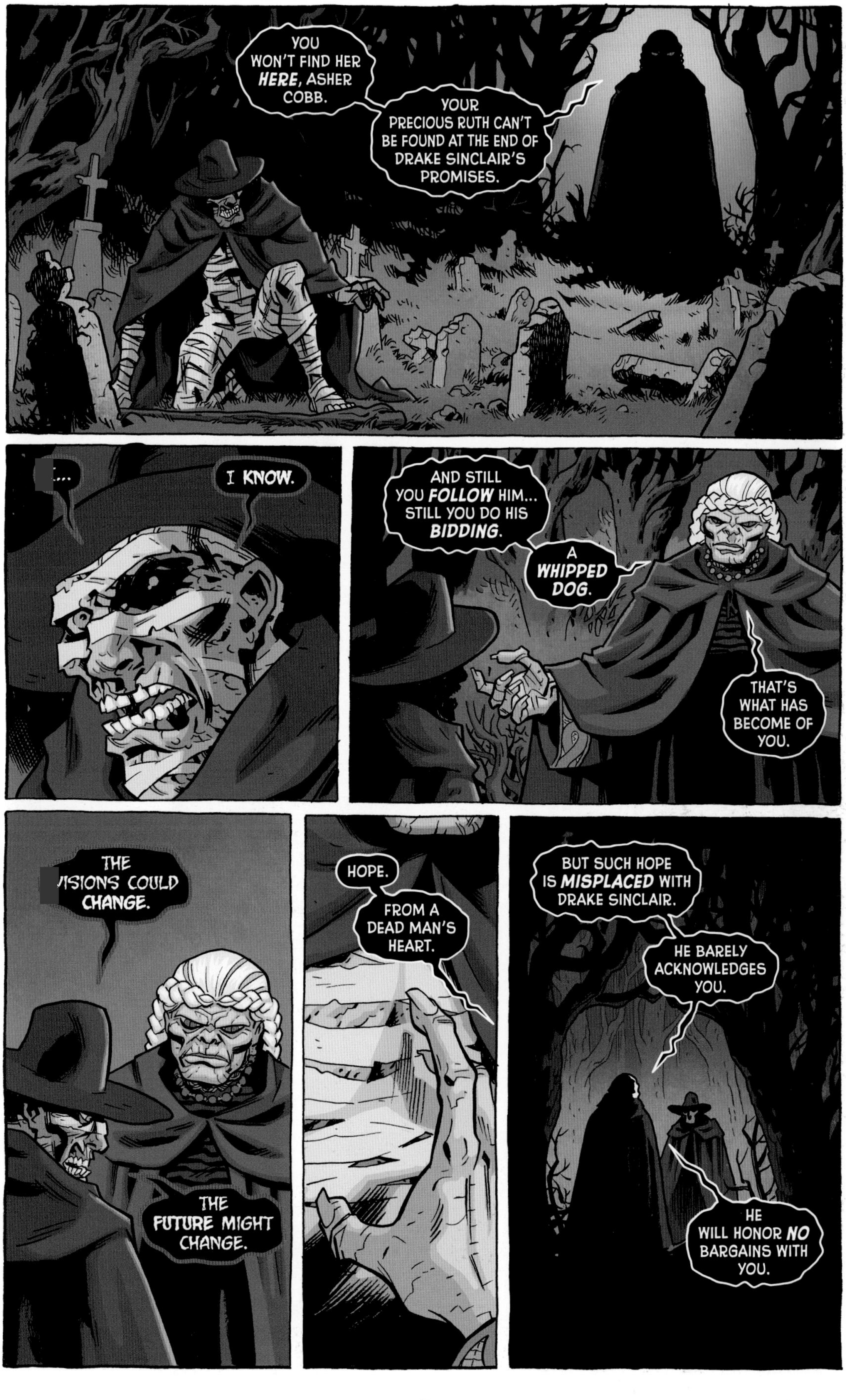
YOU WON'T FIND HER HERE, ASHER COBB.
YOUR PRECIOUS RUTH CAN'T BE FOUND AT THE END OF DRAKE SINCLAIR'S PROMISES.
[redacted]...
I KNOW.
AND STILL YOU FOLLOW HIM... STILL YOU DO HIS BIDDING.
A WHIPPED DOG.
THAT'S WHAT HAS BECOME OF YOU.
THE [redacted]ISIONS COULD CHANGE.
THE FUTURE MIGHT CHANGE.
HOPE.
FROM A DEAD MAN'S HEART.
BUT SUCH HOPE IS MISPLACED WITH DRAKE SINCLAIR.
HE BARELY ACKNOWLEDGES YOU.
HE WILL HONOR NO BARGAINS WITH YOU.

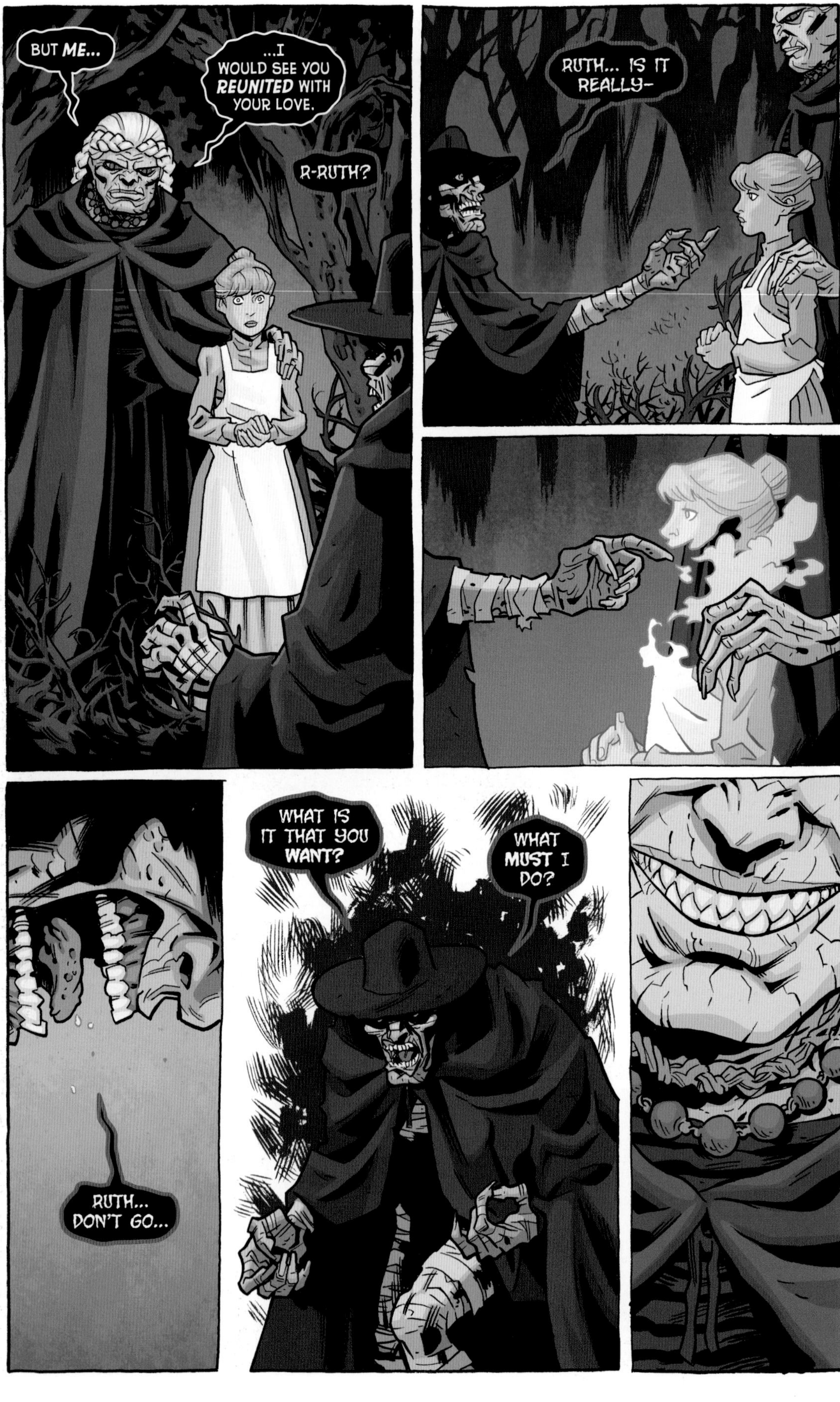
BUT ME...
...I WOULD SEE YOU REUNITED WITH YOUR LOVE.
R-RUTH?
RUTH... IS IT REALLY-
RUTH... DON'T GO...
WHAT IS IT THAT YOU WANT?
WHAT MUST I DO?

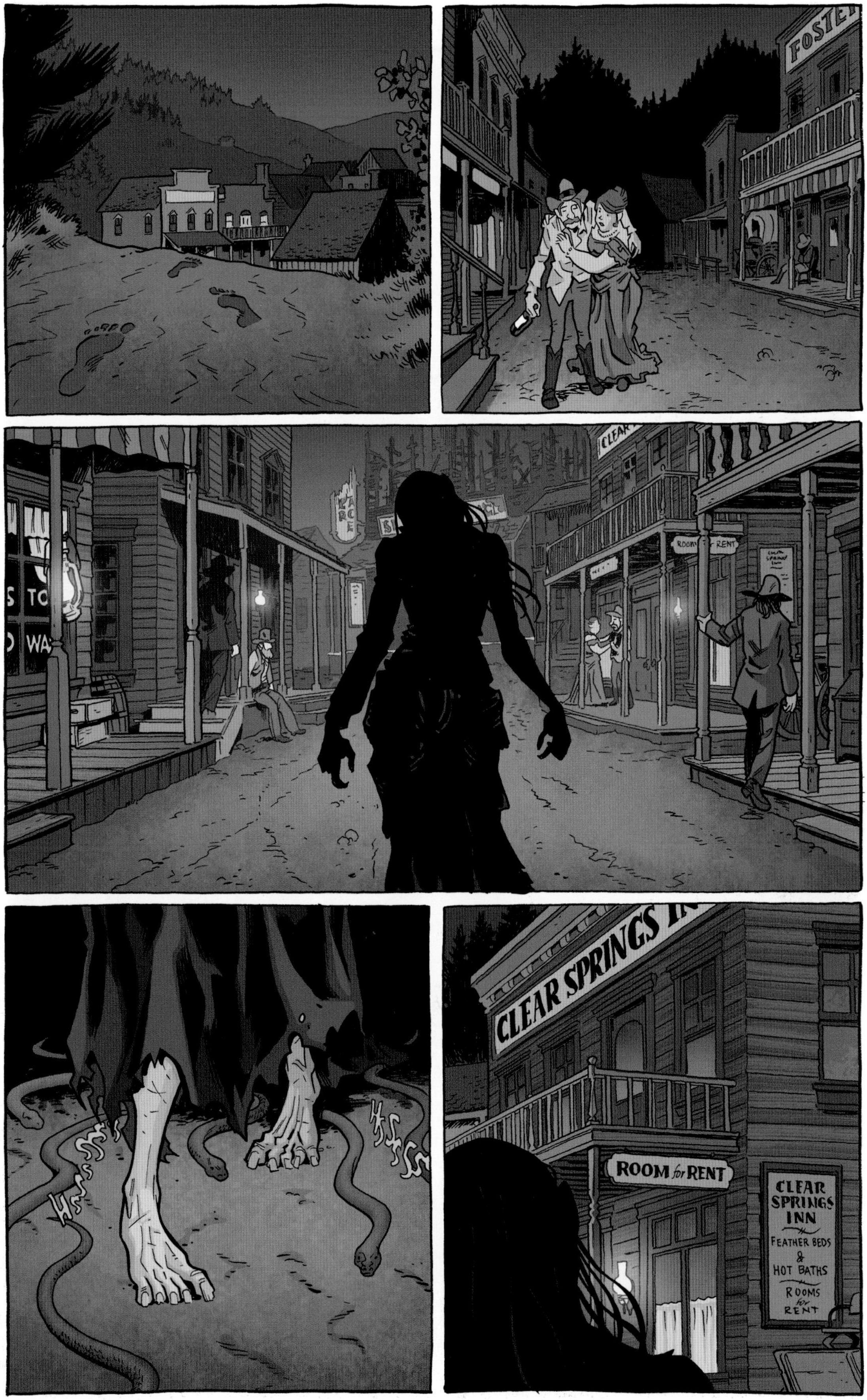
CLEAR SPRINGS IN
ROOM for RENT
CLEAR
SPRINGS
INN
FEATHER BEDS
&
HOT BATHS
ROOMS
for
RENT

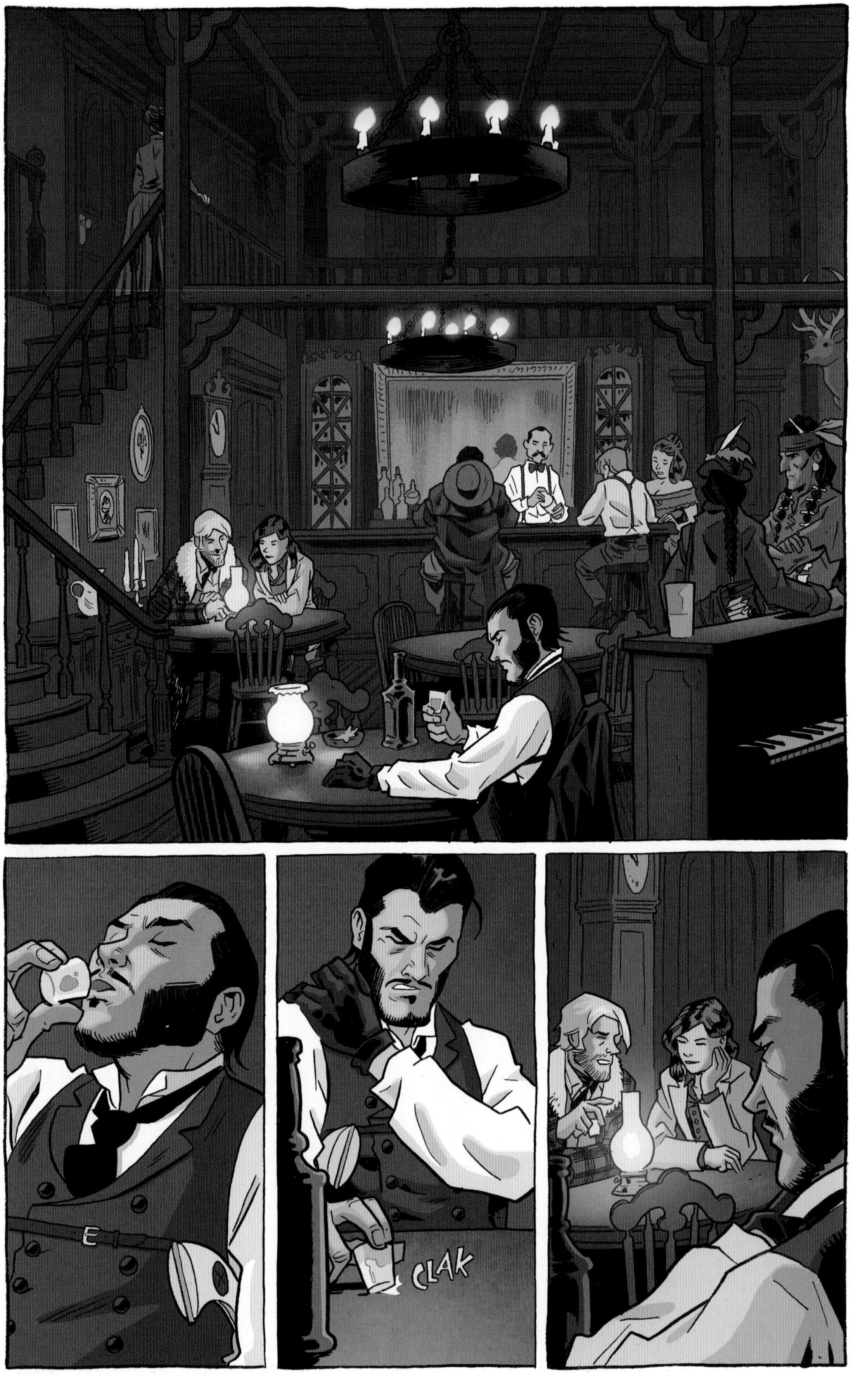
CLAK

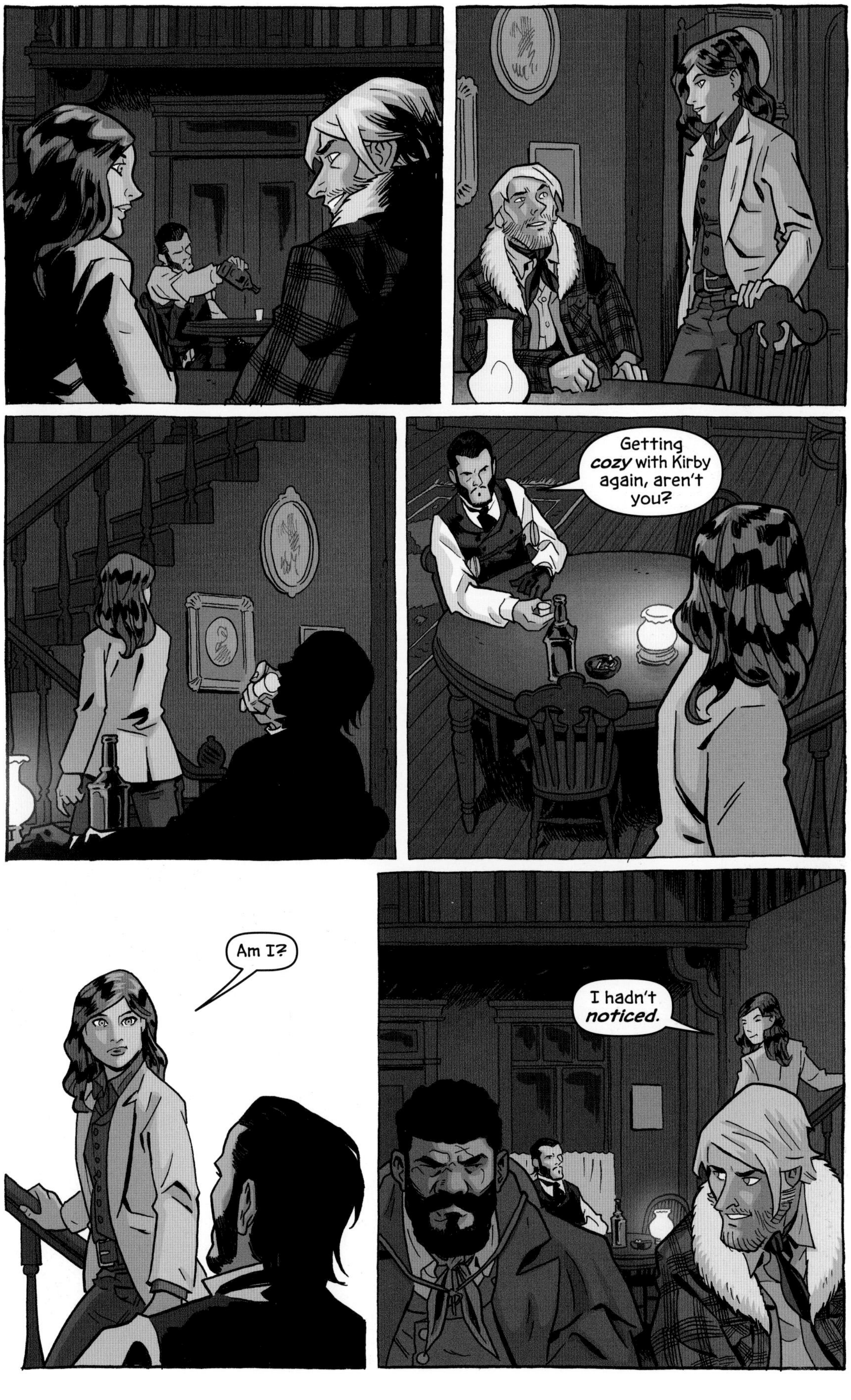
Getting cozy with Kirby again, aren't you?
Am I?
I hadn't noticed.

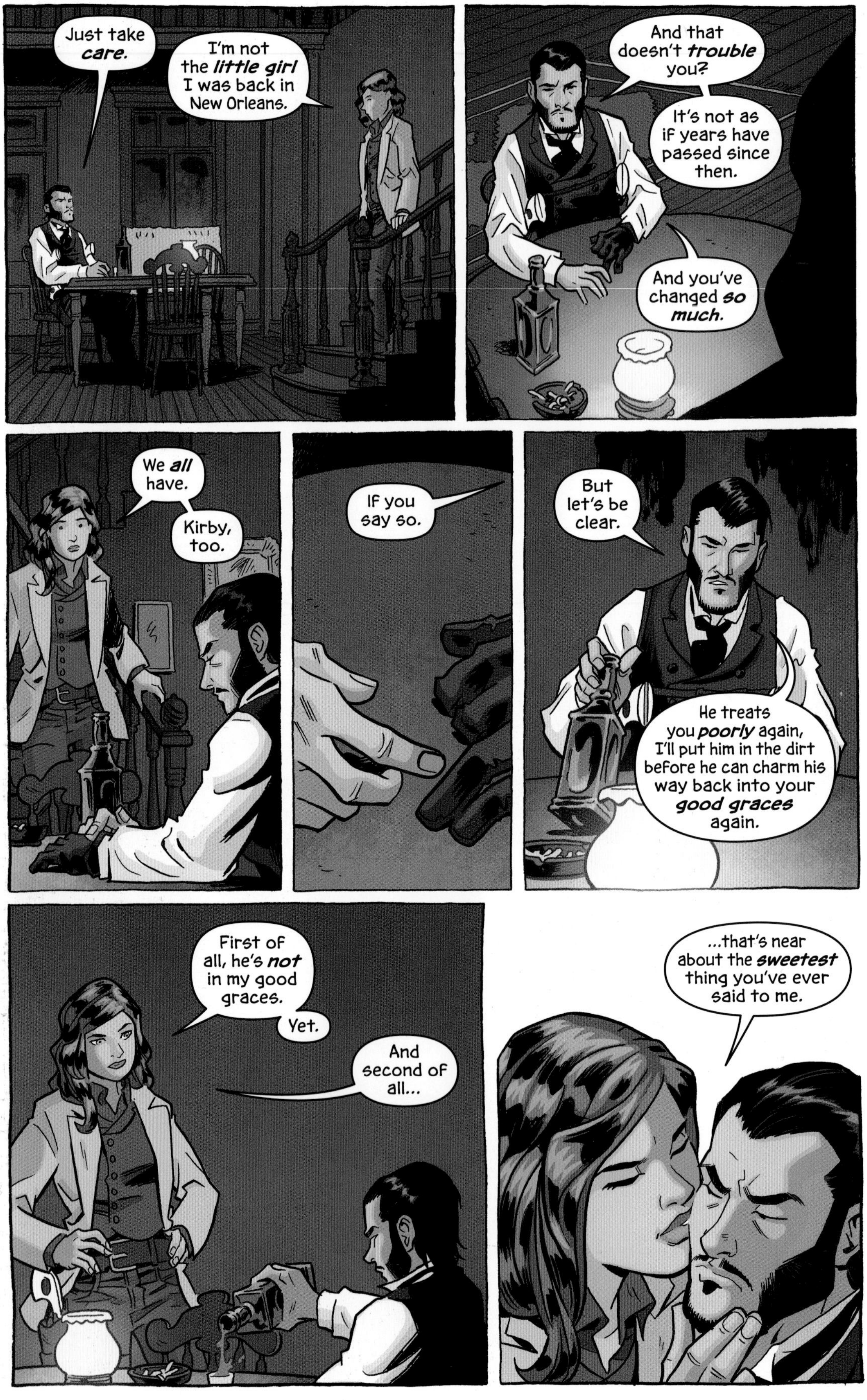
Just take care.
I'm not the little girl I was back in New Orleans.
And that doesn't trouble you?
It's not as if years have passed since then.
And you've changed so much.
We all have.
Kirby, too.
If you say so.
But let's be clear.
He treats you poorly again, I'll put him in the dirt before he can charm his way back into your good graces again.
First of all, he's not in my good graces.
Yet.
And second of all...
...that's near about the sweetest thing you've ever said to me.

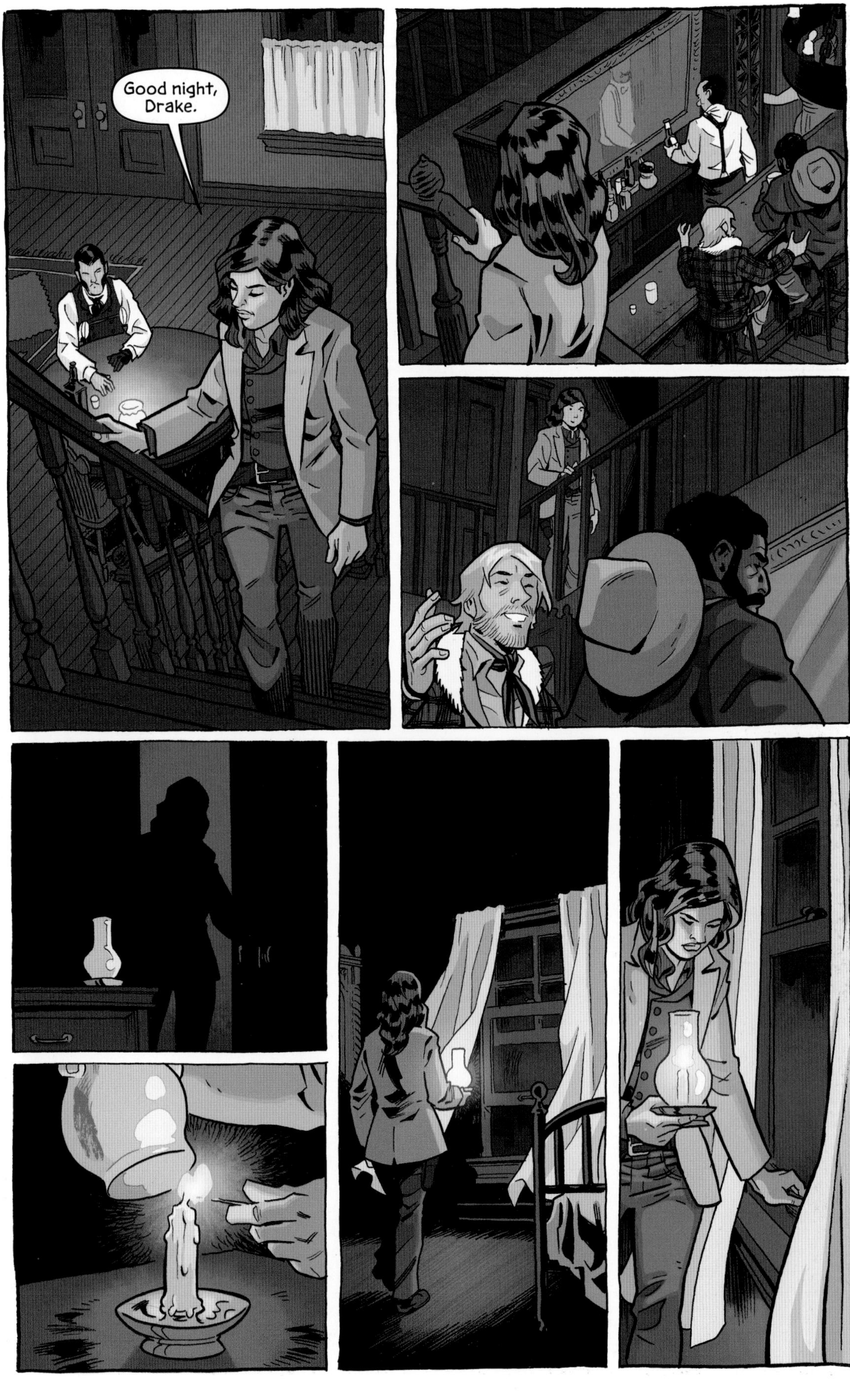
Good night,
Drake.

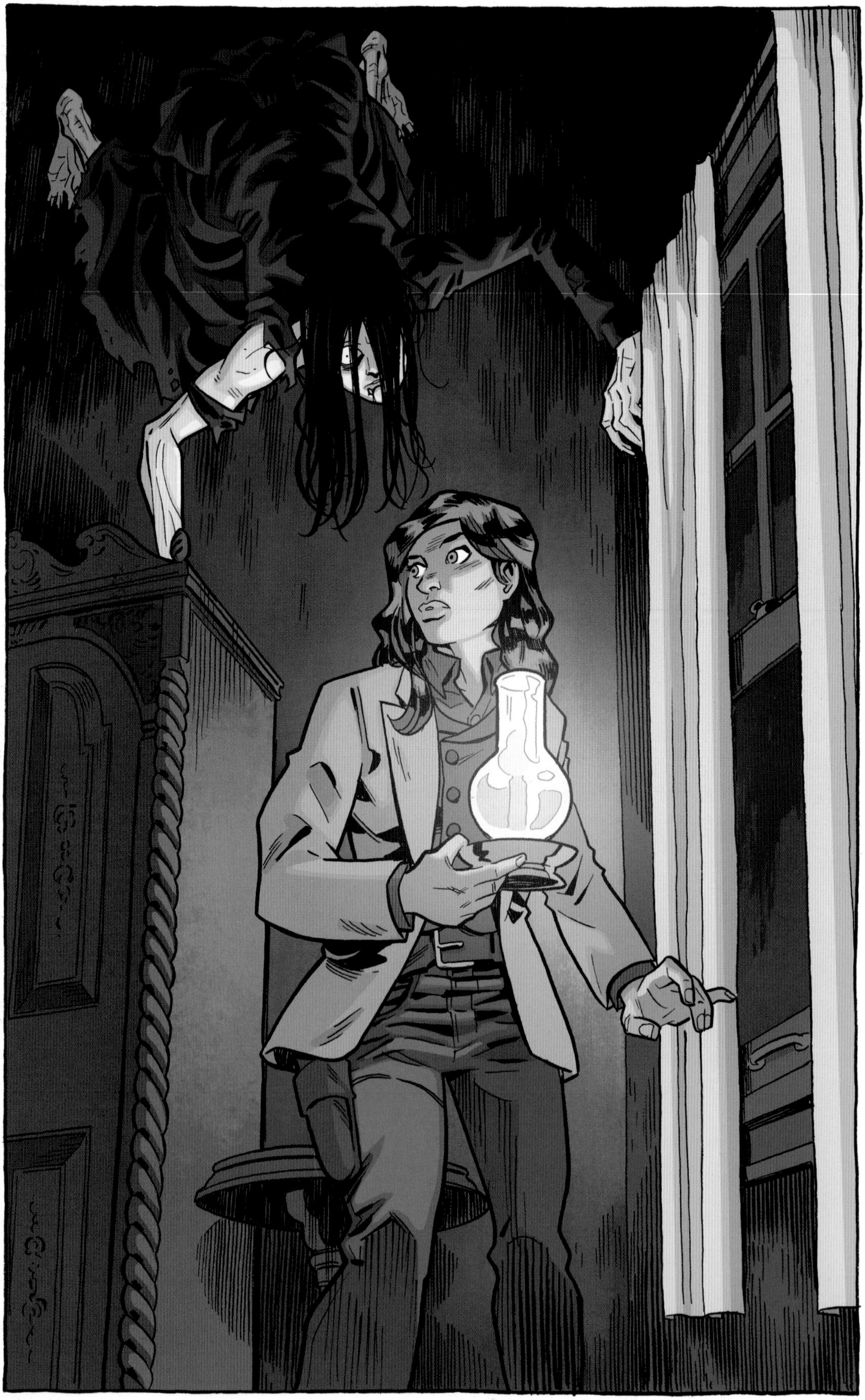

CHAPTER TWO

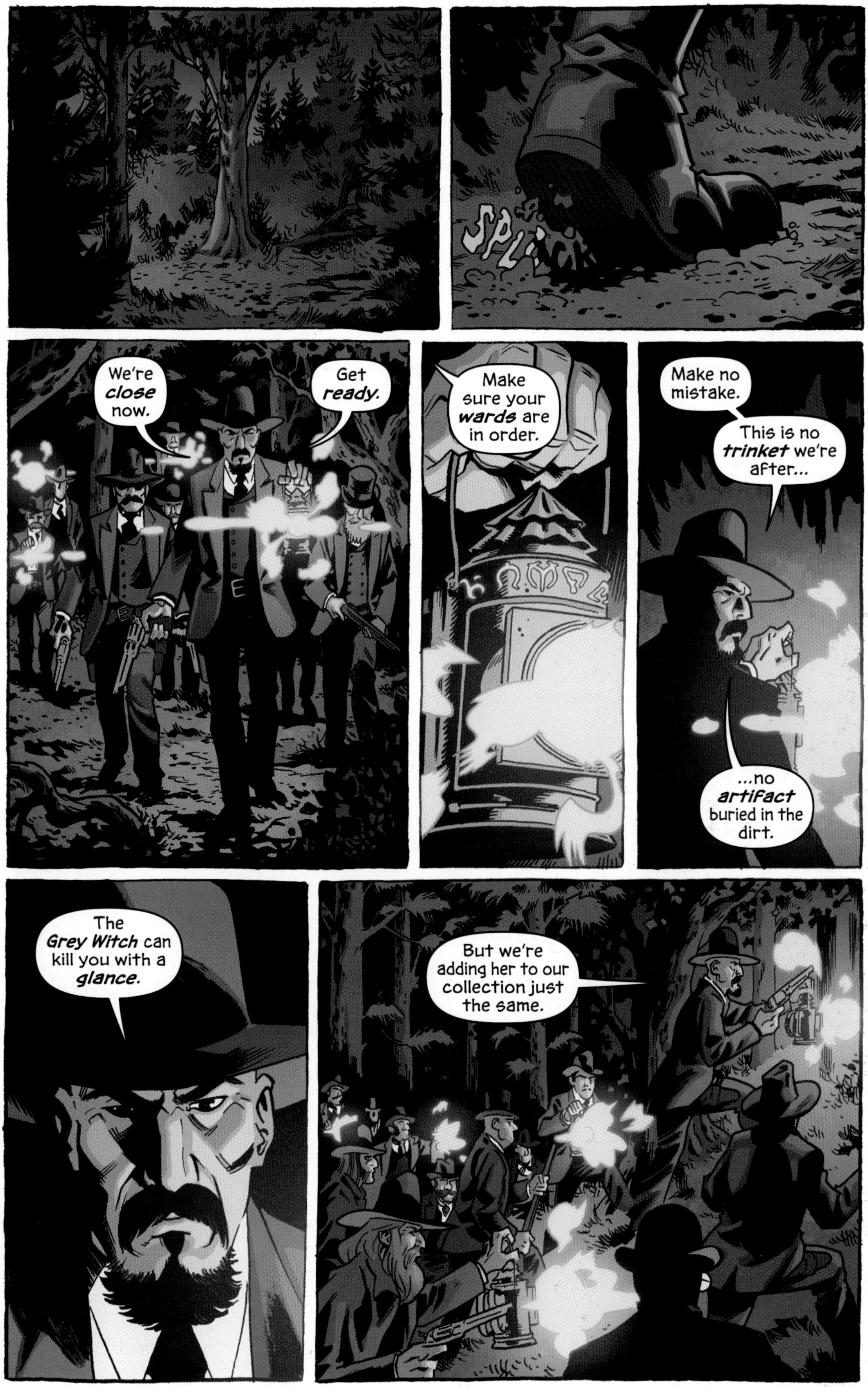
SPLICK
We're close now.
Get ready.
Make sure your wards are in order.
Make no mistake.
This is no trinket we're after...
...no artifact buried in the dirt.
The Grey Witch can kill you with a glance.
But we're adding her to our collection just the same.

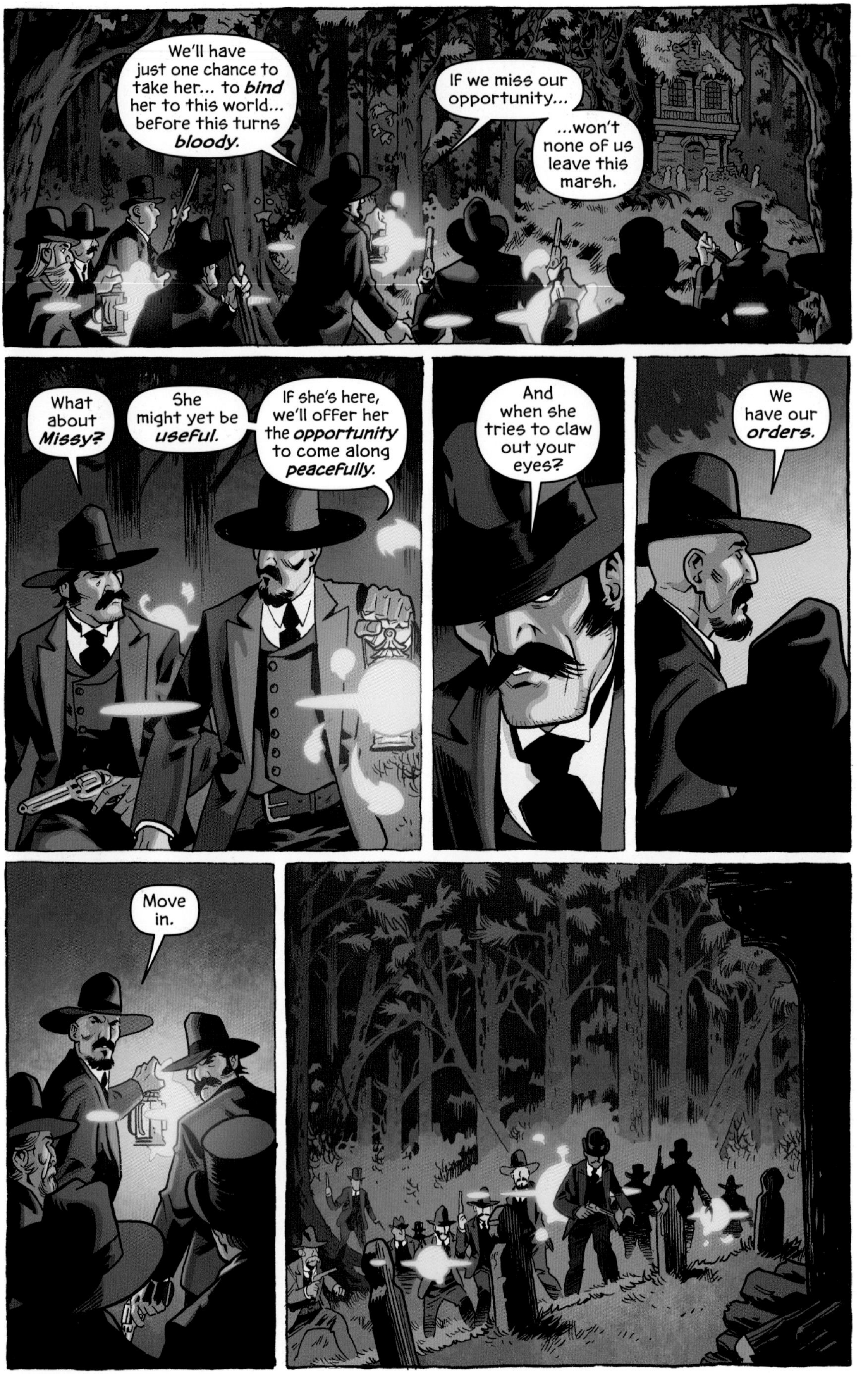
We'll have just one chance to take her... to bind her to this world... before this turns bloody.
If we miss our opportunity...
...won't none of us leave this marsh.
What about Missy?
She might yet be useful.
If she's here, we'll offer her the opportunity to come along peacefully.
And when she tries to claw out your eyes?
We have our orders.
Move in.

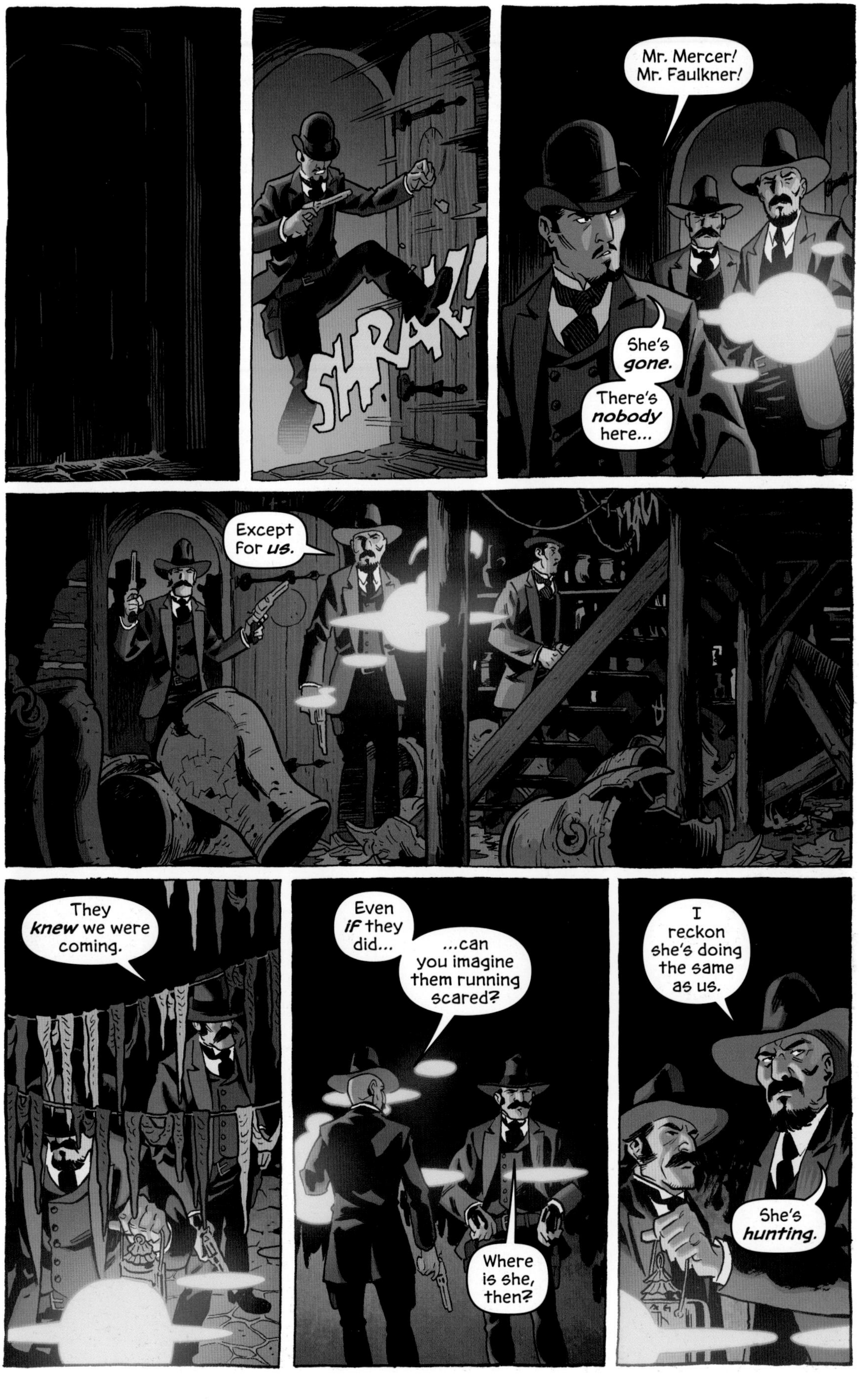
SHRAK!
Mr. Mercer! Mr. Faulkner!
She's *gone.*
There's *nobody* here...
Except for *us.*
They *knew* we were coming.
Even *if* they did...
...can you imagine them running scared?
Where is she, then?
I reckon she's doing the same as us.
She's *hunting.*

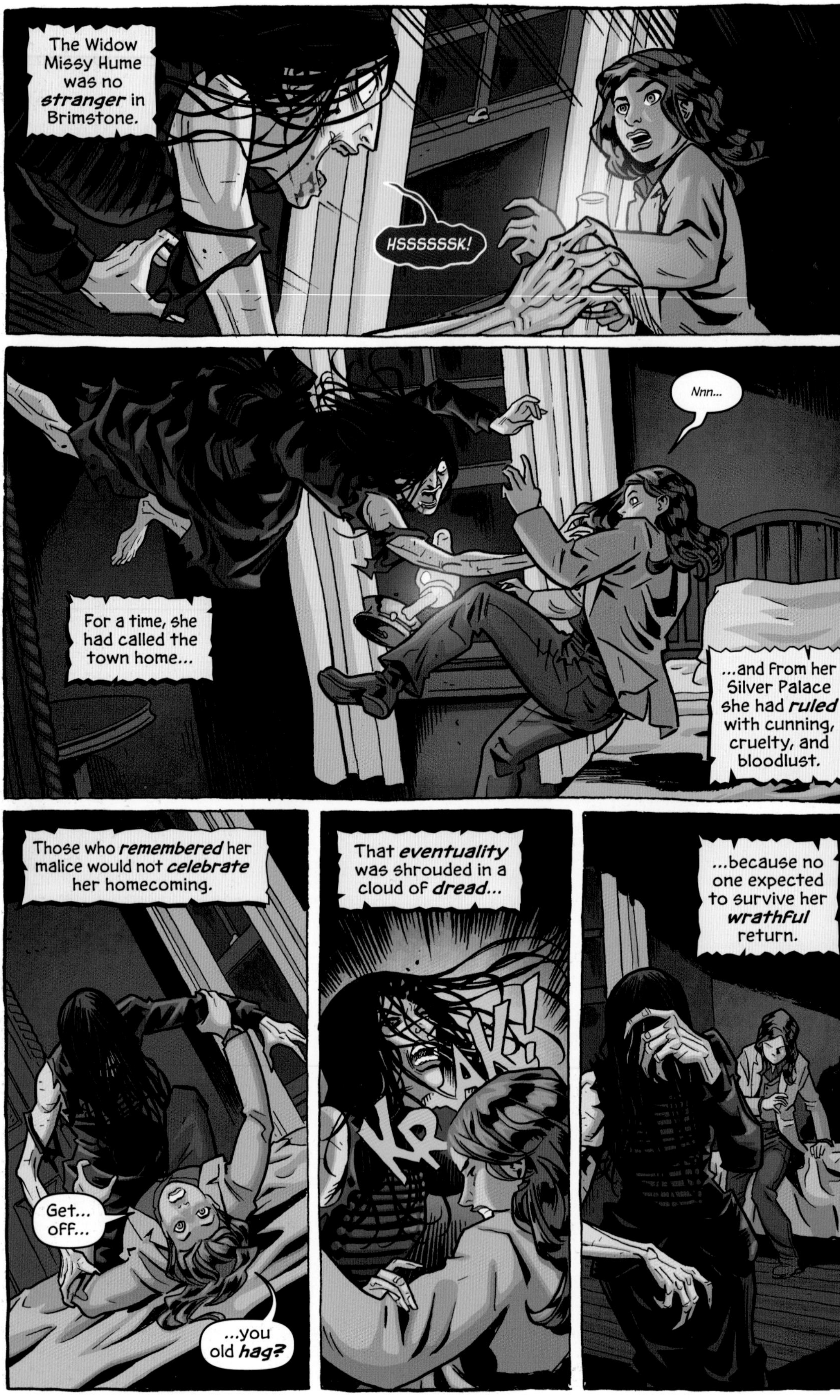
The Widow Missy Hume was no *stranger* in Brimstone.
HSSSSSSK!
For a time, she had called the town home...
Nnn...
...and from her Silver Palace she had *ruled* with cunning, cruelty, and bloodlust.
Those who *remembered* her malice would not *celebrate* her homecoming.
Get... off...
...you old *hag?*
That *eventuality* was shrouded in a cloud of *dread*...
KRAK!!
...because no one expected to survive her *wrathful* return.

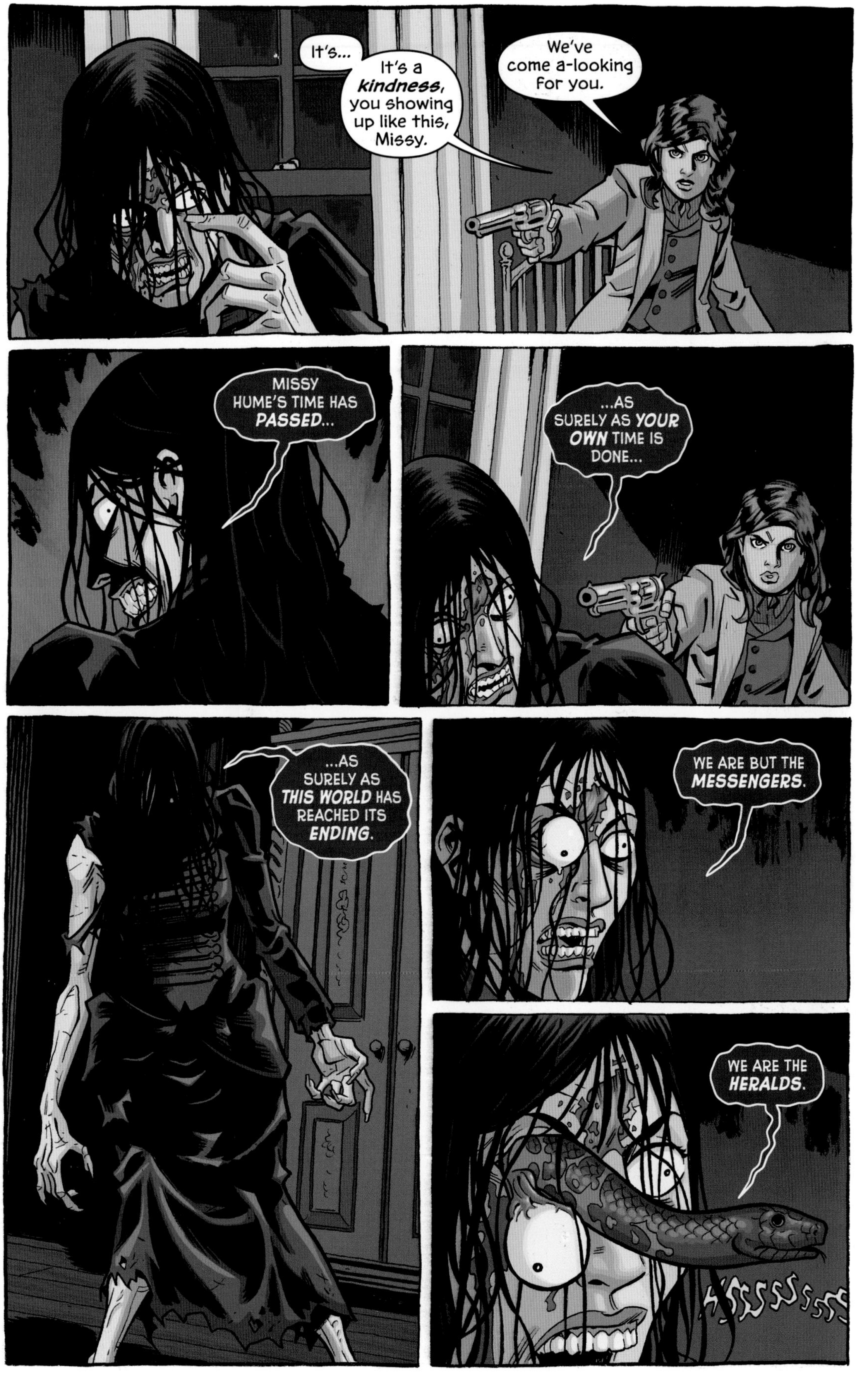
It's...
It's a *kindness*, you showing up like this, Missy.
We've come a-looking for you.
MISSY HUME'S TIME HAS *PASSED*...
...AS SURELY AS *YOUR OWN* TIME IS DONE...
...AS SURELY AS *THIS WORLD* HAS REACHED ITS *ENDING*.
WE ARE BUT THE *MESSENGERS*.
WE ARE THE *HERALDS*.

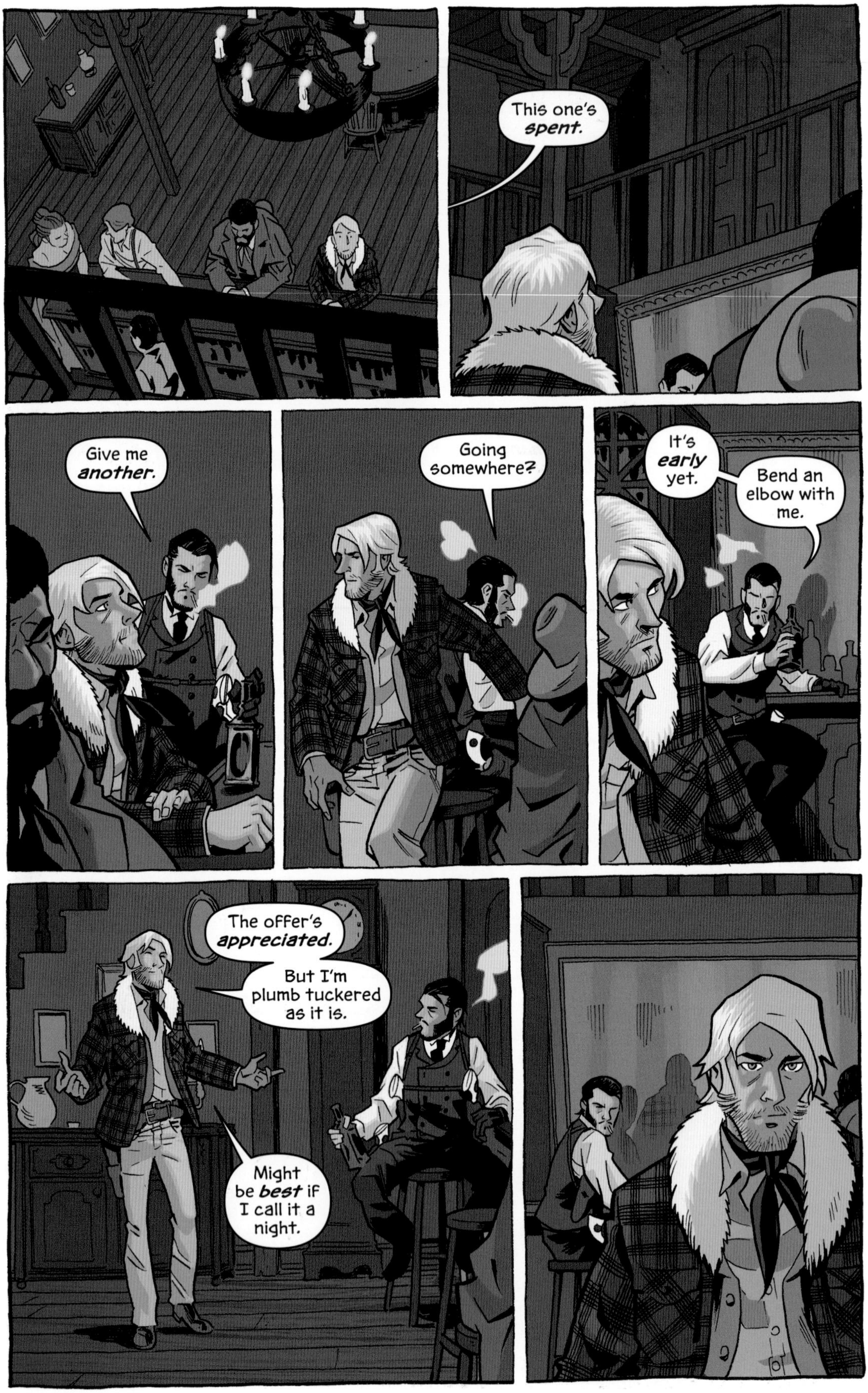
This one's *spent*.
Give me *another*.
Going somewhere?
It's *early* yet.
Bend an elbow with me.
The offer's *appreciated*.
But I'm plumb tuckered as it is.
Might be *best* if I call it a night.

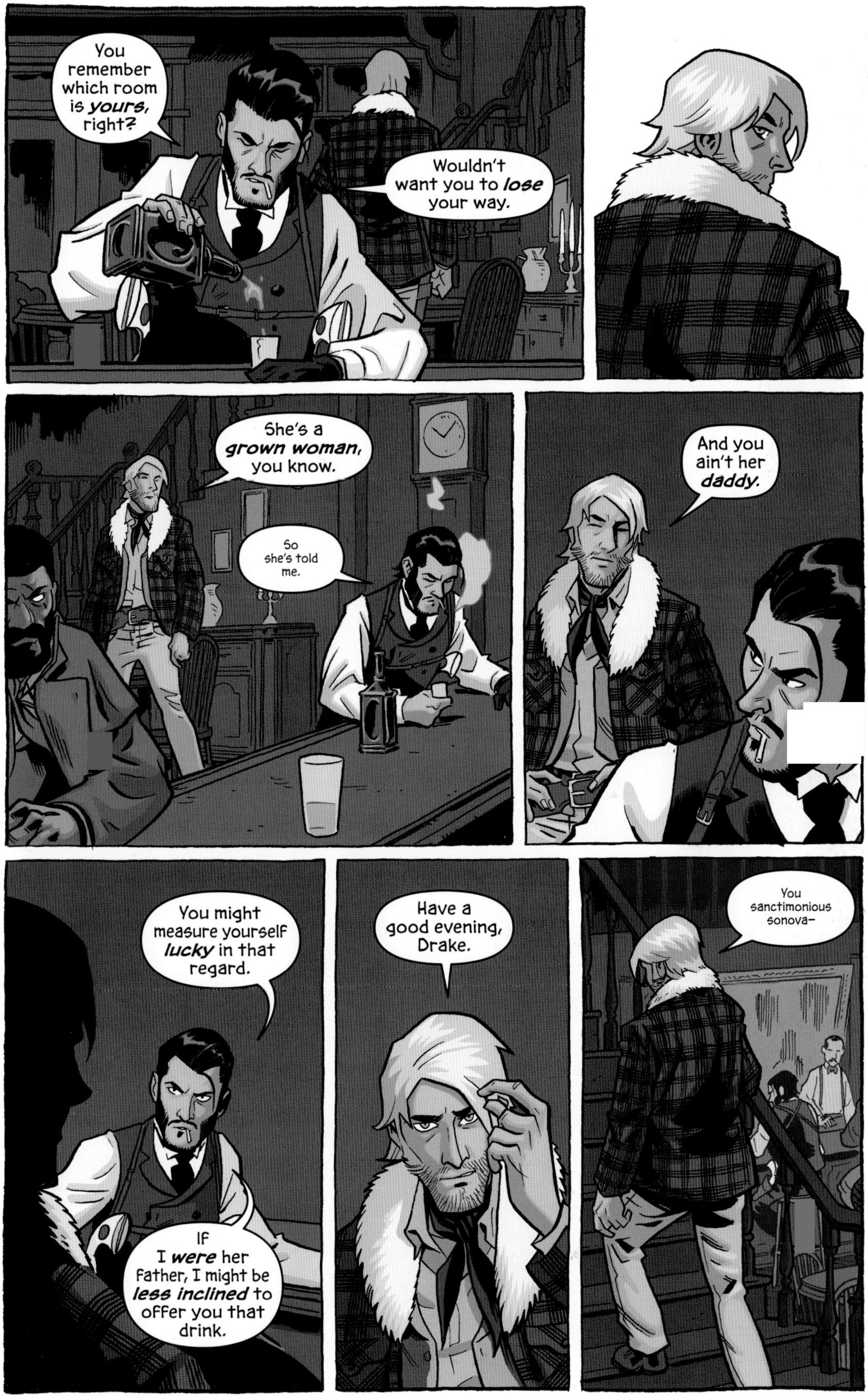
You remember which room is *yours*, right?
Wouldn't want you to *lose* your way.
She's a *grown woman*, you know.
So she's told me.
And you ain't her *daddy*.
You might measure yourself *lucky* in that regard.
If I *were* her father, I might be *less inclined* to offer you that drink.
Have a good evening, Drake.
You sanctimonious sonova—

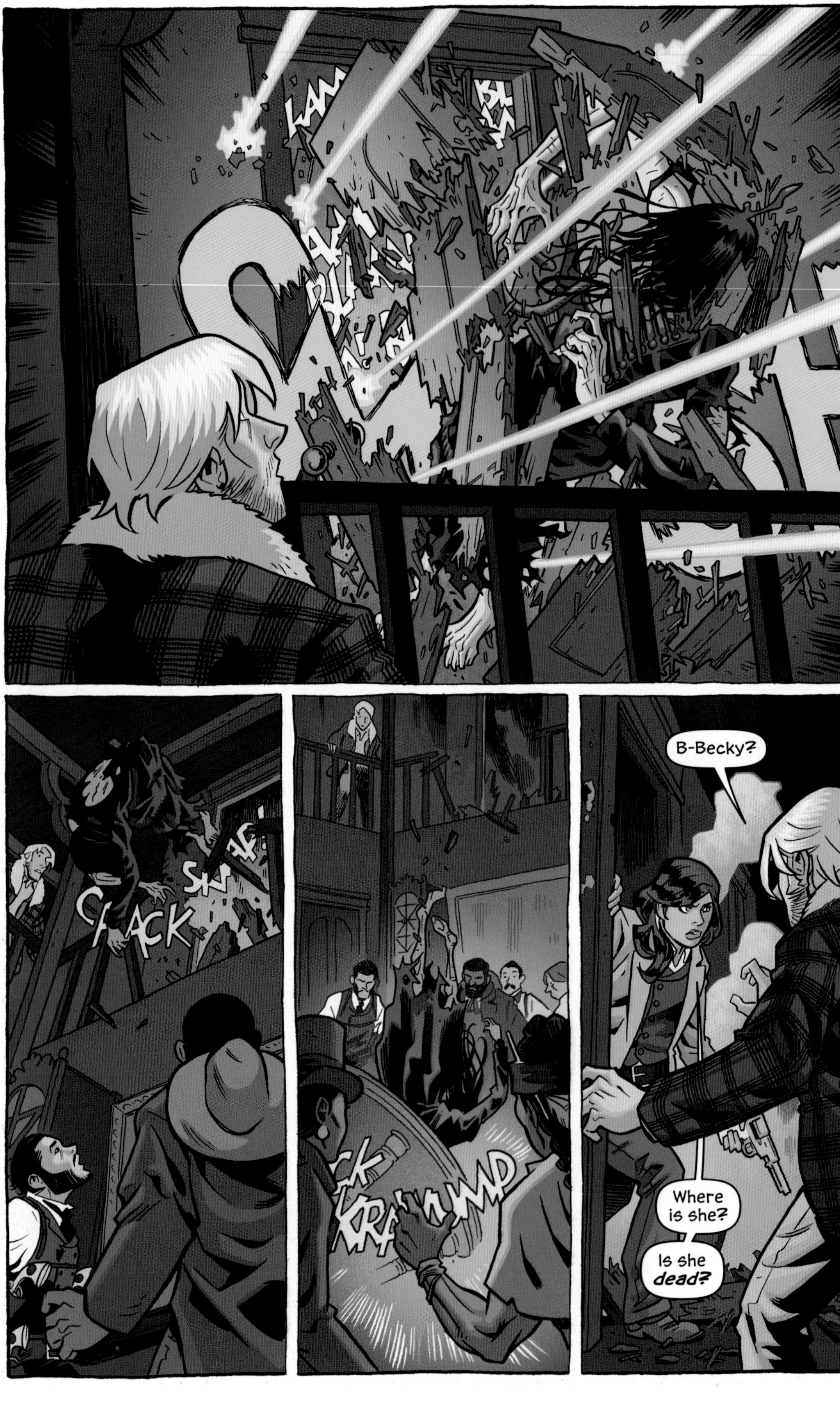

CRACK
B-Becky?
Where is she?
Is she *dead?*

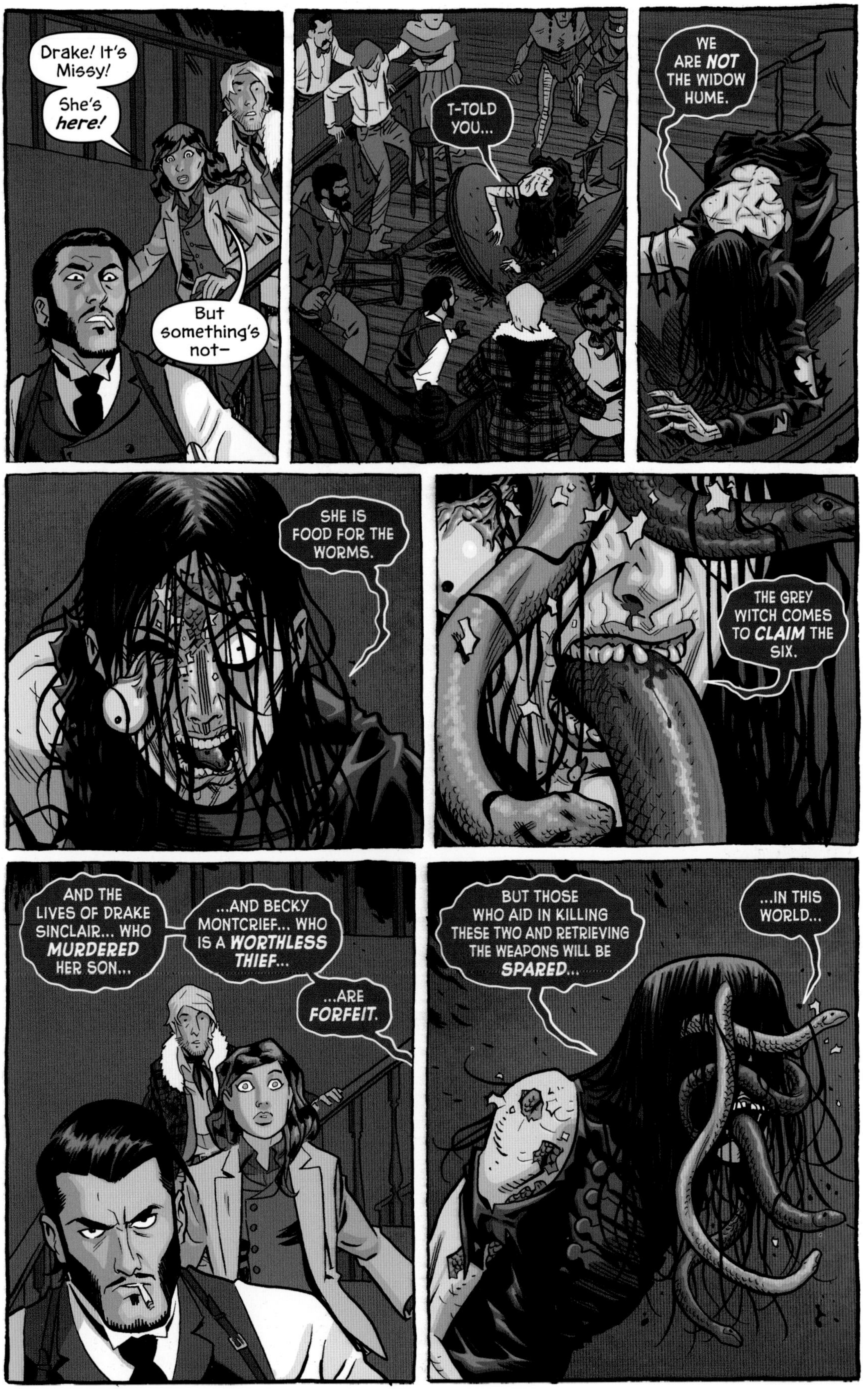

Drake! It's Missy!
She's *here!*
But something's not–
T-TOLD YOU...
WE ARE ***NOT*** THE WIDOW HUME.
SHE IS FOOD FOR THE WORMS.
THE GREY WITCH COMES TO ***CLAIM*** THE SIX.
AND THE LIVES OF DRAKE SINCLAIR... WHO ***MURDERED*** HER SON...
...AND BECKY MONTCRIEF... WHO IS A ***WORTHLESS THIEF***...
...ARE ***FORFEIT***.
BUT THOSE WHO AID IN KILLING THESE TWO AND RETRIEVING THE WEAPONS WILL BE ***SPARED***...
...IN THIS WORLD...

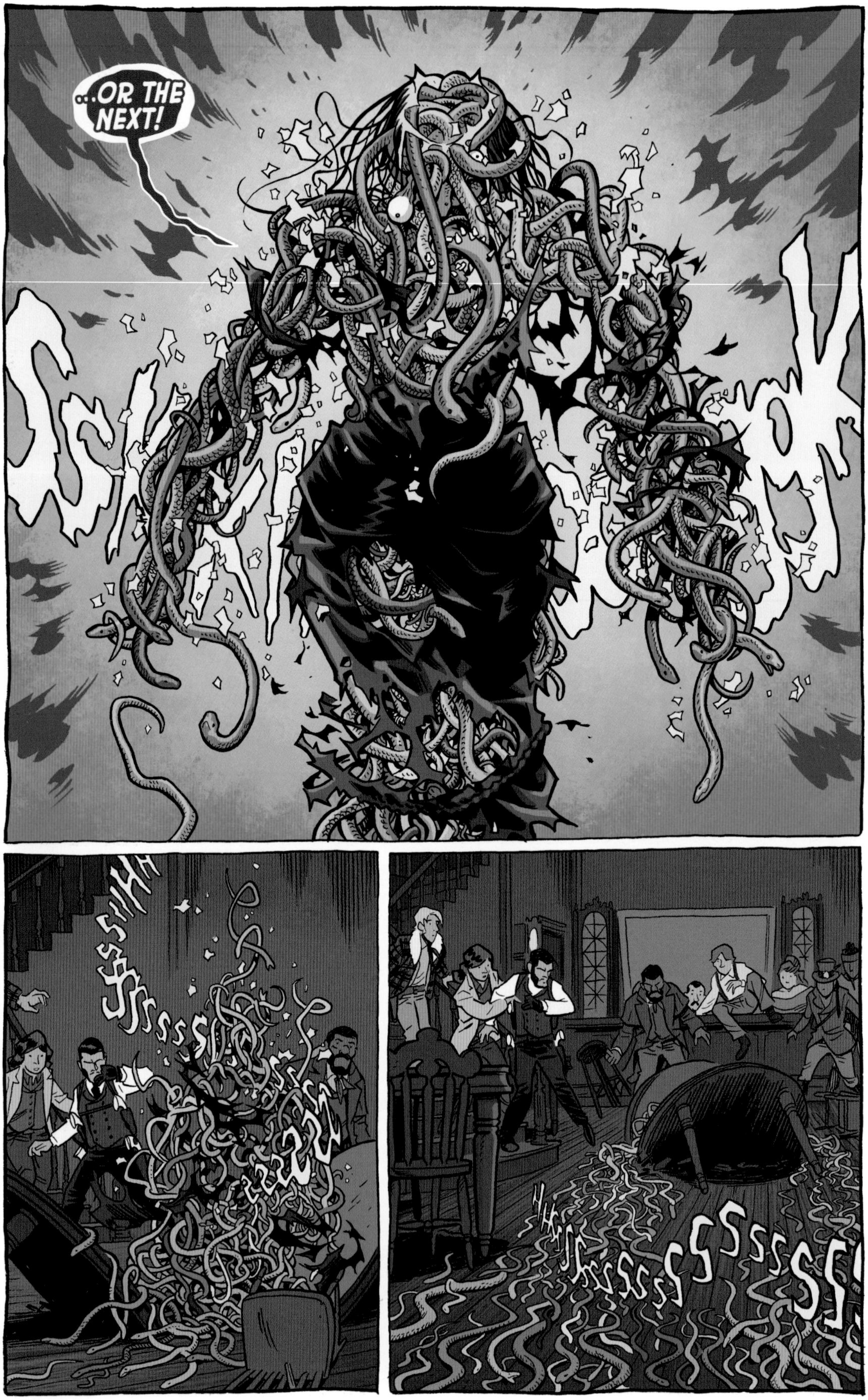
...OR THE NEXT!

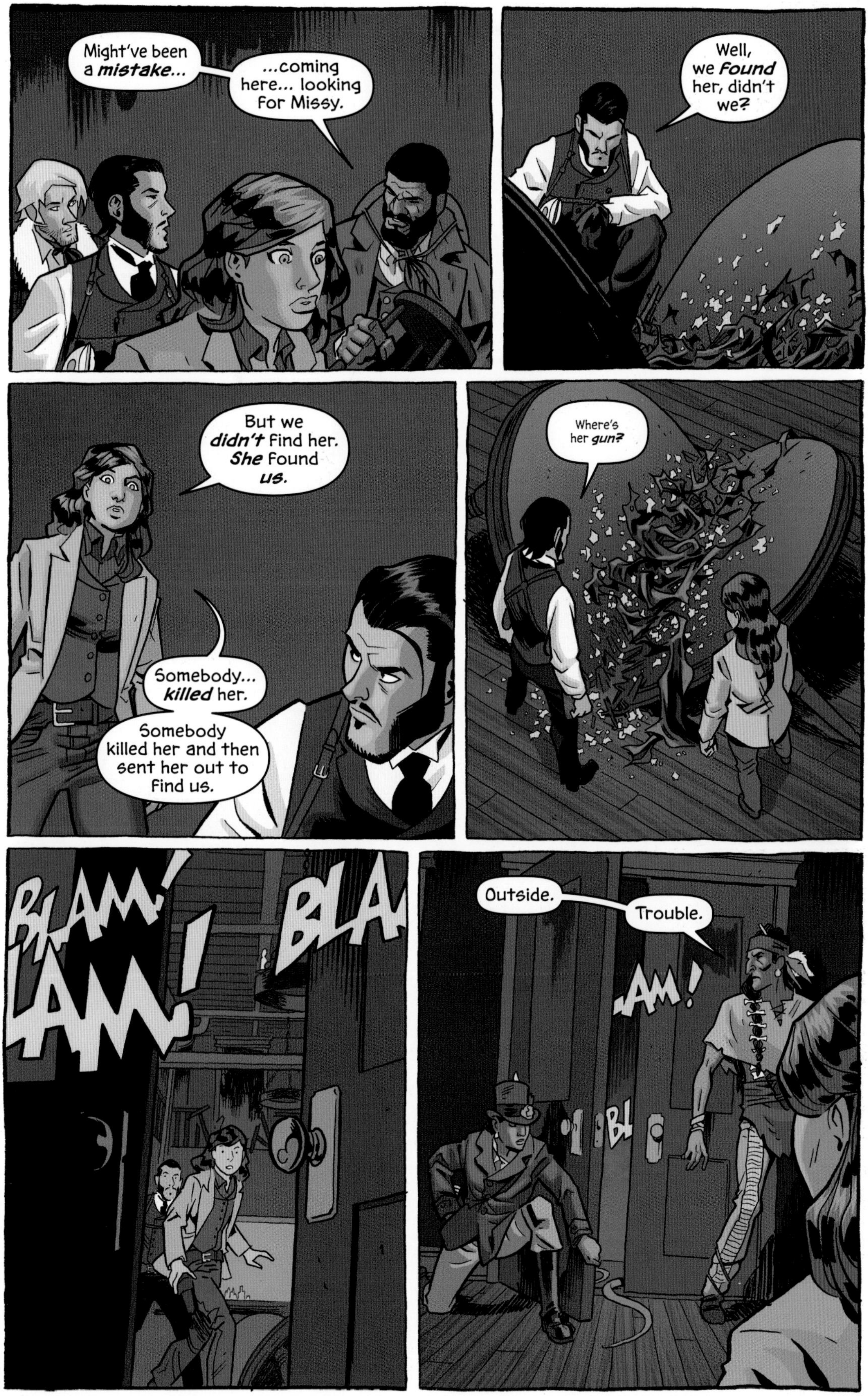
Might've been a mistake...
...coming here... looking for Missy.
Well, we found her, didn't we?
But we didn't find her. She found us.
Somebody... killed her.
Somebody killed her and then sent her out to find us.
Where's her gun?
BLAM! BLAM!
BLA
Outside.
Trouble.
AM!
BL

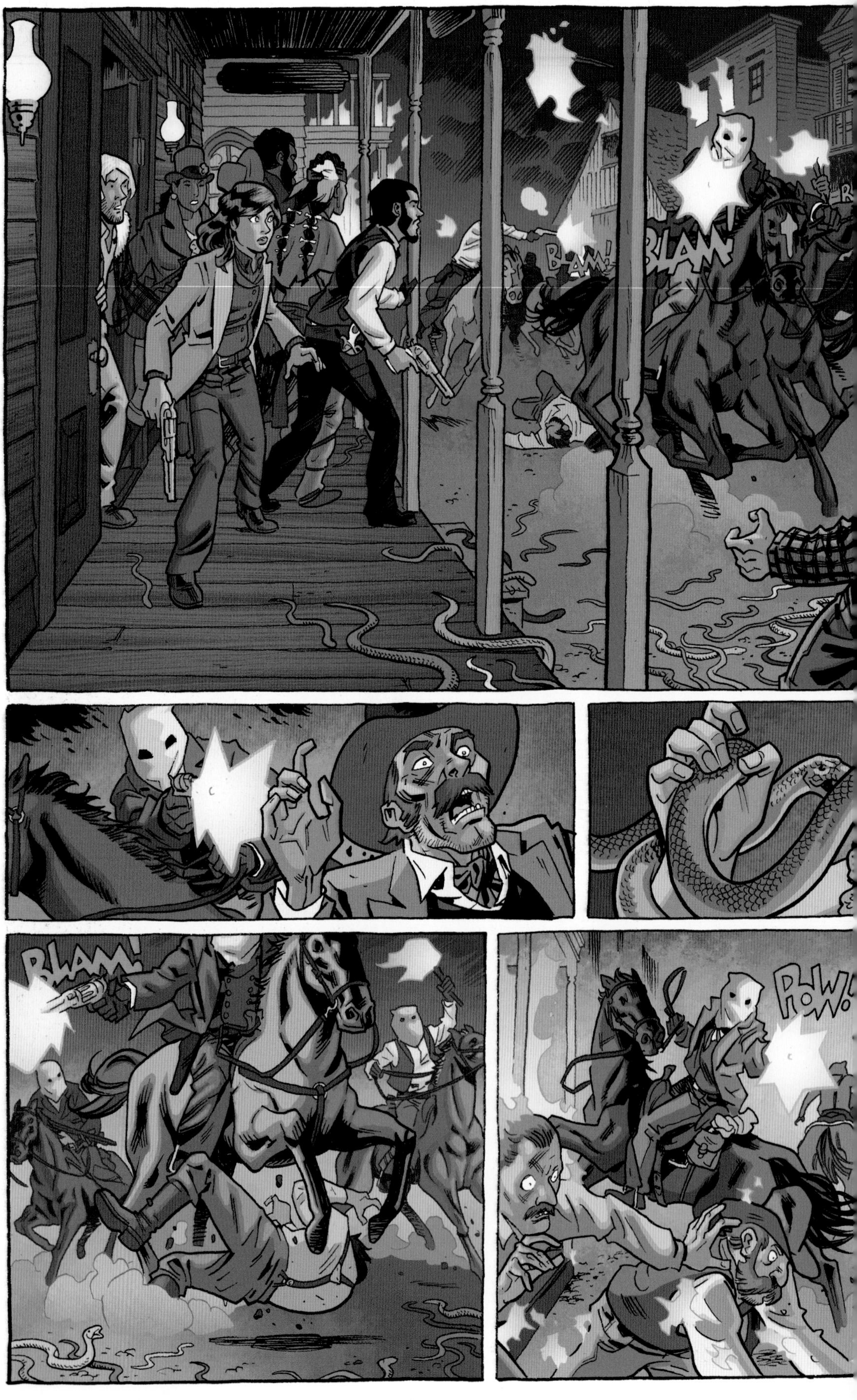
BLAM!
BLAM!
BLAM!
POW!

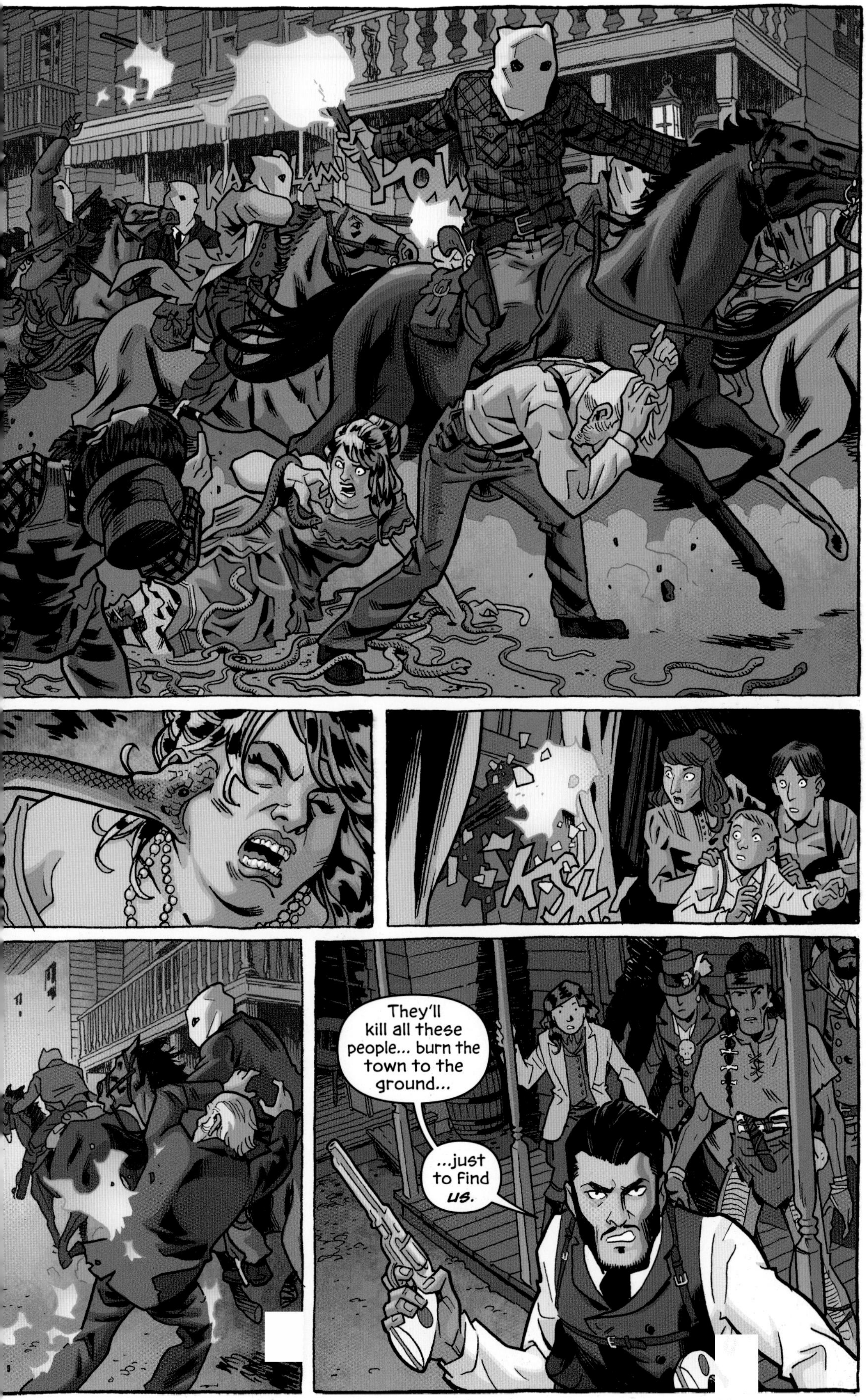
They'll kill all these people... burn the town to the ground...
...just to find *us*.

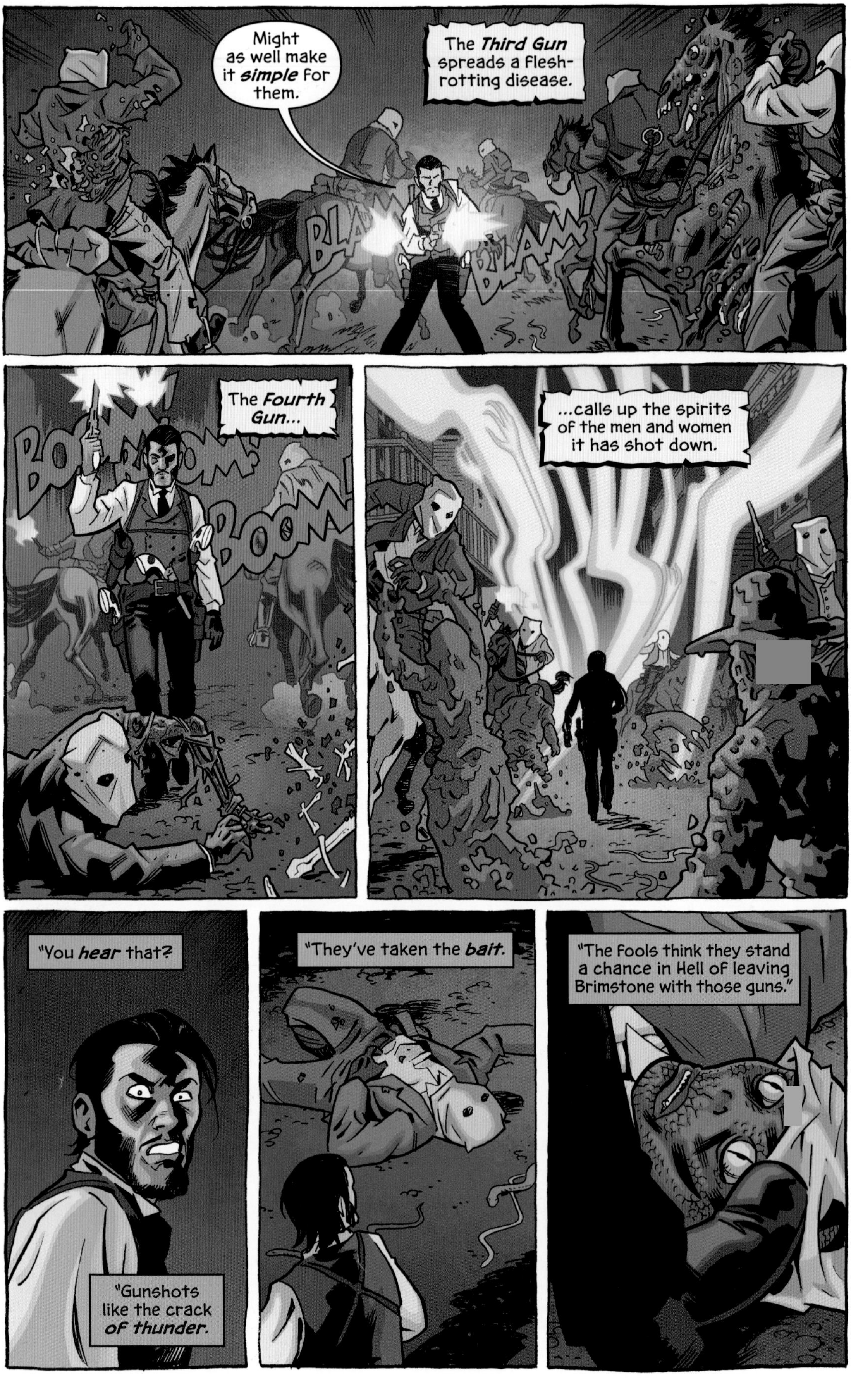
Might as well make it *simple* for them.
The *Third Gun* spreads a flesh-rotting disease.
BLAM!
BLAM!
The *Fourth Gun*...
BOOM!
BOOM!
...calls up the spirits of the men and women it has shot down.
"You *hear* that?
"Gunshots like the crack *of thunder*.
"They've taken the *bait*.
"The fools think they stand a chance in Hell of leaving Brimstone with those guns."

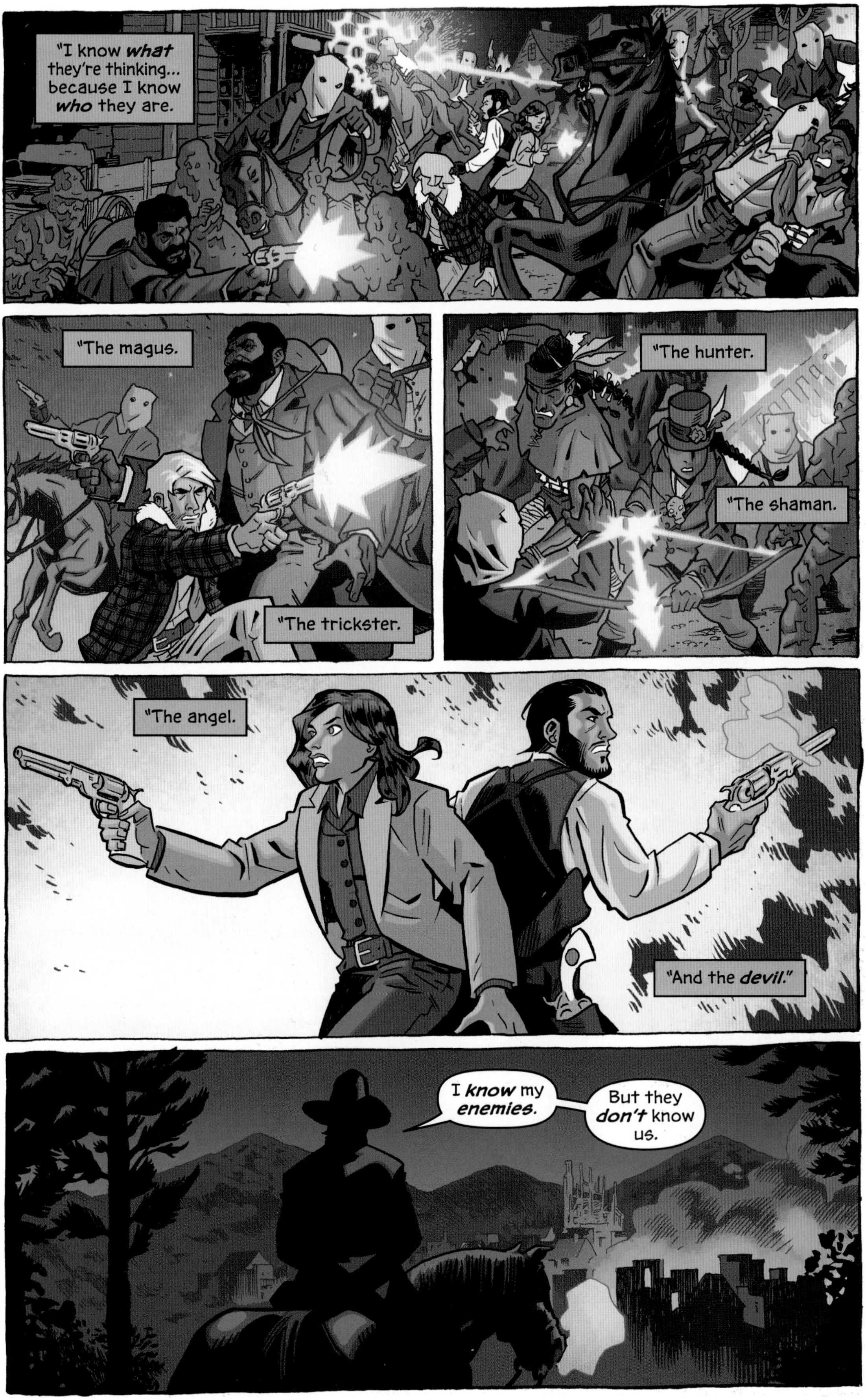
"I know *what* they're thinking... because I know *who* they are.
"The magus.
"The trickster.
"The hunter.
"The shaman.
"The angel.
"And the *devil*."
I *know* my *enemies*.
But they *don't* know us.

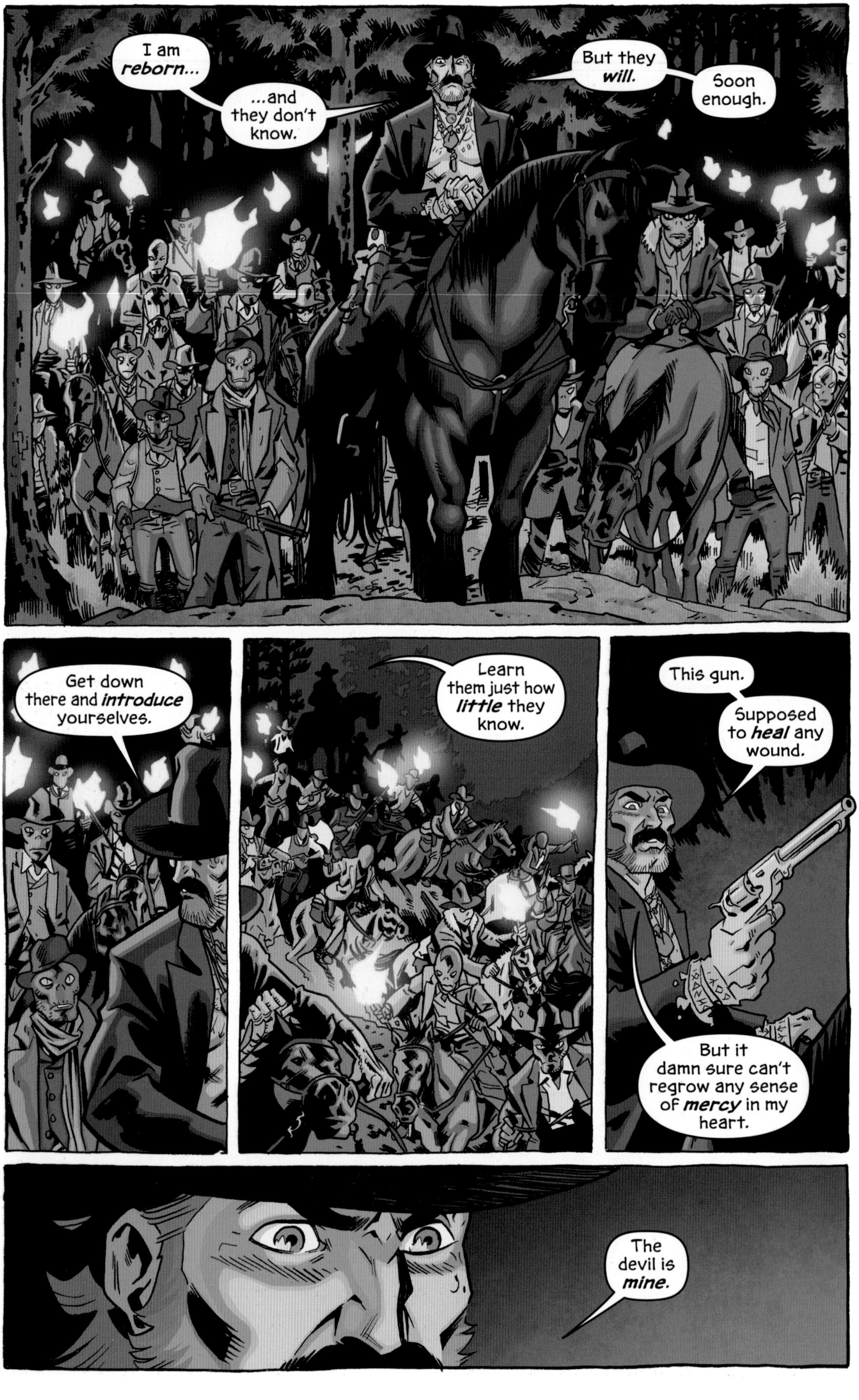

I am *reborn*...
...and they don't know.
But they *will*.
Soon enough.
Get down there and *introduce* yourselves.
Learn them just how *little* they know.
This gun.
Supposed to *heal* any wound.
But it damn sure can't regrow any sense of *mercy* in my heart.
The devil is *mine*.

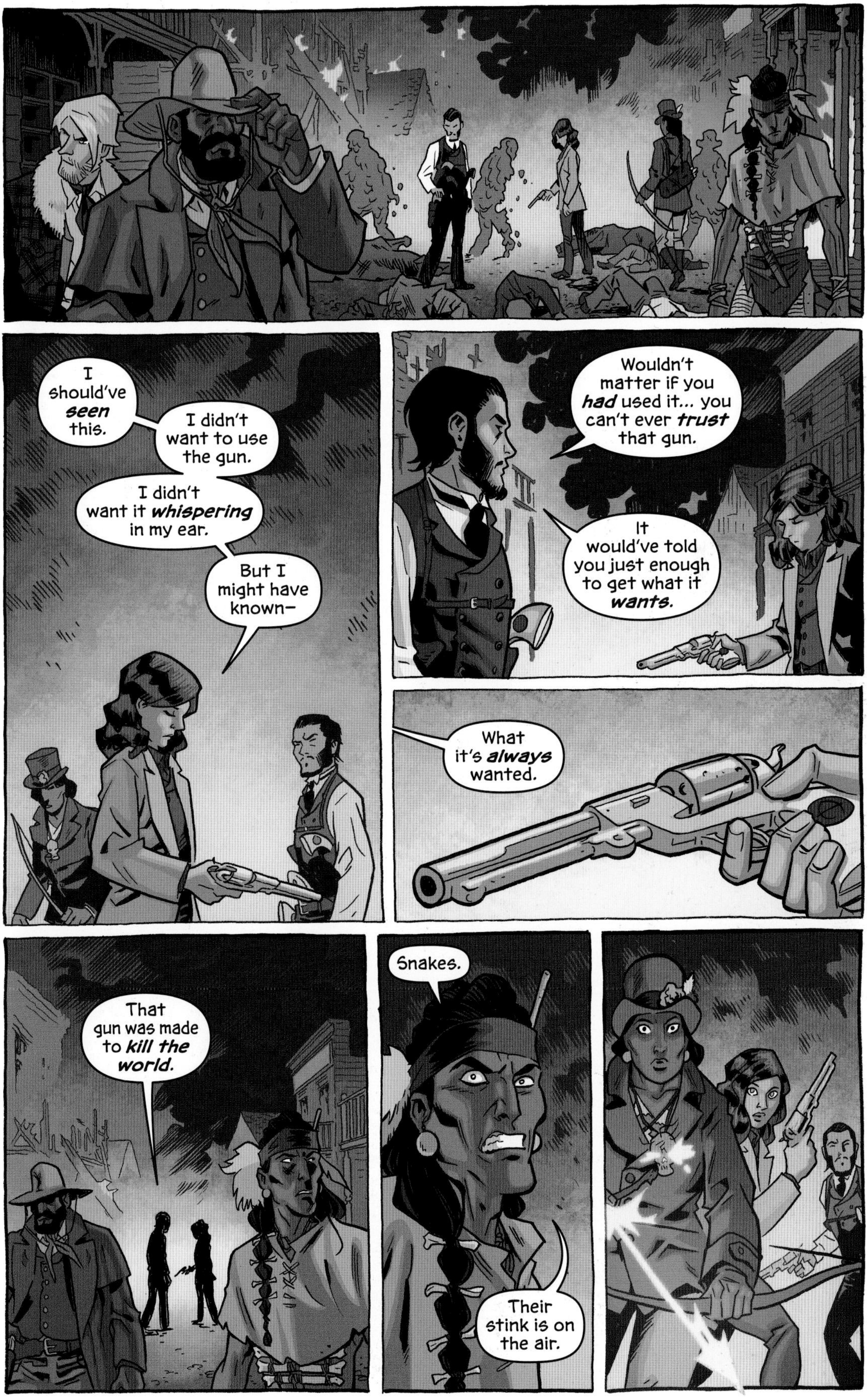
I should've seen this.
I didn't want to use the gun.
I didn't want it whispering in my ear.
But I might have known–
Wouldn't matter if you had used it... you can't ever trust that gun.
It would've told you just enough to get what it wants.
What it's always wanted.
That gun was made to kill the world.
Snakes.
Their stink is on the air.

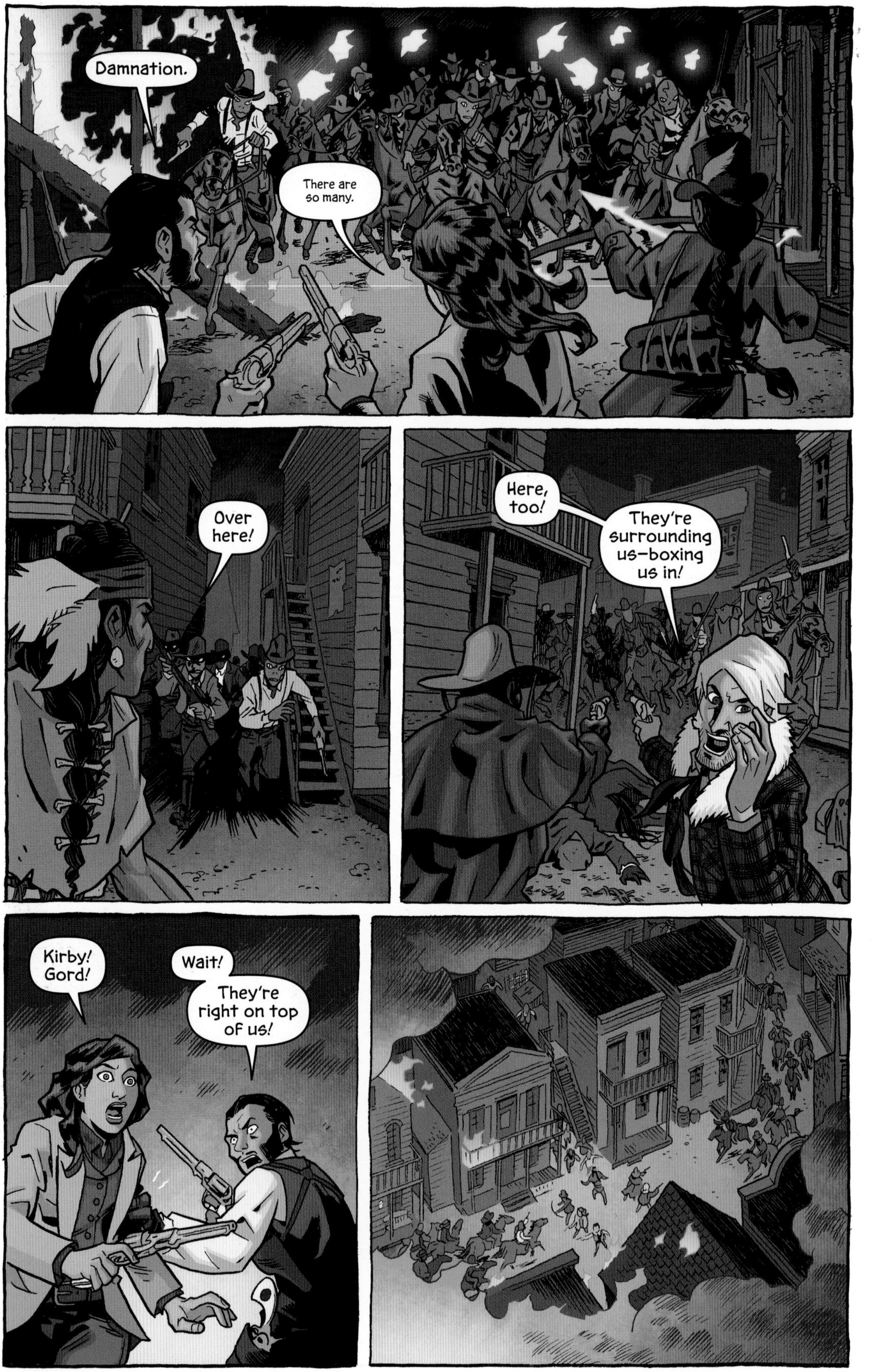

Damnation.
There are so many.
Over here!
Here, too!
They're surrounding us—boxing us in!
Kirby! Gord!
Wait!
They're right on top of us!

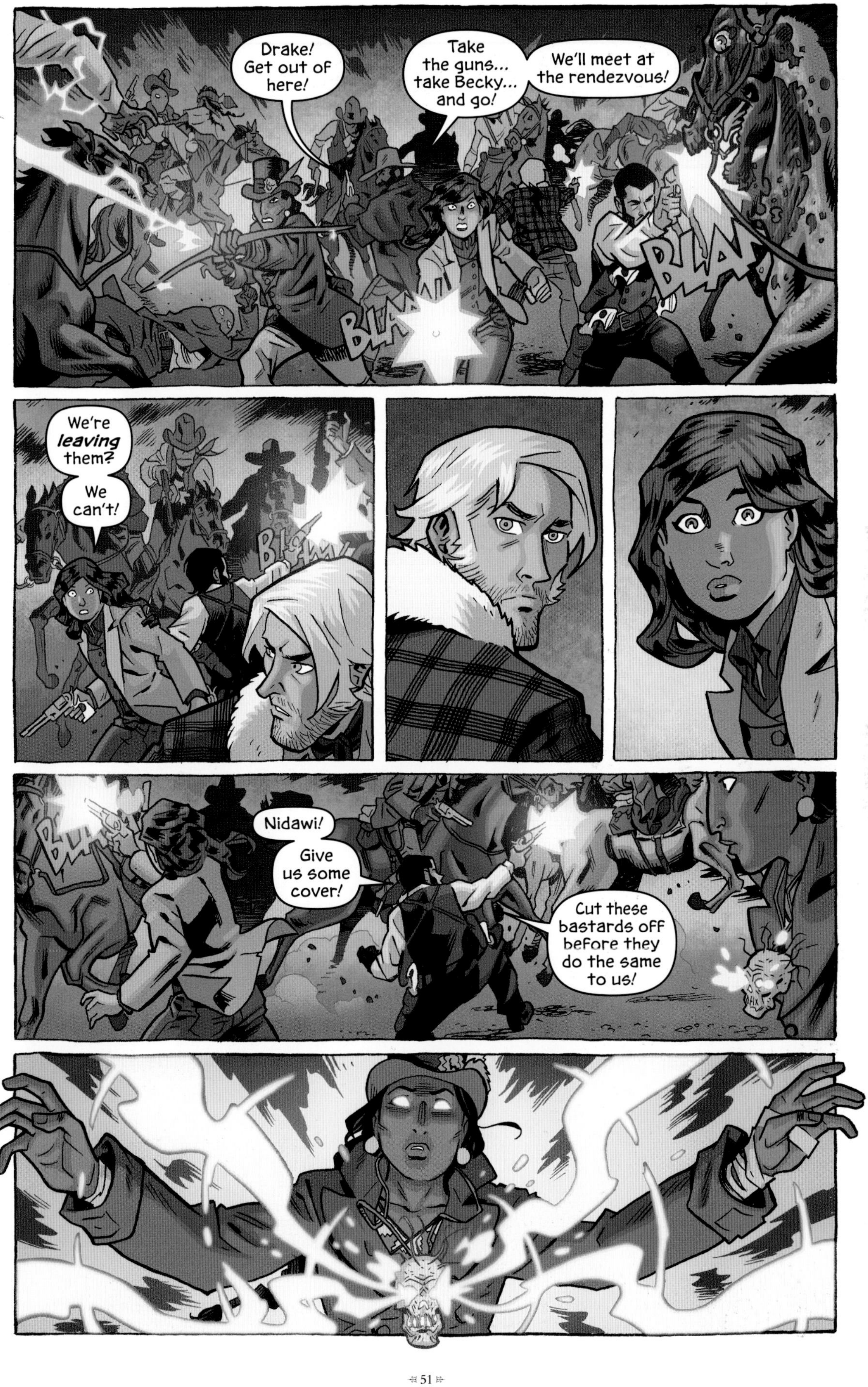
Drake! Get out of here!
Take the guns... take Becky... and go!
We'll meet at the rendezvous!
BLAM
BLAM
We're *leaving* them?
We can't!
Nidawi!
Give us some cover!
Cut these bastards off before they do the same to us!

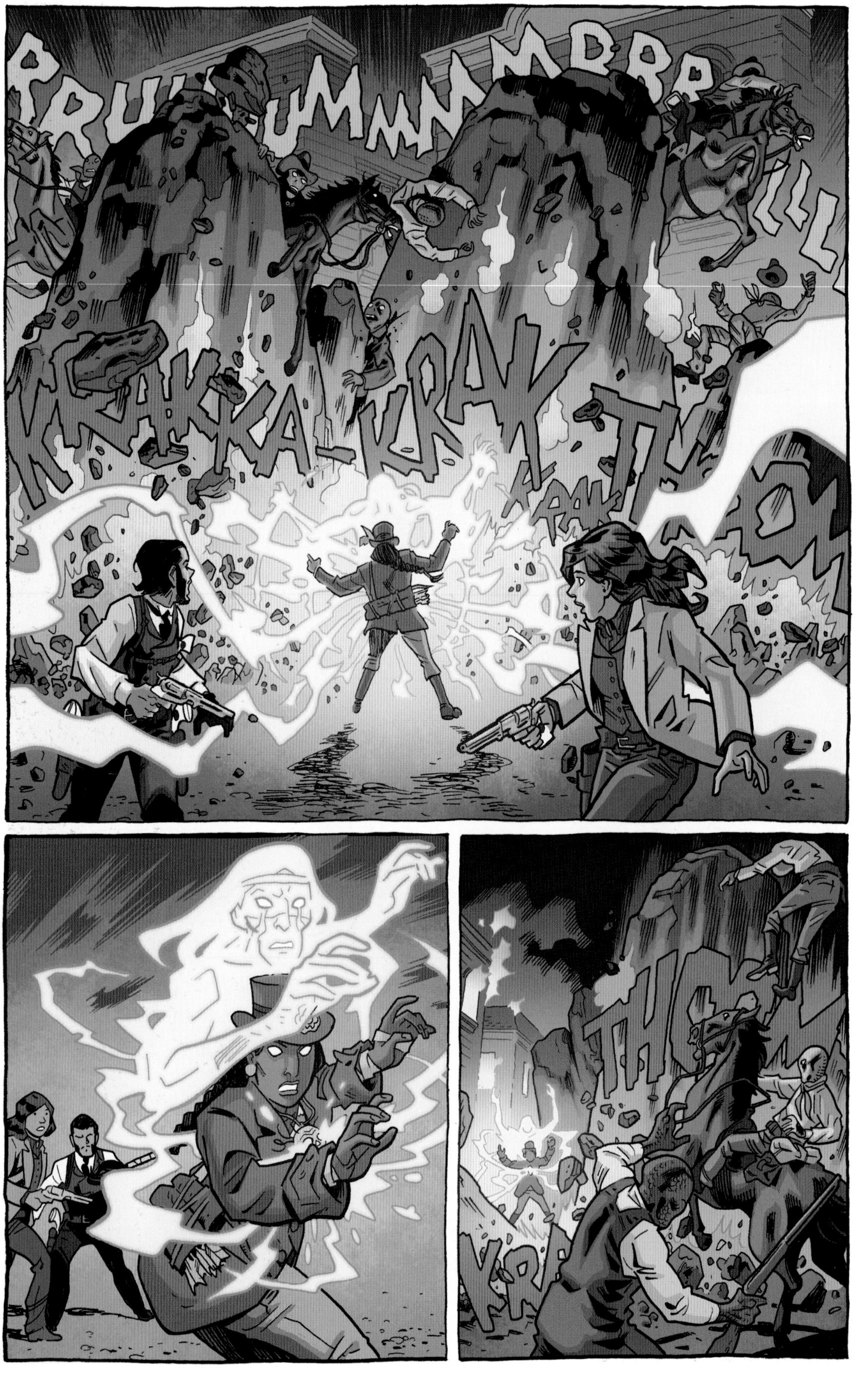
KRAKKA-KRAK

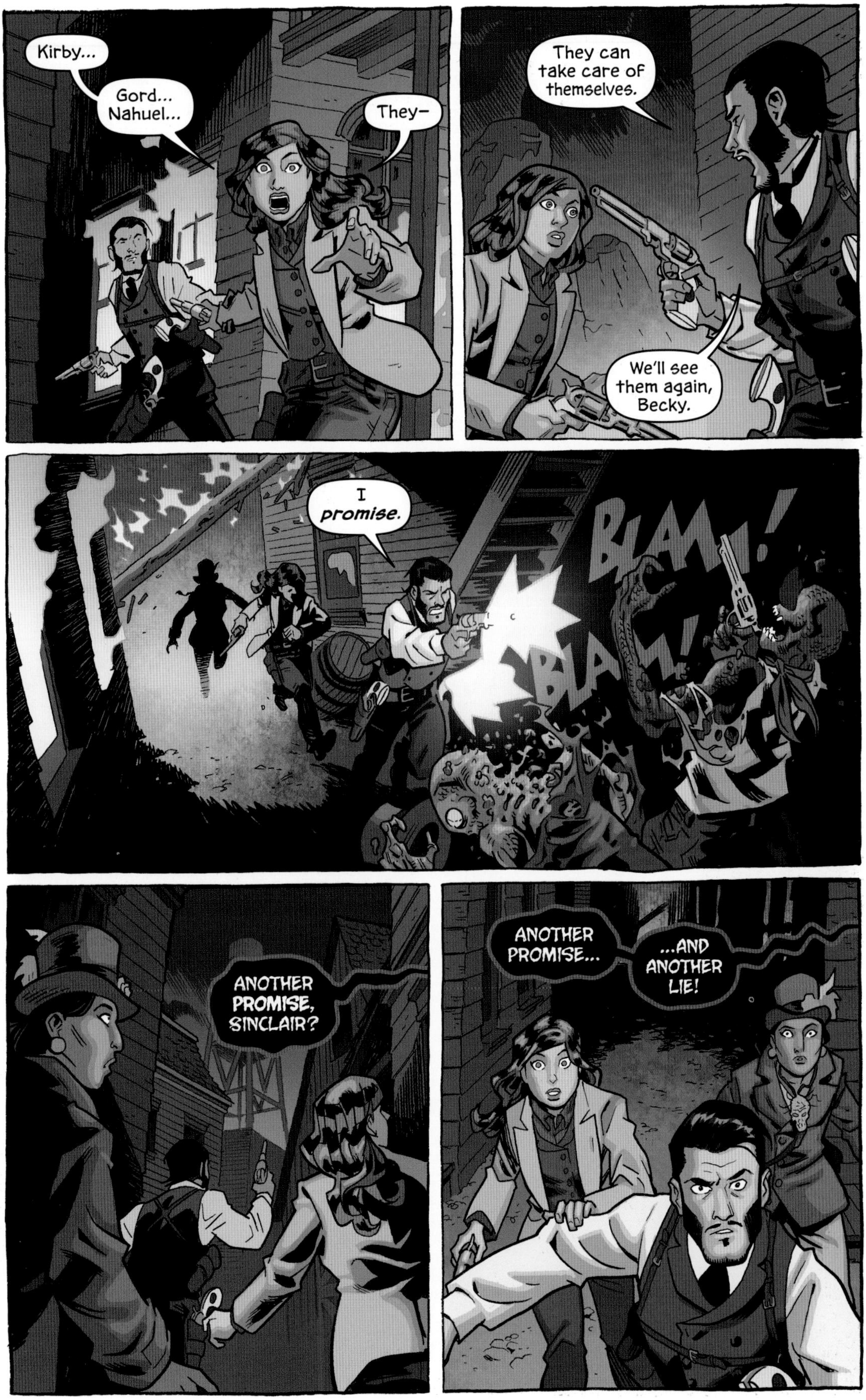
Kirby...
Gord... Nahuel...
They–
They can take care of themselves.
We'll see them again, Becky.
I *promise.*
BLAM!
BLAM!
ANOTHER PROMISE, SINCLAIR?
ANOTHER PROMISE...
...AND ANOTHER LIE!

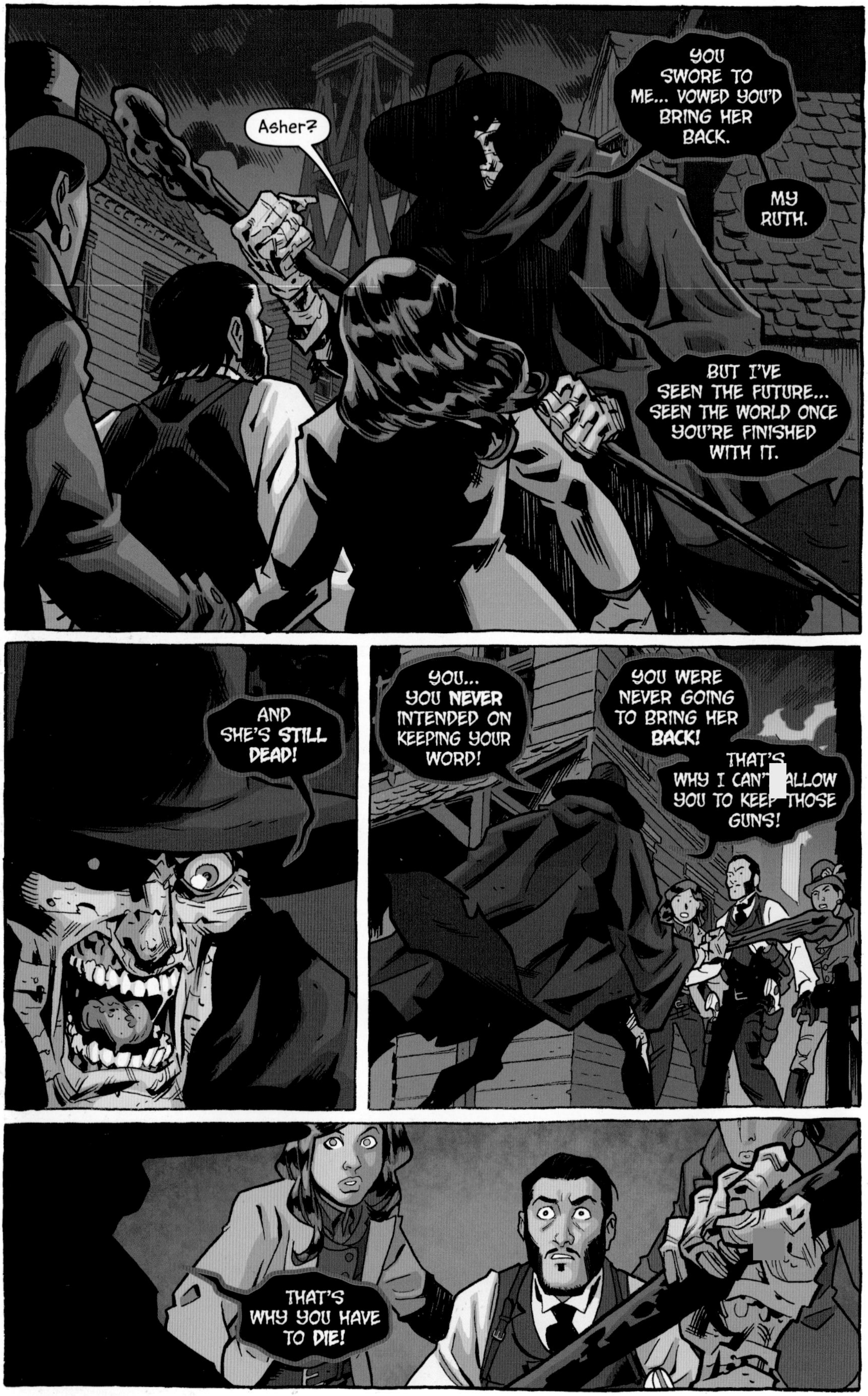

Asher?
YOU SWORE TO ME... VOWED YOU'D BRING HER BACK.
MY RUTH.
BUT I'VE SEEN THE FUTURE... SEEN THE WORLD ONCE YOU'RE FINISHED WITH IT.
AND SHE'S **STILL DEAD!**
YOU... YOU **NEVER** INTENDED ON KEEPING YOUR WORD!
YOU WERE NEVER GOING TO BRING HER **BACK!**
THAT'S WHY I CAN'T ALLOW YOU TO KEEP THOSE GUNS!
THAT'S WHY YOU HAVE TO **DIE!**

CHAPTER THREE

DRY GOO

BOOM! BOOM! BOOM! BOOM

BOOM!

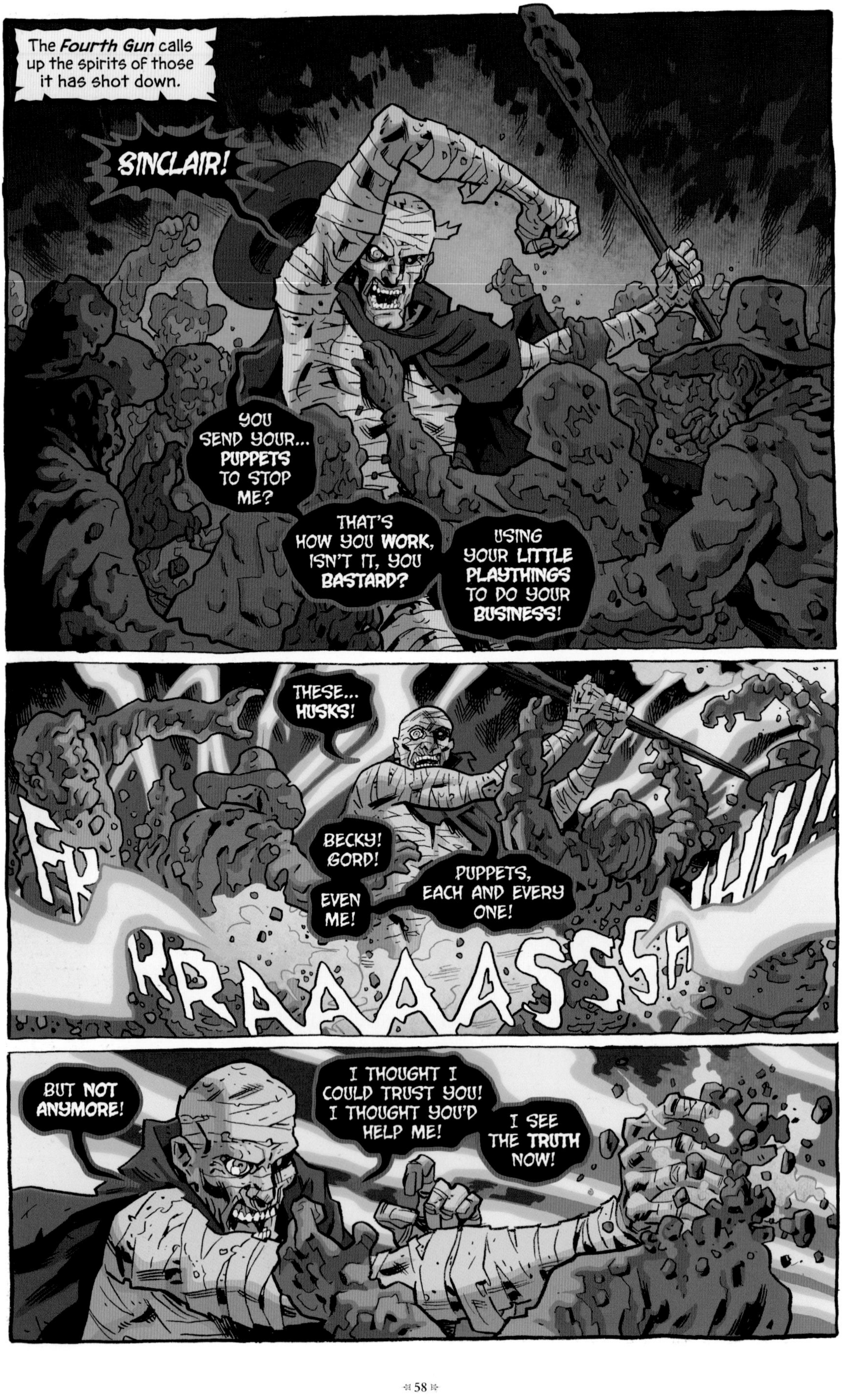
The *Fourth Gun* calls up the spirits of those it has shot down.
SINCLAIR!
YOU SEND YOUR... **PUPPETS** TO STOP ME?
THAT'S HOW YOU **WORK**, ISN'T IT, YOU **BASTARD?**
USING YOUR **LITTLE PLAYTHINGS** TO DO YOUR **BUSINESS!**
THESE... **HUSKS!**
BECKY! GORD!
EVEN ME!
PUPPETS, EACH AND EVERY ONE!
FK
RRAAAASSSH
BUT **NOT ANYMORE!**
I THOUGHT I COULD TRUST YOU! I THOUGHT YOU'D HELP ME!
I SEE THE **TRUTH** NOW!

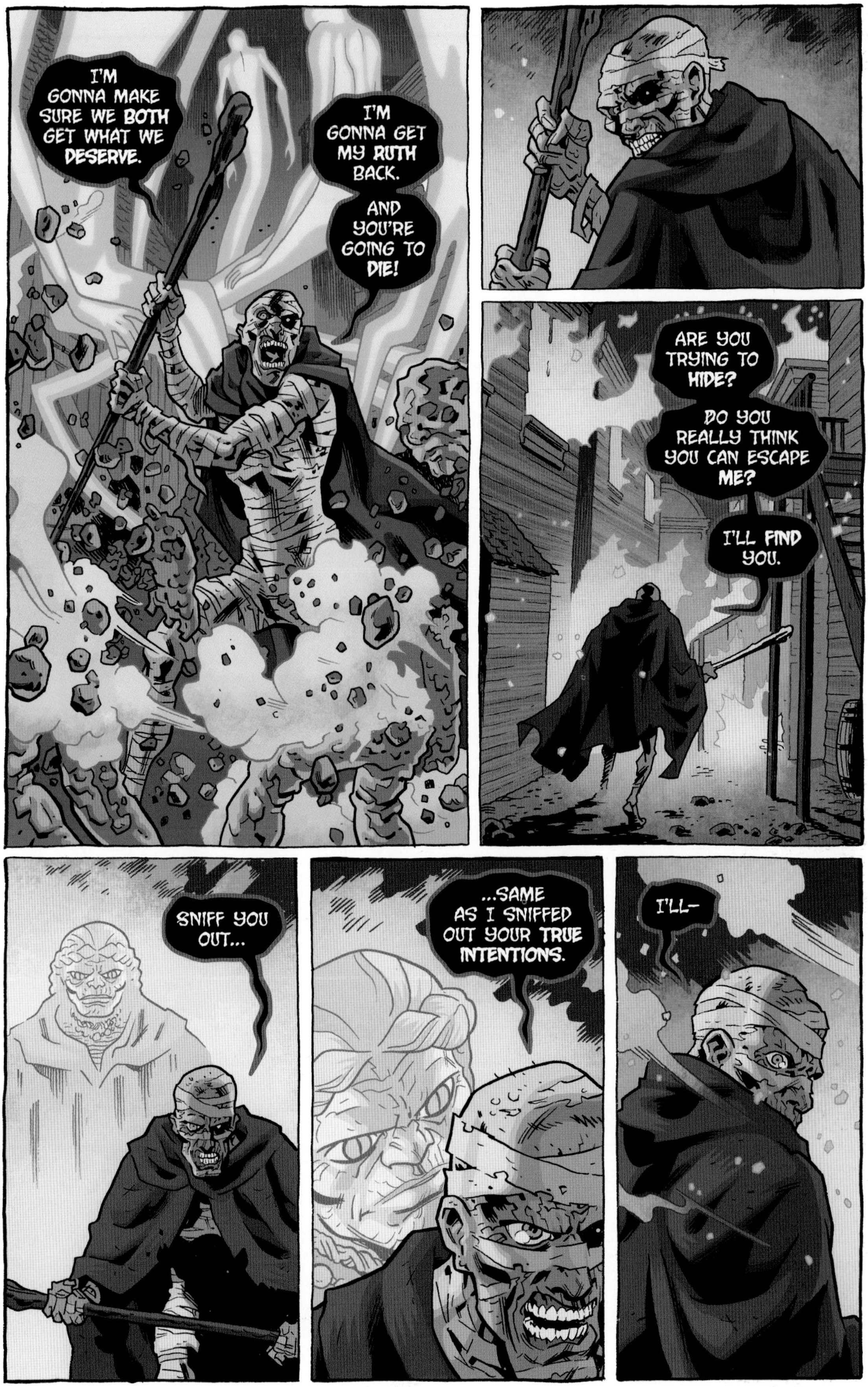
I'M GONNA MAKE SURE WE BOTH GET WHAT WE DESERVE.
I'M GONNA GET MY RUTH BACK.
AND YOU'RE GOING TO DIE!
ARE YOU TRYING TO HIDE?
DO YOU REALLY THINK YOU CAN ESCAPE ME?
I'LL FIND YOU.
SNIFF YOU OUT...
...SAME AS I SNIFFED OUT YOUR TRUE INTENTIONS.
I'LL-

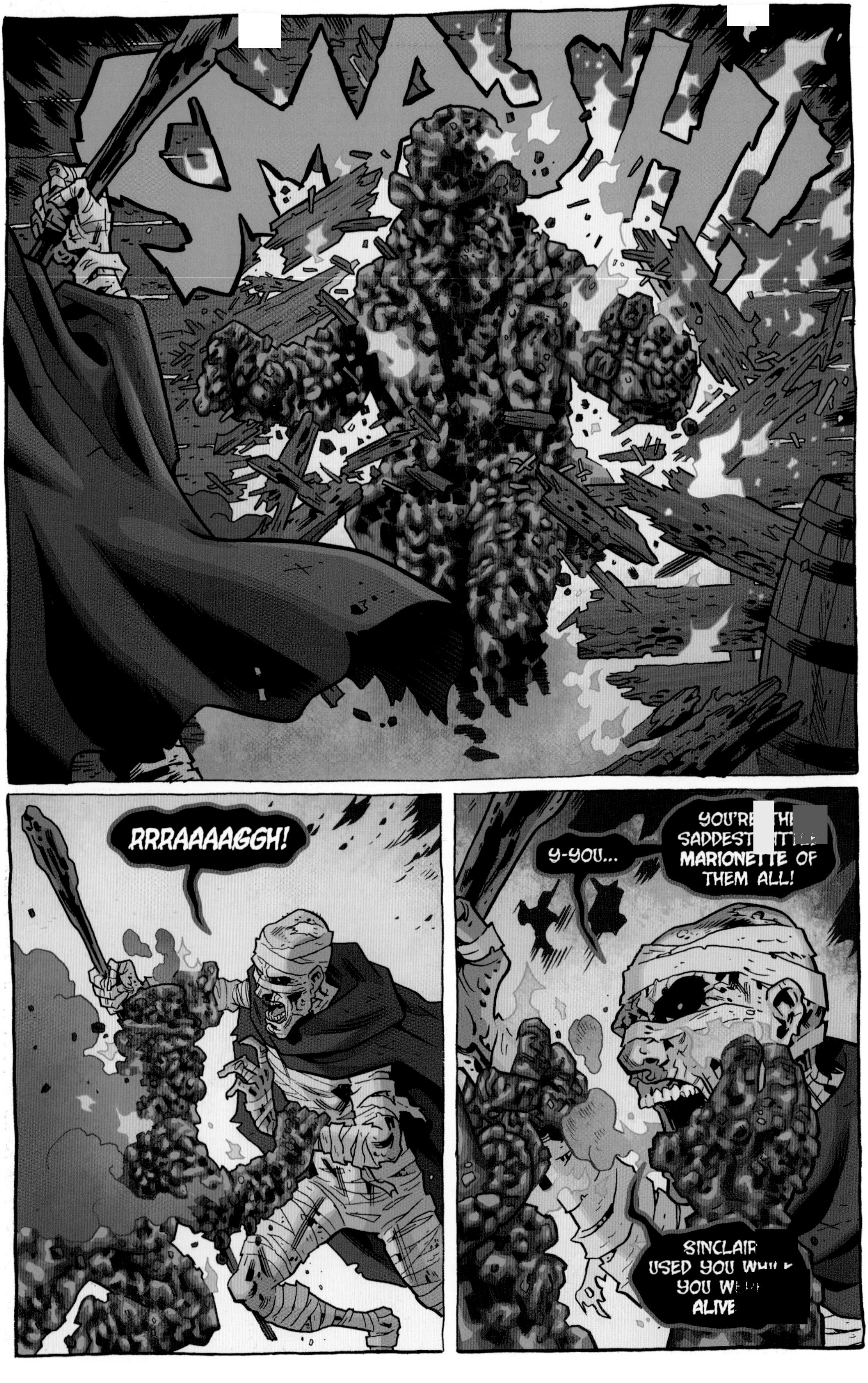
RRRAAAAGGH!
Y-YOU...
SADDEST
MARIONETTE OF THEM ALL!
SINCLAIR
USED YOU
YOU
ALIVE

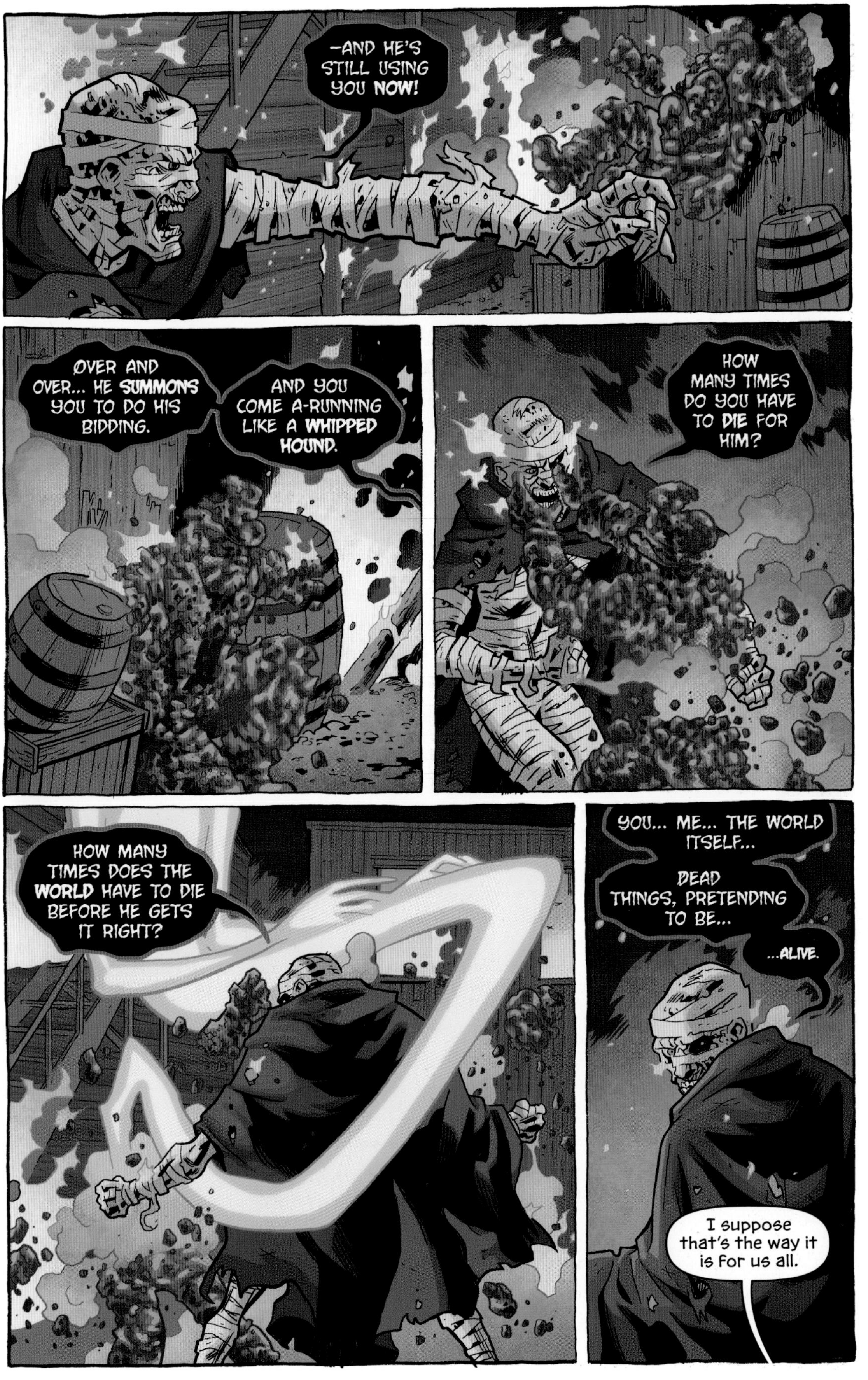

–AND HE'S STILL USING YOU **NOW!**
OVER AND OVER... HE **SUMMONS** YOU TO DO HIS BIDDING.
AND YOU COME A-RUNNING LIKE A **WHIPPED HOUND.**
HOW MANY TIMES DO YOU HAVE TO **DIE** FOR HIM?
HOW MANY TIMES DOES THE **WORLD** HAVE TO DIE BEFORE HE GETS IT RIGHT?
YOU... ME... THE WORLD ITSELF...
DEAD THINGS, PRETENDING TO BE...
...**ALIVE.**
I suppose that's the way it is for us all.

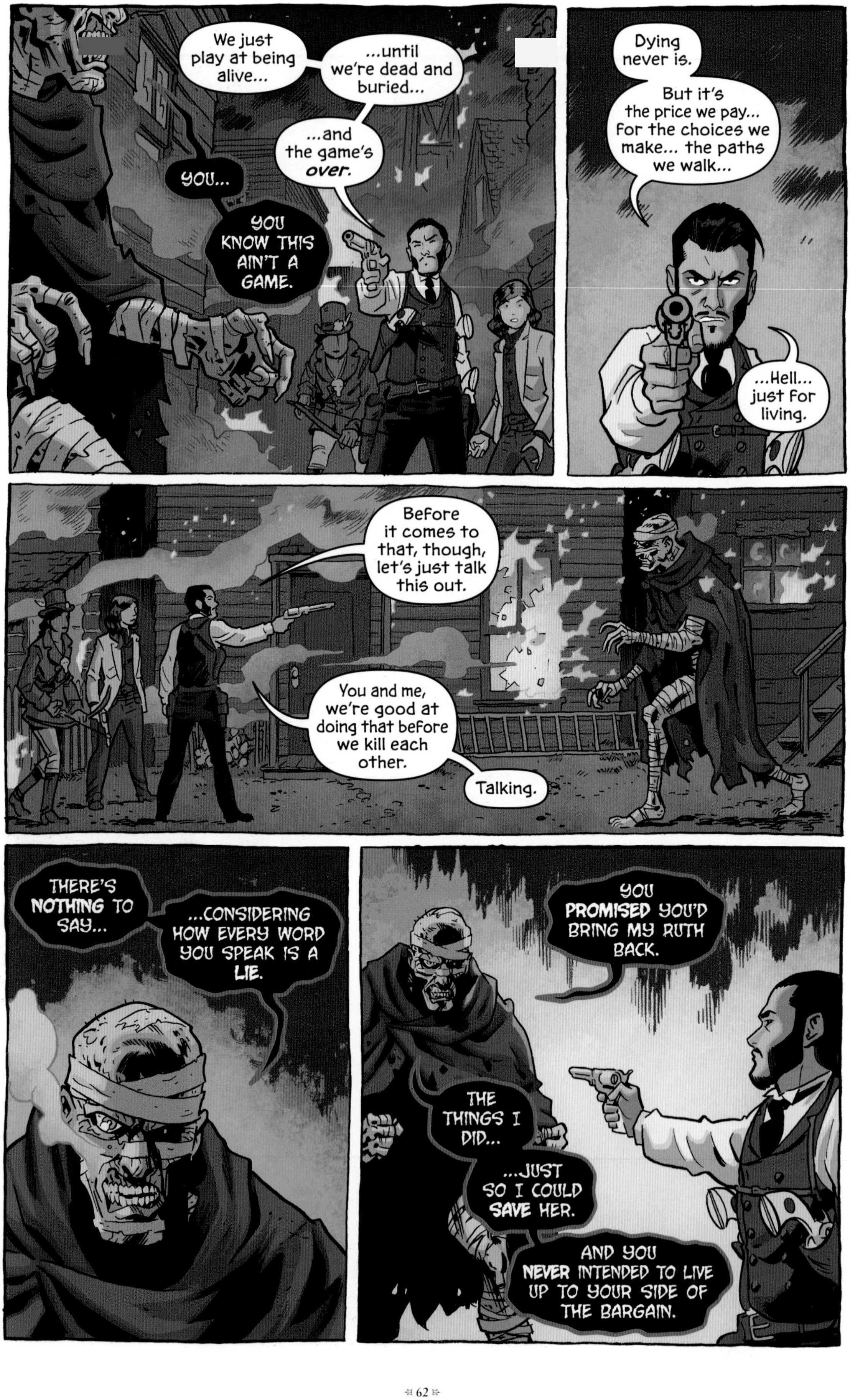

We just play at being alive...
...until we're dead and buried...
...and the game's *over*.
YOU...
YOU KNOW THIS AIN'T A GAME.
Dying never is.
But it's the price we pay... for the choices we make... the paths we walk...
...Hell... just for living.
Before it comes to that, though, let's just talk this out.
You and me, we're good at doing that before we kill each other.
Talking.
THERE'S **NOTHING** TO SAY...
...CONSIDERING HOW EVERY WORD YOU SPEAK IS A **LIE**.
YOU **PROMISED** YOU'D BRING MY RUTH BACK.
THE THINGS I DID...
...JUST SO I COULD **SAVE** HER.
AND YOU **NEVER** INTENDED TO LIVE UP TO YOUR SIDE OF THE BARGAIN.

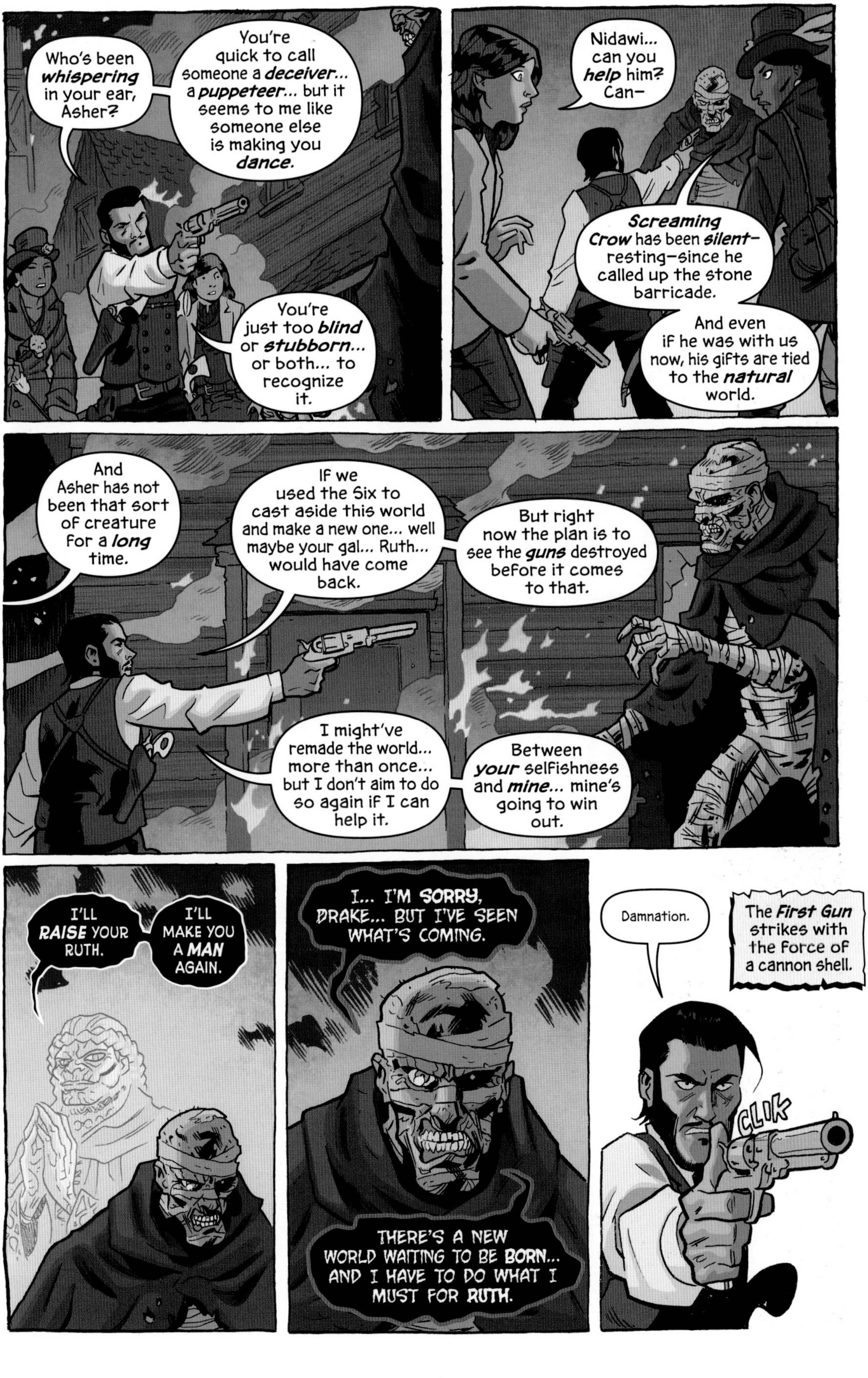
Who's been whispering in your ear, Asher?
You're quick to call someone a deceiver... a puppeteer... but it seems to me like someone else is making you dance.
You're just too blind or stubborn... or both... to recognize it.
Nidawi... can you help him? Can—
Screaming Crow has been silent—resting—since he called up the stone barricade.
And even if he was with us now, his gifts are tied to the natural world.
And Asher has not been that sort of creature for a long time.
If we used the Six to cast aside this world and make a new one... well maybe your gal... Ruth... would have come back.
But right now the plan is to see the guns destroyed before it comes to that.
I might've remade the world... more than once... but I don't aim to do so again if I can help it.
Between your selfishness and mine... mine's going to win out.
I'LL RAISE YOUR RUTH.
I'LL MAKE YOU A MAN AGAIN.
I... I'M SORRY, DRAKE... BUT I'VE SEEN WHAT'S COMING.
THERE'S A NEW WORLD WAITING TO BE BORN... AND I HAVE TO DO WHAT I MUST FOR RUTH.
Damnation.
The First Gun strikes with the force of a cannon shell.
CLIK

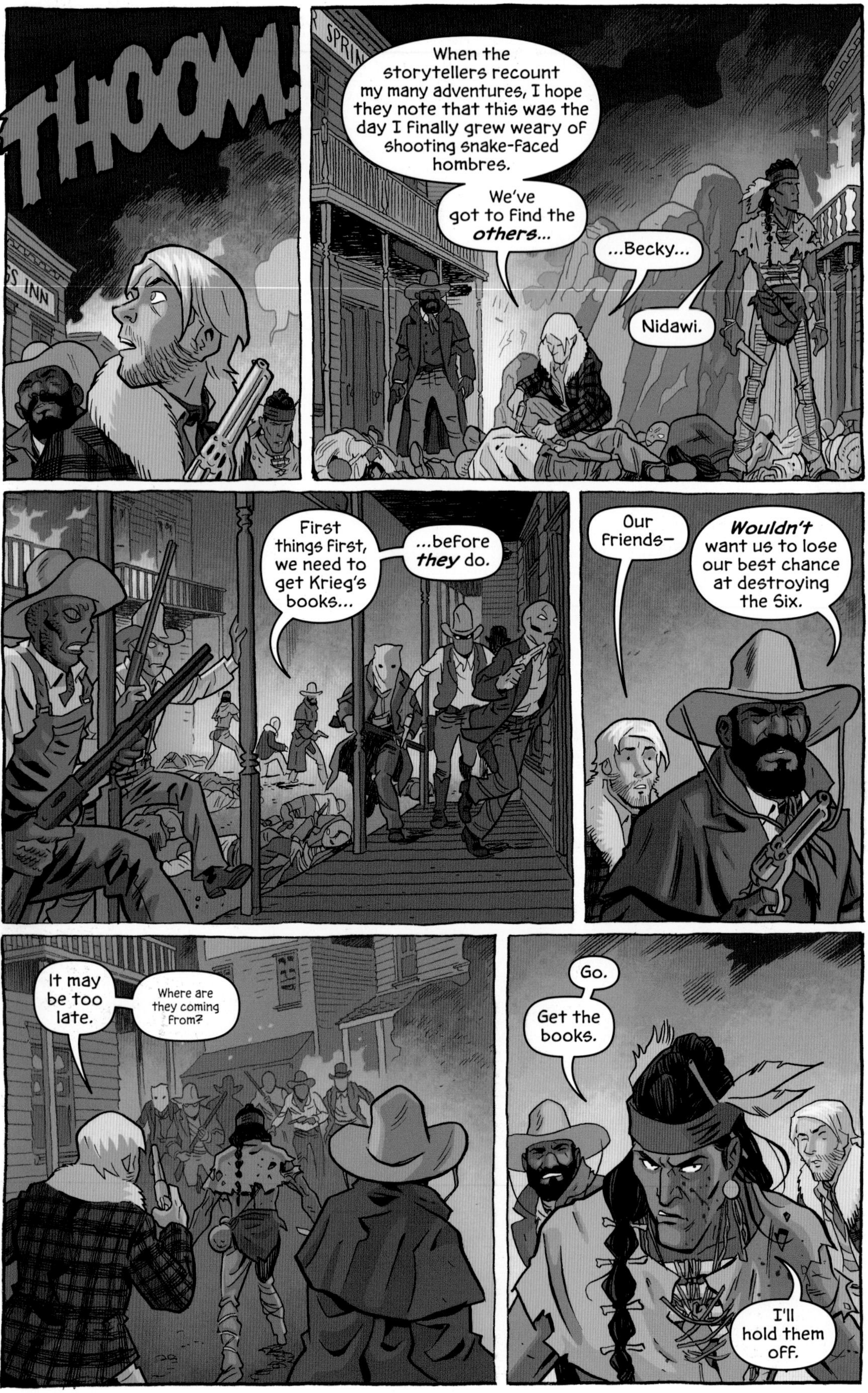
THOOM!
When the storytellers recount my many adventures, I hope they note that this was the day I finally grew weary of shooting snake-faced hombres.
We've got to find the *others*...
...Becky...
Nidawi.
First things first, we need to get Krieg's books...
...before *they* do.
Our friends–
Wouldn't want us to lose our best chance at destroying the Six.
It may be too late.
Where are they coming from?
Go.
Get the books.
I'll hold them off.

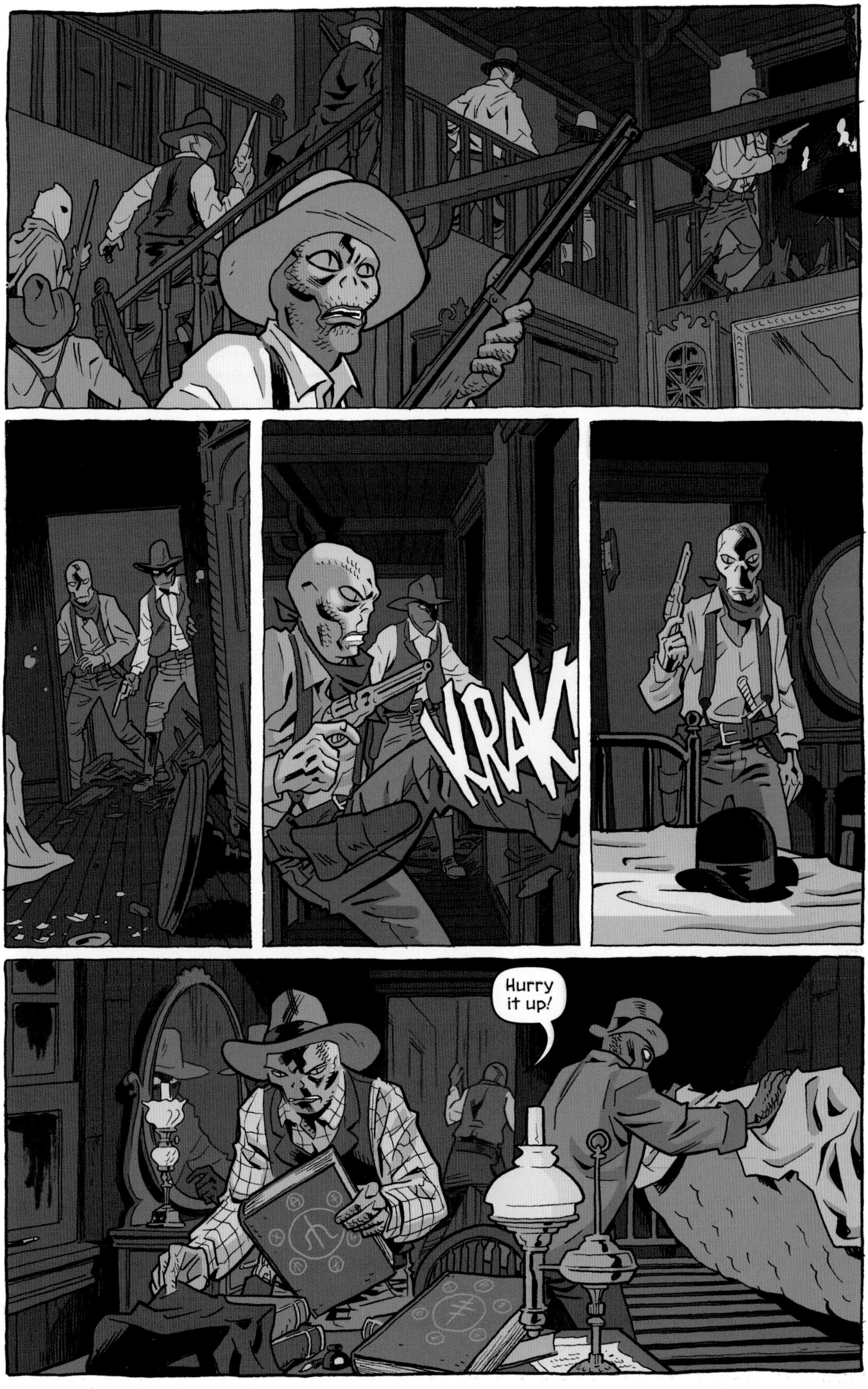
VRAK!
Hurry it up!

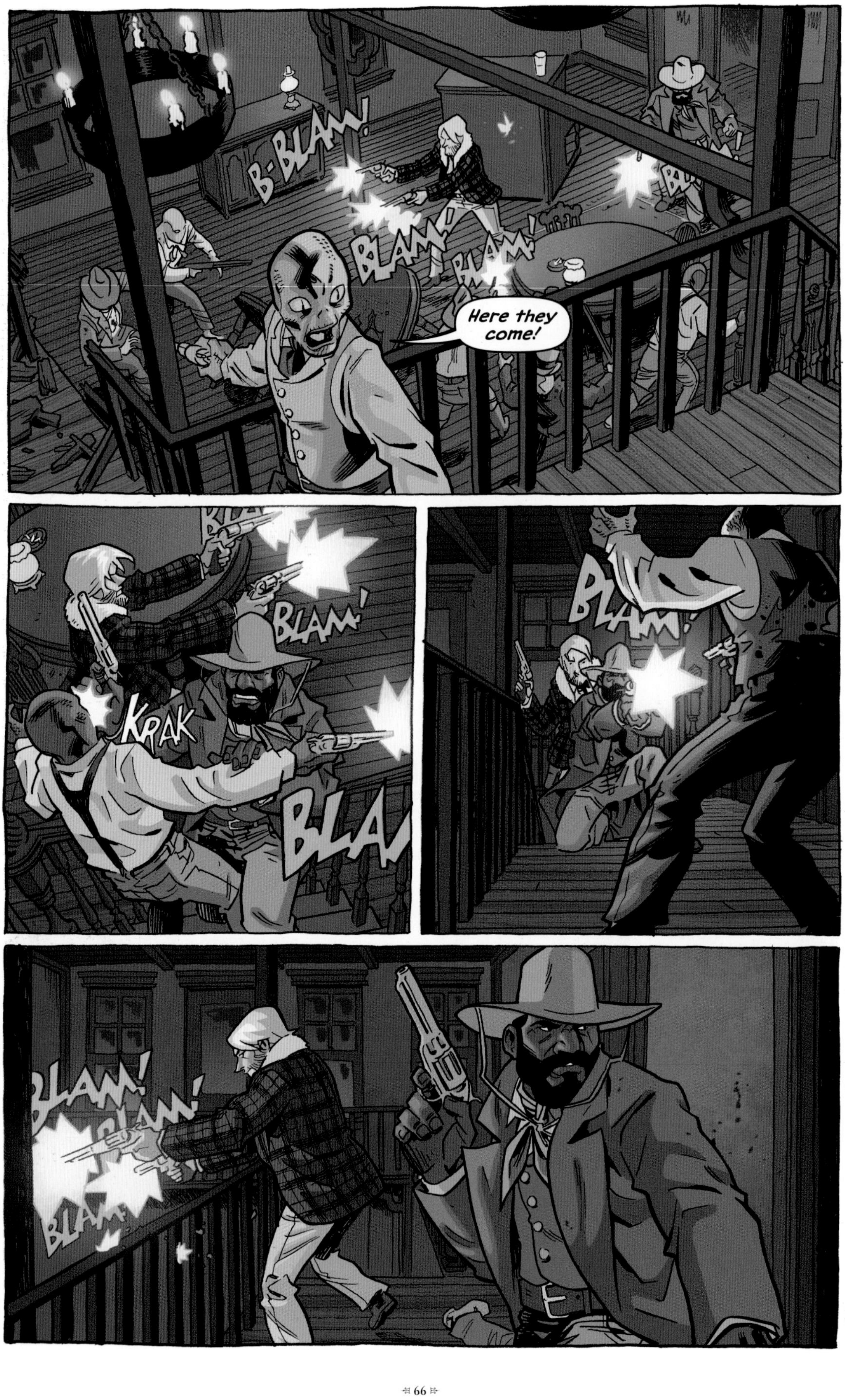
B-BLAM!
BLAM!
Here they come!
BLAM!
KRAK
BLAM!
BLAM!

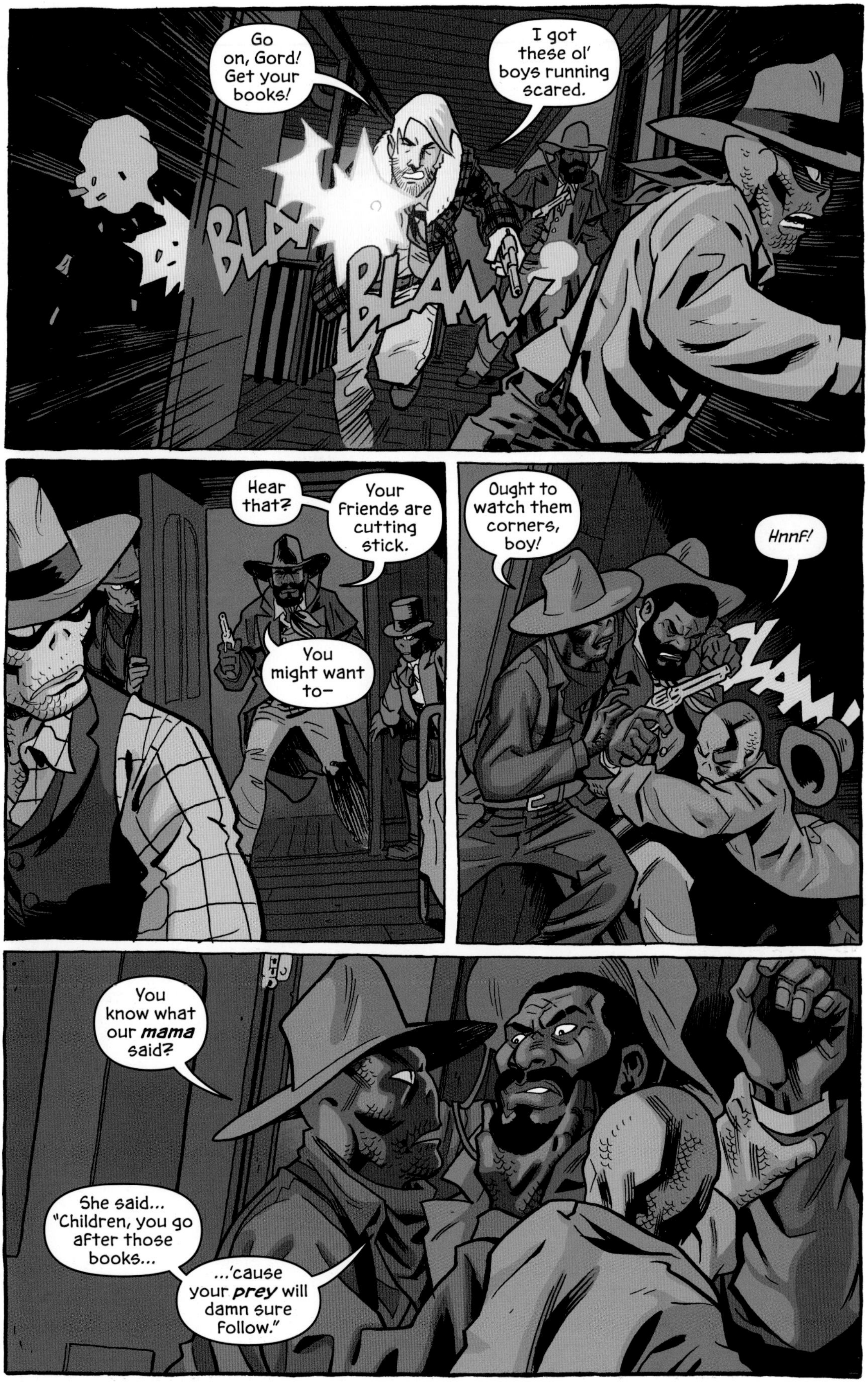
Go on, Gord! Get your books!
I got these ol' boys running scared.
BLAM
BLAM!
Hear that?
Your friends are cutting stick.
You might want to–
Ought to watch them corners, boy!
Hnnf!
You know what our *mama* said?
She said... "Children, you go after those books...
...'cause your *prey* will damn sure follow."

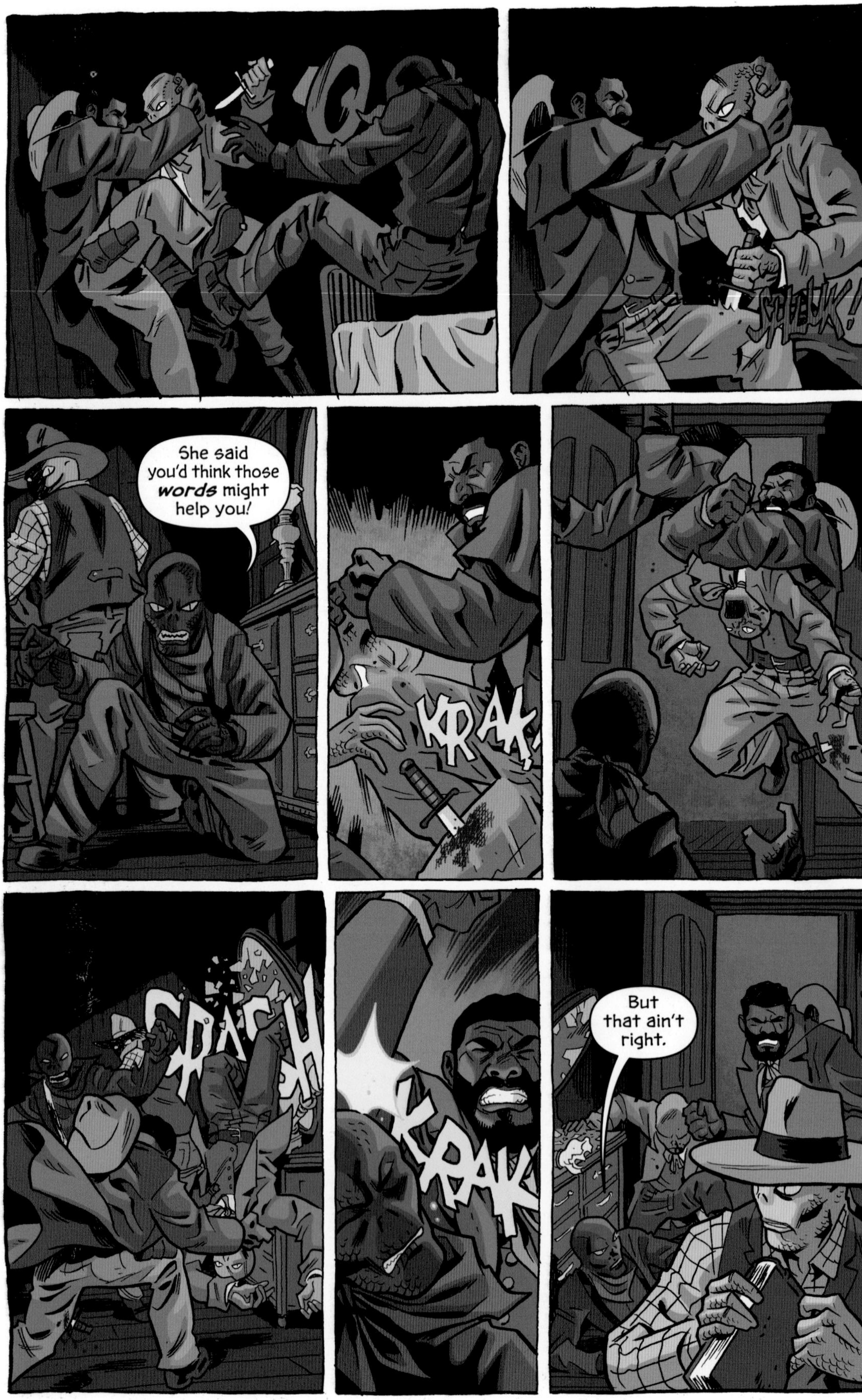
SHHUK!
She said you'd think those ***words*** might help you!
KRAK!
CRASH
KRAK
But that ain't right.

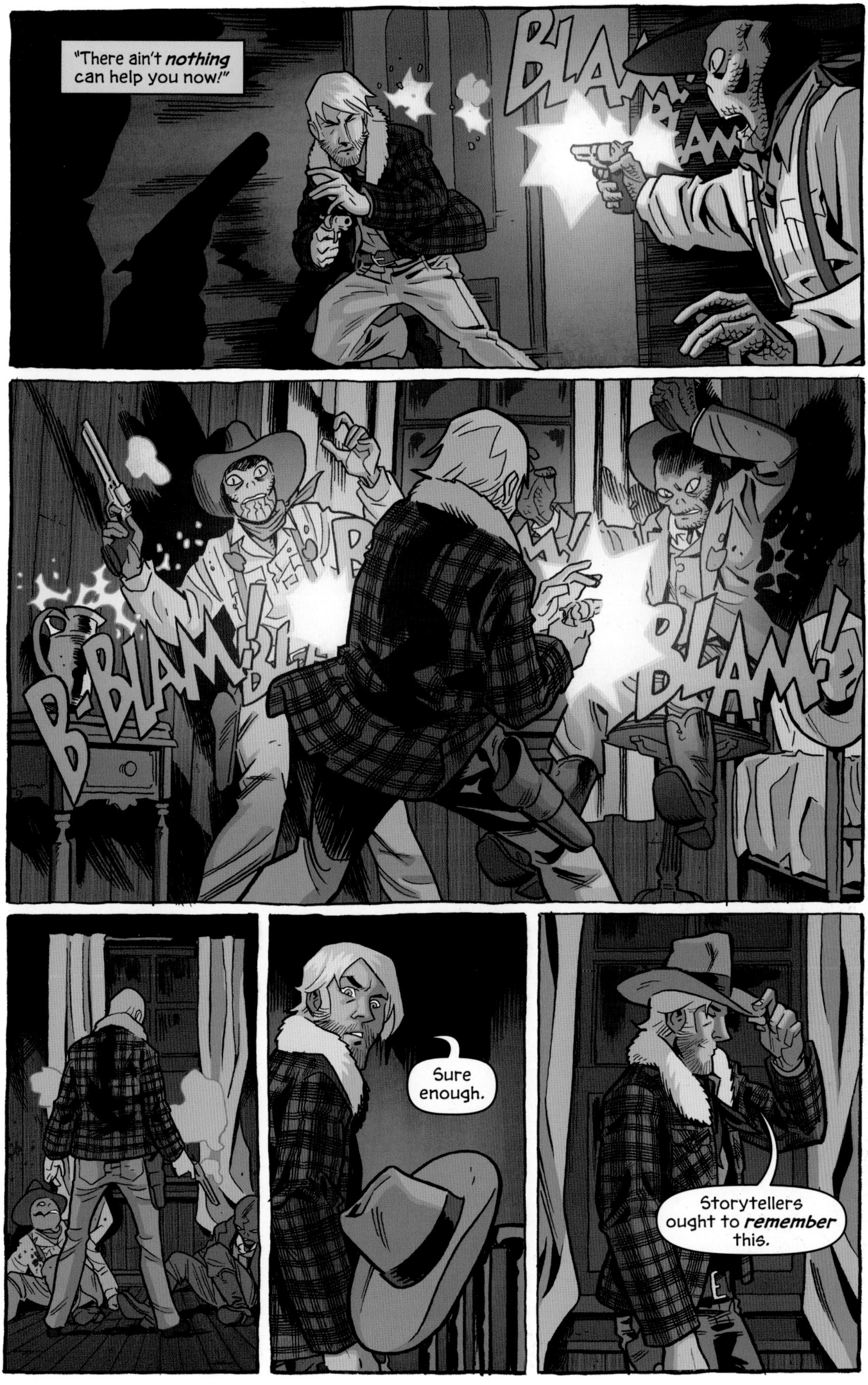
"There ain't ***nothing*** can help you now!"
BLAM! BLAM!
B-BLAM! BLAM!
BLAM!
Sure enough.
Storytellers ought to ***remember*** this.

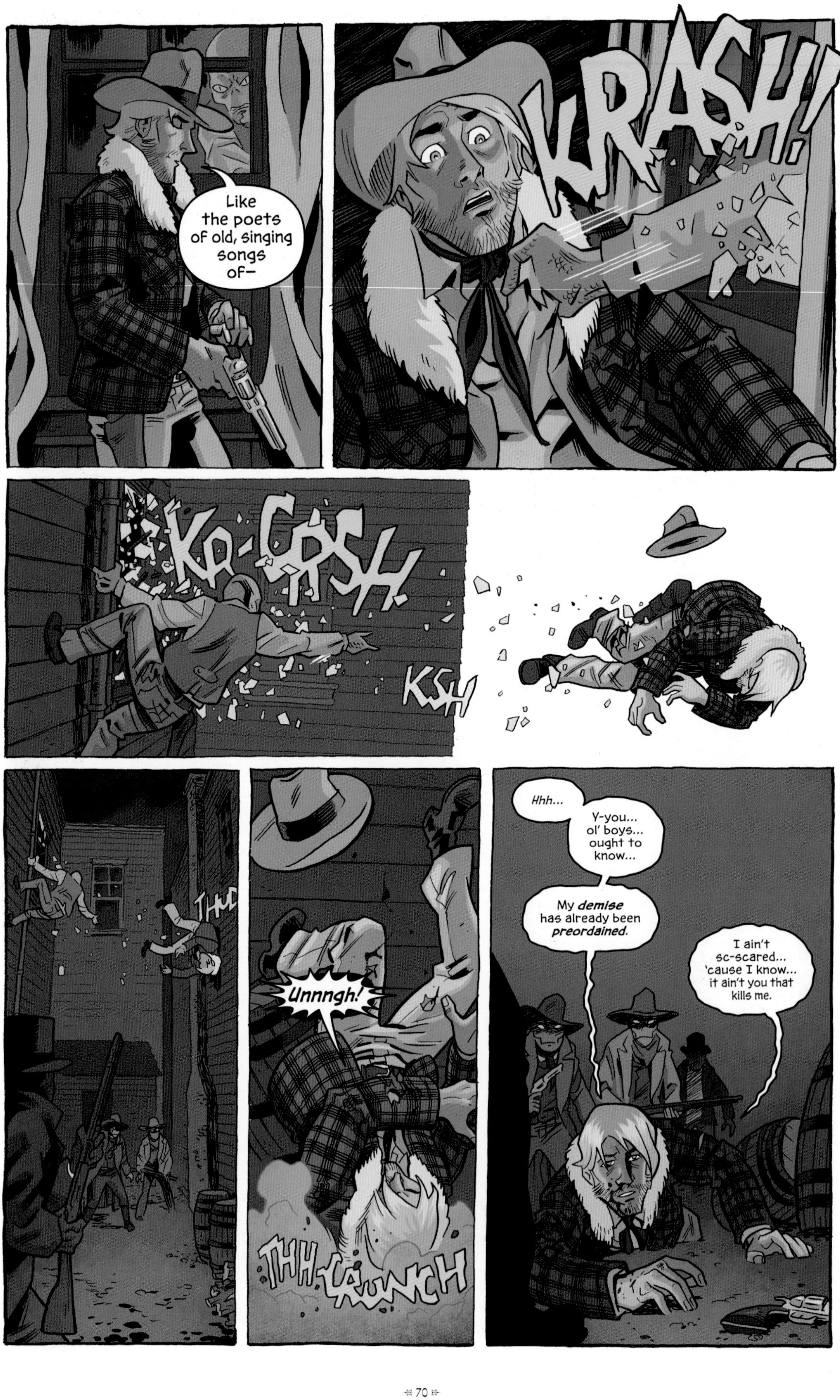
Like the poets of old, singing songs of—
KRASH!!
KA-CRSH
KSH
THUD
Unnngh!
THH-CRUNCH
Hhh...
Y-you... ol' boys... ought to know...
My *demise* has already been *preordained*.
I ain't sc-scared... 'cause I know... it ain't you that kills me.

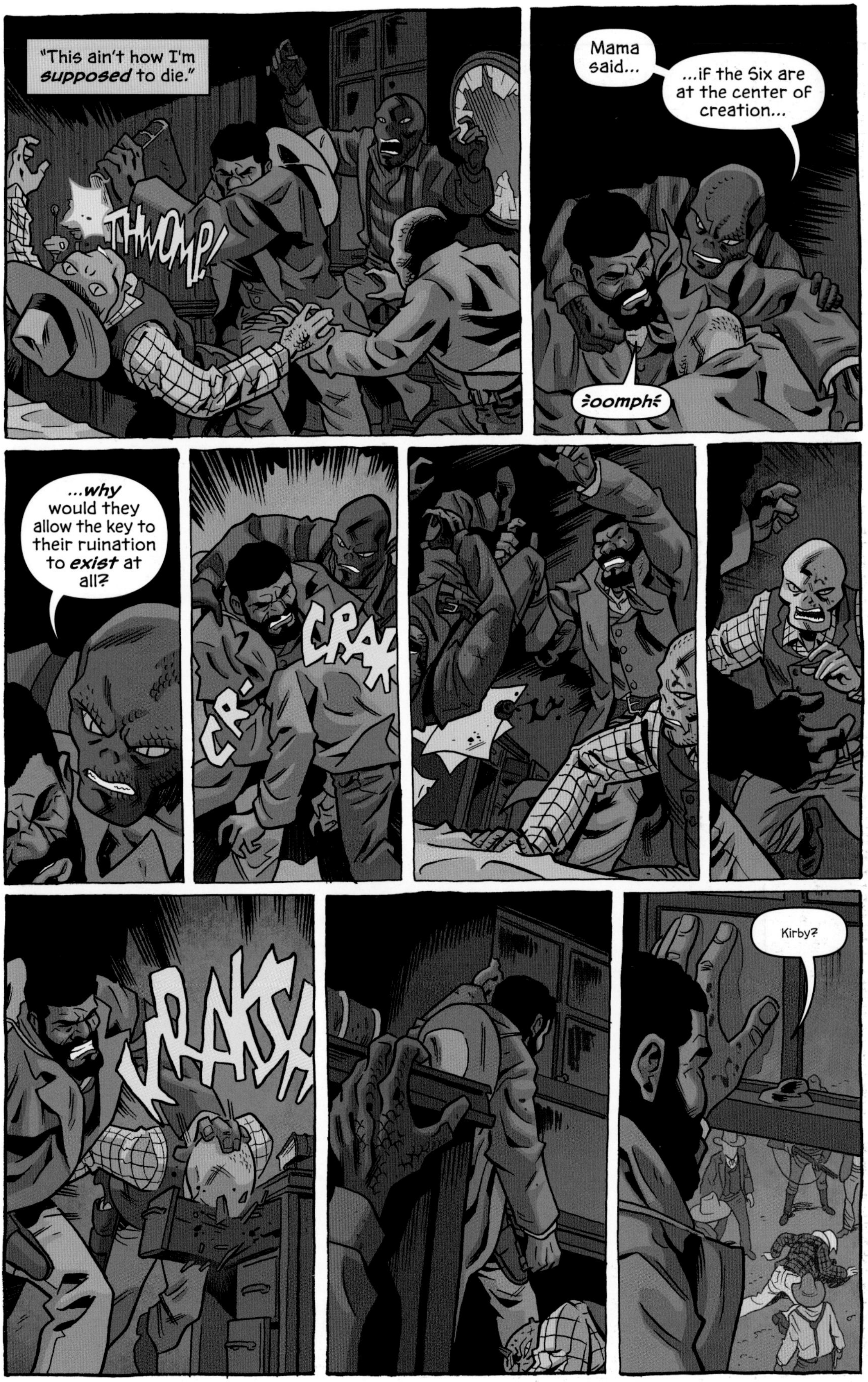

"This ain't how I'm supposed to die."
THWOMP!
Mama said...
...if the Six are at the center of creation...
oomph
...why would they allow the key to their ruination to exist at all?
CRAK
CR-
VRAKK
Kirby?

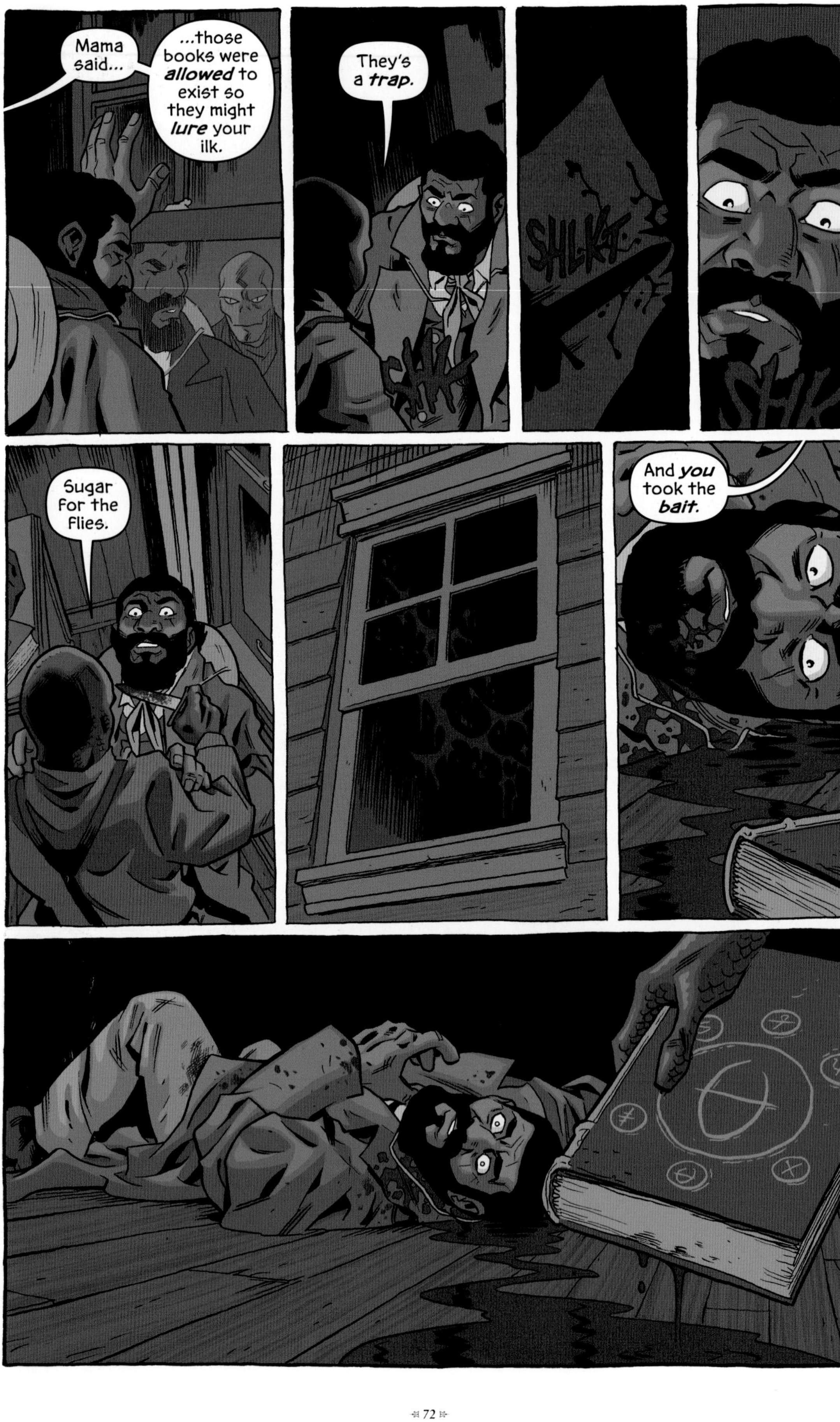
Mama said...
...those books were *allowed* to exist so they might *lure* your ilk.
They's a *trap.*
SHLK-T
SHK
SHK
Sugar for the Flies.
And *you* took the *bait.*

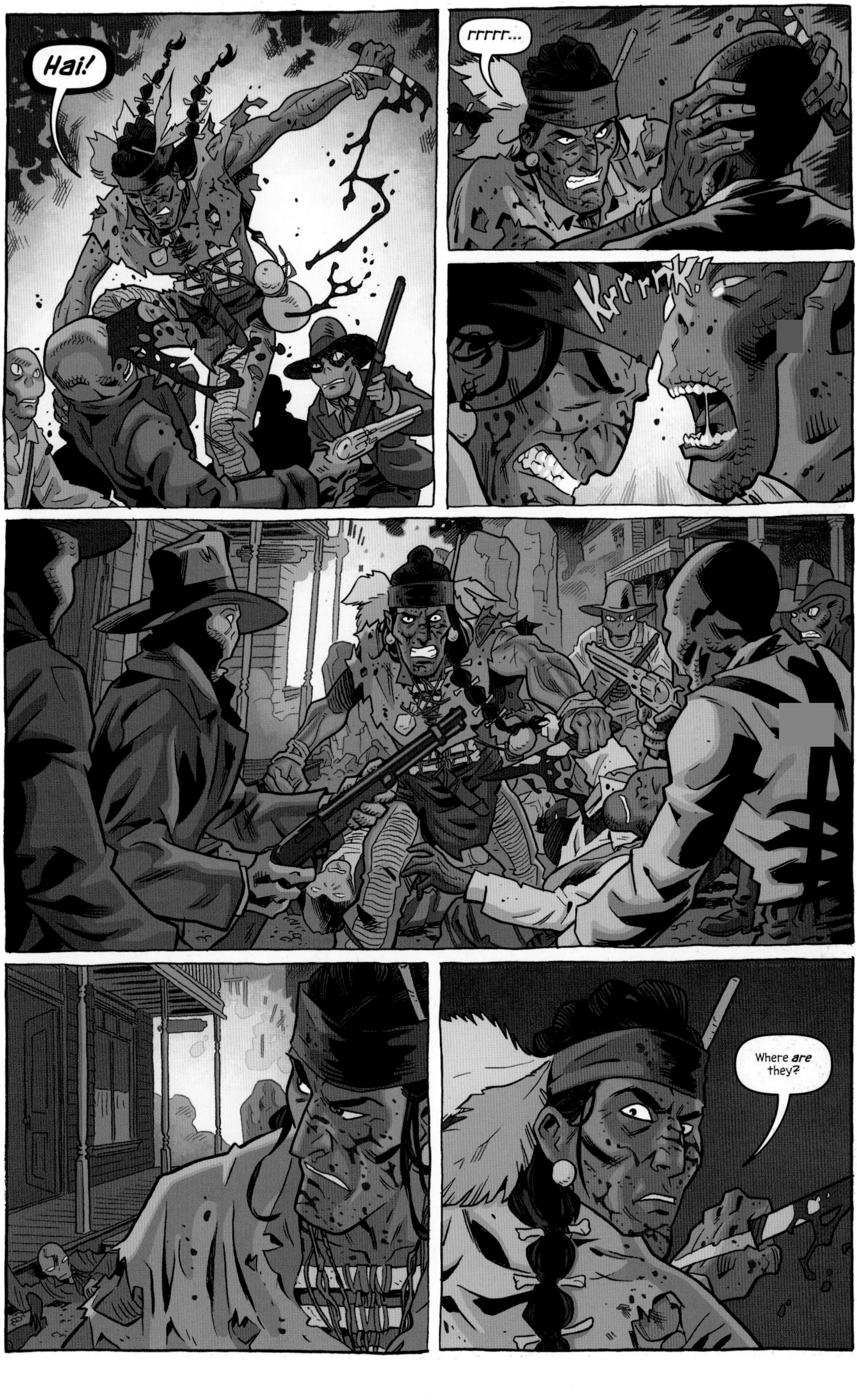
Hai!
rrrrr...
Krrrrk!
Where are they?

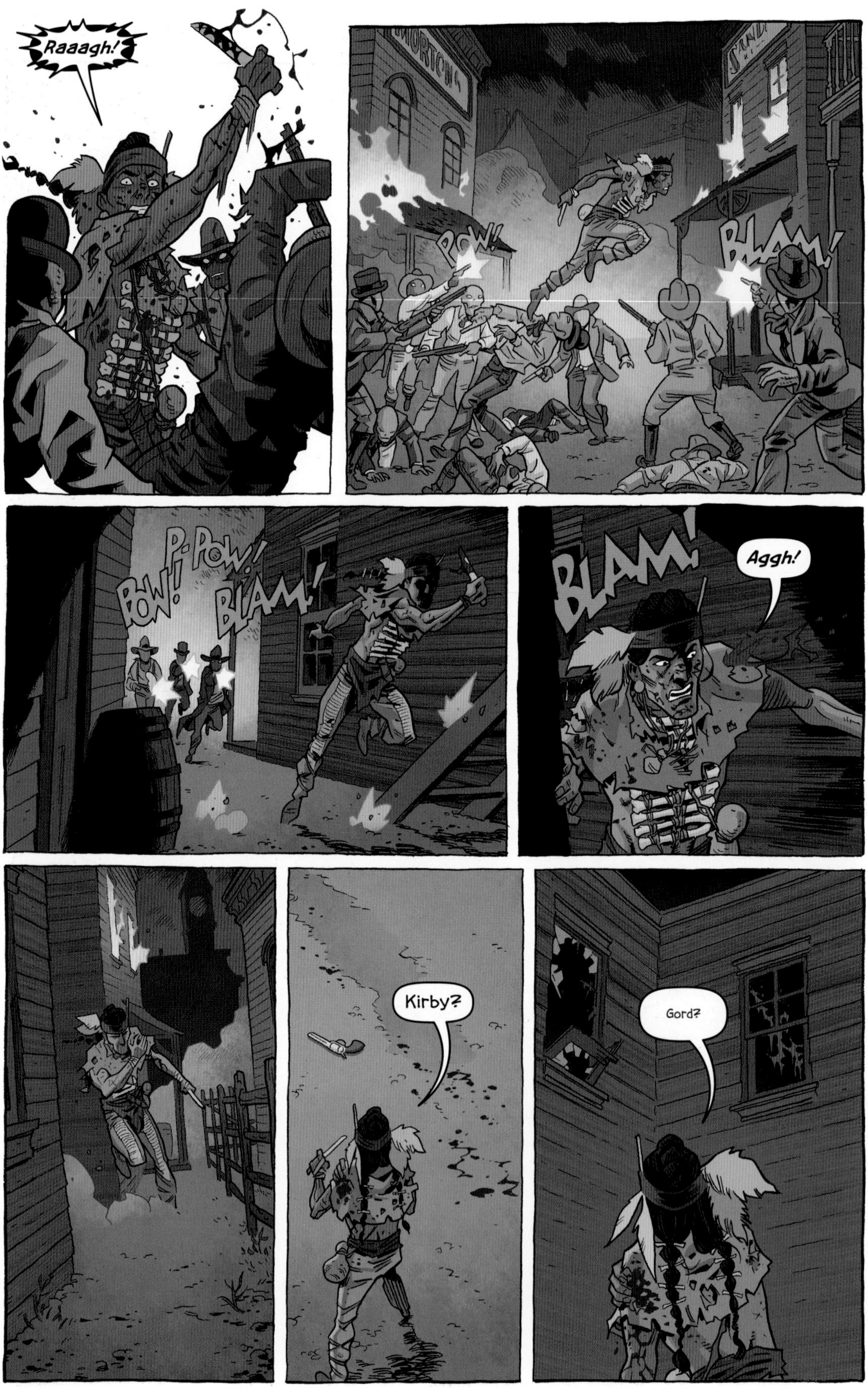

Raaagh!
POW!
BLAM!
POW!
P-POW!
BLAM!
BLAM!
Aggh!
Kirby?
Gord?

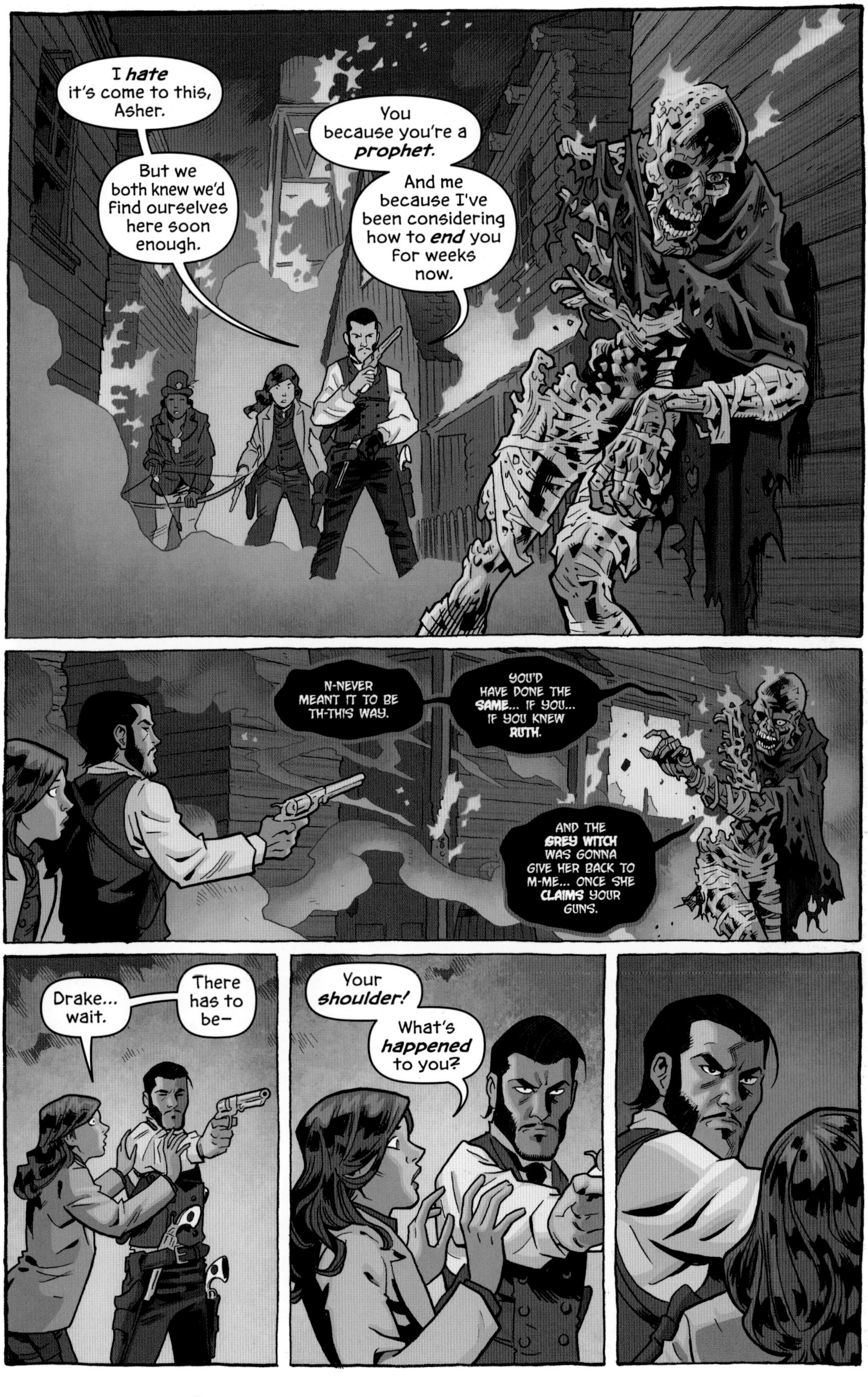
I *hate* it's come to this, Asher.
But we both knew we'd find ourselves here soon enough.
You because you're a *prophet*.
And me because I've been considering how to *end* you for weeks now.
N-NEVER MEANT IT TO BE TH-THIS WAY.
YOU'D HAVE DONE THE **SAME**... IF YOU... IF YOU KNEW **RUTH**.
AND THE **GREY WITCH** WAS GONNA GIVE HER BACK TO M-ME... ONCE SHE **CLAIMS** YOUR GUNS.
Drake... wait.
There has to be–
Your *shoulder!*
What's *happened* to you?

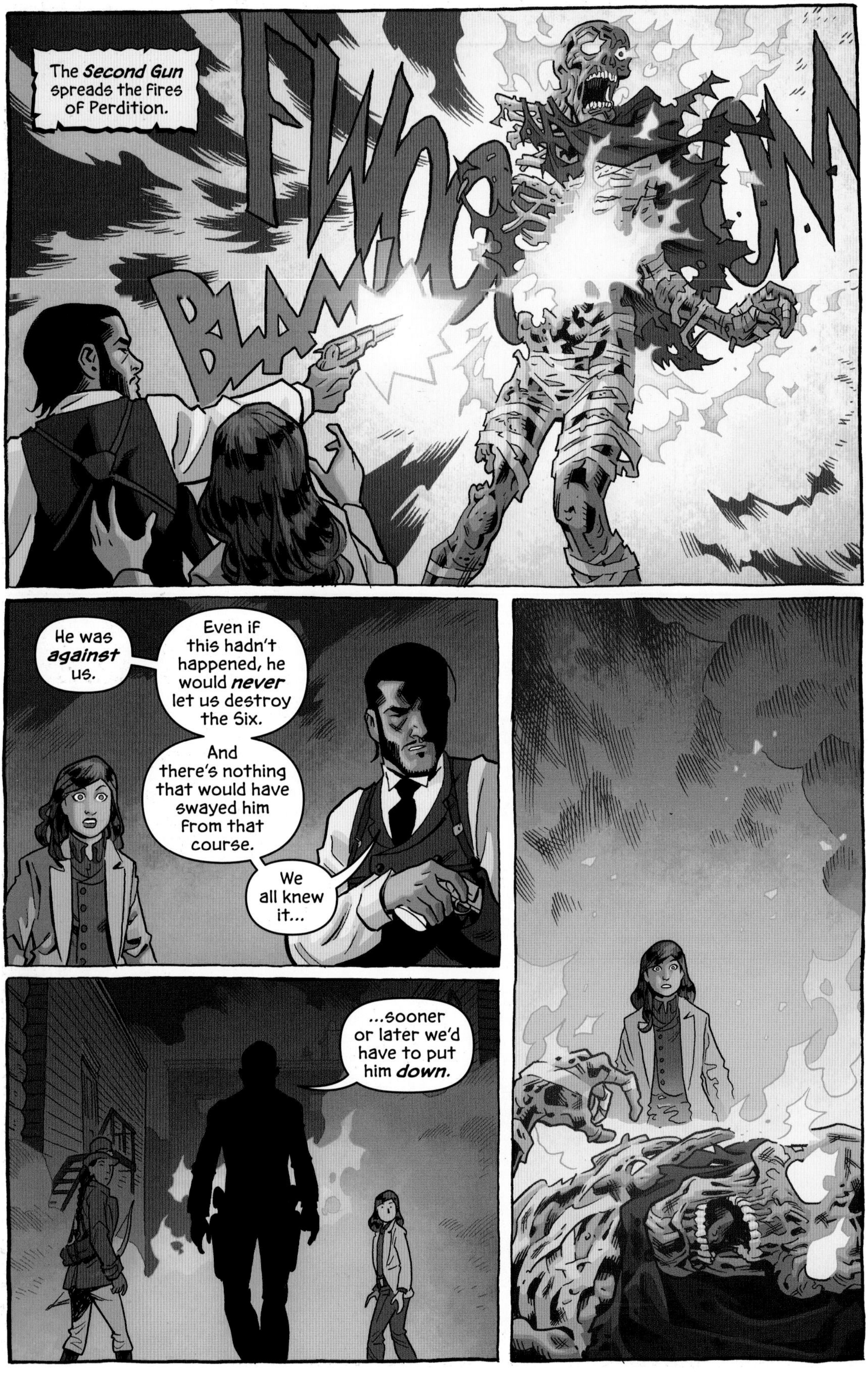

The Second Gun spreads the fires of Perdition.
FWOOOM
BLAM
He was against us.
Even if this hadn't happened, he would never let us destroy the Six.
And there's nothing that would have swayed him from that course.
We all knew it...
...sooner or later we'd have to put him down.

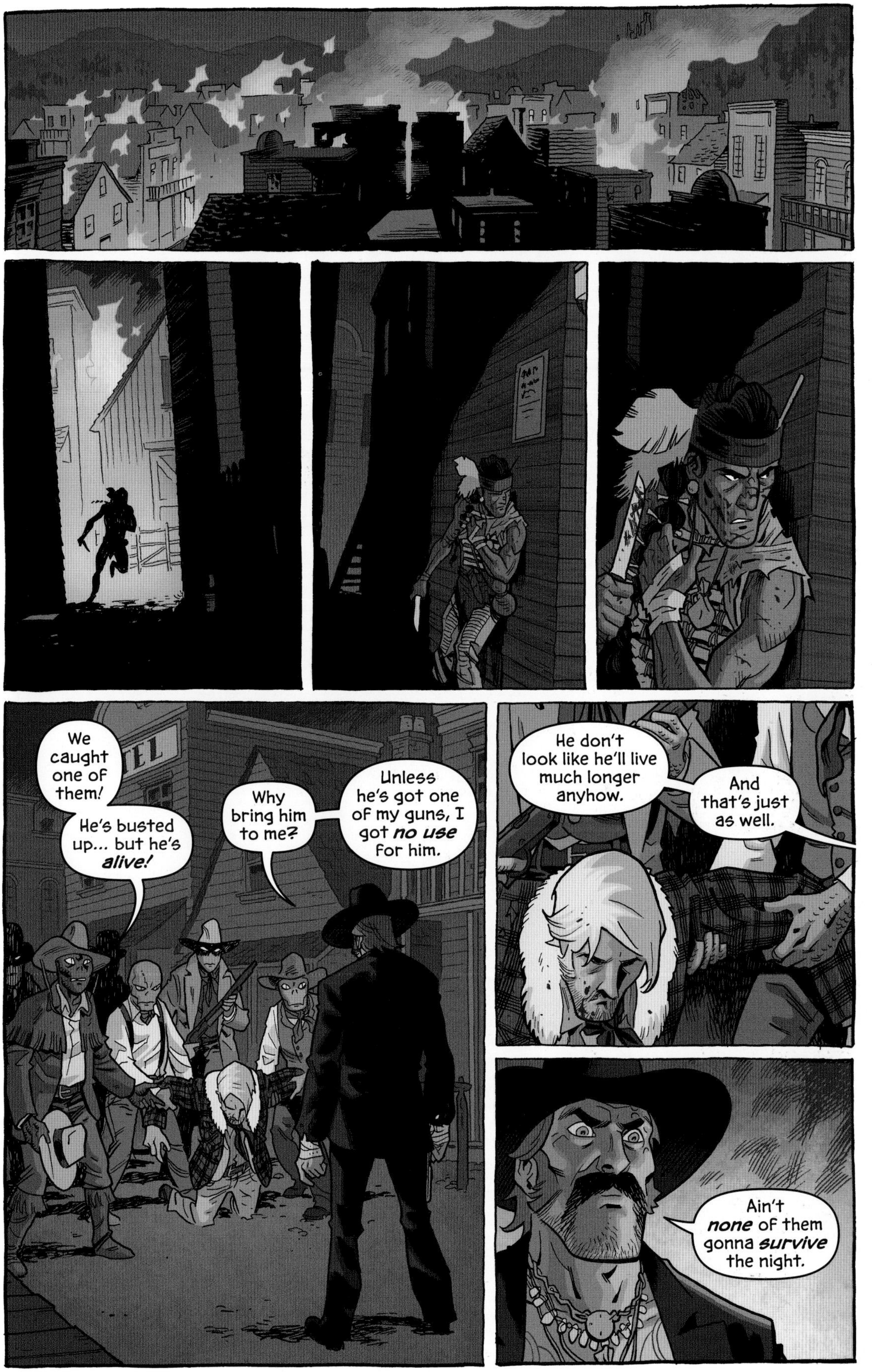
We caught one of them!
He's busted up... but he's *alive!*
Why bring him to me?
Unless he's got one of my guns, I got *no use* for him.
He don't look like he'll live much longer anyhow.
And that's just as well.
Ain't *none* of them gonna *survive* the night.

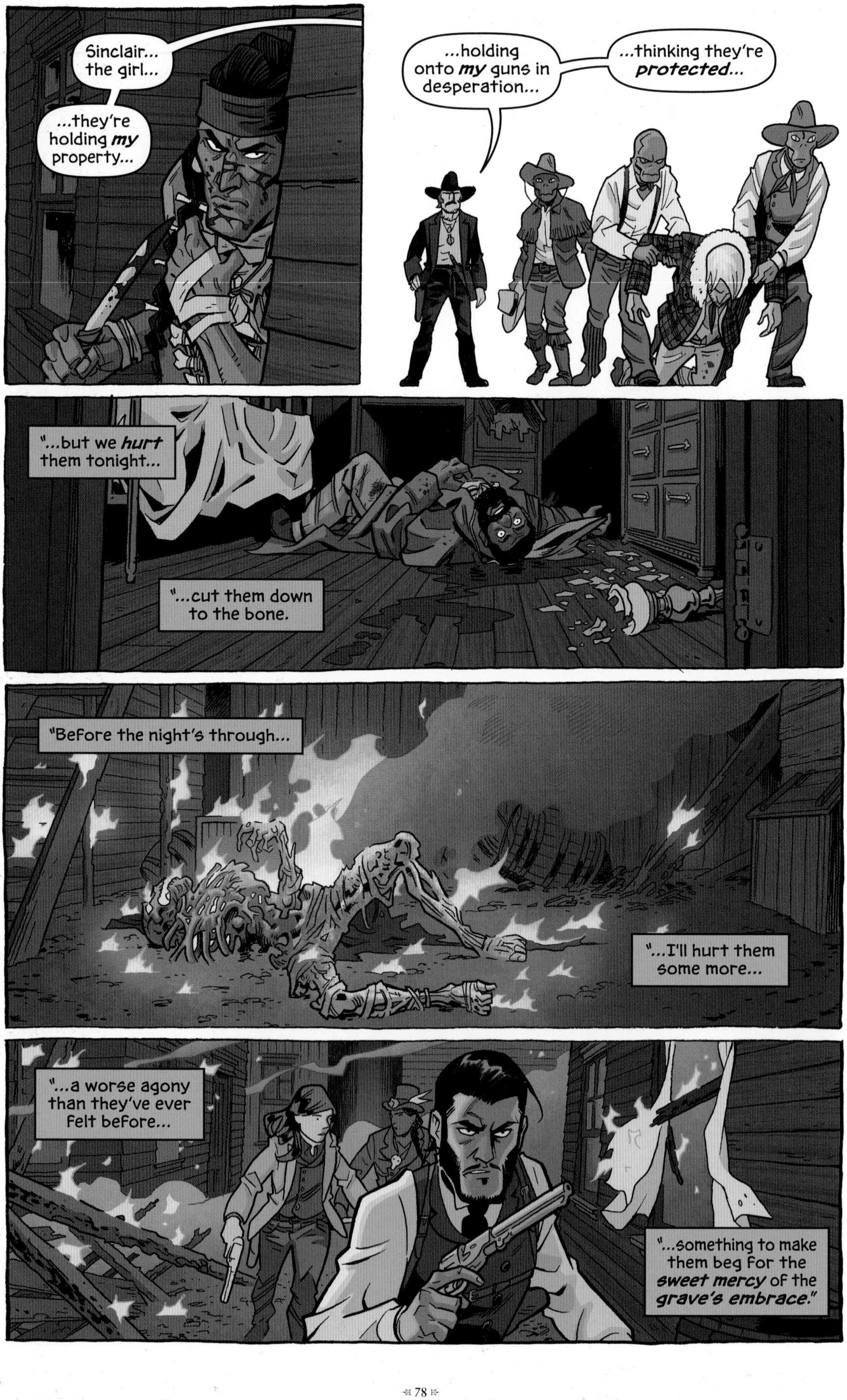

Sinclair... the girl...
...they're holding *my* property...
...holding onto *my* guns in desperation...
...thinking they're *protected*...
"...but we *hurt* them tonight...
"...cut them down to the bone.
"Before the night's through...
"...I'll hurt them some more...
"...a worse agony than they've ever felt before...
"...something to make them beg for the *sweet mercy* of the *grave's embrace*."

CHAPTER FOUR

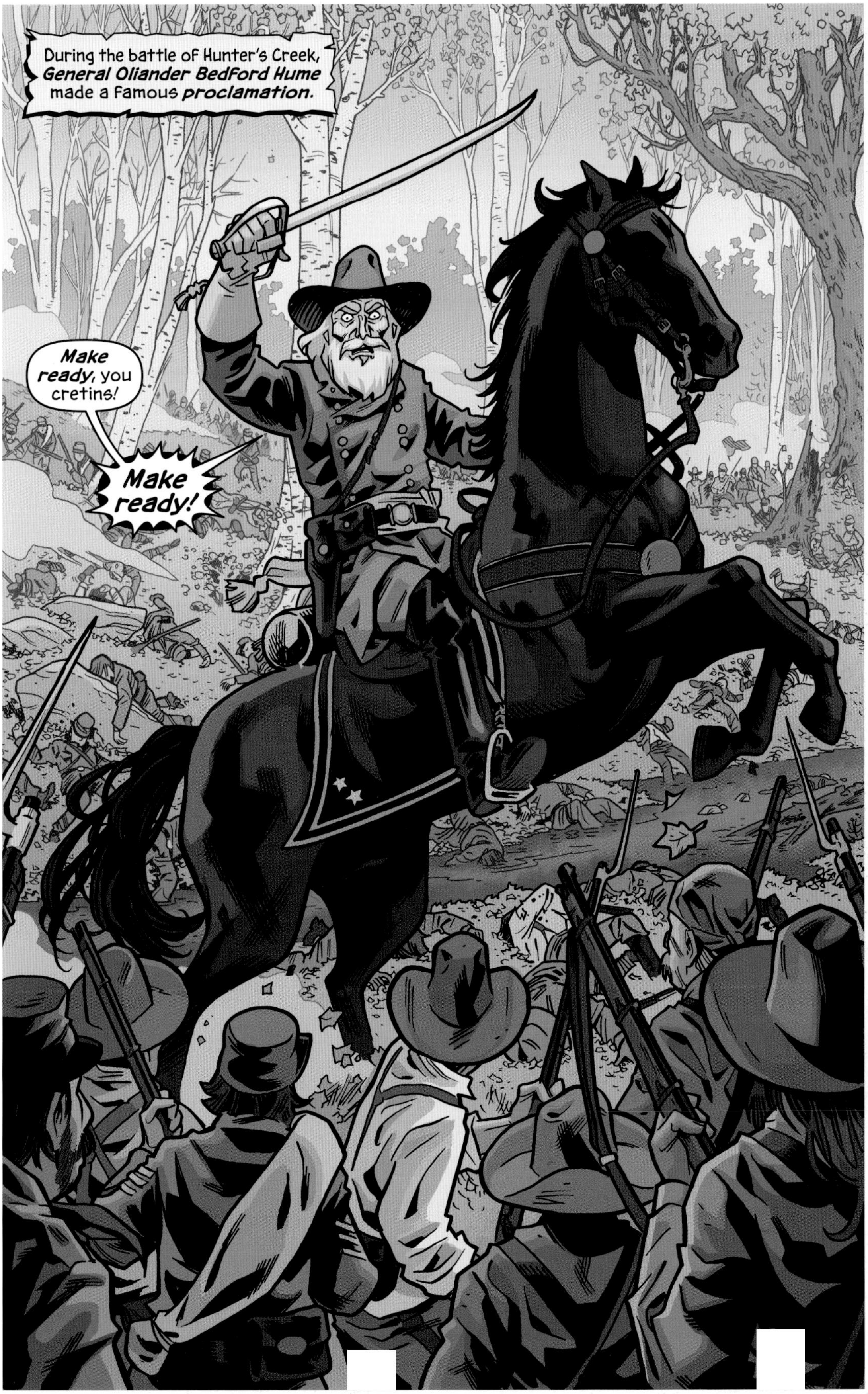

During the battle of Hunter's Creek, *General Oliander Bedford Hume* made a famous *proclamation.*
Make ready, you cretins!
Make ready!

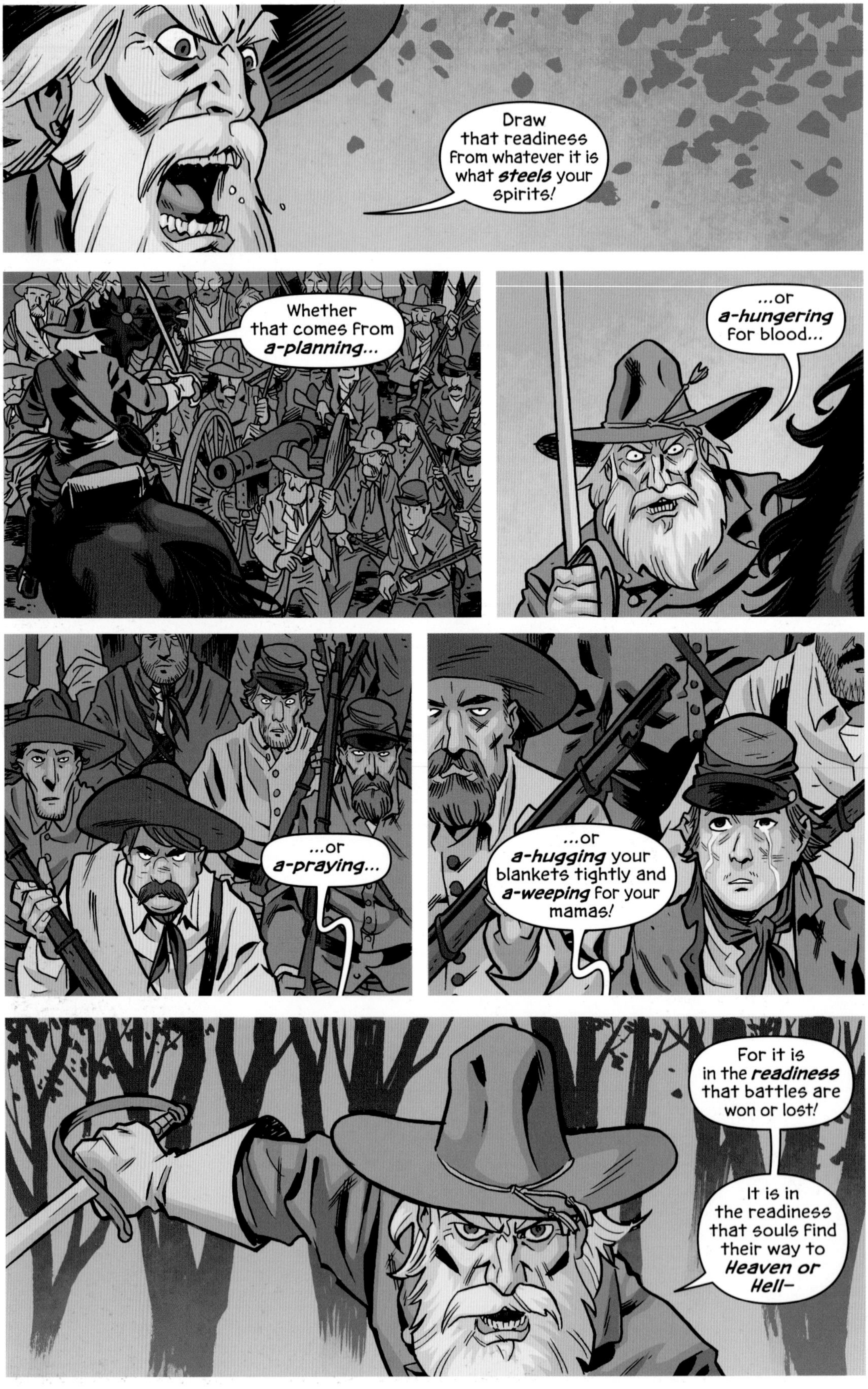
Draw that readiness from whatever it is what *steels* your spirits!
Whether that comes from *a-planning...*
...or *a-hungering* for blood...
...or *a-praying...*
...or *a-hugging* your blankets tightly and *a-weeping* for your mamas!
For it is in the *readiness* that battles are won or lost!
It is in the readiness that souls find their way to *Heaven or Hell—*

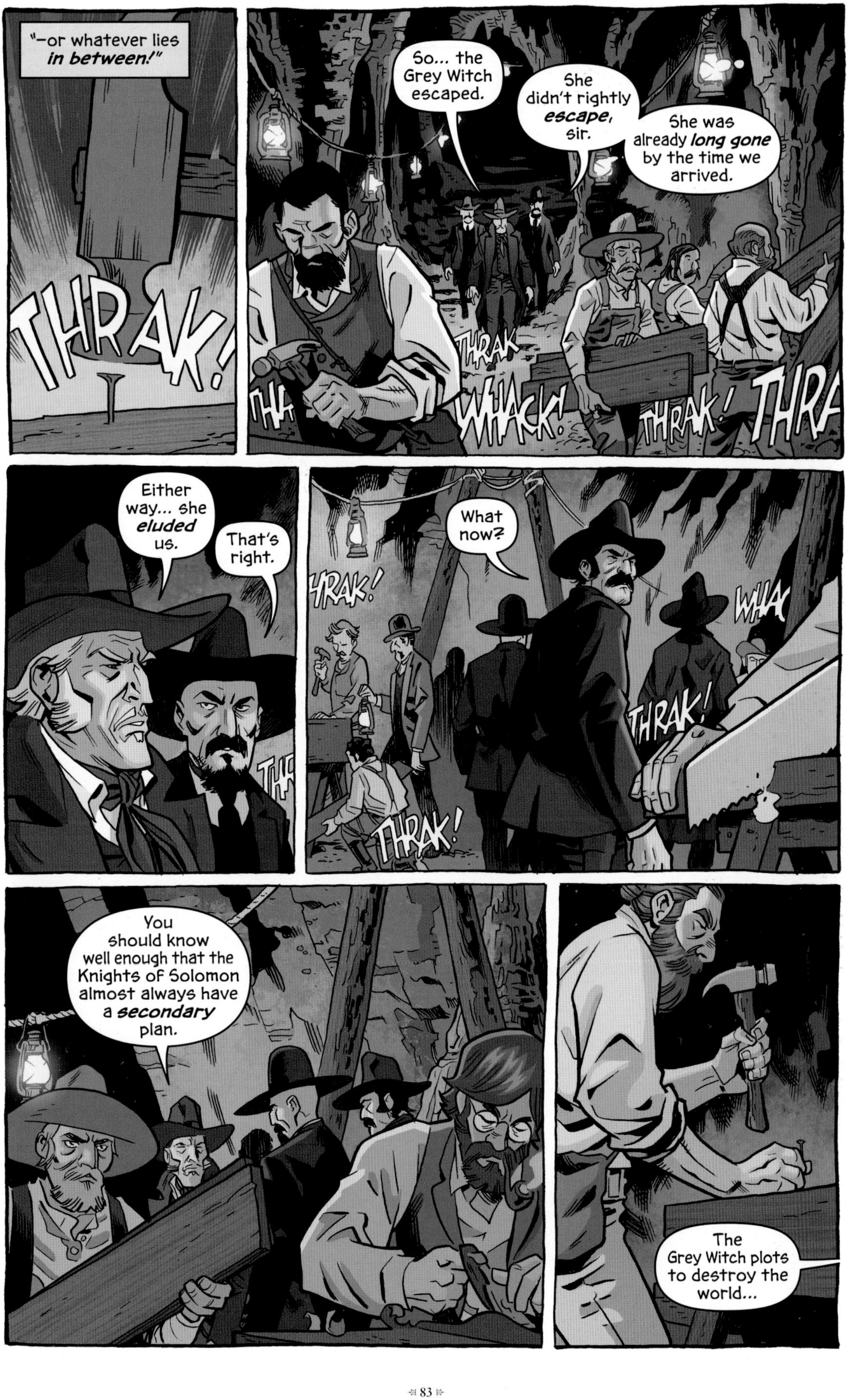
"–or whatever lies *in between!*"
THRAK!
So... the Grey Witch escaped.
She didn't rightly *escape,* sir.
She was already *long gone* by the time we arrived.
THRAK
THRA
WHACK!
THRAK!
THRA
Either way... she *eluded* us.
That's right.
THR
What now?
THRAK!
WHAC
THRAK!
THRAK!
You should know well enough that the Knights of Solomon almost always have a *secondary* plan.
The Grey Witch plots to destroy the world...

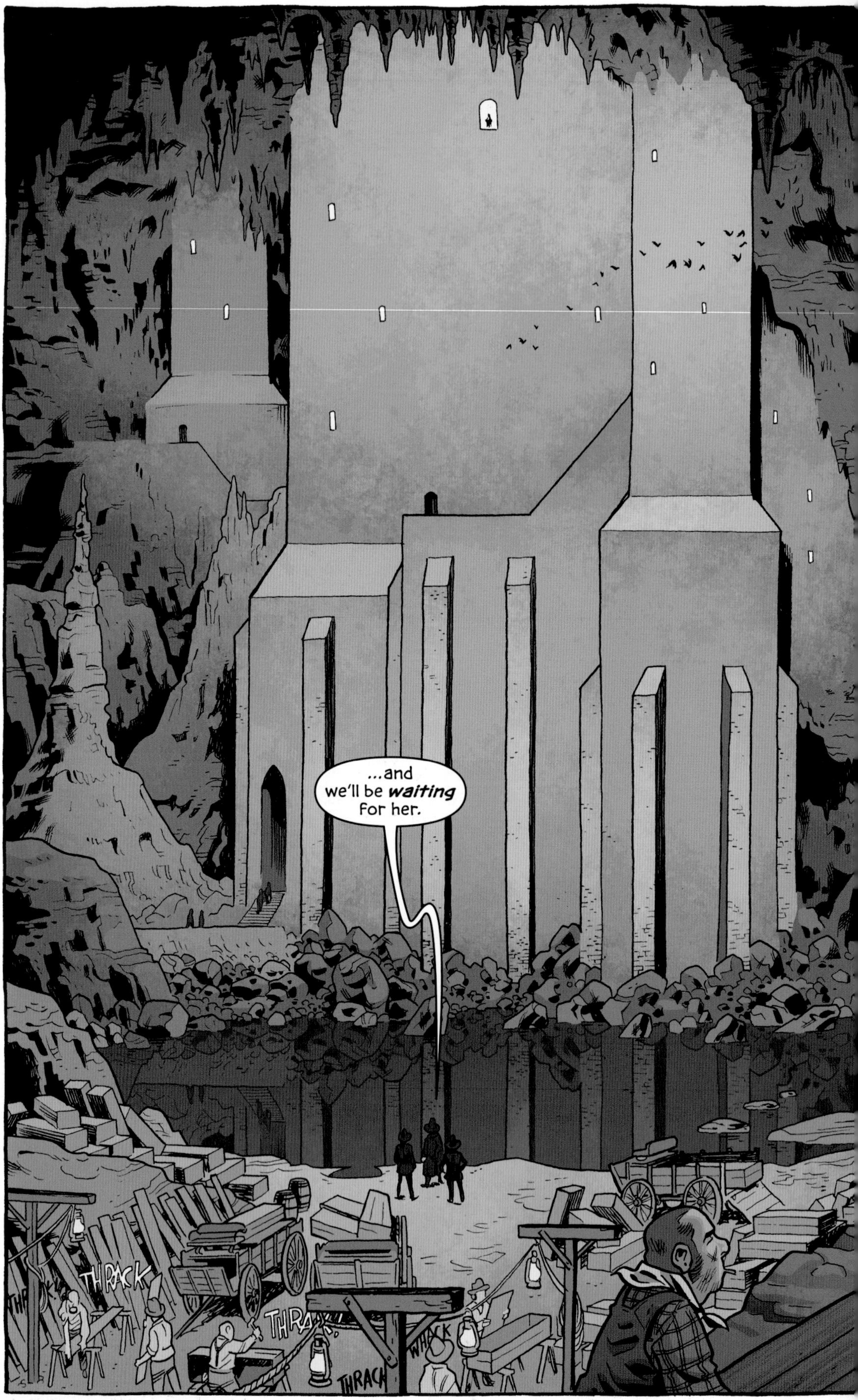
...and we'll be *waiting* for her.
THRACK
WHACK
THRACK

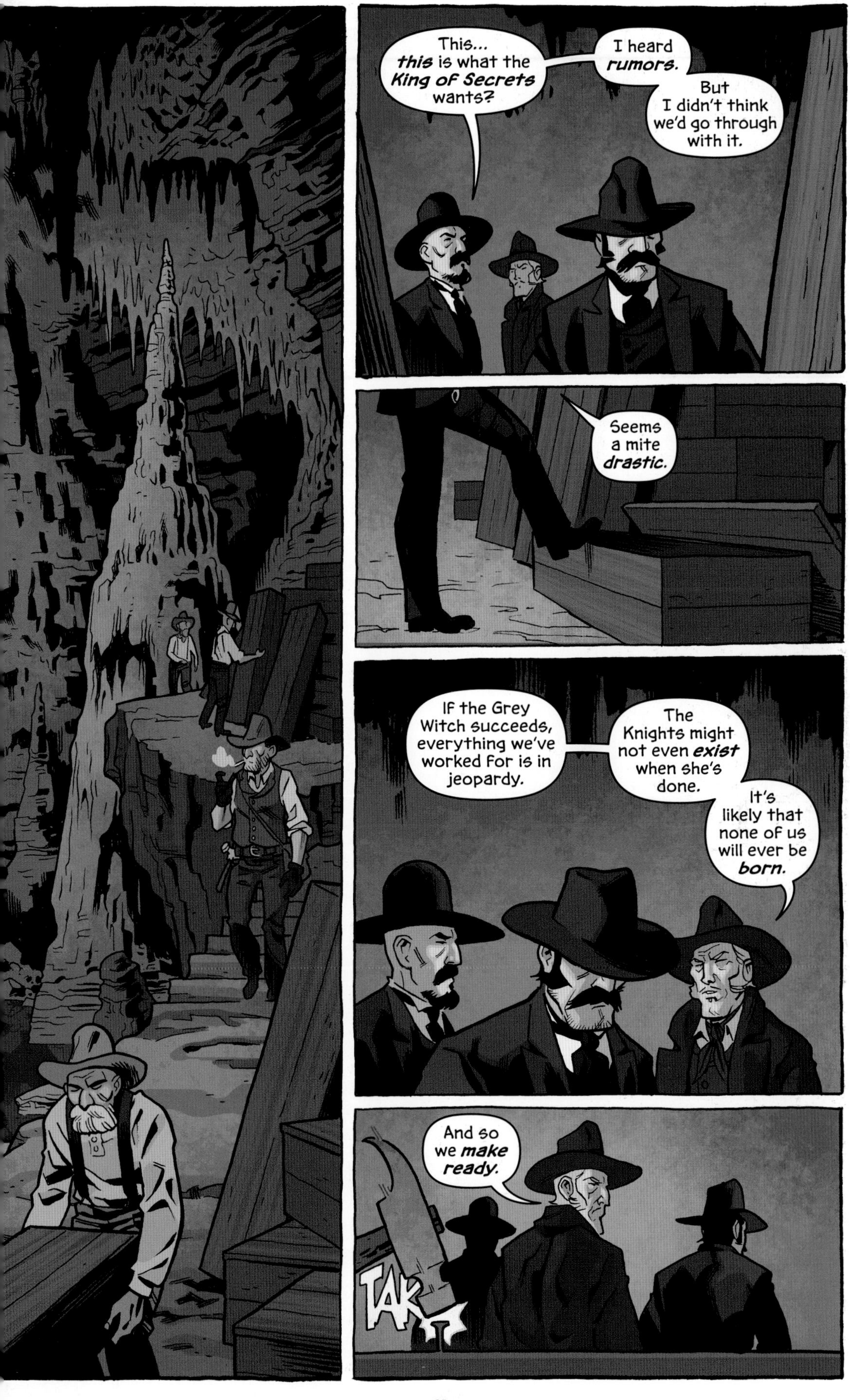
This... this is what the King of Secrets wants?
I heard rumors.
But I didn't think we'd go through with it.
Seems a mite drastic.
If the Grey Witch succeeds, everything we've worked for is in jeopardy.
The Knights might not even exist when she's done.
It's likely that none of us will ever be born.
And so we make ready.
TAK

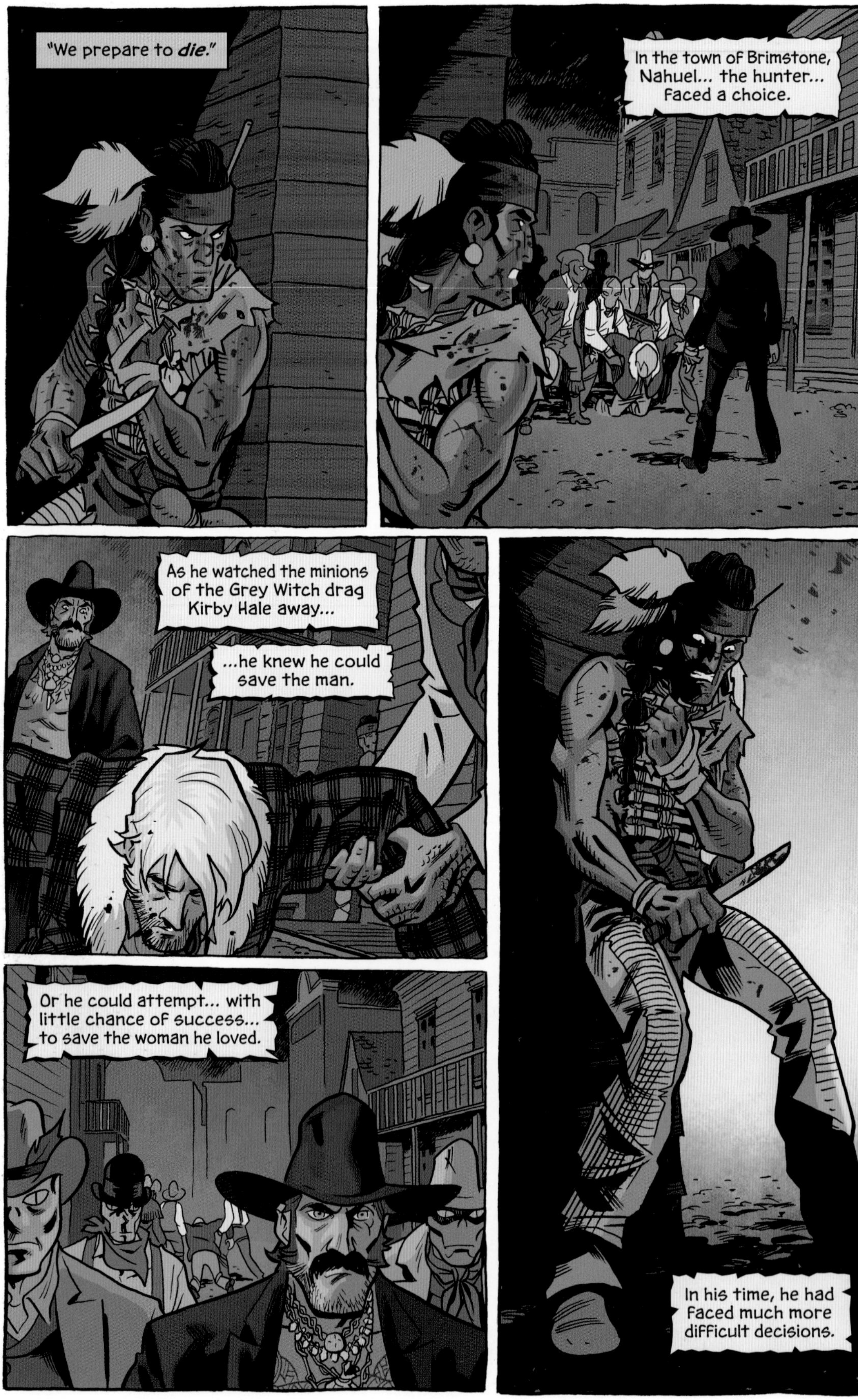
"We prepare to *die*."
In the town of Brimstone, Nahuel... the hunter... faced a choice.
As he watched the minions of the Grey Witch drag Kirby Hale away...
...he knew he could save the man.
Or he could attempt... with little chance of success... to save the woman he loved.
In his time, he had faced much more difficult decisions.

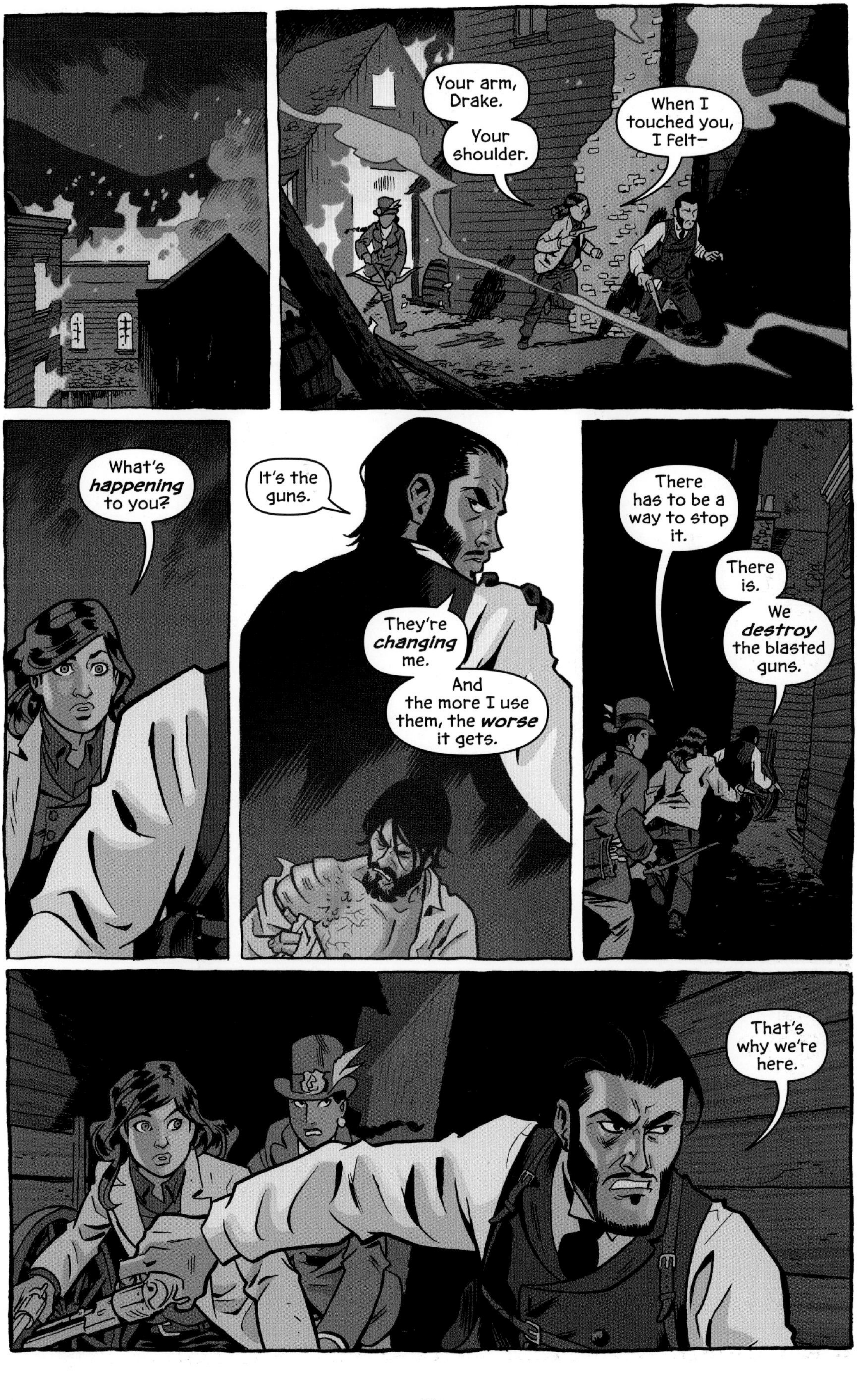
Your arm, Drake.
Your shoulder.
When I touched you, I felt—
What's *happening* to you?
It's the guns.
They're *changing* me.
And the more I use them, the *worse* it gets.
There has to be a way to stop it.
There is.
We *destroy* the blasted guns.
That's why we're here.

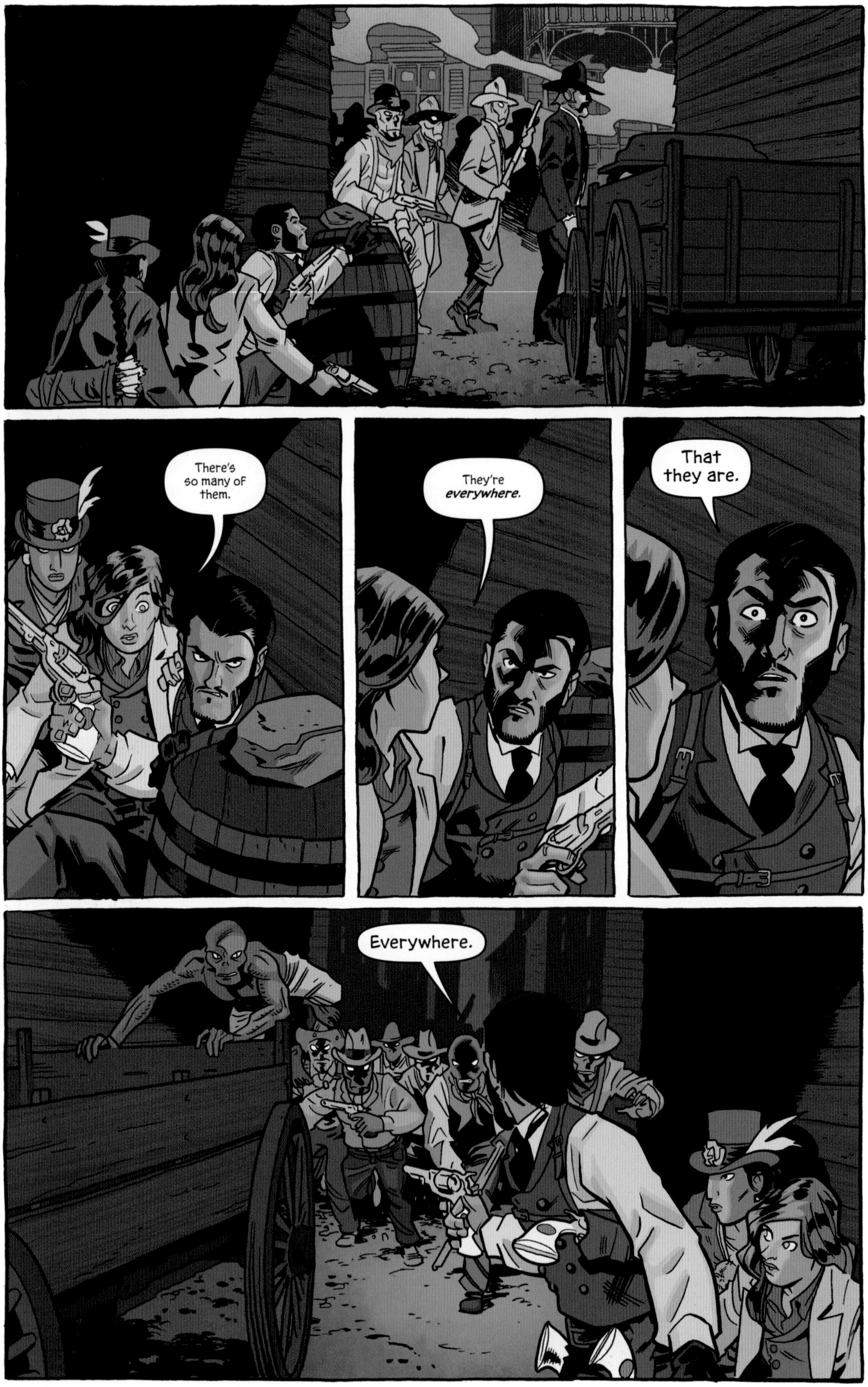

There's so many of them.
They're *everywhere*.
That they are.
Everywhere.

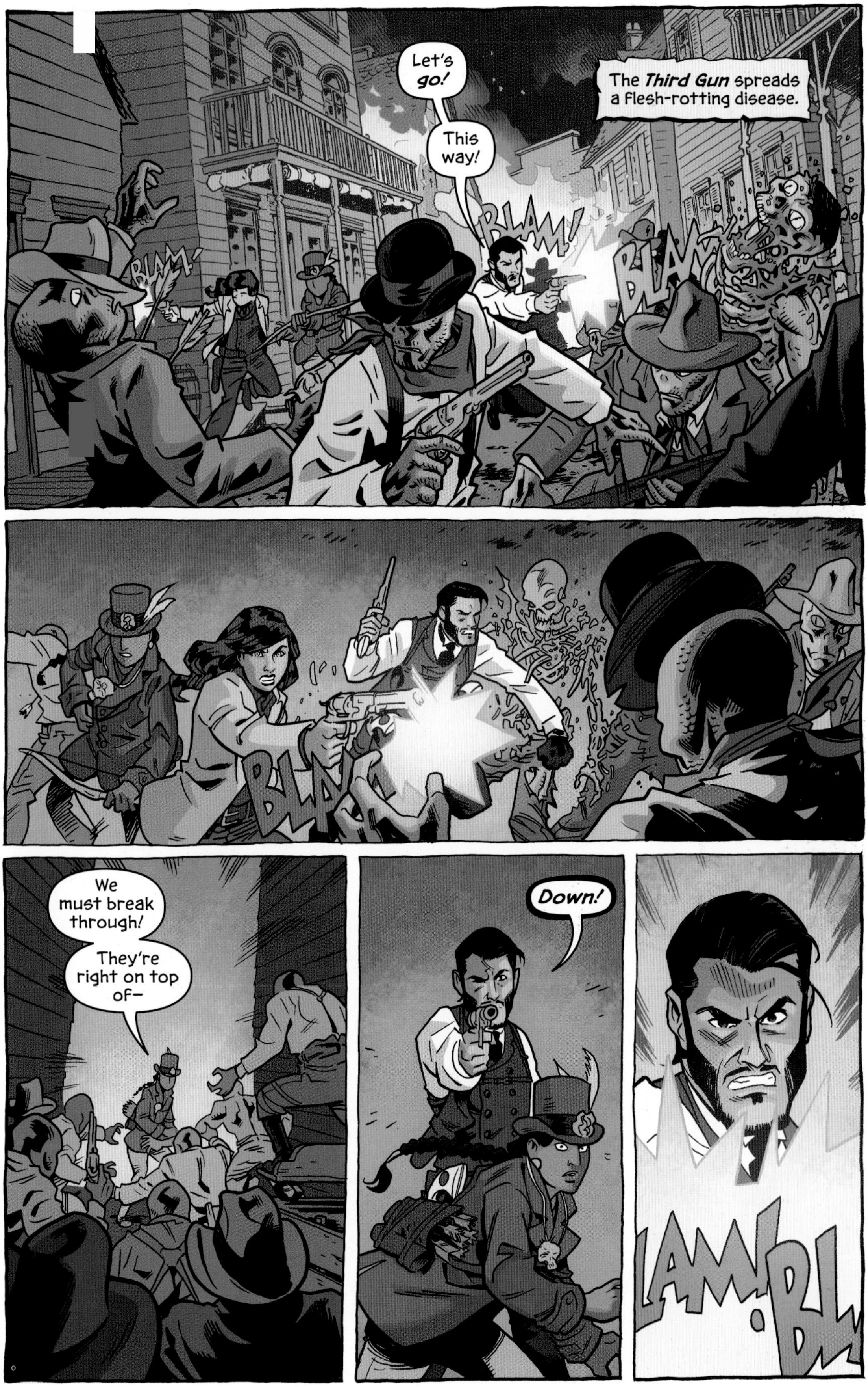

Let's go!
This way!
The Third Gun spreads a flesh-rotting disease.
BLAM!
BLAM!
We must break through!
They're right on top of–
Down!

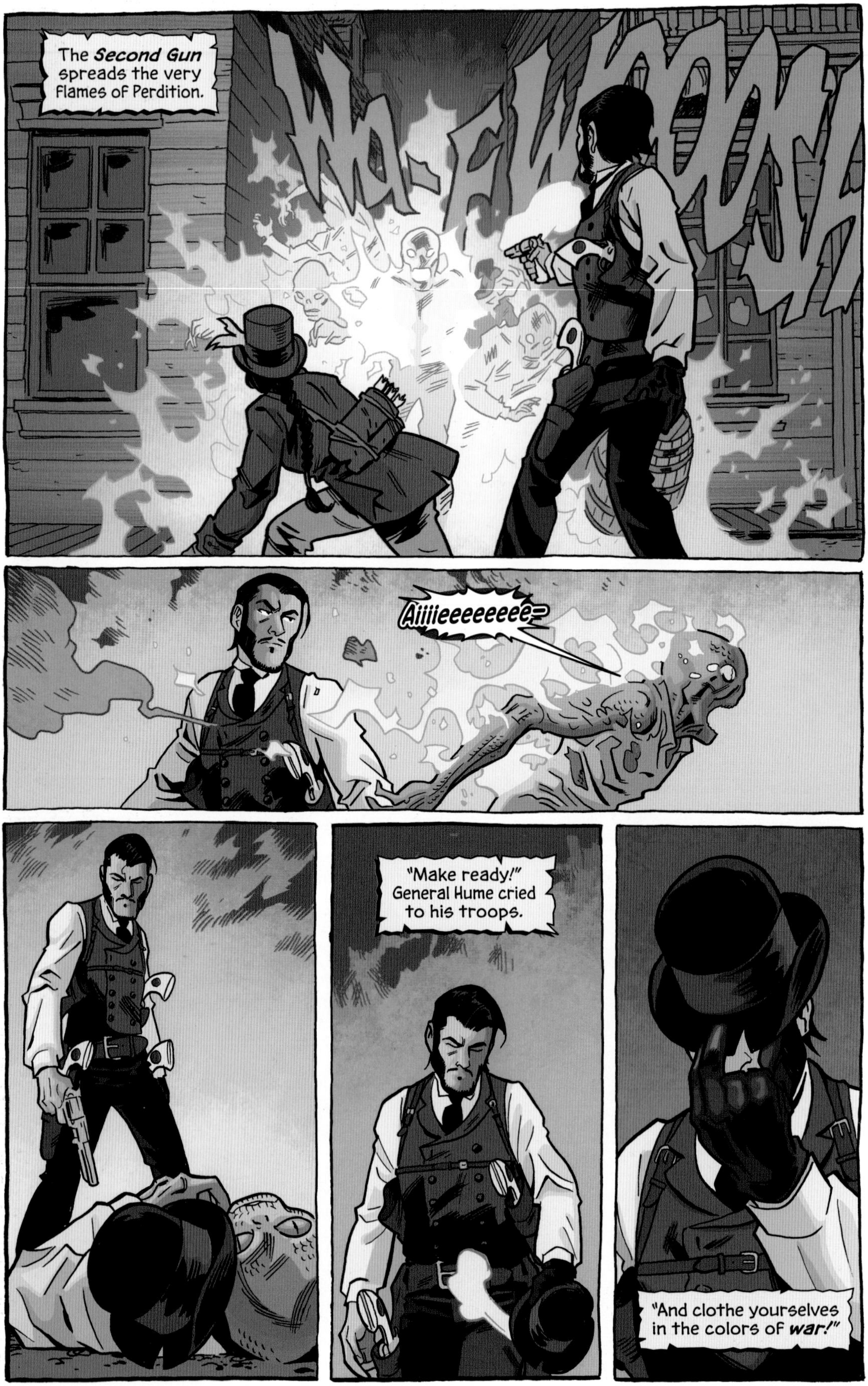
The *Second Gun* spreads the very flames of Perdition.
WA-FUWOOM!
Aiiiieeeeeeee—
"Make ready!" General Hume cried to his troops.
"And clothe yourselves in the colors of *war!*"

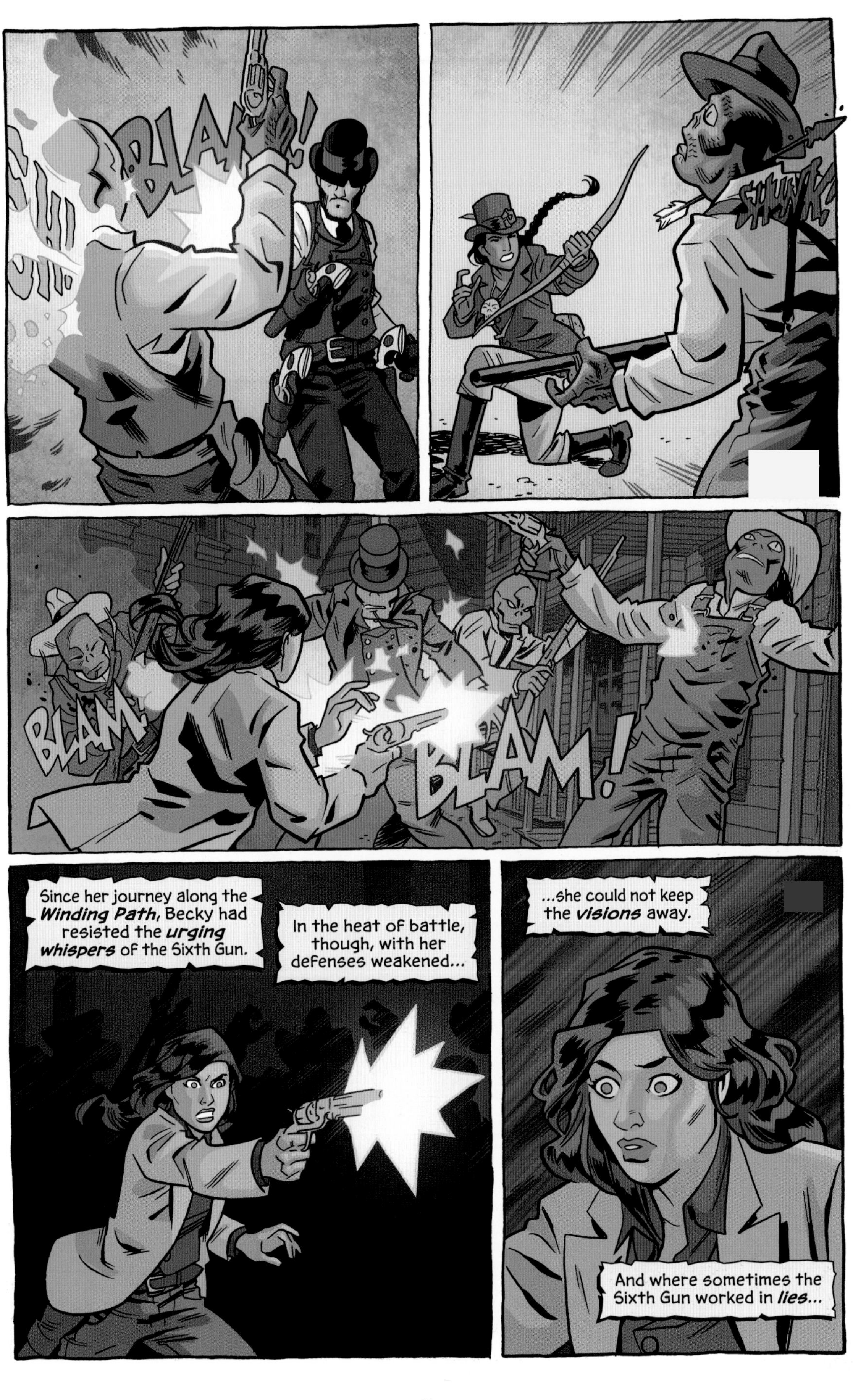
BLAM
BLAM!
Since her journey along the *Winding Path*, Becky had resisted the *urging whispers* of the Sixth Gun.
In the heat of battle, though, with her defenses weakened...
...she could not keep the *visions* away.
And where sometimes the Sixth Gun worked in *lies*...

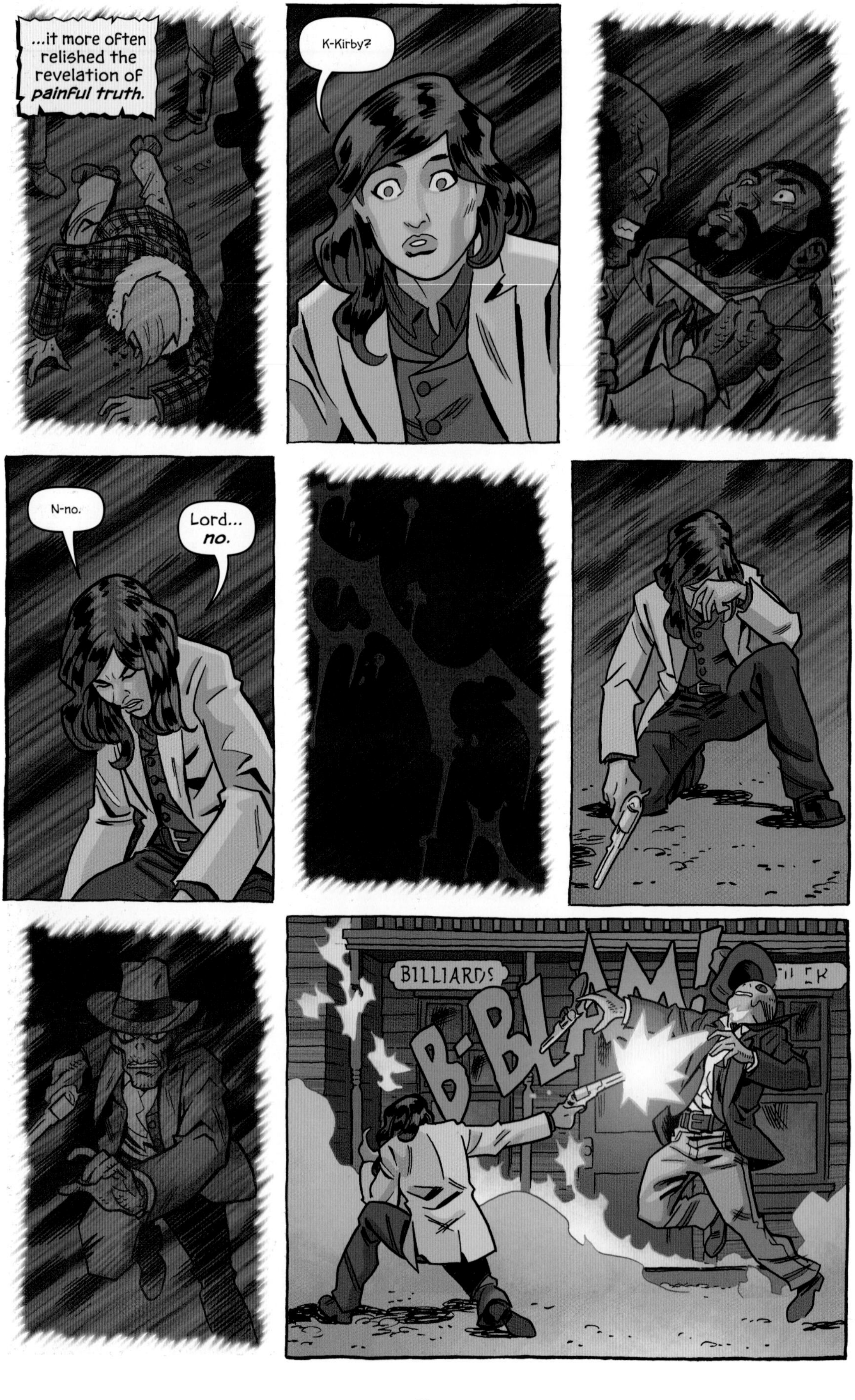
...it more often relished the revelation of ***painful truth.***
K-Kirby?
N-no.
Lord... ***no.***
BILLIARDS
B-BLAM!

P-Pleasssse.

BLAM!
SSH-BLA
BLAM
BLAM

BLAM! BLAM! AM!
BLA BLAM! BLA

Enough! He's *dead!*

That's just it.

N-Nidawi.

They're *all—*

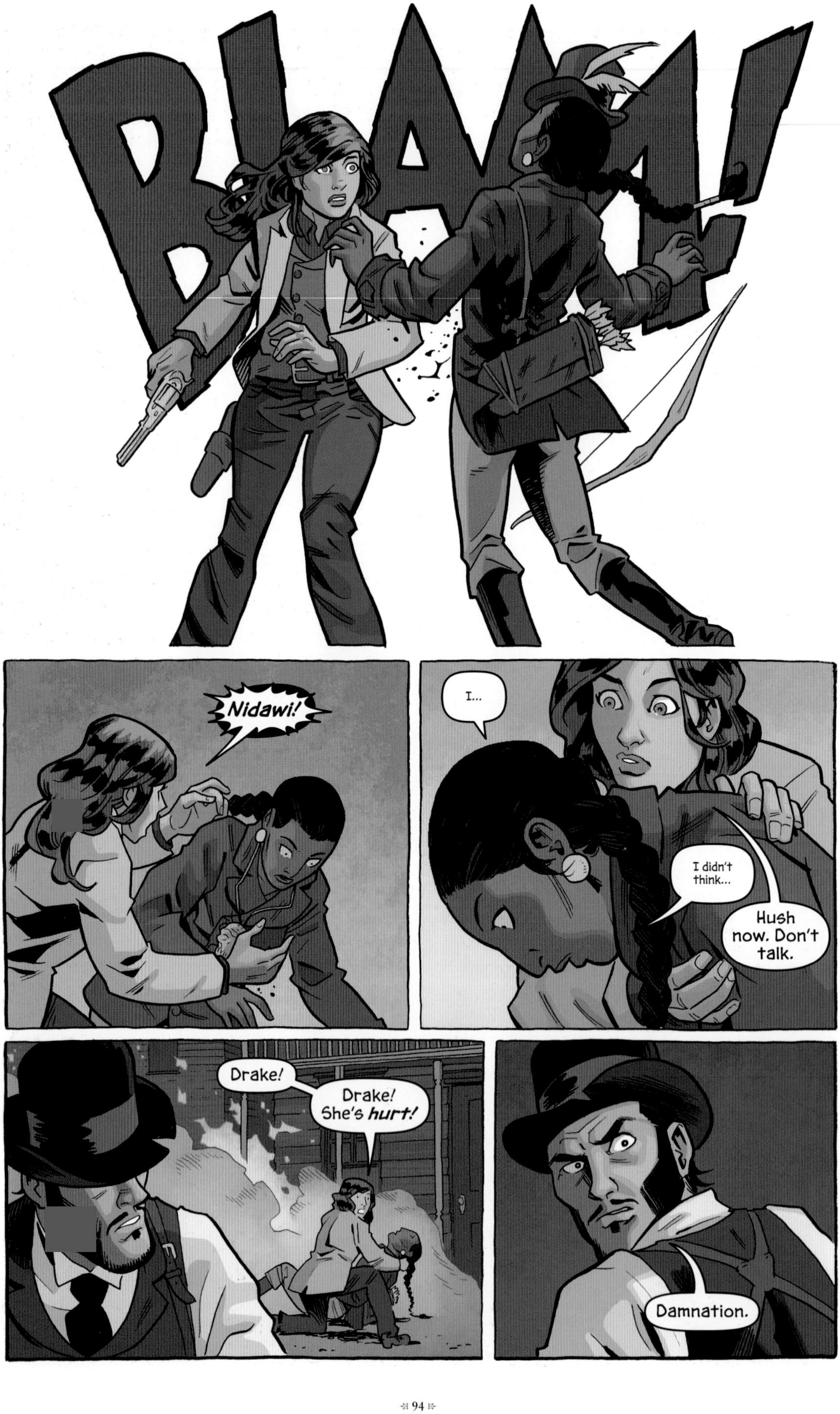
BLAM!
Nidawi!
I...
I didn't think...
Hush now. Don't talk.
Drake!
Drake! She's *hurt!*
Damnation.

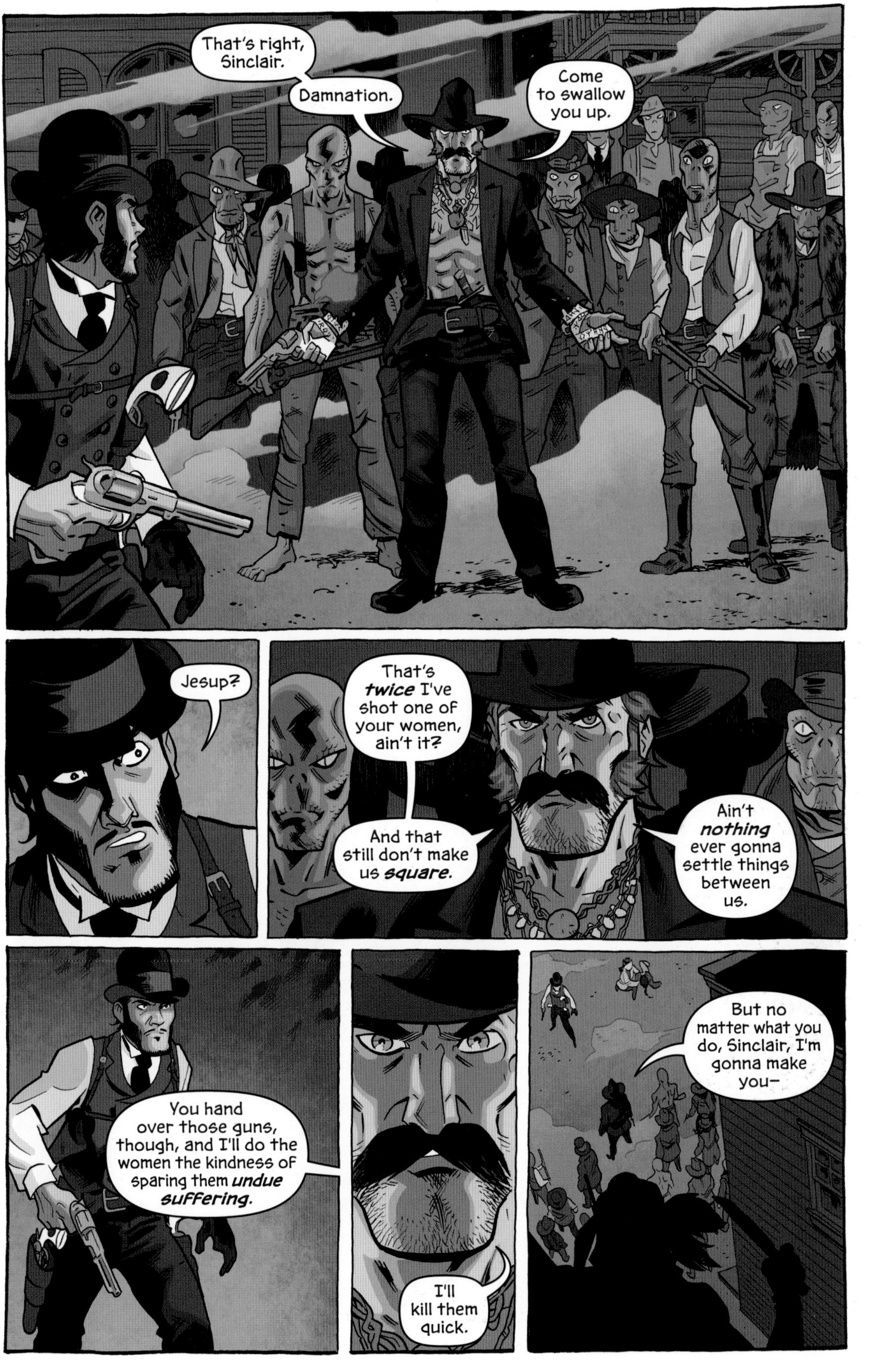
That's right, Sinclair.
Damnation.
Come to swallow you up.
Jesup?
That's *twice* I've shot one of your women, ain't it?
And that still don't make us ***square.***
Ain't ***nothing*** ever gonna settle things between us.
You hand over those guns, though, and I'll do the women the kindness of sparing them ***undue suffering.***
I'll kill them quick.
But no matter what you do, Sinclair, I'm gonna make you–

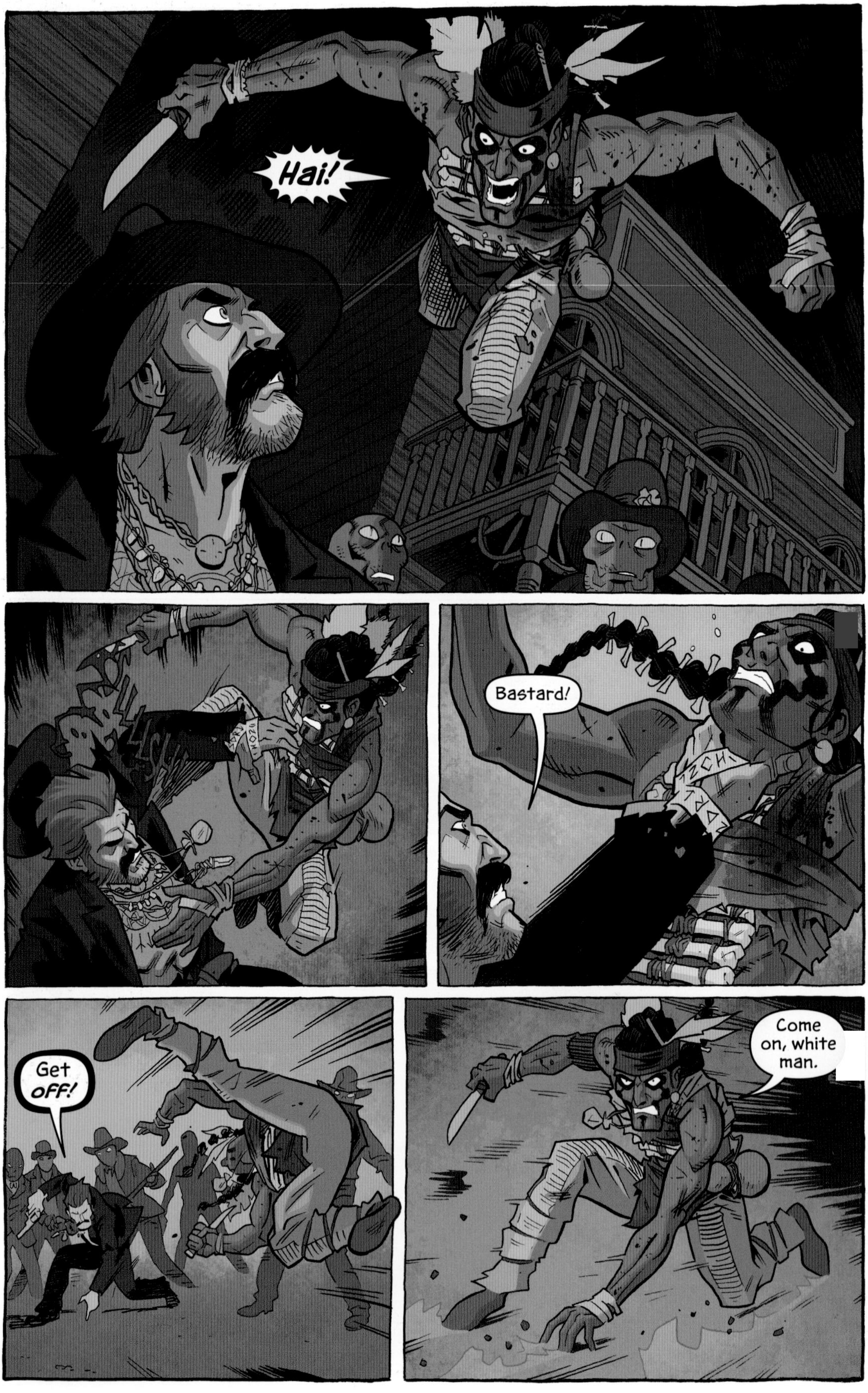
Hai!
Bastard!
Get off!
Come on, white man.

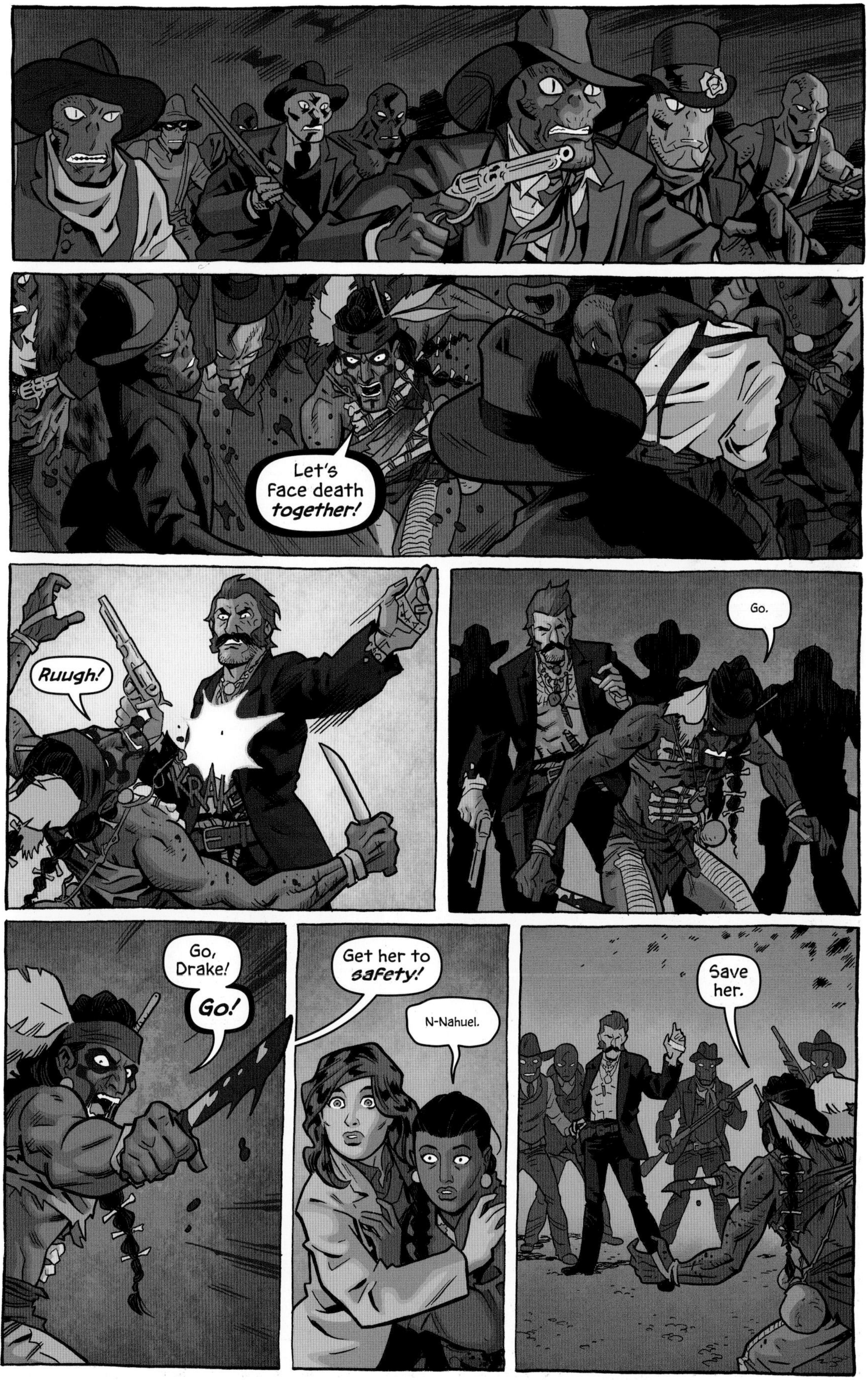

Let's face death together!
Ruugh!
KRAK
Go.
Go, Drake! Go!
Get her to safety!
N-Nahuel.
Save her.

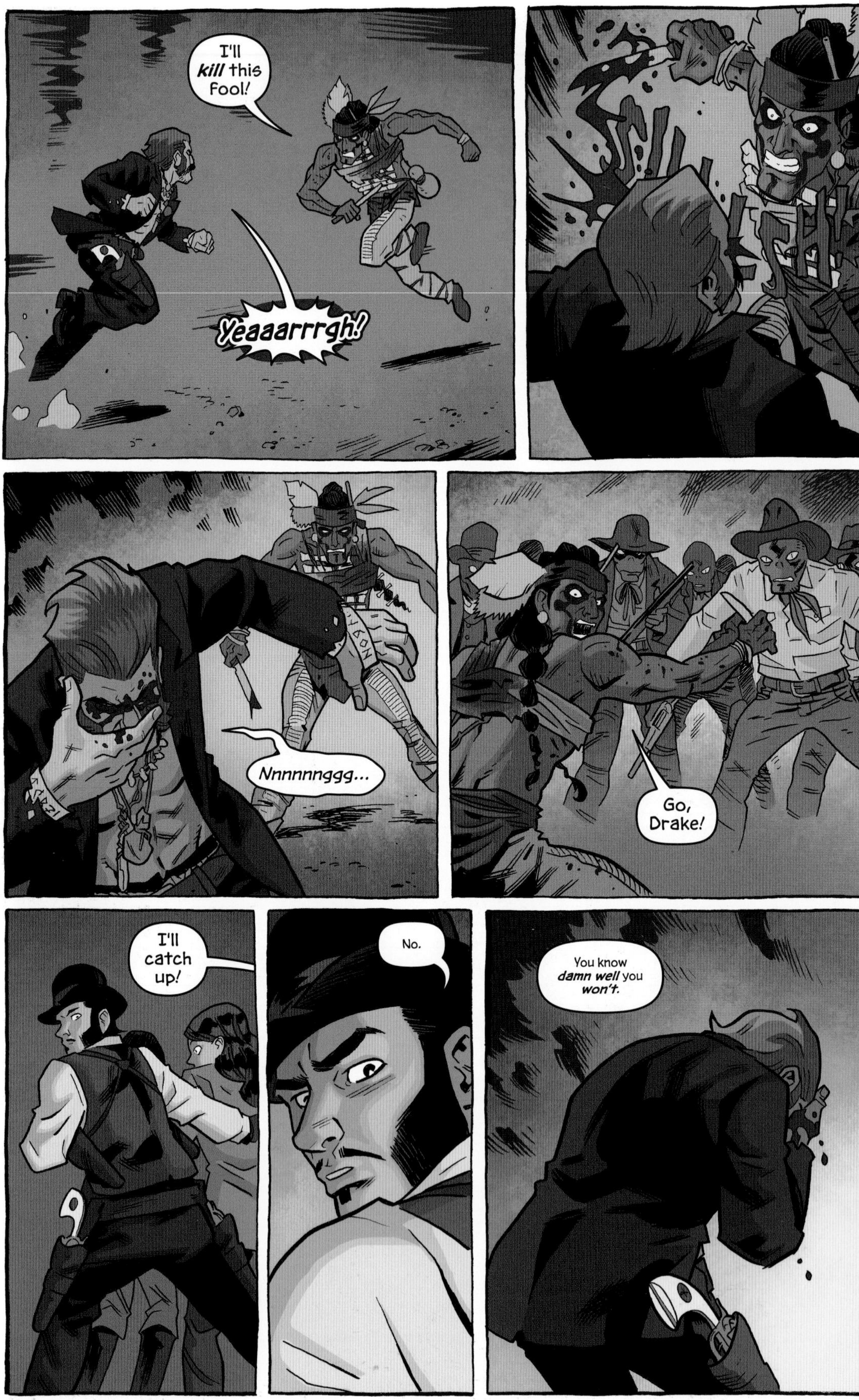
I'll *kill* this fool!
Yeaaarrrgh!
Nnnnnnggg...
Go, Drake!
I'll catch up!
No.
You know *damn well* you *won't*.

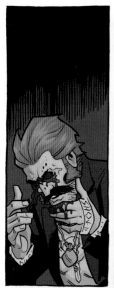

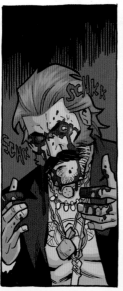

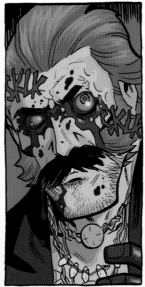

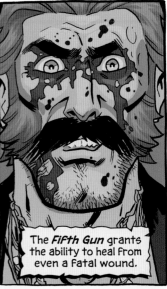

SCHKK
SCHK
SCHK
SCHLK
SCHLK
The Fifth Gun grants the ability to heal from even a fatal wound.
Want you to know, boy.
If that squaw of yours don't bleed out...
...I'll—
You won't touch her!
SHANK

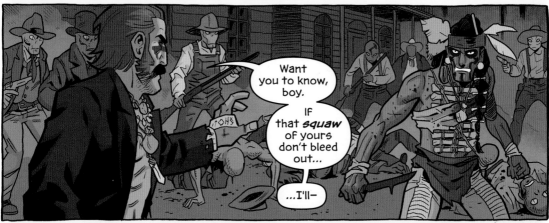

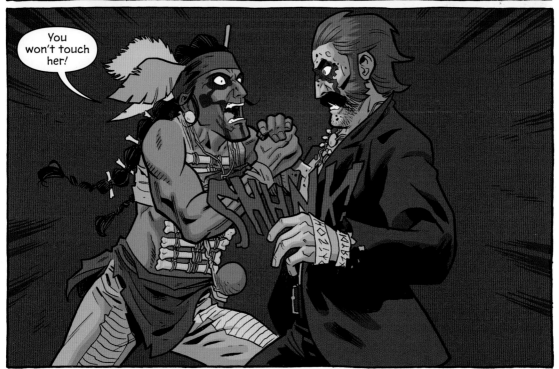

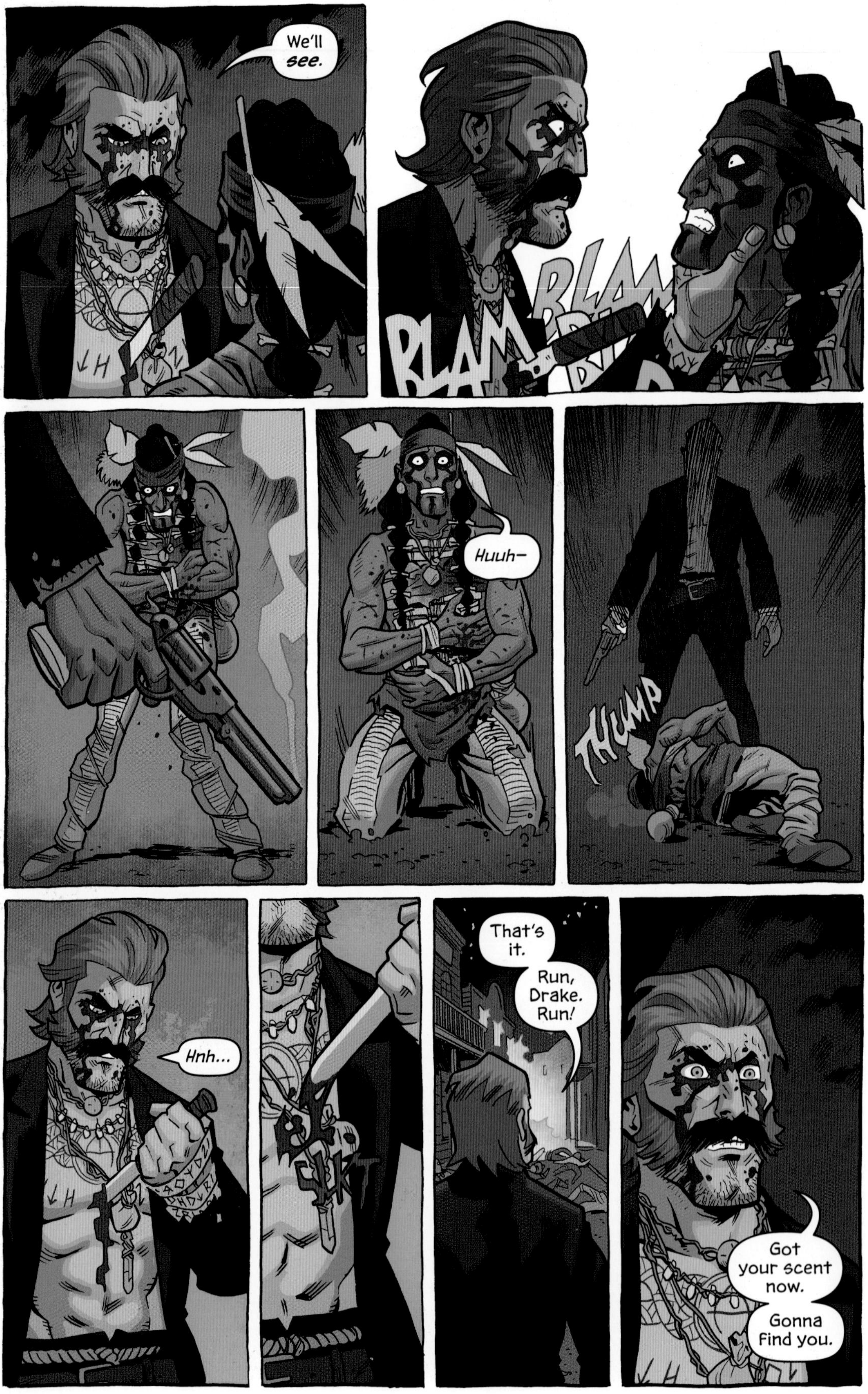

We'll *see.*
BLAM BLAM
Huuh–
THUMP
Hnh...
That's it.
Run, Drake. Run!
Got your scent now.
Gonna find you.

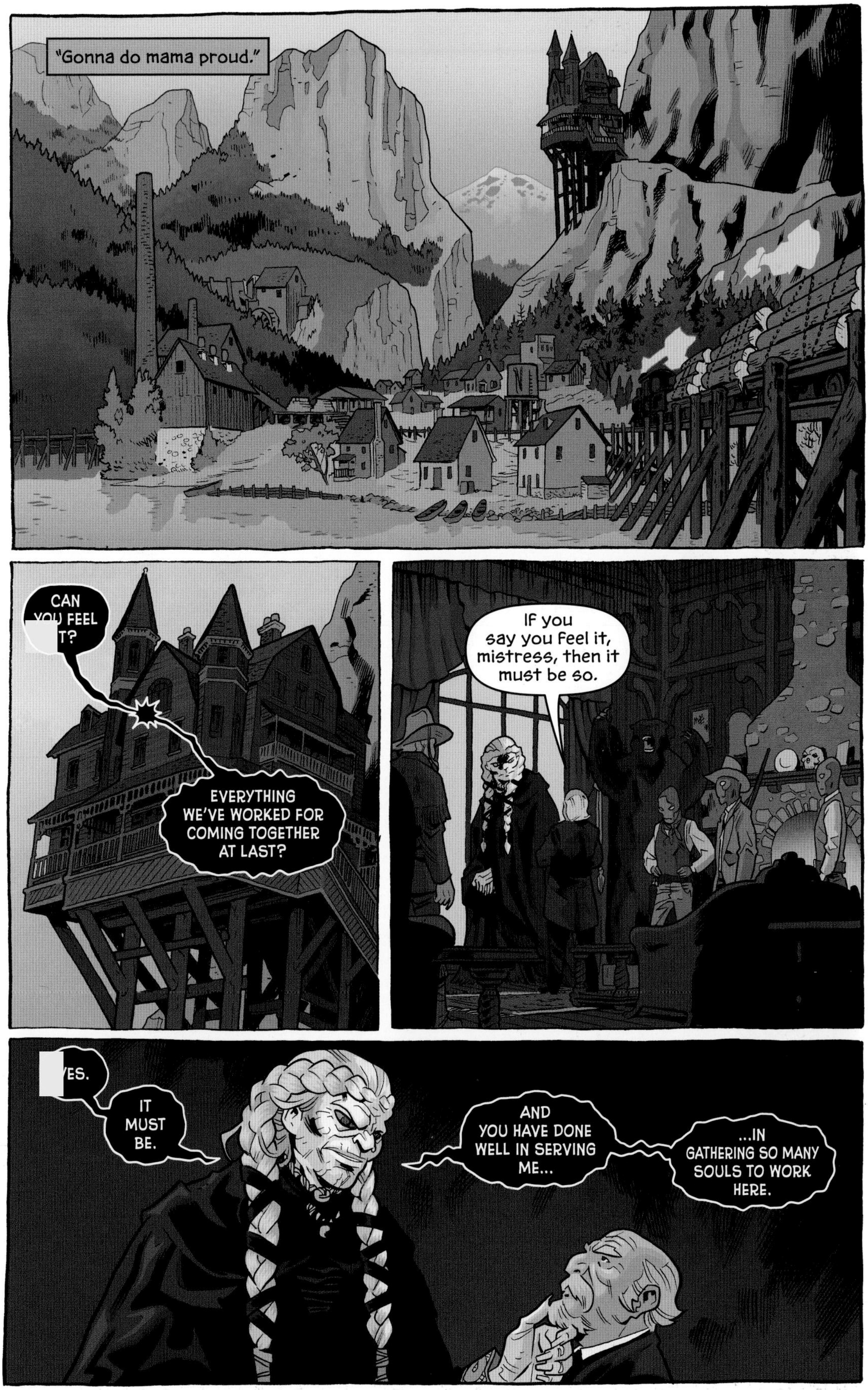
"Gonna do mama proud."
CAN YOU FEEL T?
EVERYTHING WE'VE WORKED FOR COMING TOGETHER AT LAST?
If you say you feel it, mistress, then it must be so.
ES.
IT MUST BE.
AND YOU HAVE DONE WELL IN SERVING ME...
...IN GATHERING SO MANY SOULS TO WORK HERE.

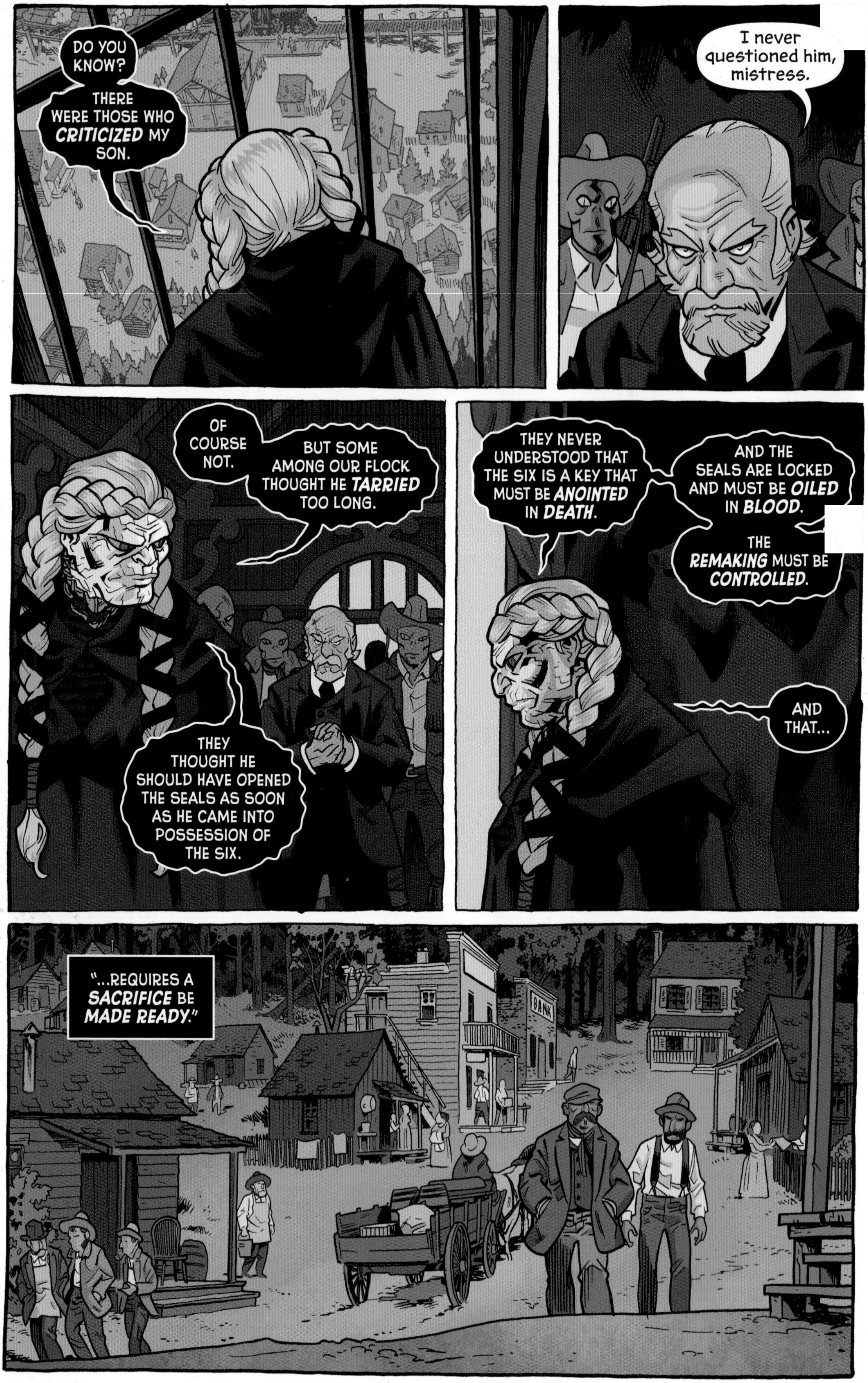
DO YOU KNOW?
THERE WERE THOSE WHO *CRITICIZED* MY SON.
I never questioned him, mistress.
OF COURSE NOT.
BUT SOME AMONG OUR FLOCK THOUGHT HE *TARRIED* TOO LONG.
THEY THOUGHT HE SHOULD HAVE OPENED THE SEALS AS SOON AS HE CAME INTO POSSESSION OF THE SIX.
THEY NEVER UNDERSTOOD THAT THE SIX IS A KEY THAT MUST BE *ANOINTED* IN *DEATH*.
AND THE SEALS ARE LOCKED AND MUST BE *OILED* IN *BLOOD*.
THE *REMAKING* MUST BE *CONTROLLED*.
AND THAT...
"...REQUIRES A *SACRIFICE* BE *MADE READY*."
BANK

CHAPTER FIVE

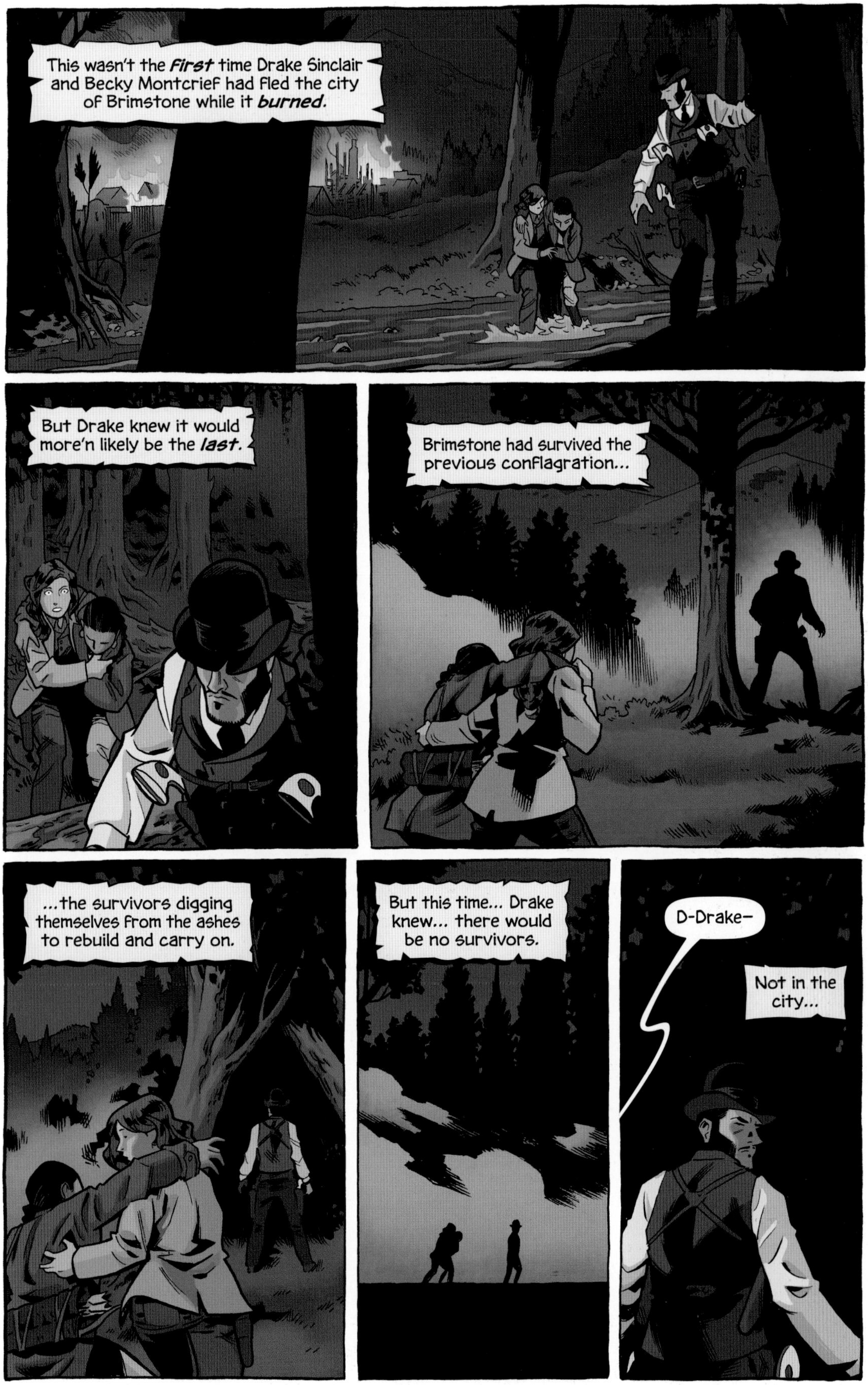
This wasn't the *first* time Drake Sinclair and Becky Montcrief had fled the city of Brimstone while it *burned.*
But Drake knew it would more'n likely be the *last.*
Brimstone had survived the previous conflagration...
...the survivors digging themselves from the ashes to rebuild and carry on.
But this time... Drake knew... there would be no survivors.
D-Drake–
Not in the city...

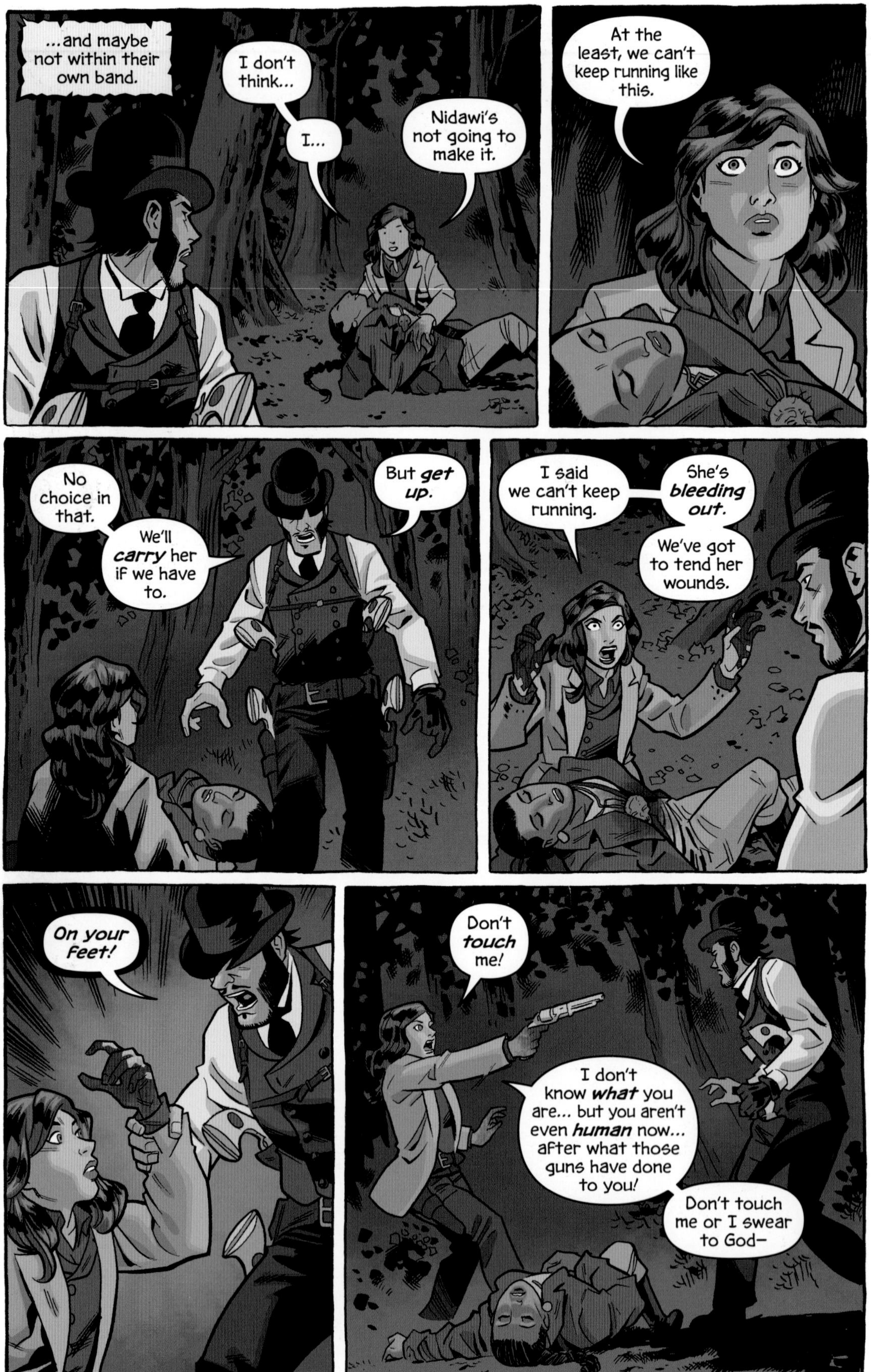
...and maybe not within their own band.
I don't think...
I...
Nidawi's not going to make it.
At the least, we can't keep running like this.
No choice in that.
We'll carry her if we have to.
But get up.
I said we can't keep running.
She's bleeding out.
We've got to tend her wounds.
On your feet!
Don't touch me!
I don't know what you are... but you aren't even human now... after what those guns have done to you!
Don't touch me or I swear to God—

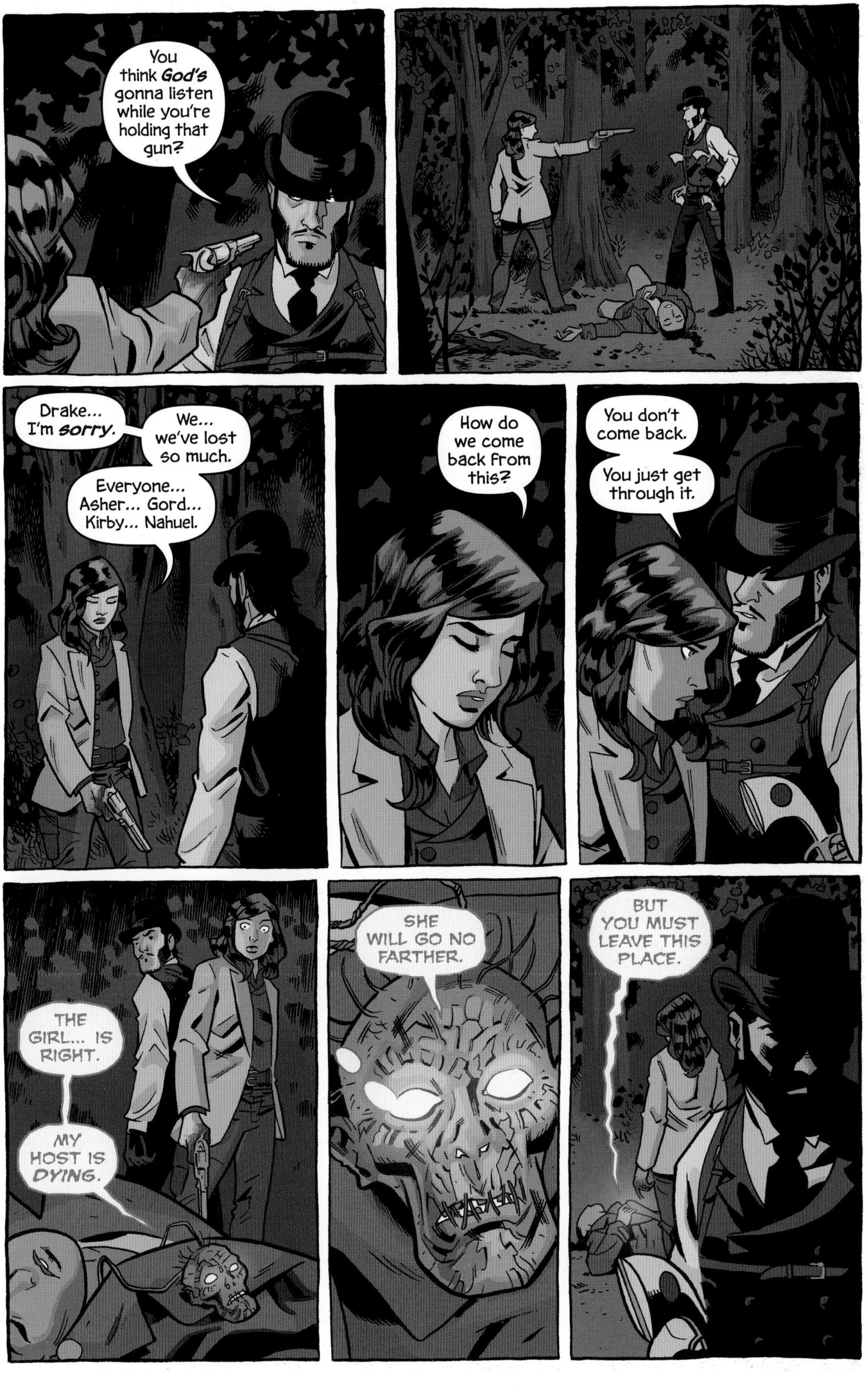
You think God's gonna listen while you're holding that gun?
Drake... I'm sorry.
We... we've lost so much.
Everyone... Asher... Gord... Kirby... Nahuel.
How do we come back from this?
You don't come back.
You just get through it.
THE GIRL... IS RIGHT.
MY HOST IS DYING.
SHE WILL GO NO FARTHER.
BUT YOU MUST LEAVE THIS PLACE.

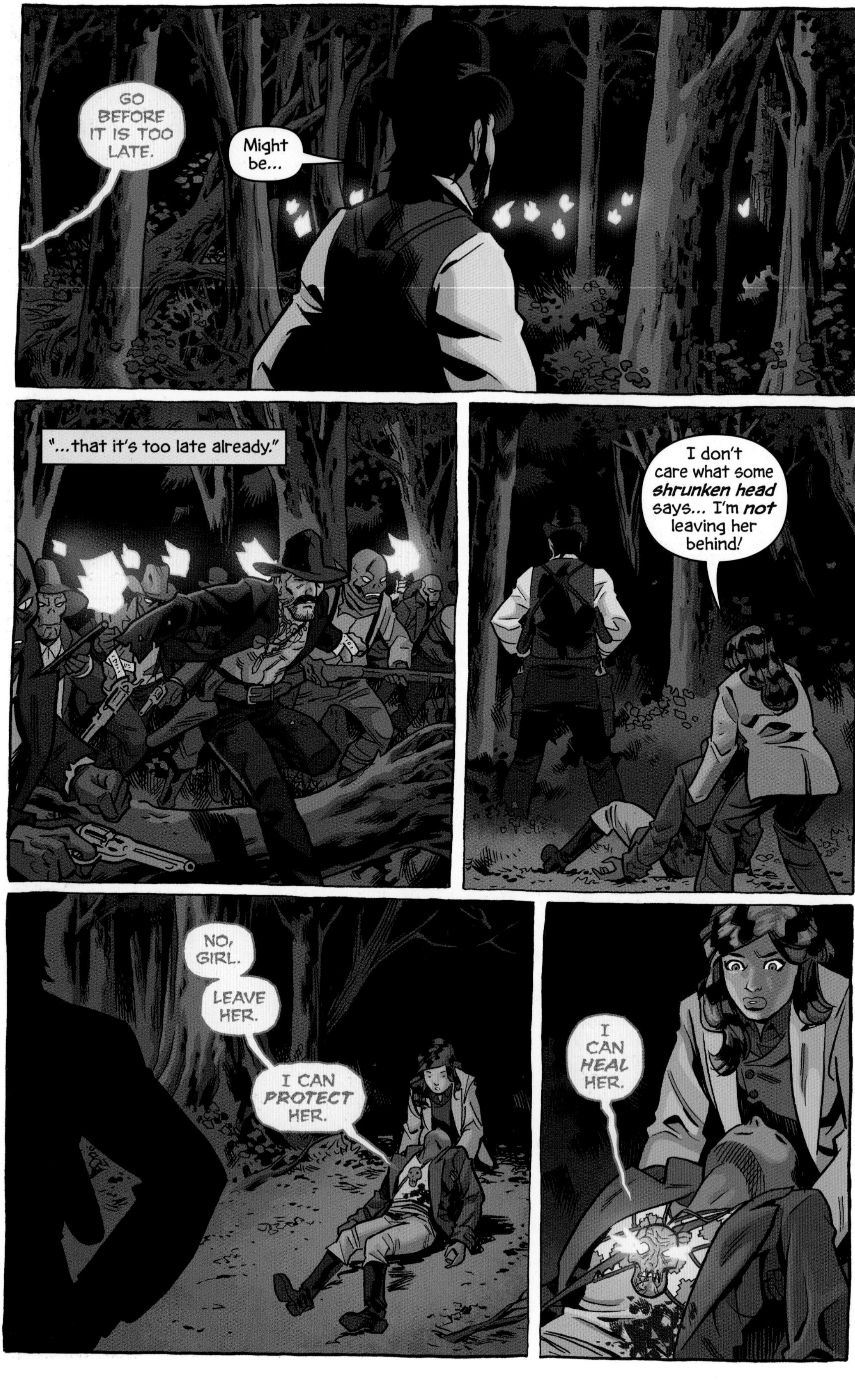

GO BEFORE IT IS TOO LATE.
Might be...
"...that it's too late already."
I don't care what some **shrunken head** says... I'm **not** leaving her behind!
NO, GIRL.
LEAVE HER.
I CAN **PROTECT** HER.
I CAN **HEAL** HER.

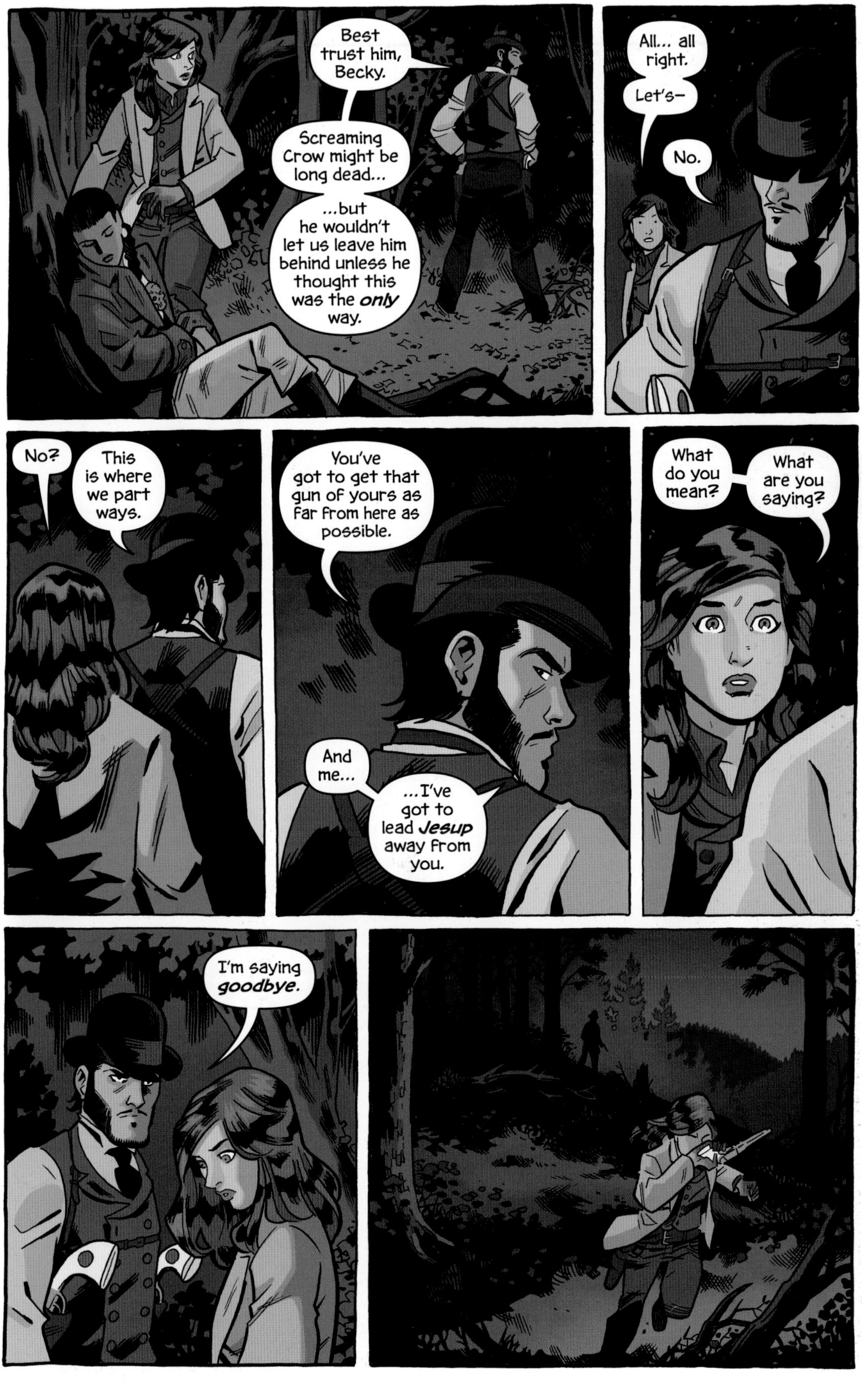
Best trust him, Becky.
Screaming Crow might be long dead...
...but he wouldn't let us leave him behind unless he thought this was the *only* way.
All... all right.
Let's—
No.
No?
This is where we part ways.
You've got to get that gun of yours as far from here as possible.
And me...
...I've got to lead *Jesup* away from you.
What do you mean?
What are you saying?
I'm saying *goodbye*.

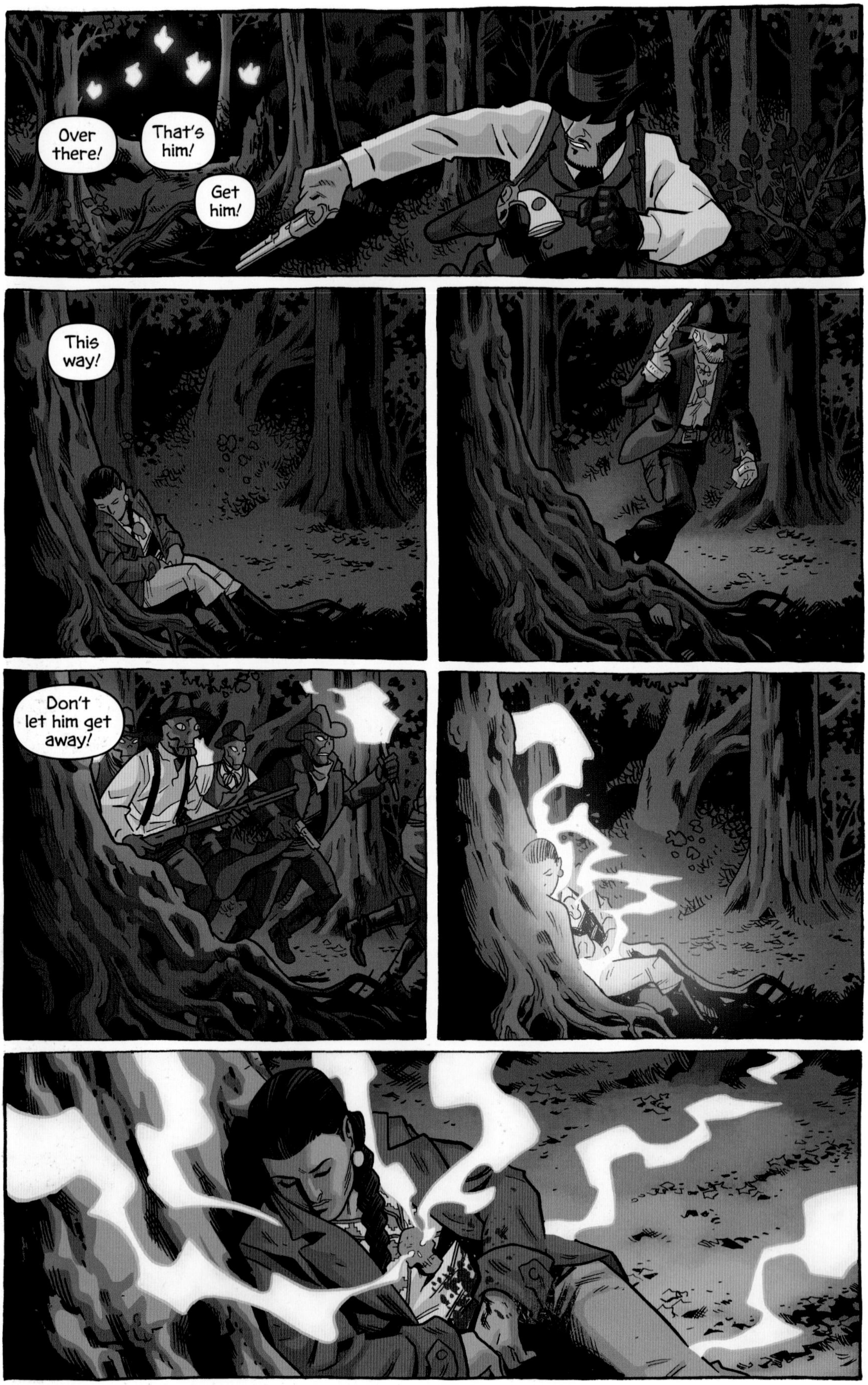
Over there!
That's him!
Get him!
This way!
Don't let him get away!

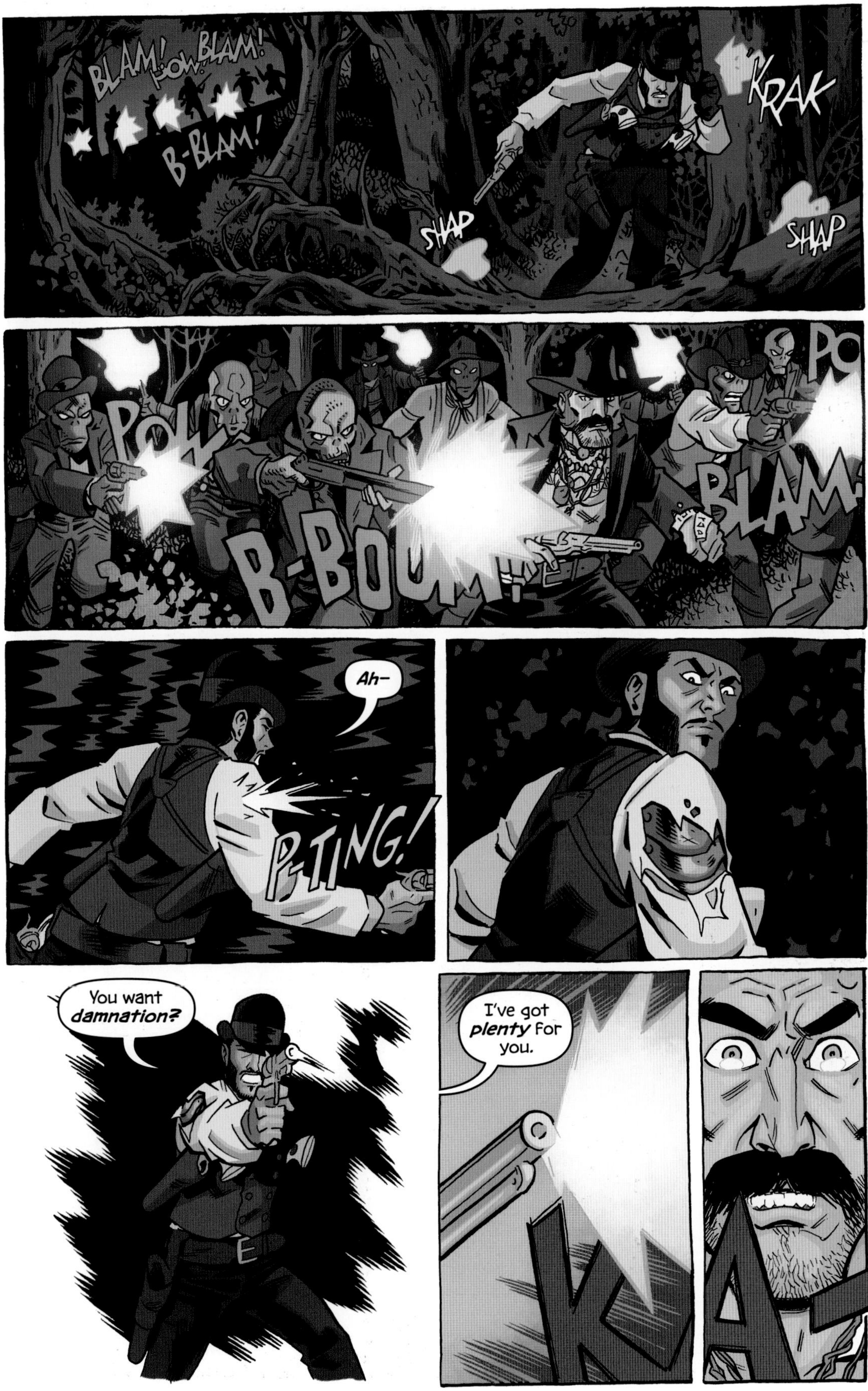
BLAM! POW! BLAM!
B-BLAM!
KRAK
SHAP
SHAP
POW
B-BOOM
BLAM
PO
Ah-
P-TING!
You want *damnation?*
I've got *plenty* for you.
KA-

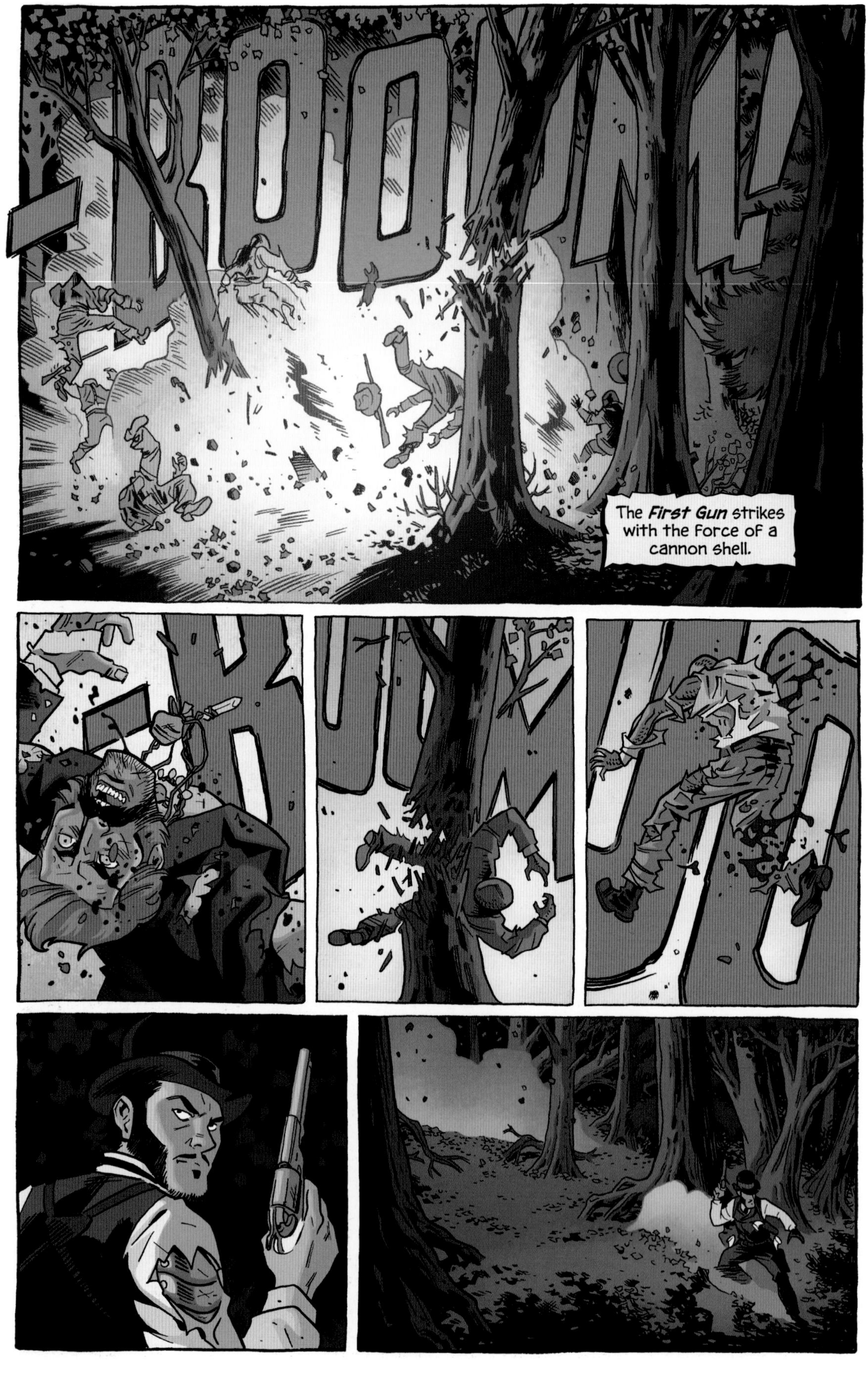
The *First Gun* strikes with the force of a cannon shell.

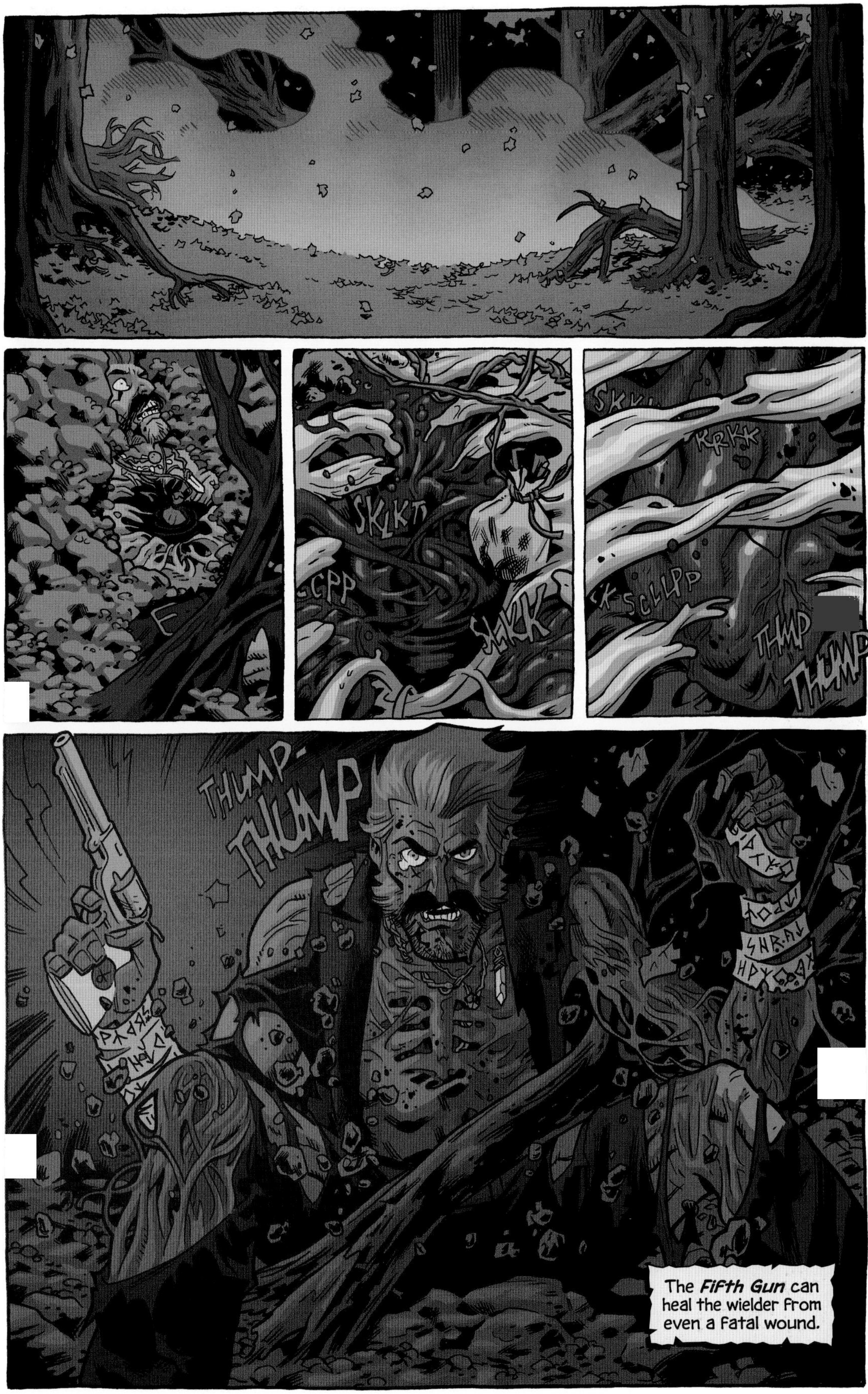
SKLKT
SKLKK
KRKK
K-SCLLPP
THUMP
THUMP
THUMP-
THUMP
The *Fifth Gun* can heal the wielder from even a fatal wound.

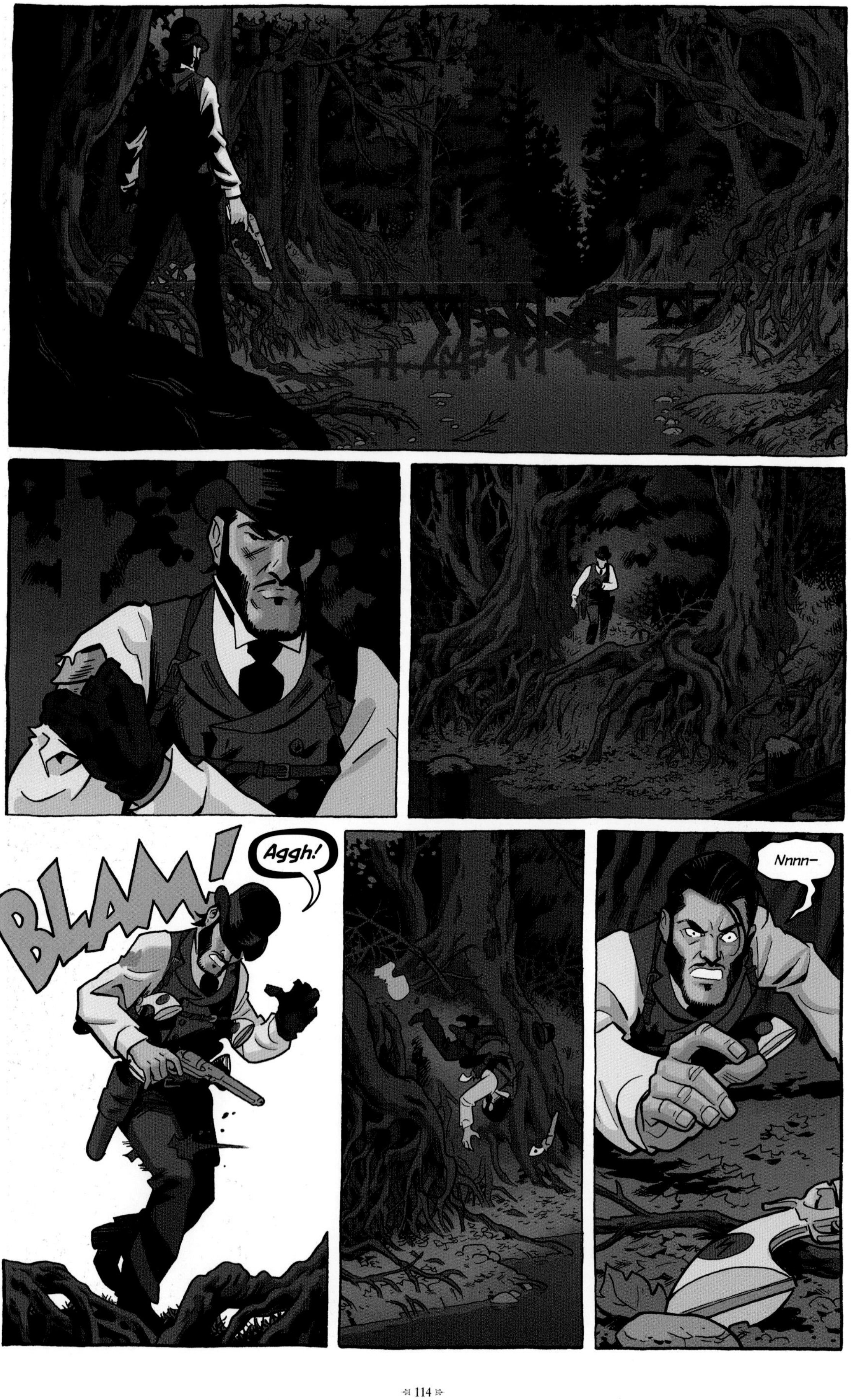
BLAM!
Aggh!
Nnnn-

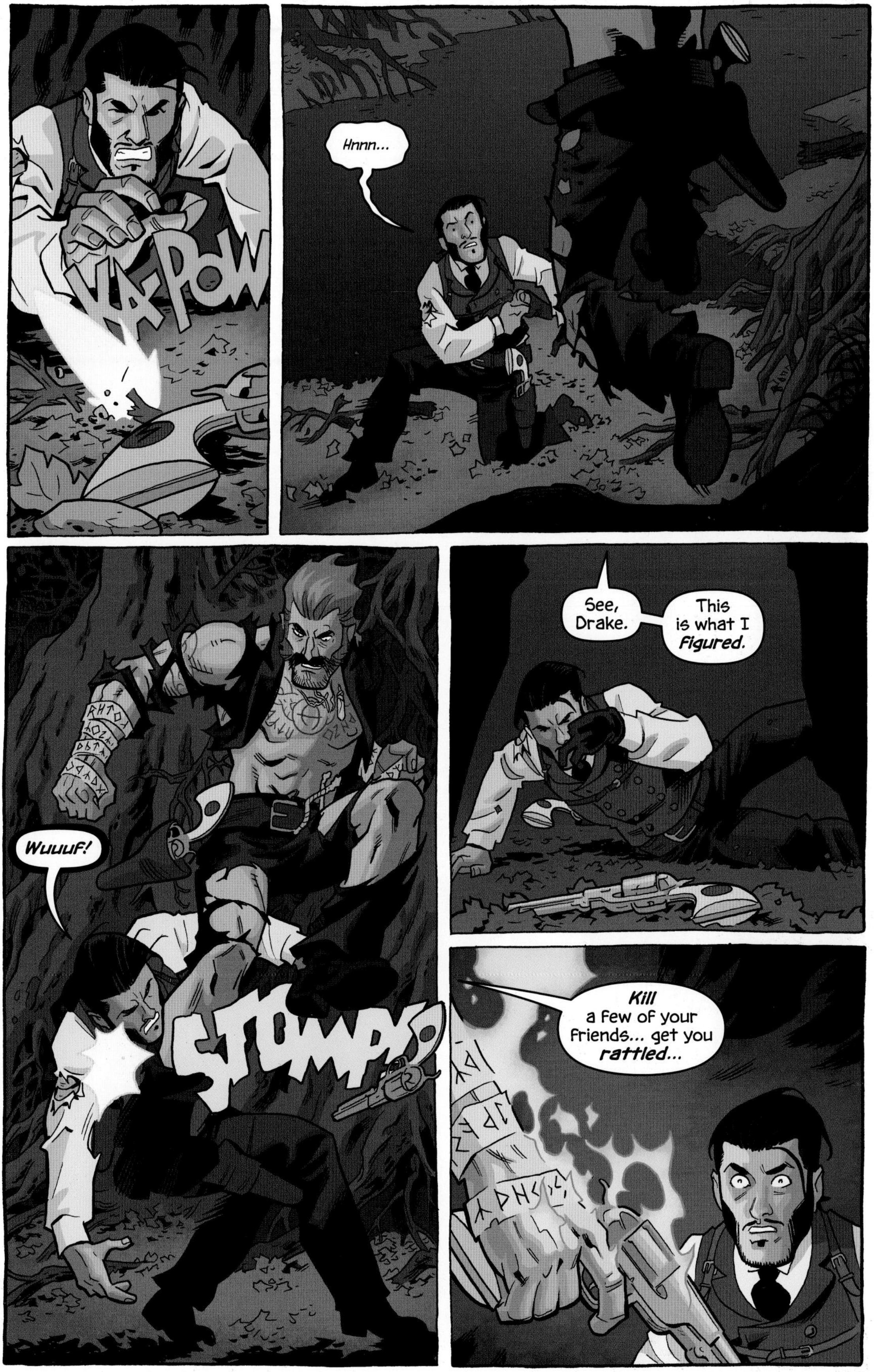
KA-POW
Hnnn...
Wuuuf!
STOMP
See, Drake.
This is what I *figured*.
Kill a few of your friends... get you *rattled*...

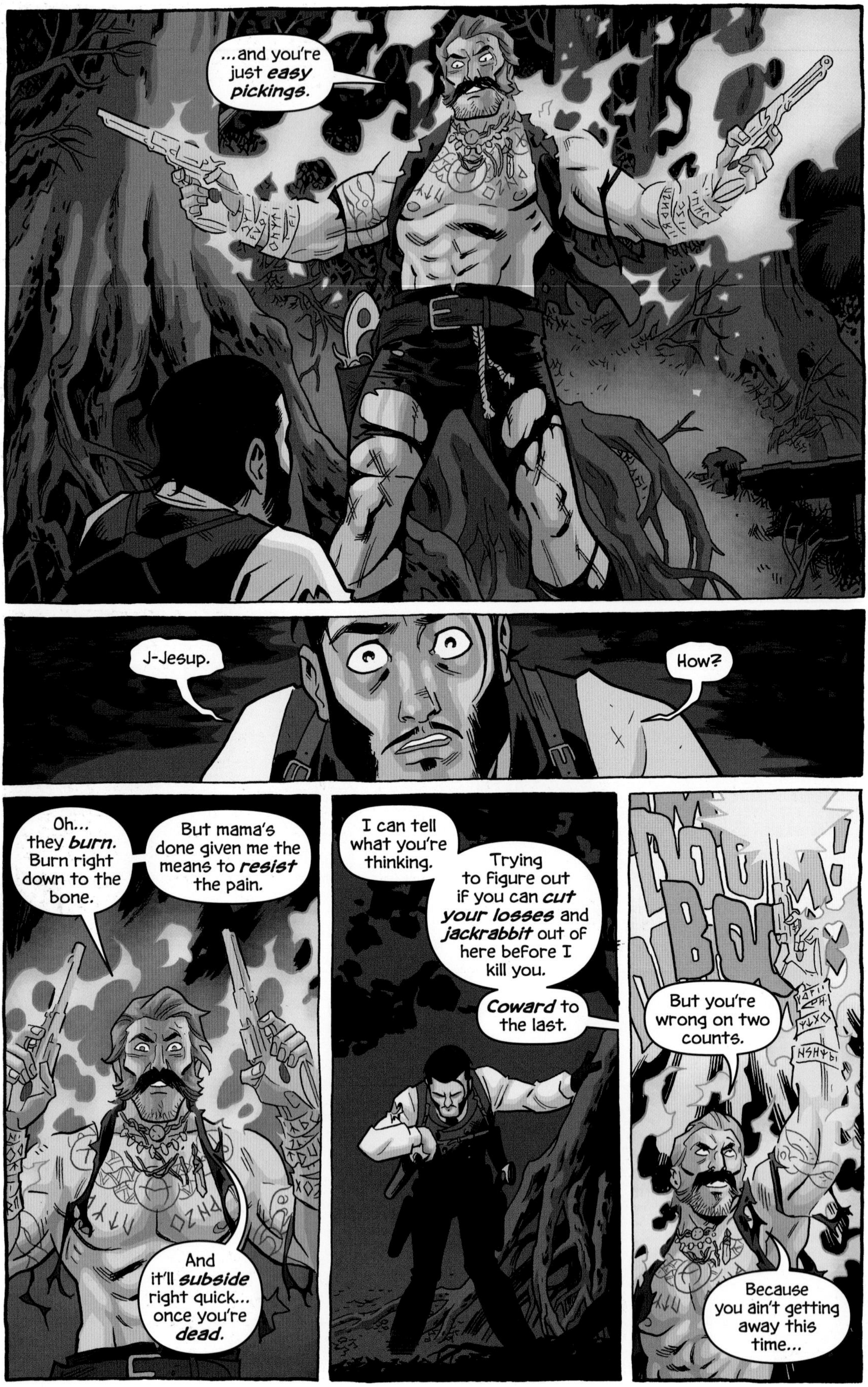
...and you're just *easy pickings.*
J-Jesup.
How?
Oh... they *burn.* Burn right down to the bone.
But mama's done given me the means to *resist* the pain.
And it'll *subside* right quick... once you're *dead.*
I can tell what you're thinking.
Trying to figure out if you can *cut your losses* and *jackrabbit* out of here before I kill you.
Coward to the last.
But you're wrong on two counts.
Because you ain't getting away this time...

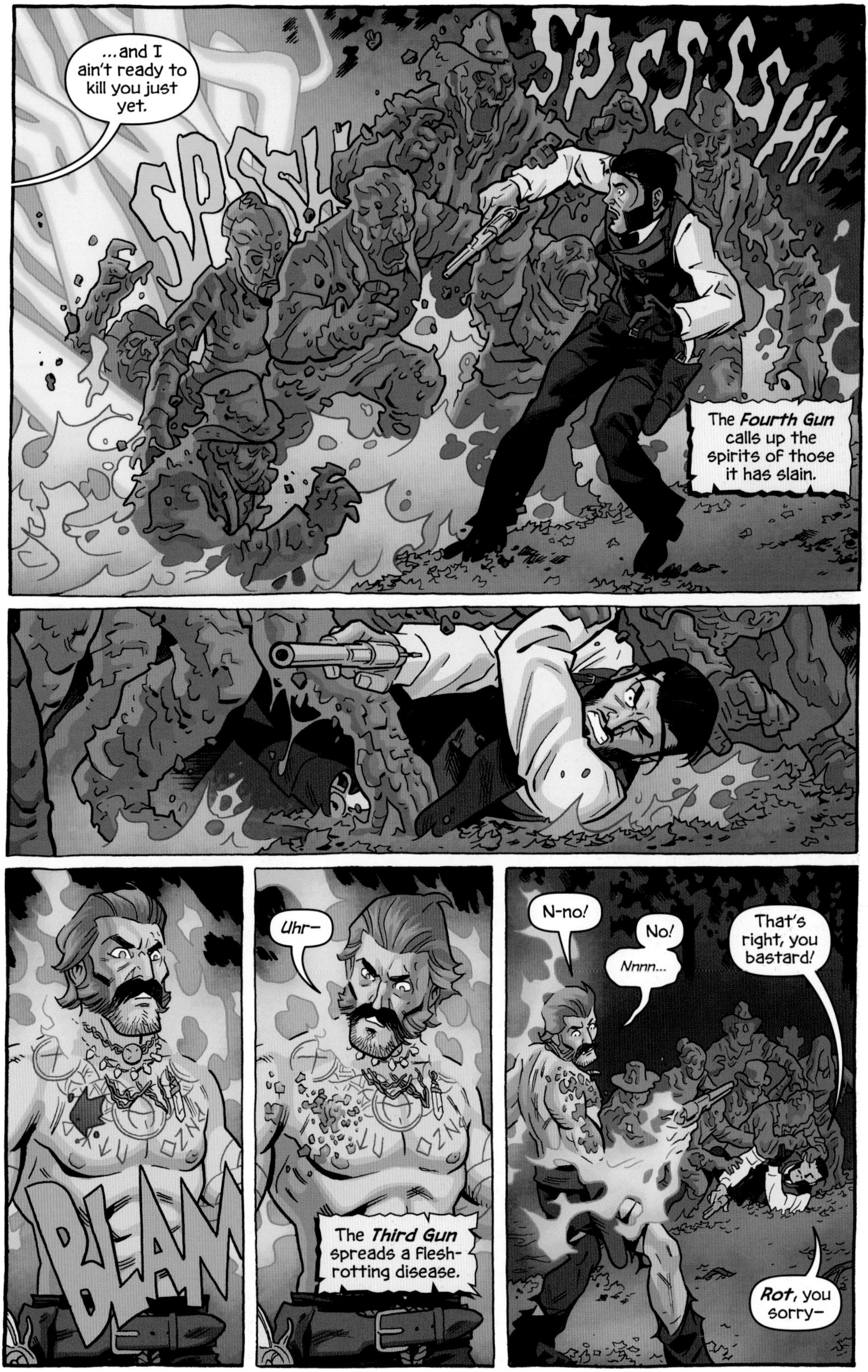
...and I ain't ready to kill you just yet.
SPSSH
SPSSSHH
The *Fourth Gun* calls up the spirits of those it has slain.
BLAM
Uhr–
The *Third Gun* spreads a flesh-rotting disease.
N-no!
No!
Nnnn...
That's right, you bastard!
Rot, you sorry–

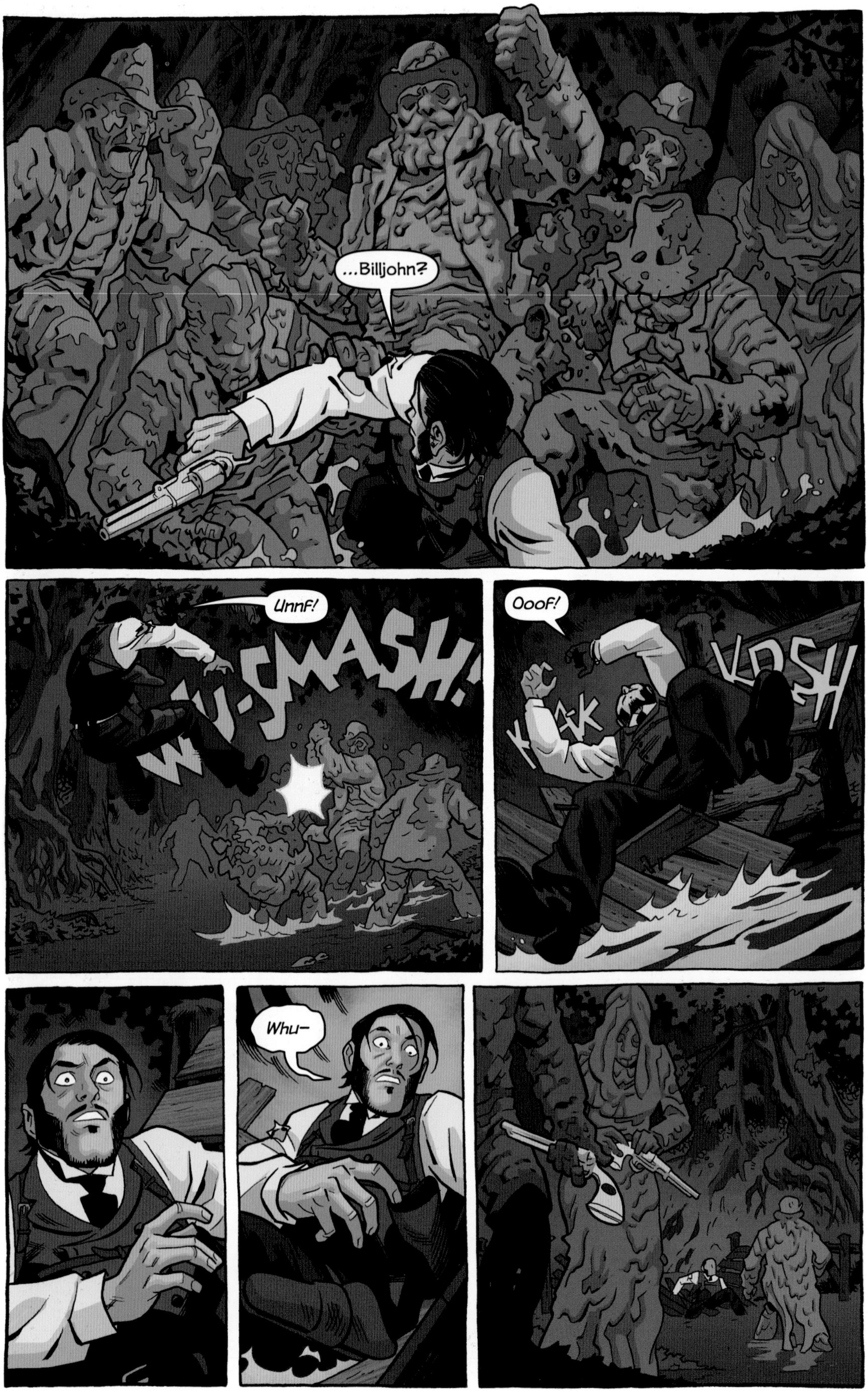

...Billjohn?
Unnf!
WU-SMASH!
Ooof!
Whu-

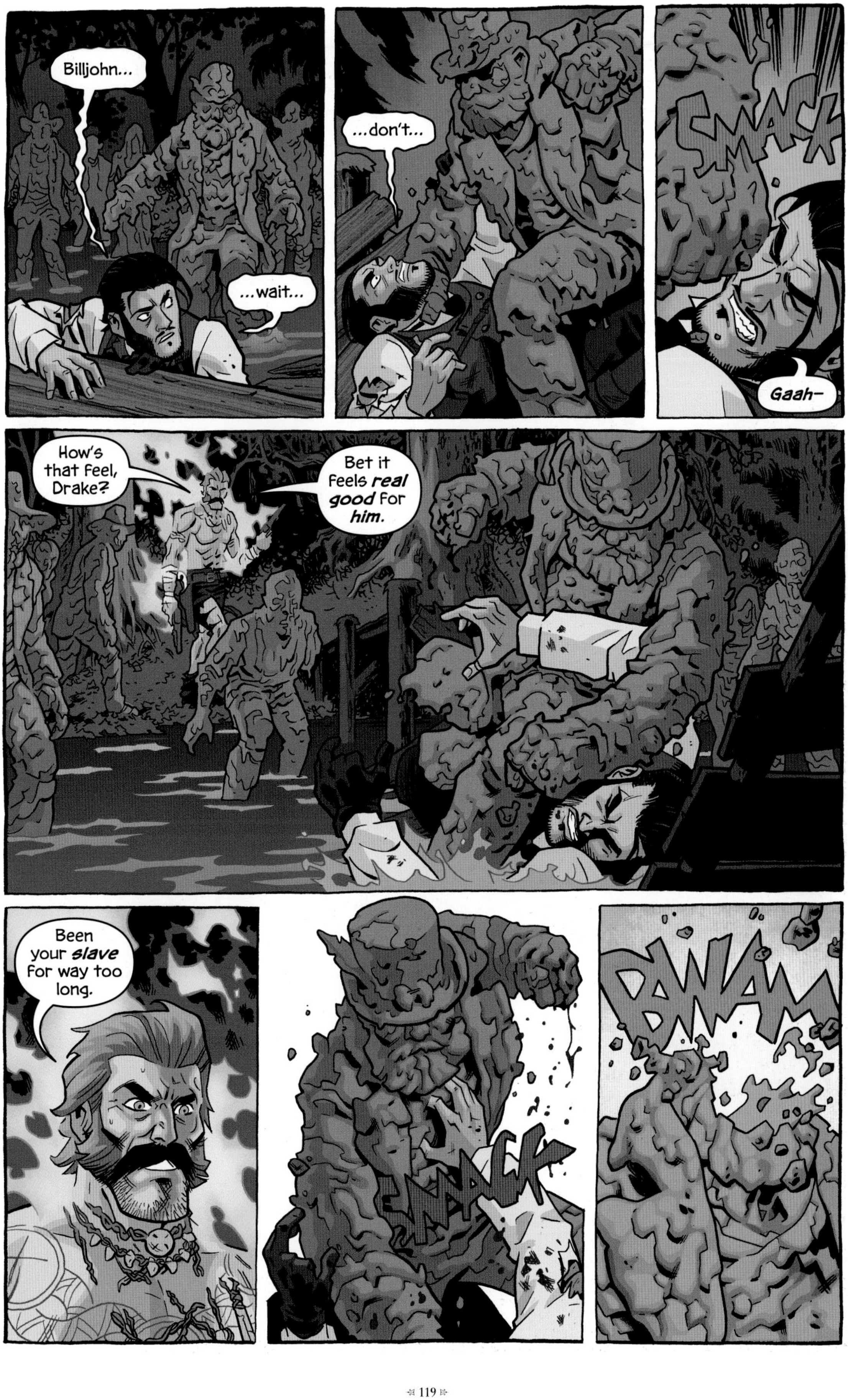
Billjohn...
...wait...
...don't...
SMACK
Gaah–
How's that feel, Drake?
Bet it feels *real good* for *him.*
Been your *slave* for way too long.
SMACK
BAWAM

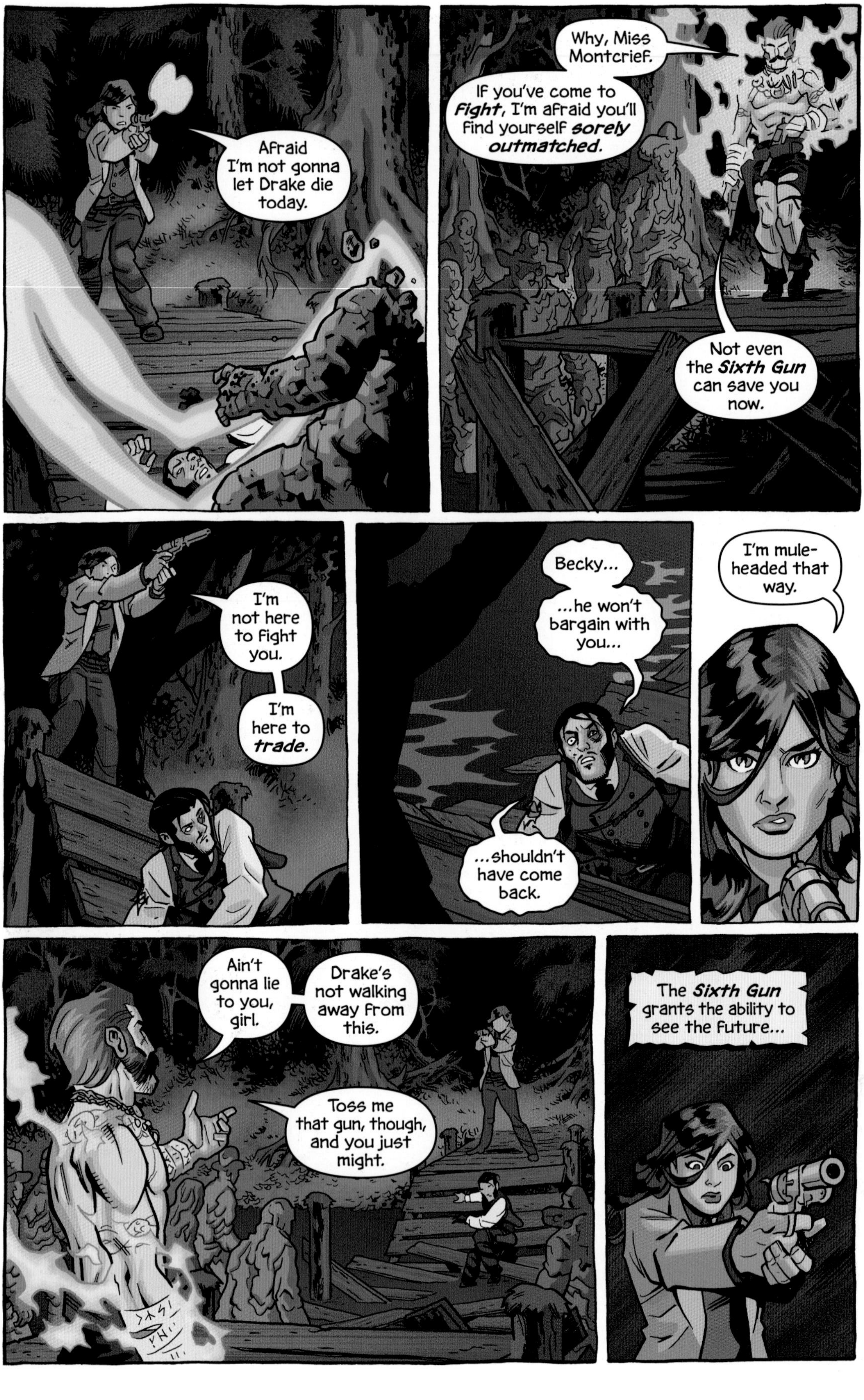
Afraid I'm not gonna let Drake die today.
Why, Miss Montcrief.
If you've come to *fight*, I'm afraid you'll find yourself *sorely outmatched.*
Not even the *Sixth Gun* can save you now.
I'm not here to fight you.
I'm here to *trade.*
Becky...
...he won't bargain with you...
...shouldn't have come back.
I'm mule-headed that way.
Ain't gonna lie to you, girl.
Drake's not walking away from this.
Toss me that gun, though, and you just might.
The *Sixth Gun* grants the ability to see the future...

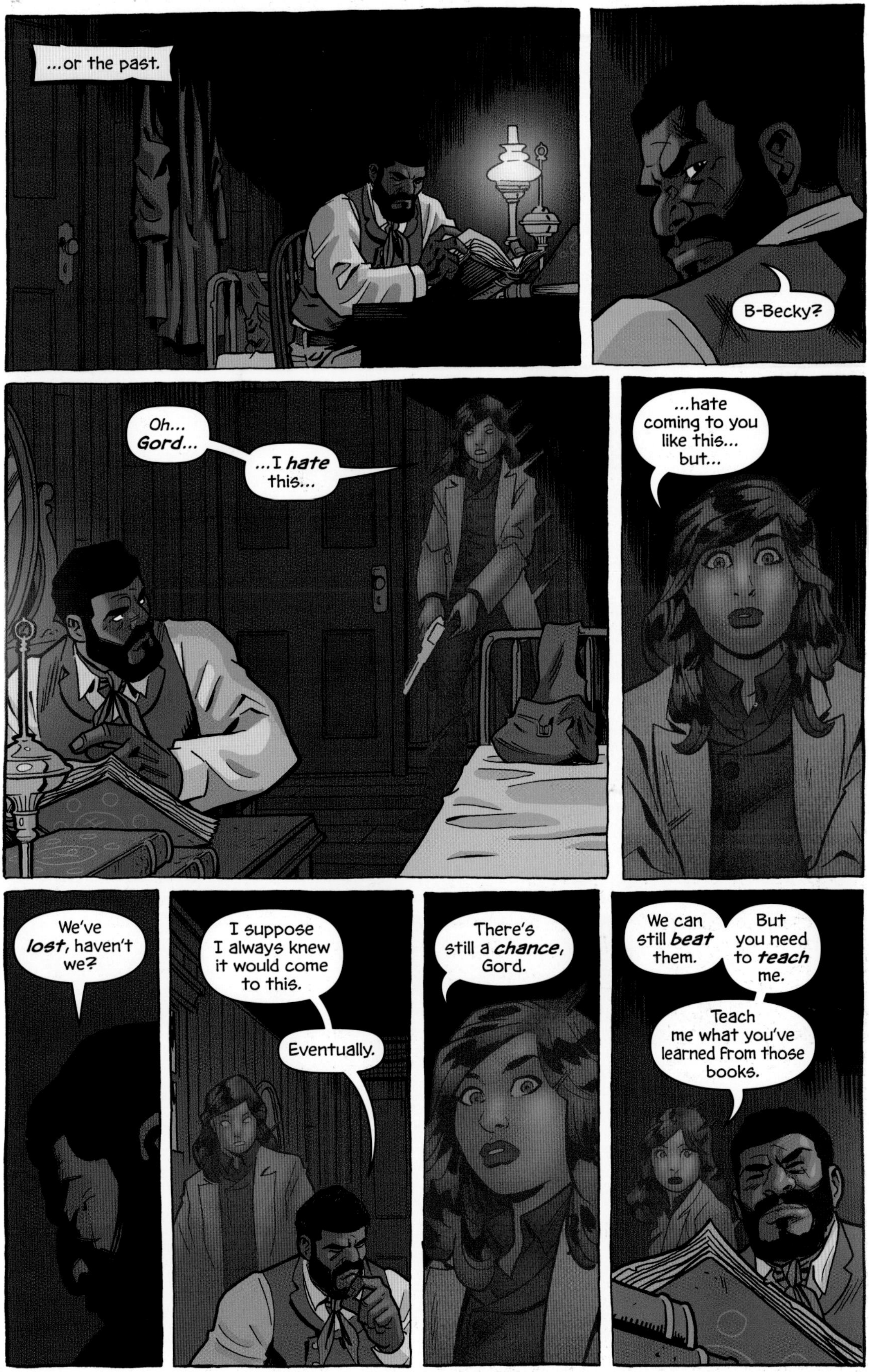
...or the past.
B-Becky?
Oh... Gord...
...I hate this...
...hate coming to you like this... but...
We've lost, haven't we?
I suppose I always knew it would come to this.
Eventually.
There's still a chance, Gord.
We can still beat them.
But you need to teach me.
Teach me what you've learned from those books.

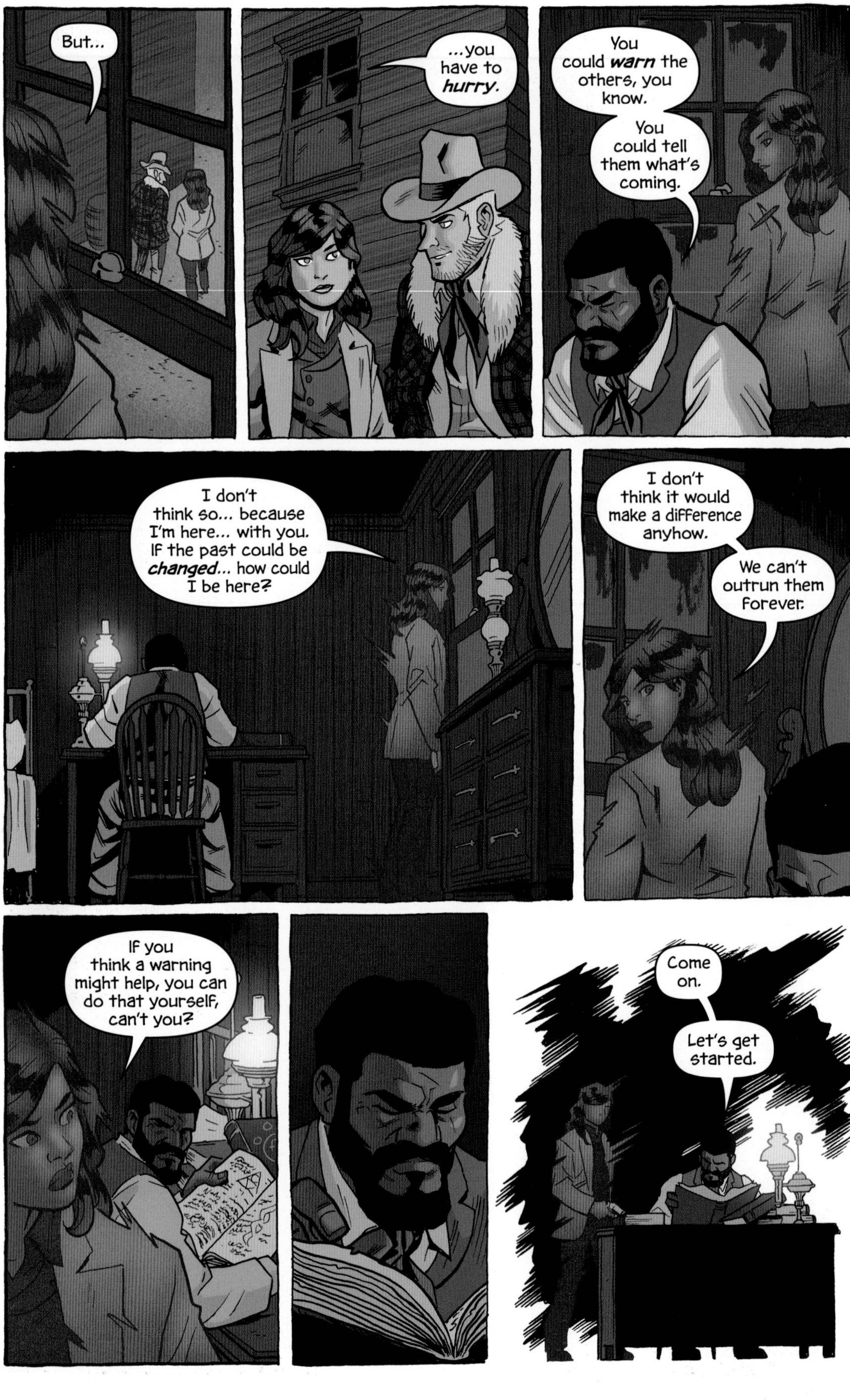
But...
...you have to *hurry.*
You could *warn* the others, you know.
You could tell them what's coming.
I don't think so... because I'm here... with you. If the past could be *changed*... how could I be here?
I don't think it would make a difference anyhow.
We can't outrun them forever.
If you think a warning might help, you can do that yourself, can't you?
Come on.
Let's get started.

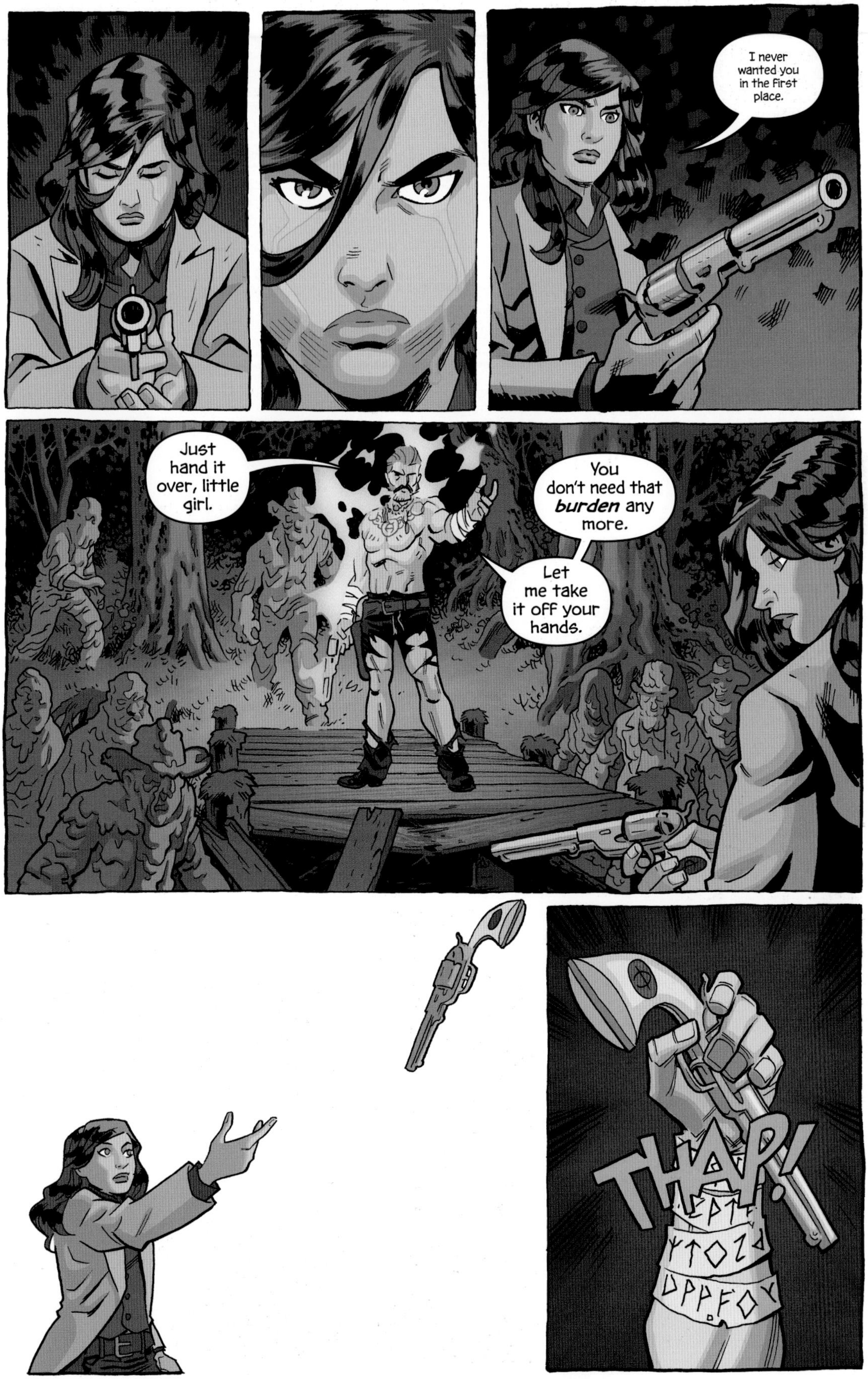
I never wanted you in the first place.
Just hand it over, little girl.
You don't need that ***burden*** any more.
Let me take it off your hands.
THAP!

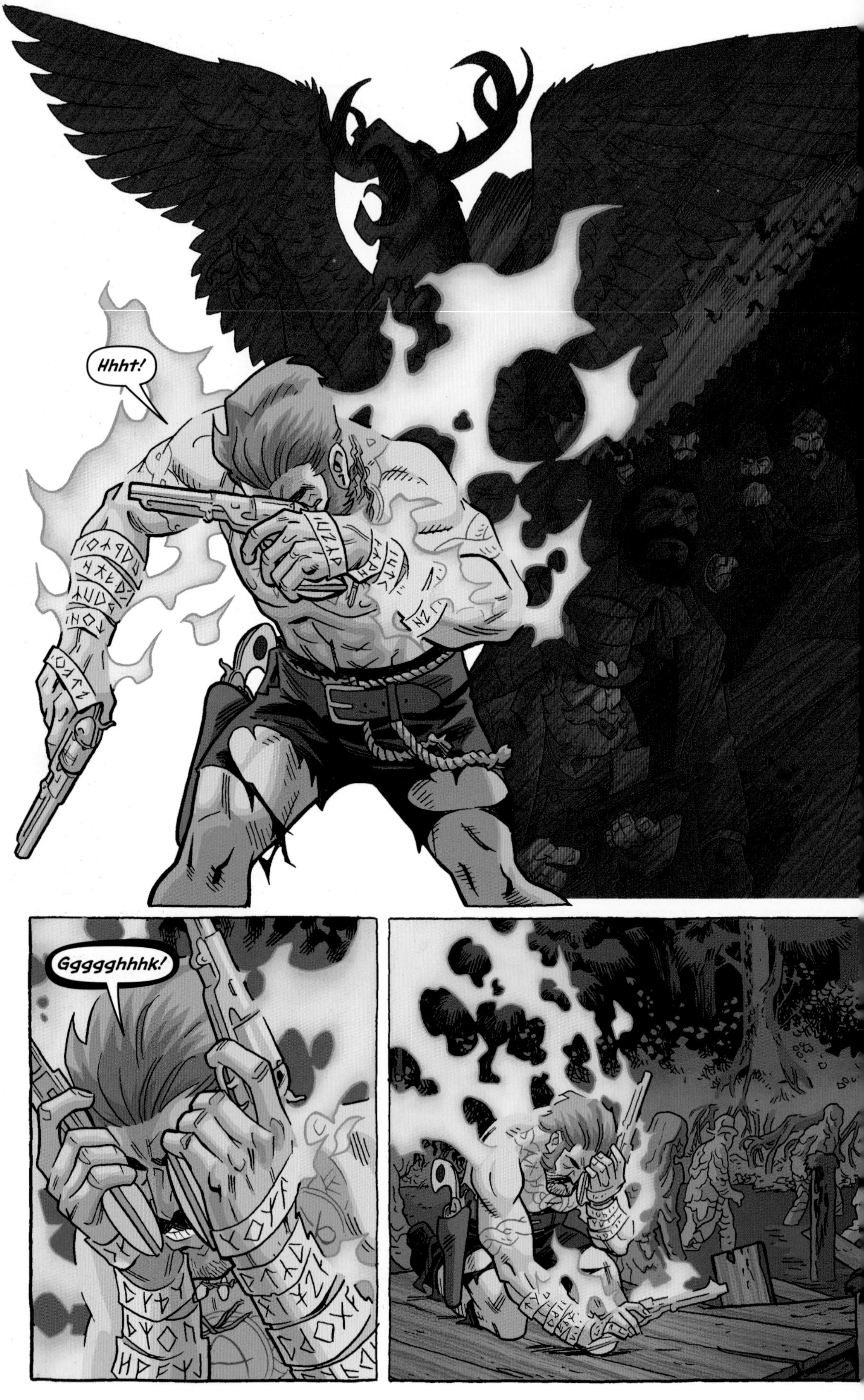
Hhht!
Gggggghhhk!

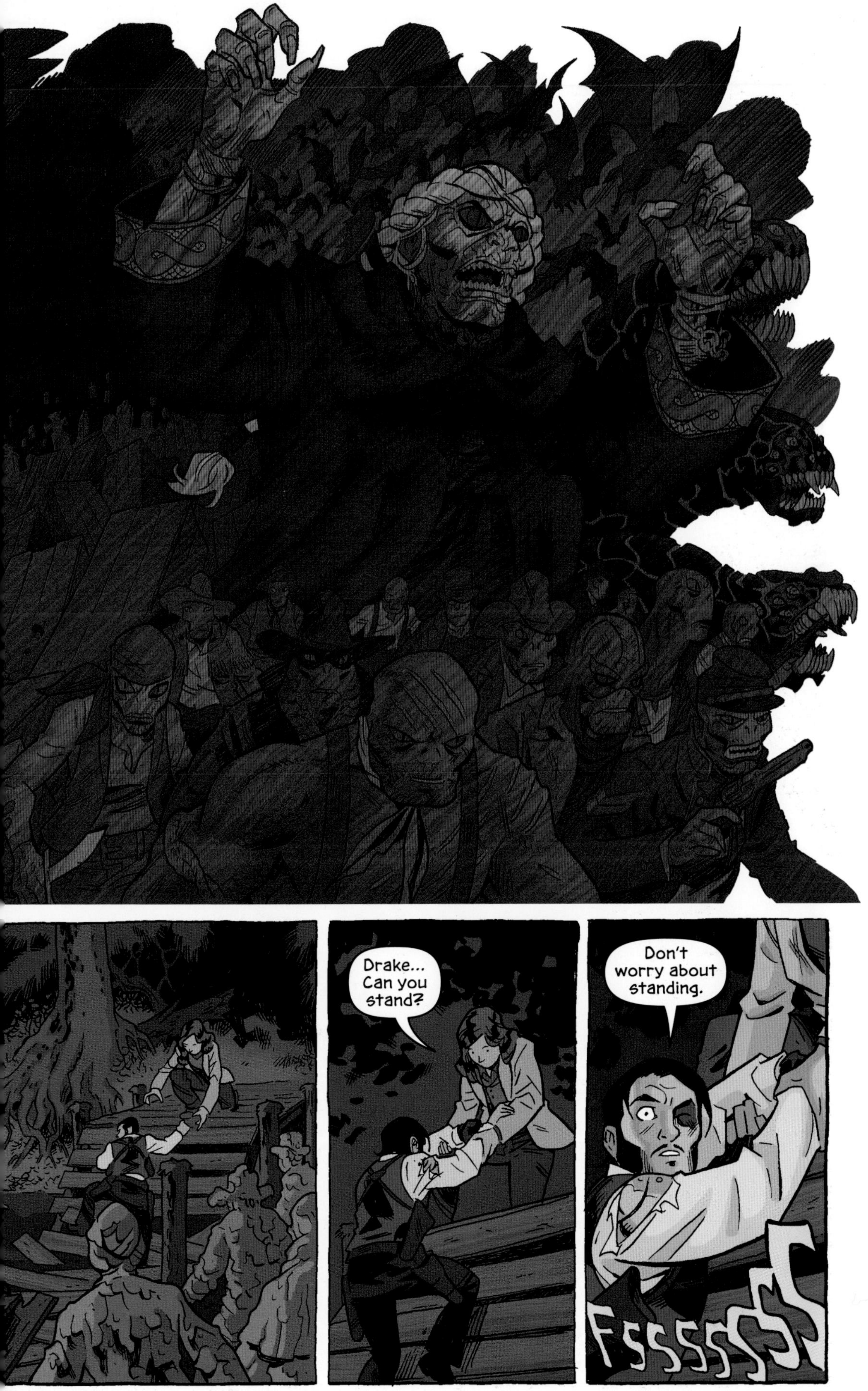

Drake...
Can you
stand?
Don't
worry about
standing.
FSSSSSS

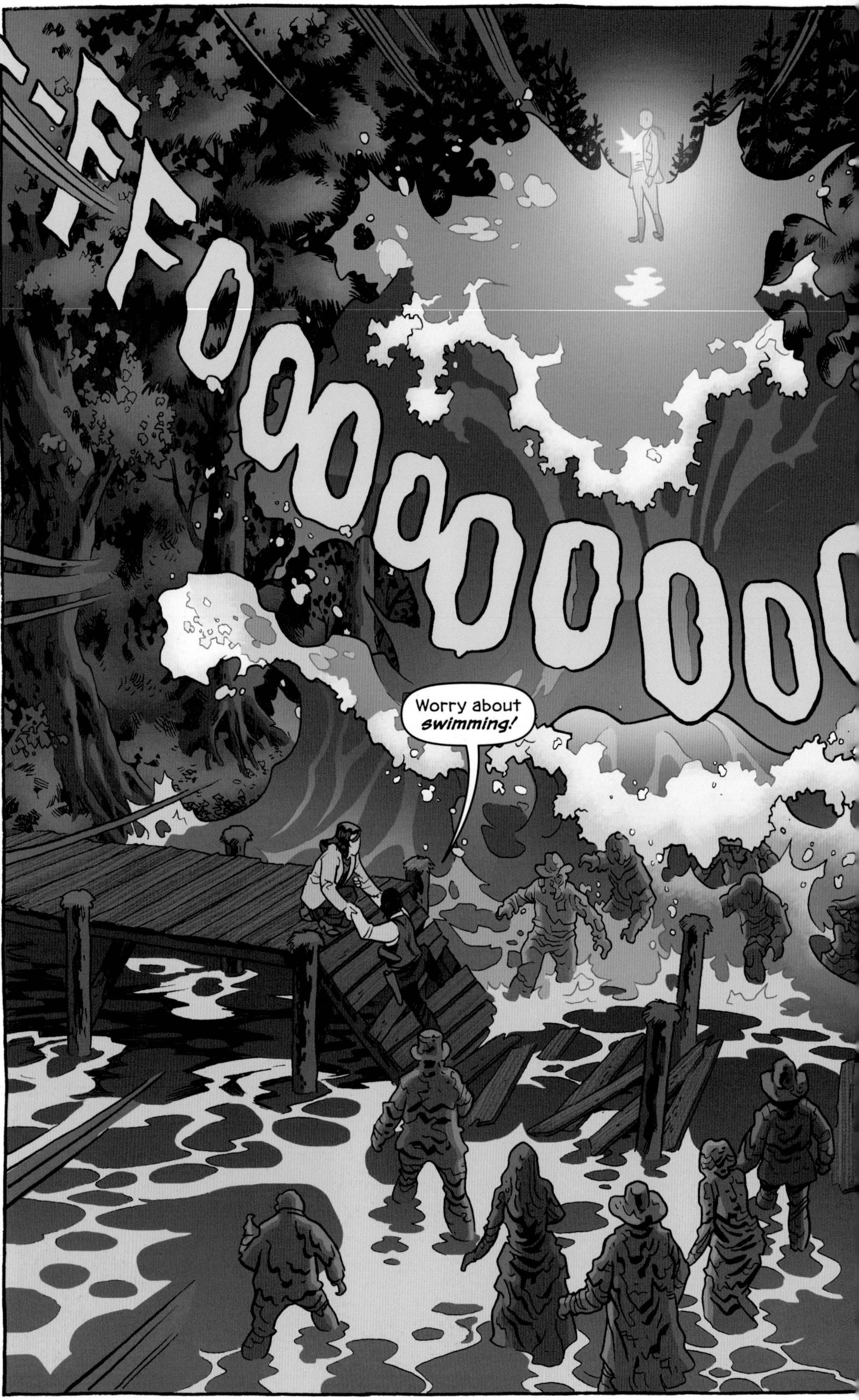
-FFOOOOOOOOOO
Worry about *swimming!*

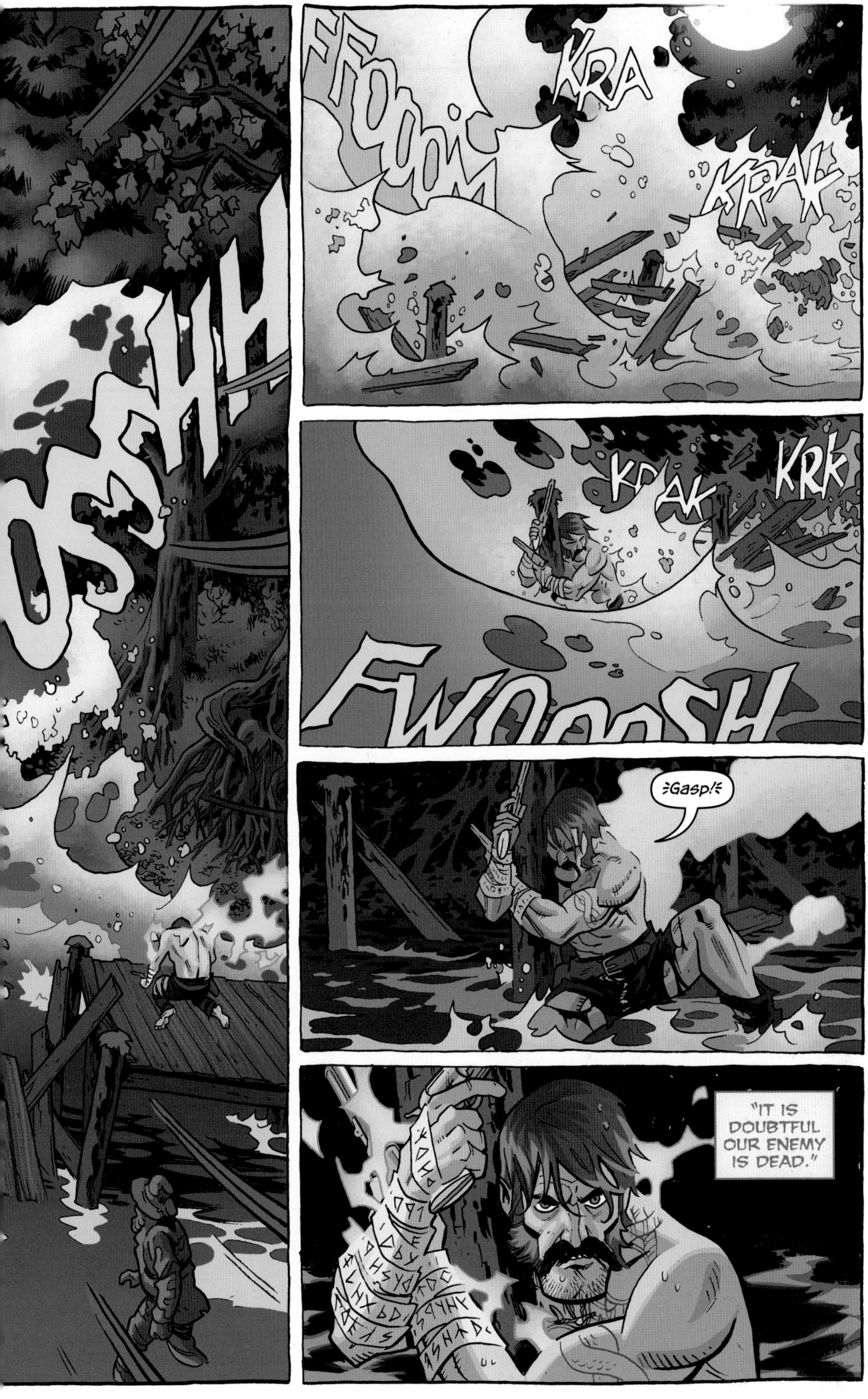

FFOOOOM
KRA
KRAK
KRAK
KRK
FWOOOSH
Gasp!
"IT IS DOUBTFUL OUR ENEMY IS DEAD."

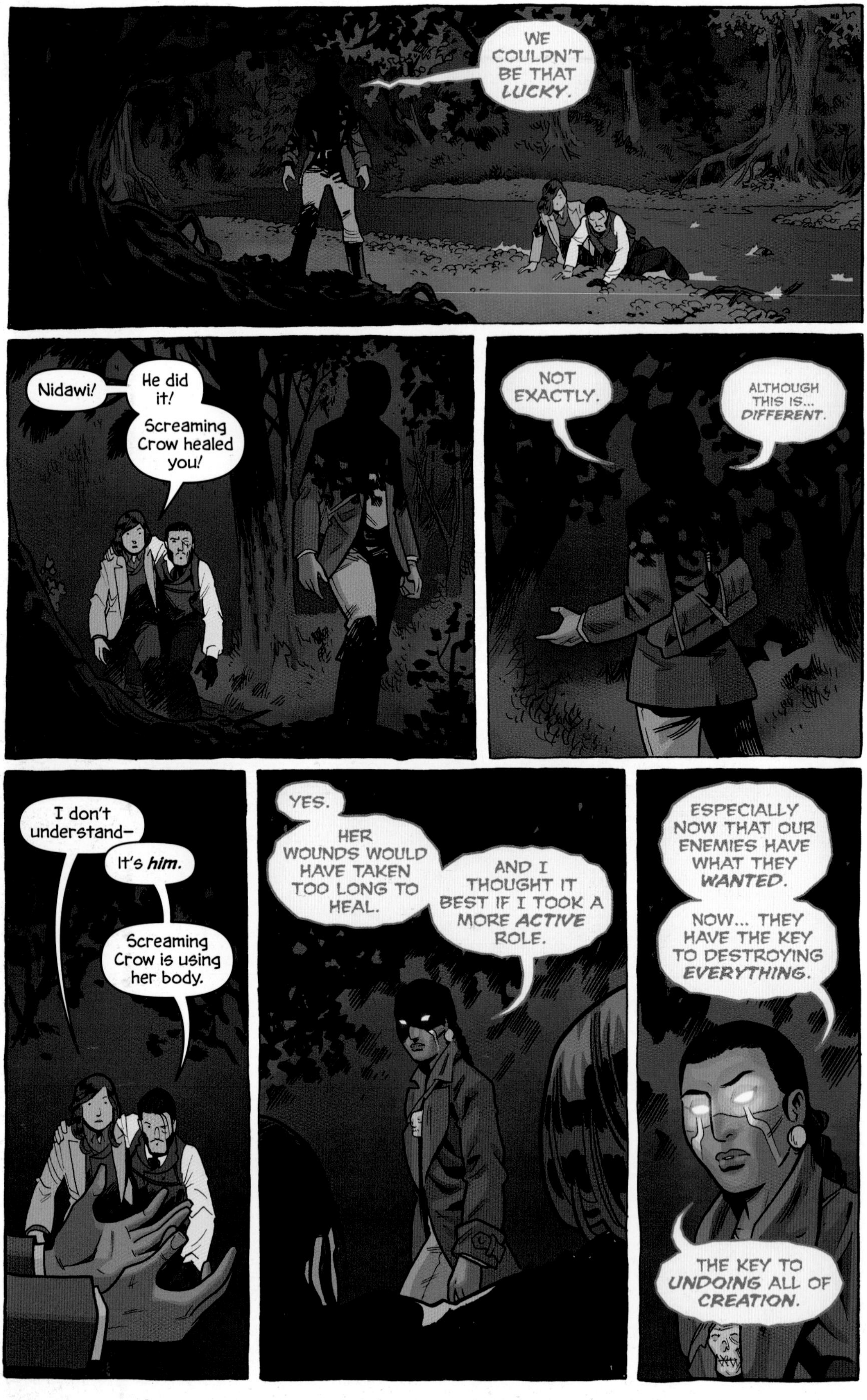
WE COULDN'T BE THAT LUCKY.
Nidawi!
He did it!
Screaming Crow healed you!
NOT EXACTLY.
ALTHOUGH THIS IS... DIFFERENT.
I don't understand–
It's him.
Screaming Crow is using her body.
YES.
HER WOUNDS WOULD HAVE TAKEN TOO LONG TO HEAL.
AND I THOUGHT IT BEST IF I TOOK A MORE ACTIVE ROLE.
ESPECIALLY NOW THAT OUR ENEMIES HAVE WHAT THEY WANTED.
NOW... THEY HAVE THE KEY TO DESTROYING EVERYTHING.
THE KEY TO UNDOING ALL OF CREATION.

CHAPTER
SIX

It won't be long now.

Even the lowliest of *sorceries* has a *cost*.

The *Cold Sleep* will take her soon.

Mama?

You have *questions*. *Of course* you do.

Don't fret.

Your mother prepared me for this day.

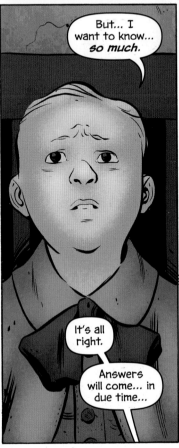

But... I want to know... *so much*.

It's all right.

Answers will come... in due time...

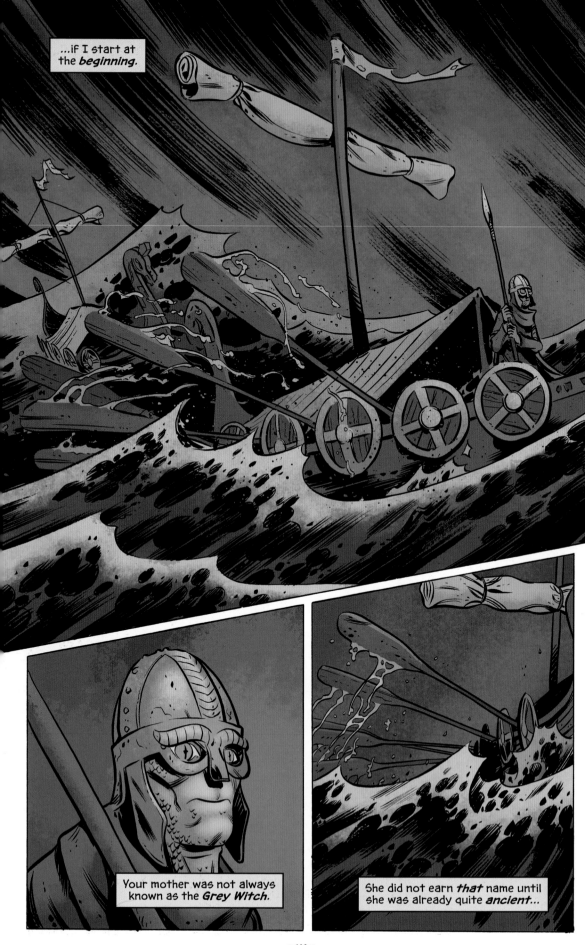

...if I start at the *beginning*.

Your mother was not always known as the *Grey Witch*.

She did not earn *that* name until she was already quite *ancient*...

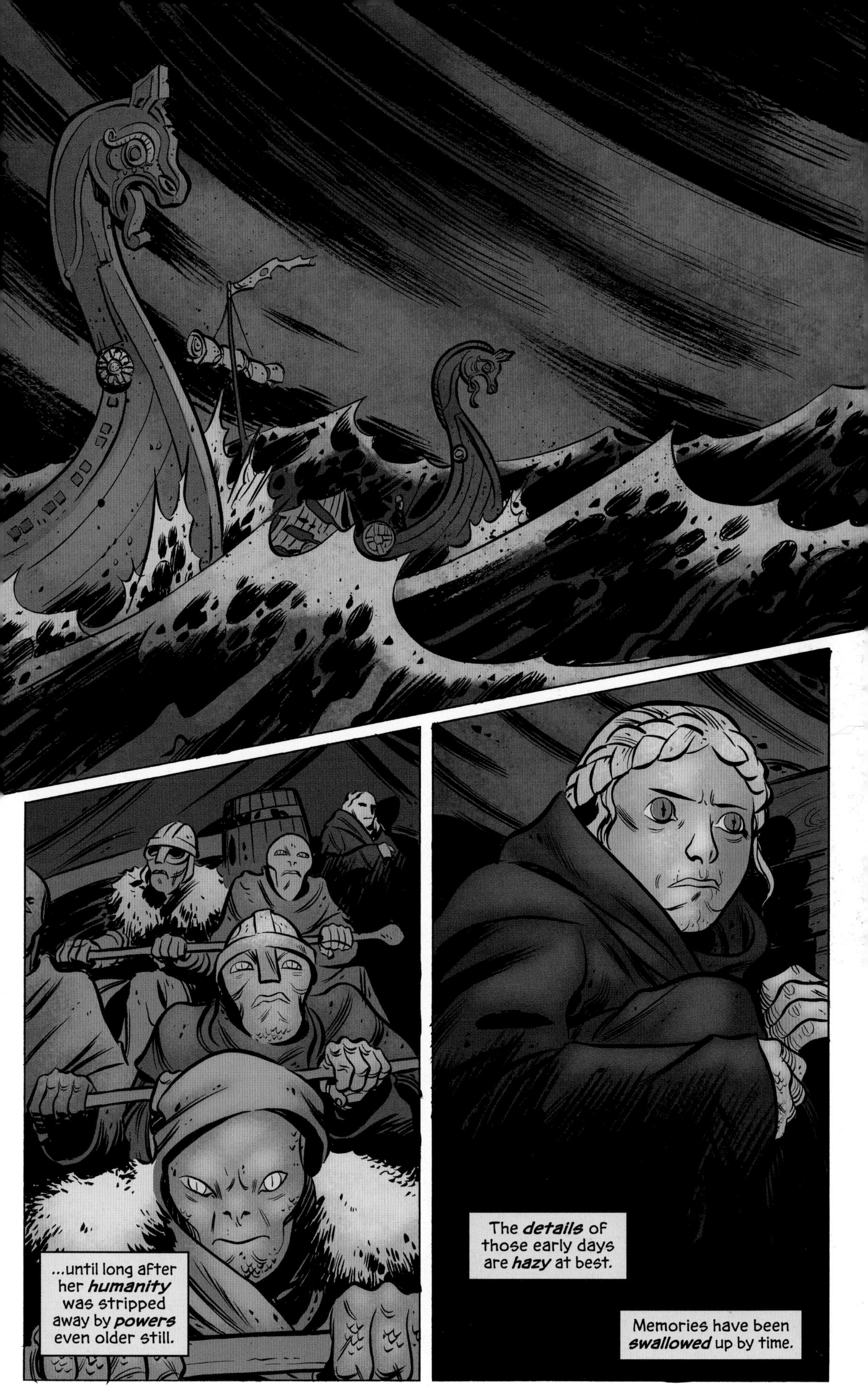
...until long after her *humanity* was stripped away by *powers* even older still.
The *details* of those early days are *hazy* at best.
Memories have been *swallowed* up by time.

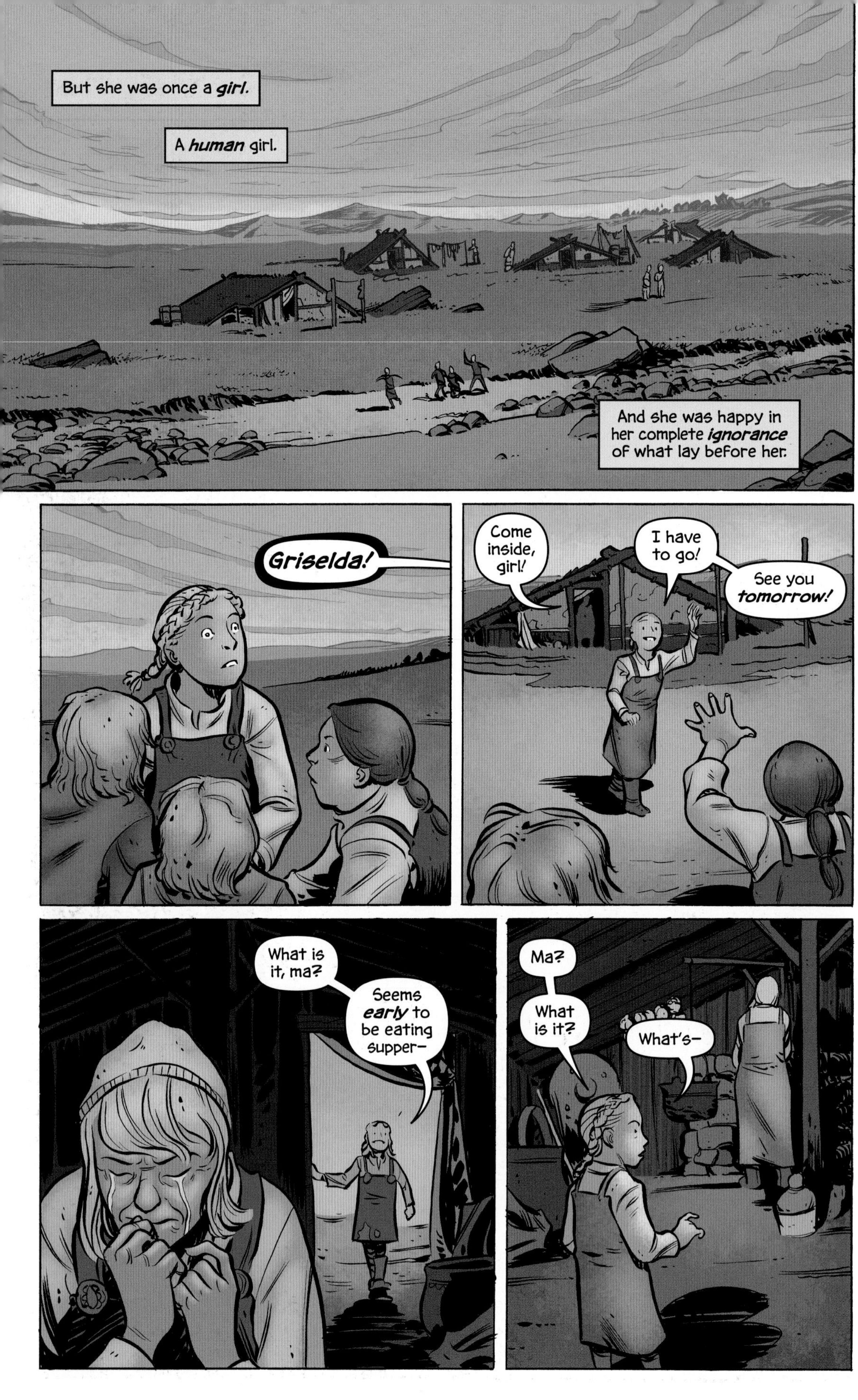
But she was once a *girl.*
A *human* girl.
And she was happy in her complete *ignorance* of what lay before her.
Griselda!
Come inside, girl!
I have to go!
See you *tomorrow!*
What is it, ma?
Seems *early* to be eating supper–
Ma?
What is it?
What's–

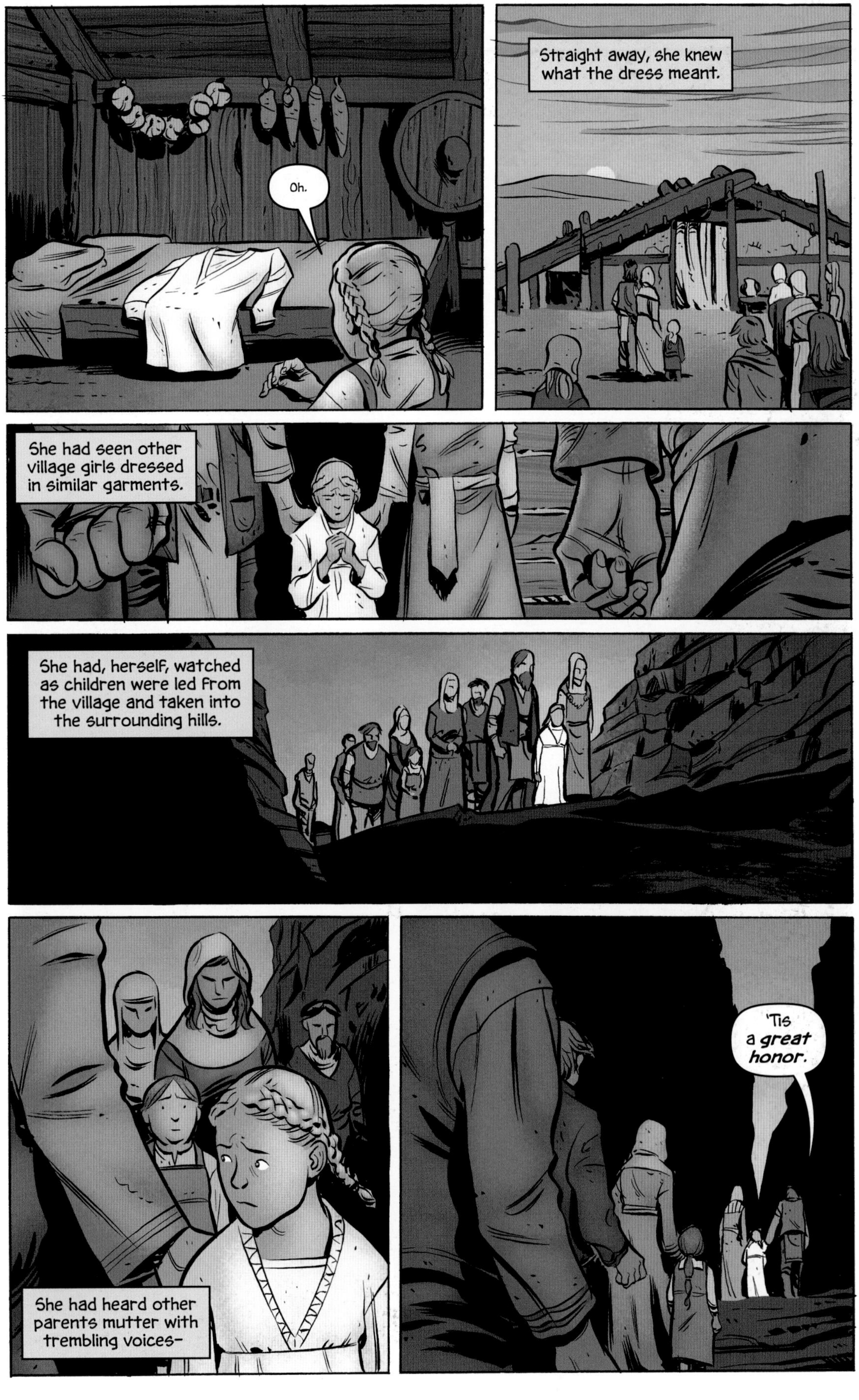
Oh.
Straight away, she knew what the dress meant.
She had seen other village girls dressed in similar garments.
She had, herself, watched as children were led from the village and taken into the surrounding hills.
She had heard other parents mutter with trembling voices–
'Tis a *great* *honor*.

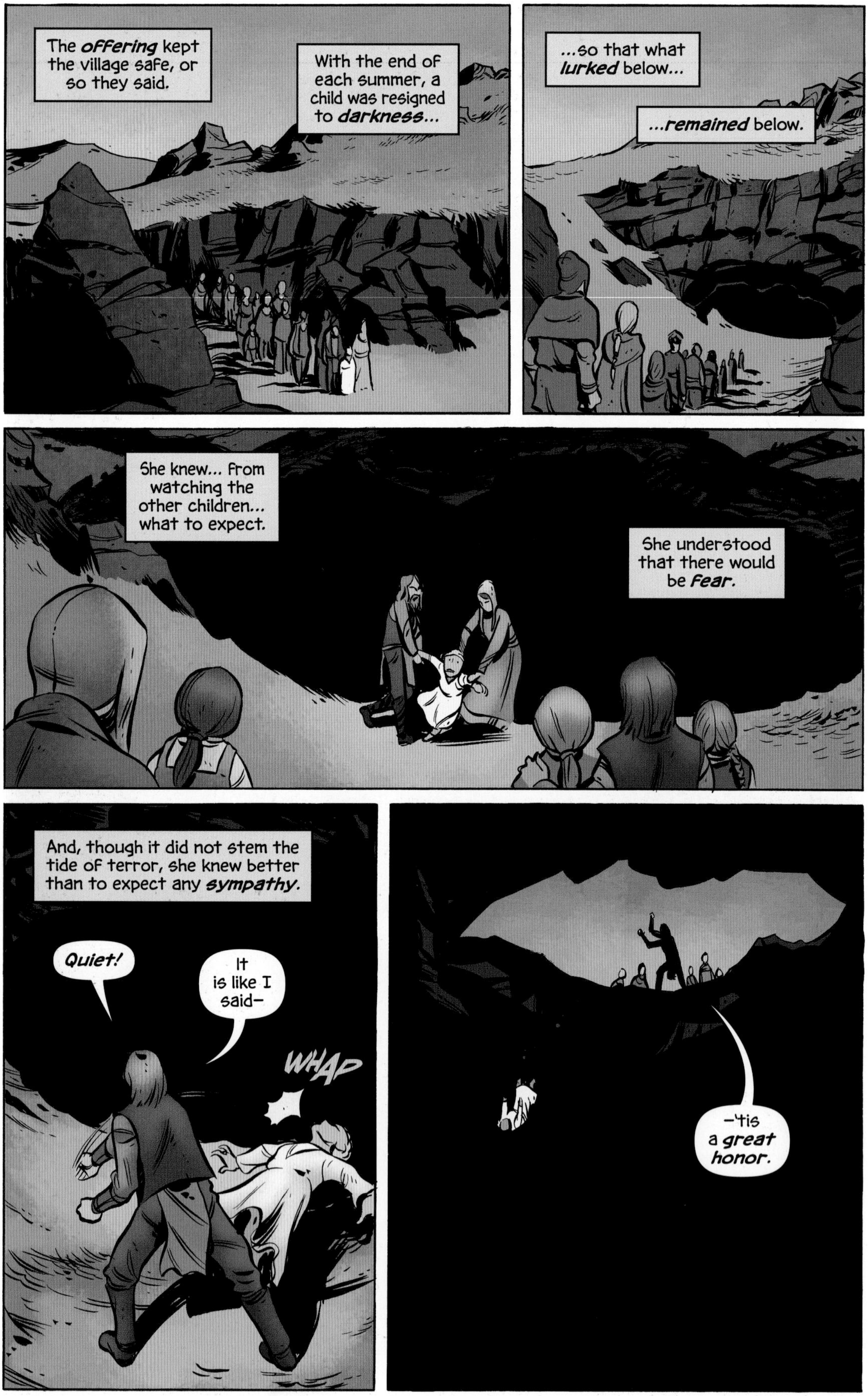
The offering kept the village safe, or so they said.
With the end of each summer, a child was resigned to darkness...
...so that what lurked below...
...remained below.
She knew... from watching the other children... what to expect.
She understood that there would be fear.
And, though it did not stem the tide of terror, she knew better than to expect any sympathy.
Quiet!
It is like I said–
WHAP
–'tis a great honor.

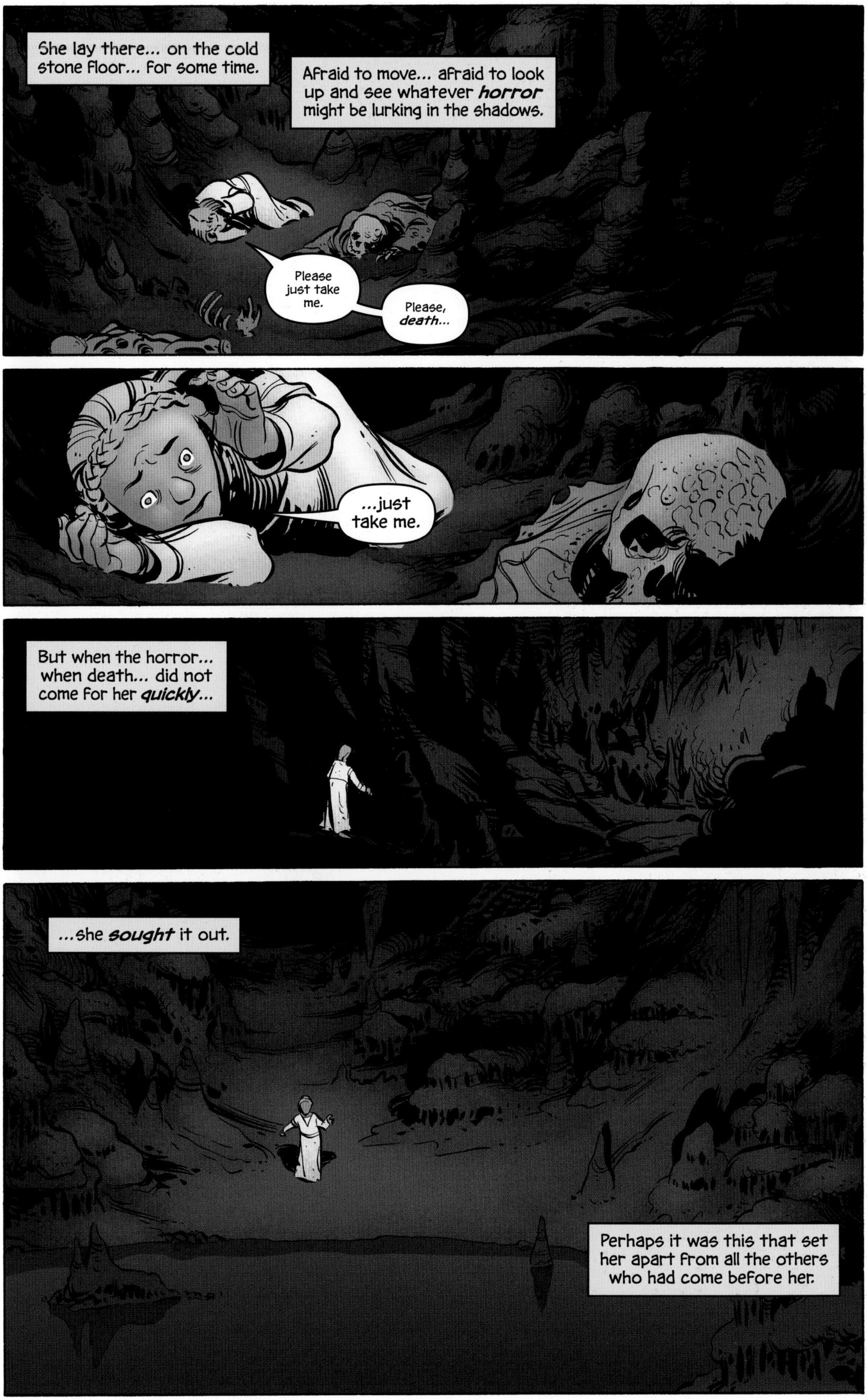
She lay there... on the cold stone floor... for some time.
Afraid to move... afraid to look up and see whatever *horror* might be lurking in the shadows.
Please just take me.
Please, *death*...
...just take me.
But when the horror... when death... did not come for her *quickly*...
...she *sought* it out.
Perhaps it was this that set her apart from all the others who had come before her.

The Great Wyrms that rose before the girl spoke no *intelligible* language.

And yet she *understood* them.

"You came," they whispered.

"Step closer so that we might gaze upon you."

NNNNRRRGGGNNNNNRRRGGNNN

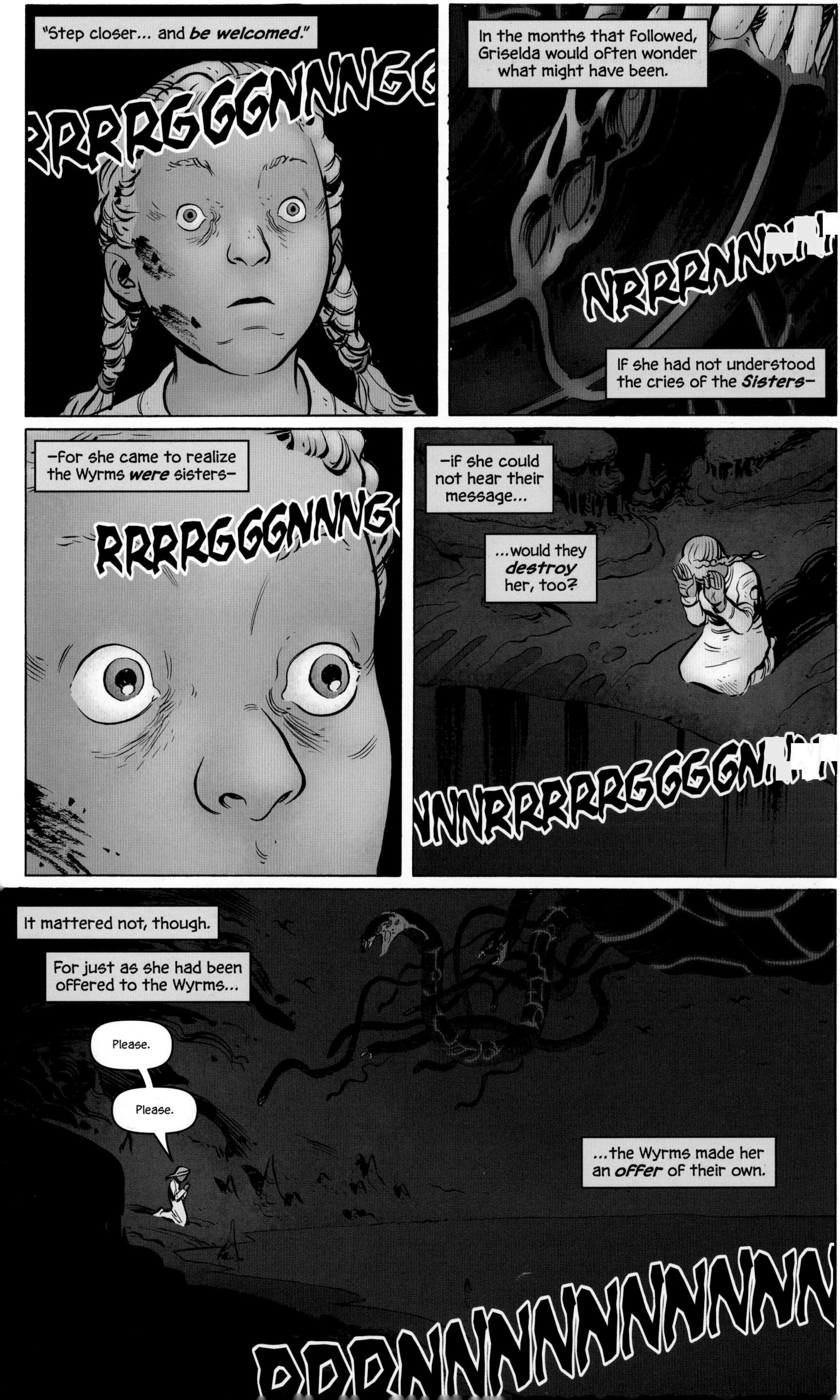
"Step closer... and *be welcomed.*"
RRRRGGGNNNGG
In the months that followed, Griselda would often wonder what might have been.
NRRRNNN
If she had not understood the cries of the *Sisters*–
–for she came to realize the Wyrms *were* sisters–
RRRRGGGNNNG
–if she could not hear their message...
...would they *destroy* her, too?
NNNRRRRRGGGN
It mattered not, though.
For just as she had been offered to the Wyrms...
Please.
Please.
...the Wyrms made her an *offer* of their own.
DDDNNNNNNNNNNN

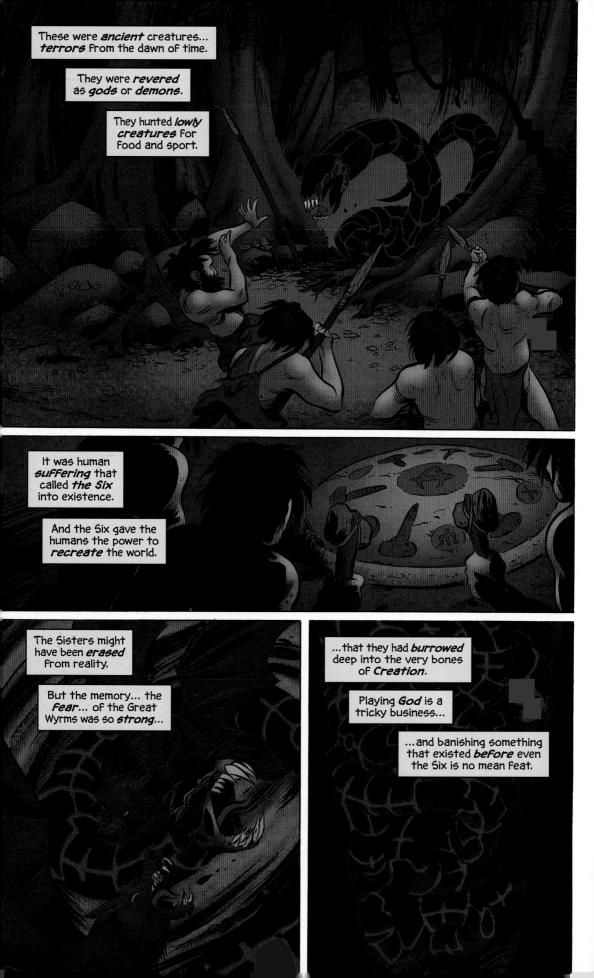

These were *ancient* creatures... *terrors* from the dawn of time.

They were *revered* as *gods* or *demons*.

They hunted *lowly creatures* for food and sport.

It was human *suffering* that called *the Six* into existence.

And the Six gave the humans the power to *recreate* the world.

The Sisters might have been *erased* from reality.

But the memory... the *fear*... of the Great Wyrms was so *strong*...

...that they had *burrowed* deep into the very bones of *Creation*.

Playing *God* is a tricky business...

...and banishing something that existed *before* even the Six is no mean feat.

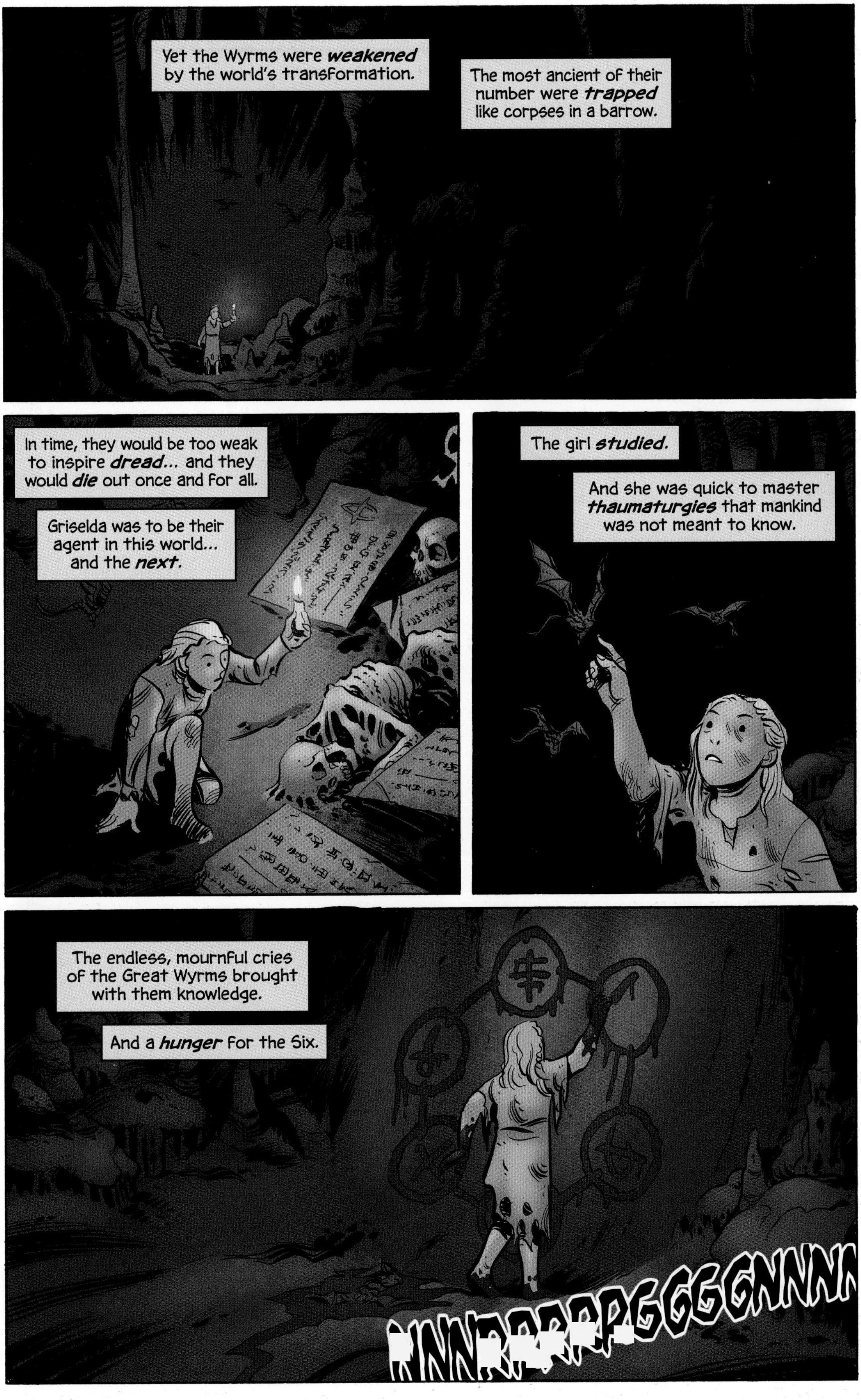
Yet the Wyrms were *weakened* by the world's transformation.
The most ancient of their number were *trapped* like corpses in a barrow.
In time, they would be too weak to inspire *dread*... and they would *die* out once and for all.
Griselda was to be their agent in this world... and the *next*.
The girl *studied*.
And she was quick to master *thaumaturgies* that mankind was not meant to know.
The endless, mournful cries of the Great Wyrms brought with them knowledge.
And a *hunger* for the Six.
NNNRRRRGGGGNNNN

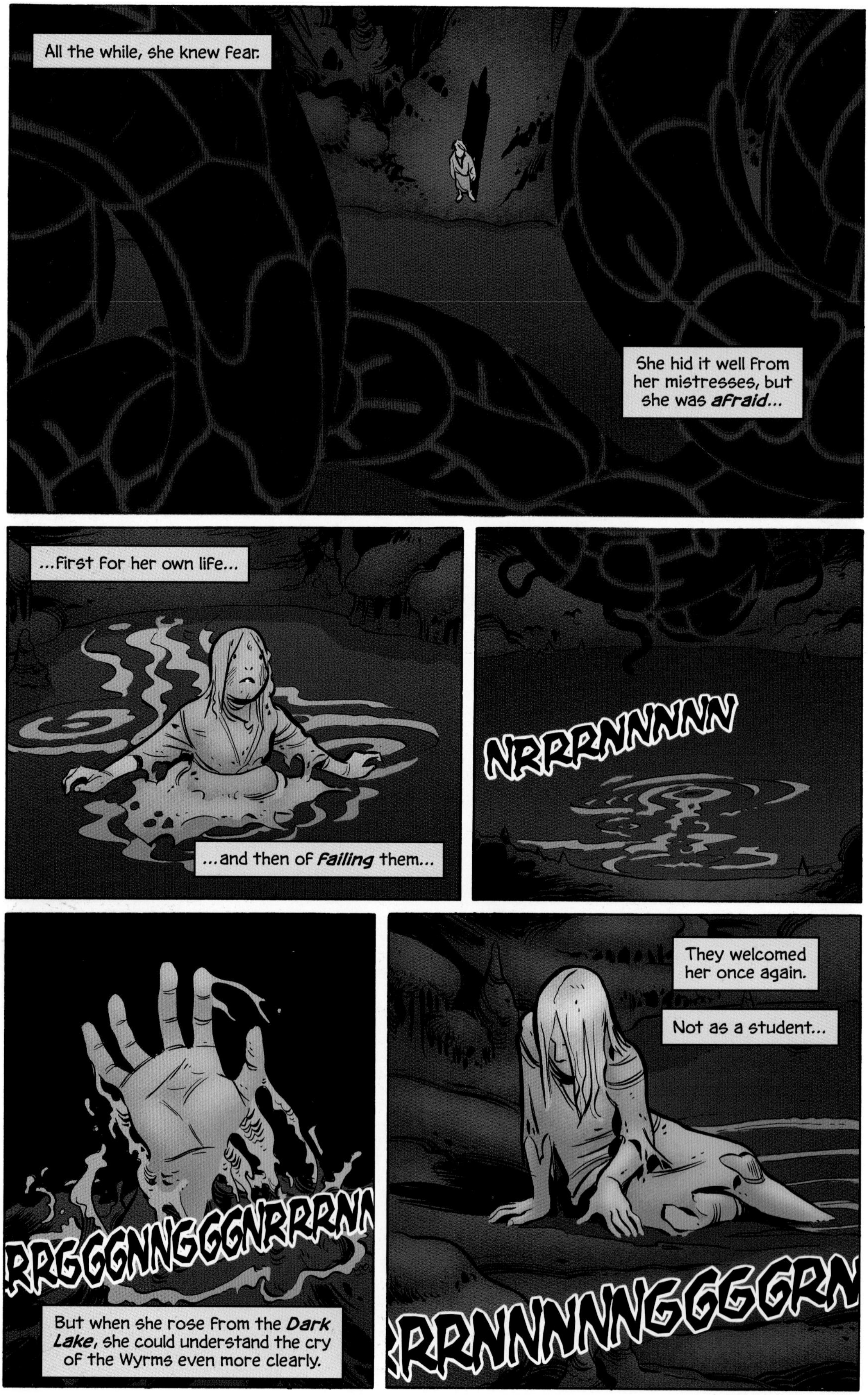
All the while, she knew fear.
She hid it well from her mistresses, but she was *afraid*...
...first for her own life...
...and then of *failing* them...
NRRRNNNNN
RRGGGNNGGGNRRRN
But when she rose from the *Dark Lake*, she could understand the cry of the Wyrms even more clearly.
They welcomed her once again.
Not as a student...
RRNNNNNGGGRN

...but as a *sister*.

And when the next summer ended... when *another* village girl was cast into the *darkness*...

...Griselda was no longer a child who felt fear.

She was instead a beast that *inspired* it.

GRRRAAAA!

N-no! Nnno!

GRRRRRRRR...

She was barely recognizable to the girl from her village.

Gr-Griselda?

GRRNNNCK!

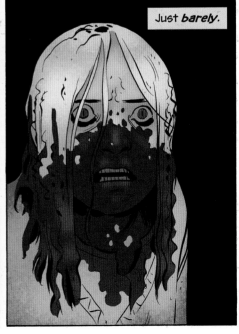

Just *barely*.

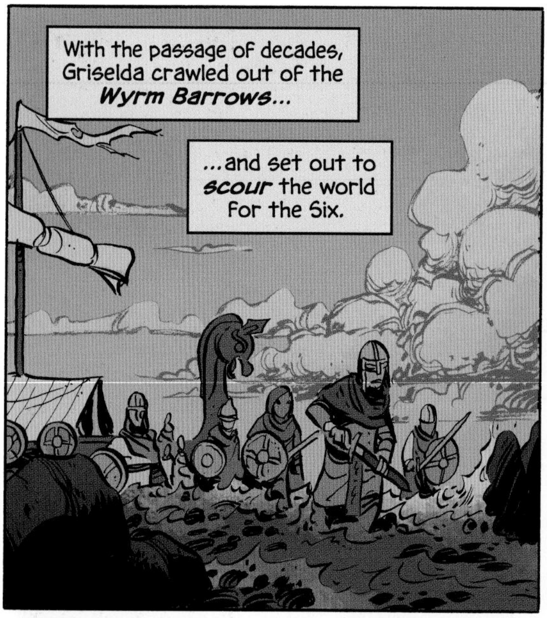
With the passage of decades, Griselda crawled out of the *Wyrm Barrows*...
...and set out to *scour* the world for the Six.

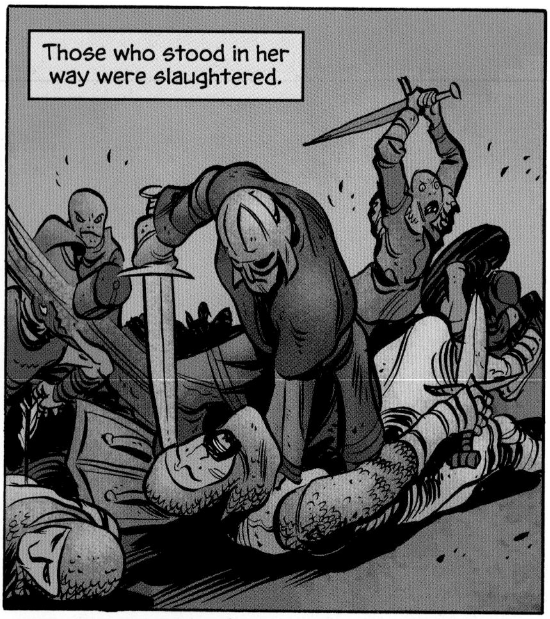
Those who stood in her way were slaughtered.

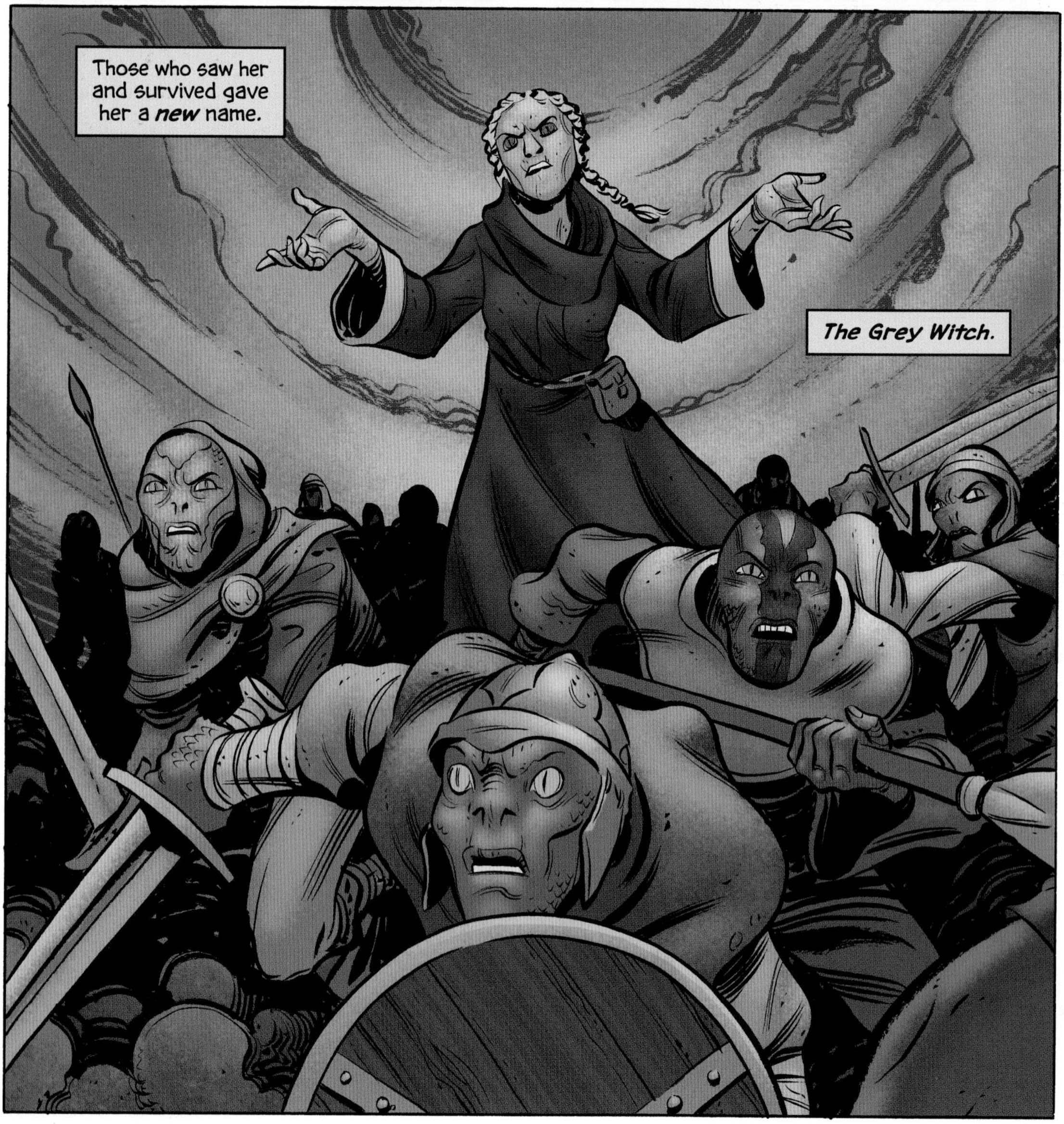
Those who saw her and survived gave her a *new* name.
The Grey Witch.

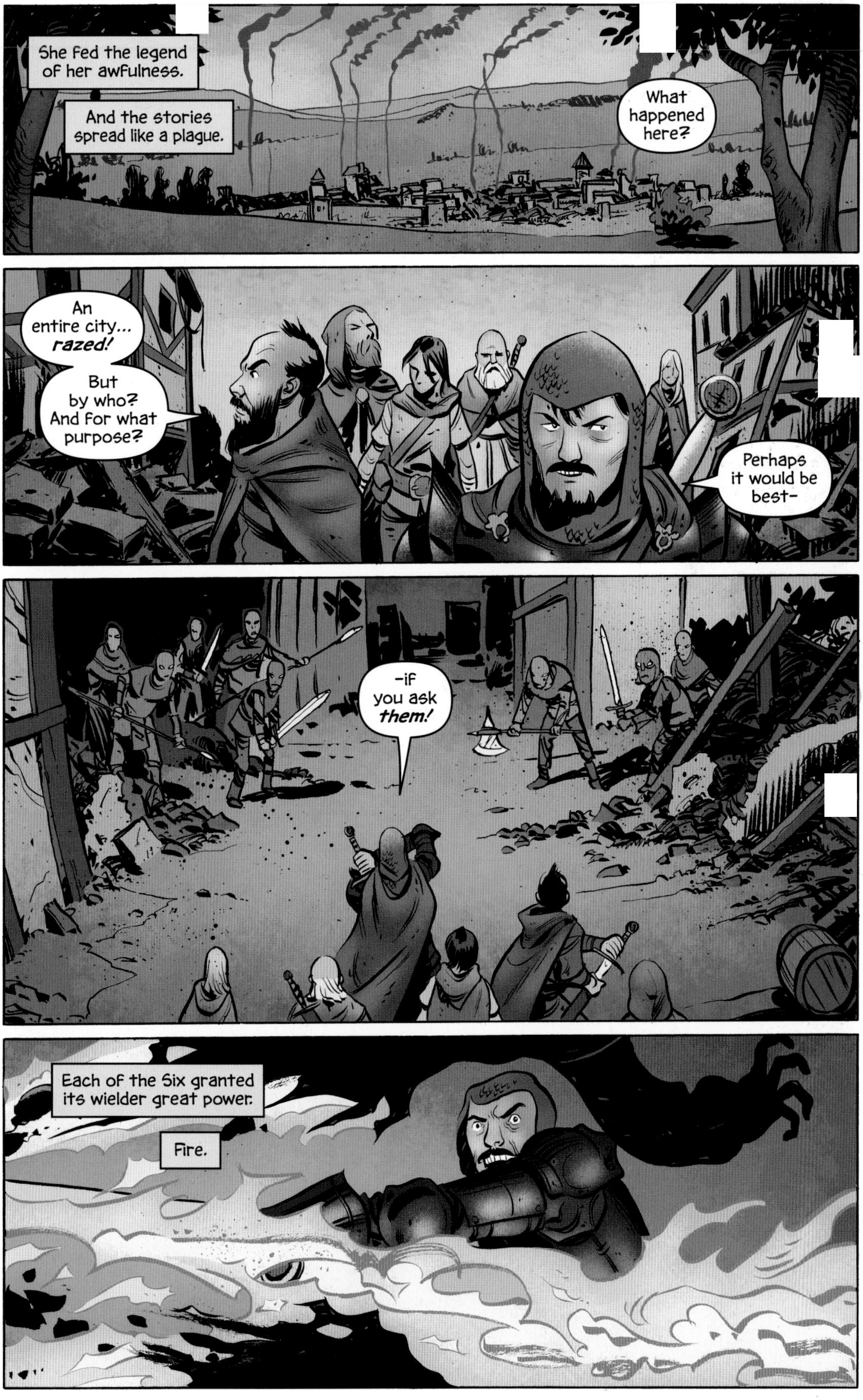
She fed the legend of her awfulness.
And the stories spread like a plague.
What happened here?
An entire city... *razed!*
But by who? And for what purpose?
Perhaps it would be best-
-if you ask *them!*
Each of the Six granted its wielder great power.
Fire.

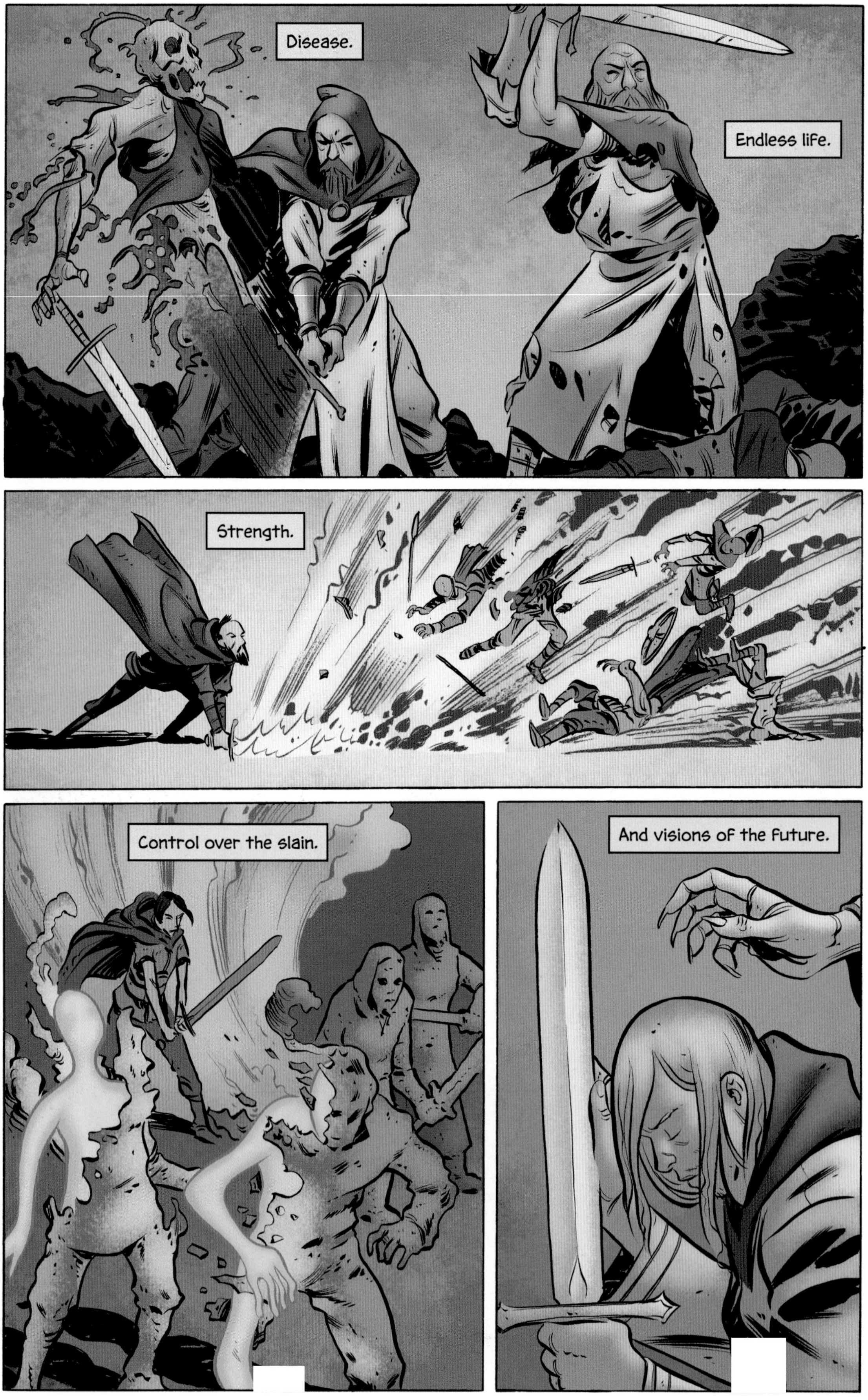
Disease.
Endless life.
Strength.
Control over the slain.
And visions of the future.

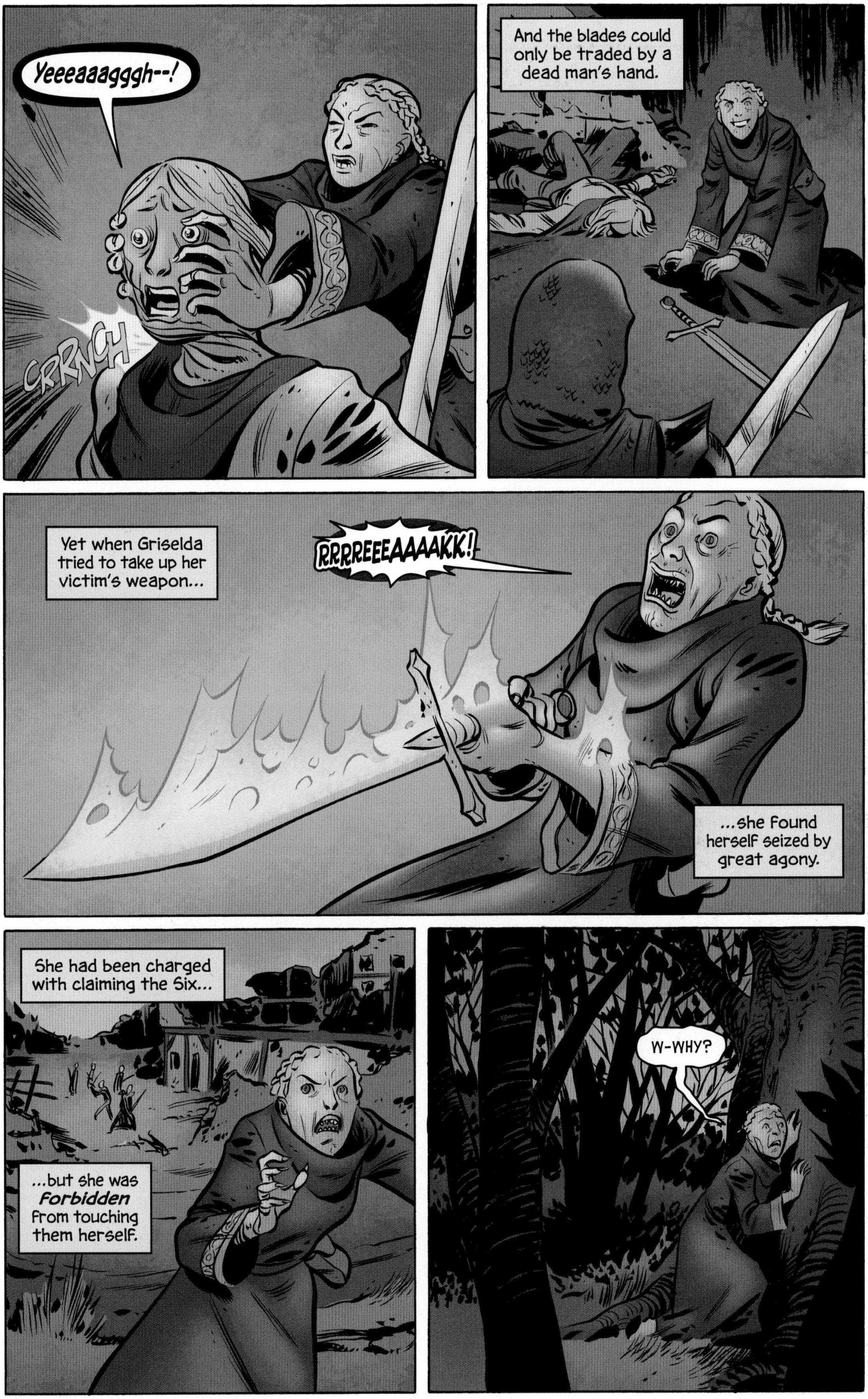

Yeeeaaagggh--!
CRRNCH
And the blades could only be traded by a dead man's hand.
Yet when Griselda tried to take up her victim's weapon...
RRRREEEAAAAKK!
...she found herself seized by great agony.
She had been charged with claiming the Six...
...but she was *Forbidden* from touching them herself.
W-WHY?

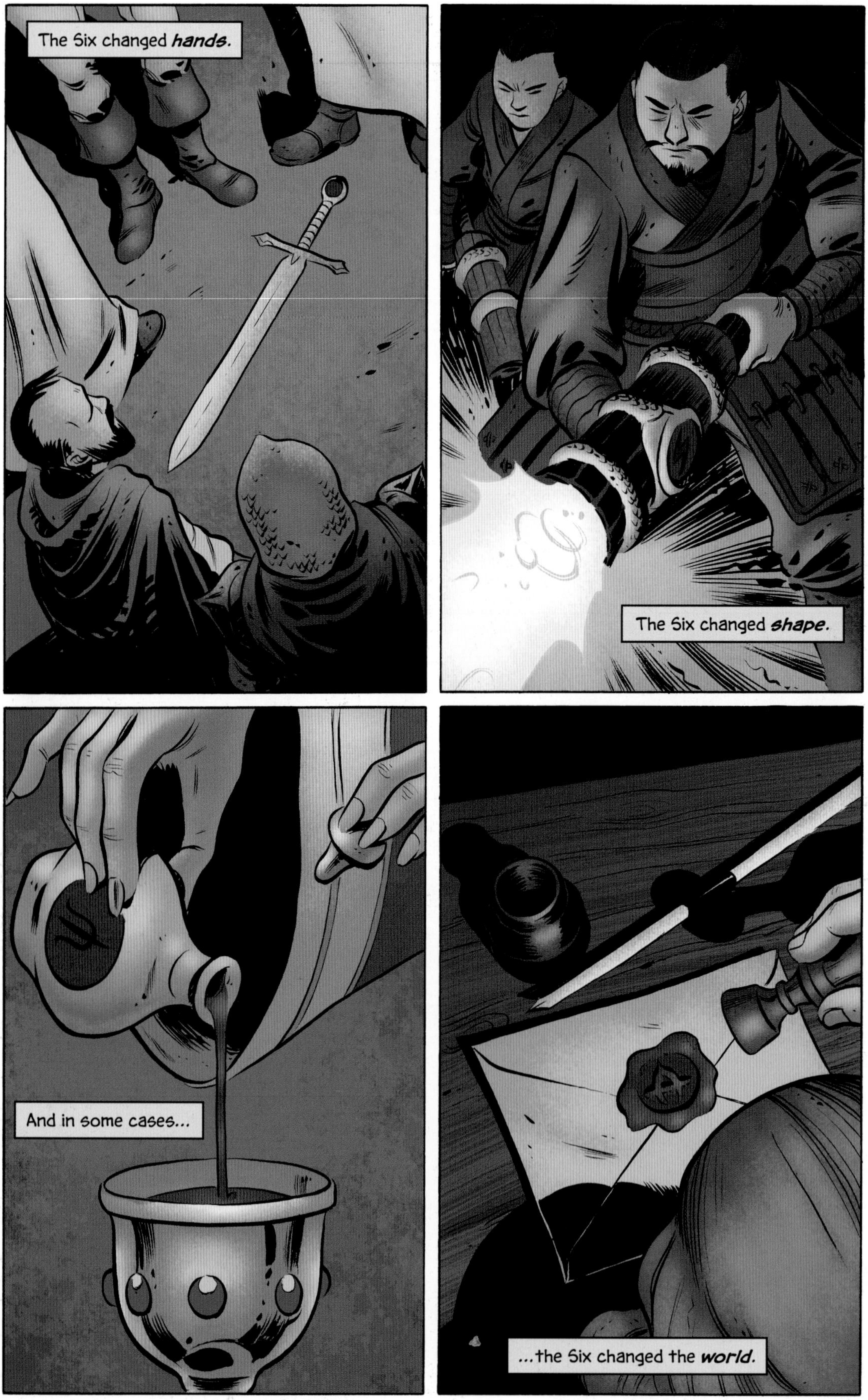
The Six changed hands.
The Six changed shape.
And in some cases...
...the Six changed the world.

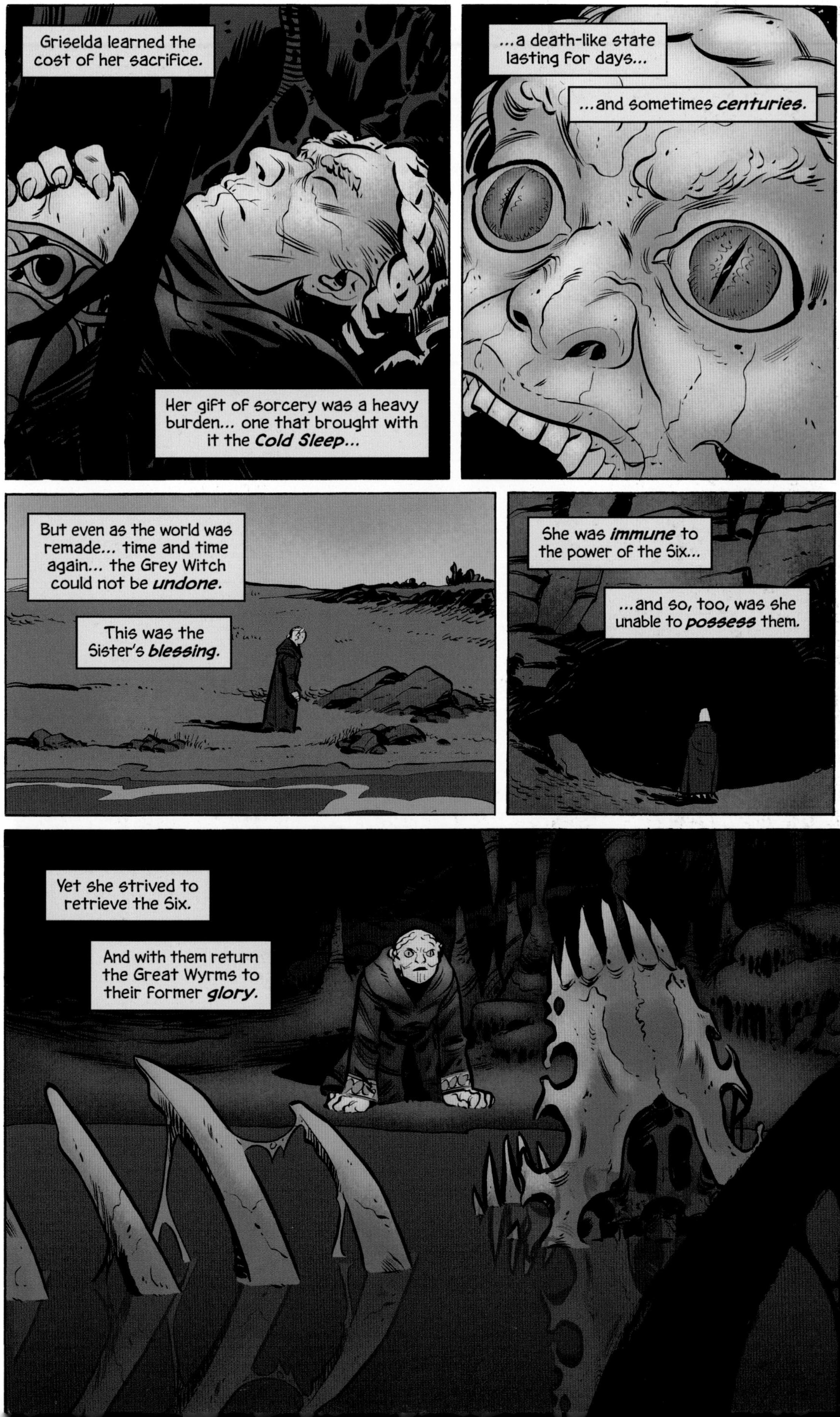
Griselda learned the cost of her sacrifice.
Her gift of sorcery was a heavy burden... one that brought with it the Cold Sleep...
...a death-like state lasting for days...
...and sometimes centuries.
But even as the world was remade... time and time again... the Grey Witch could not be undone.
This was the Sister's blessing.
She was immune to the power of the Six...
...and so, too, was she unable to possess them.
Yet she strived to retrieve the Six.
And with them return the Great Wyrms to their former glory.

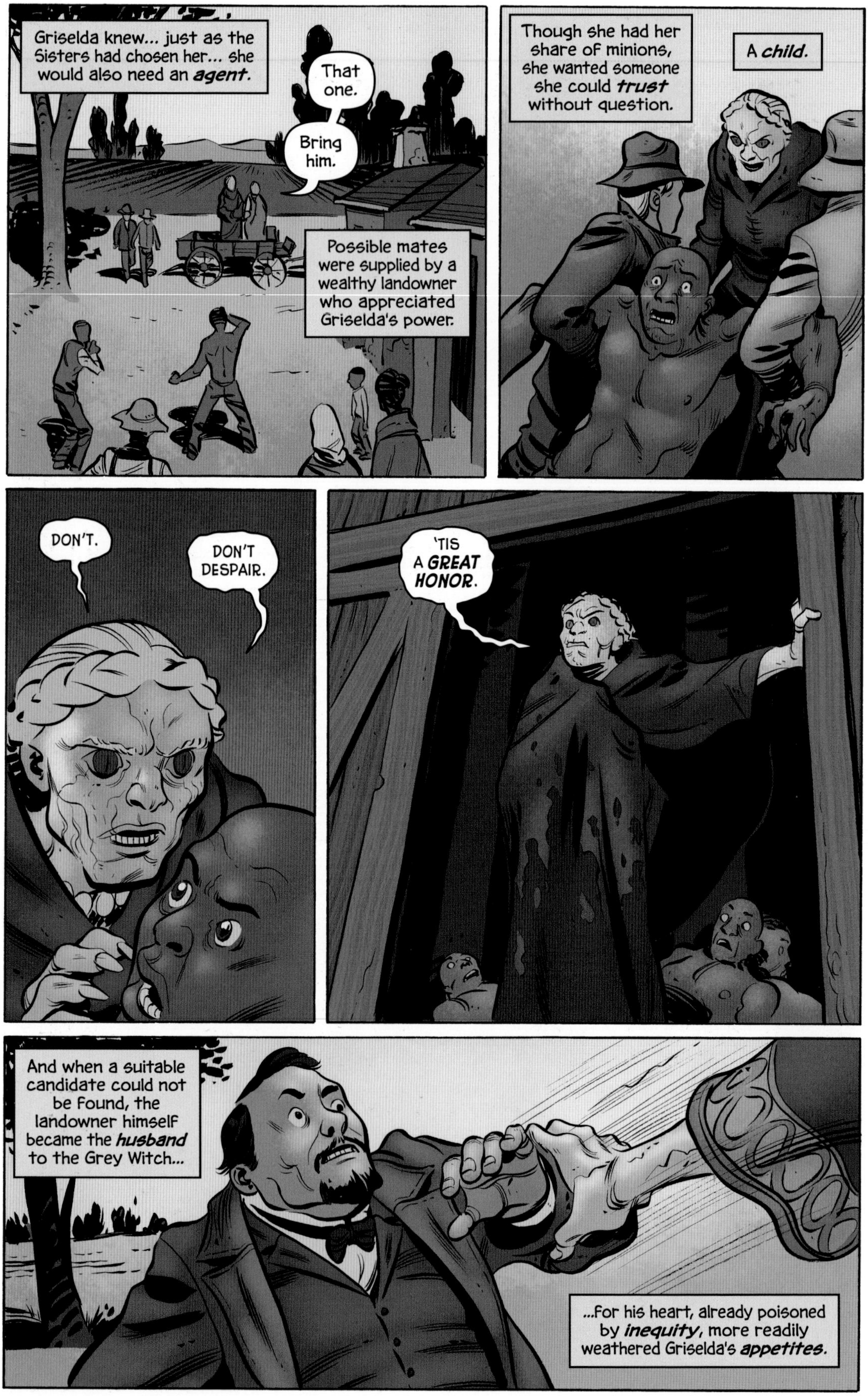
Griselda knew... just as the Sisters had chosen her... she would also need an *agent*.
That one.
Bring him.
Possible mates were supplied by a wealthy landowner who appreciated Griselda's power.
Though she had her share of minions, she wanted someone she could *trust* without question.
A *child*.
DON'T.
DON'T DESPAIR.
'TIS A **GREAT HONOR**.
And when a suitable candidate could not be found, the landowner himself became the *husband* to the Grey Witch...
...for his heart, already poisoned by *inequity*, more readily weathered Griselda's *appetites*.

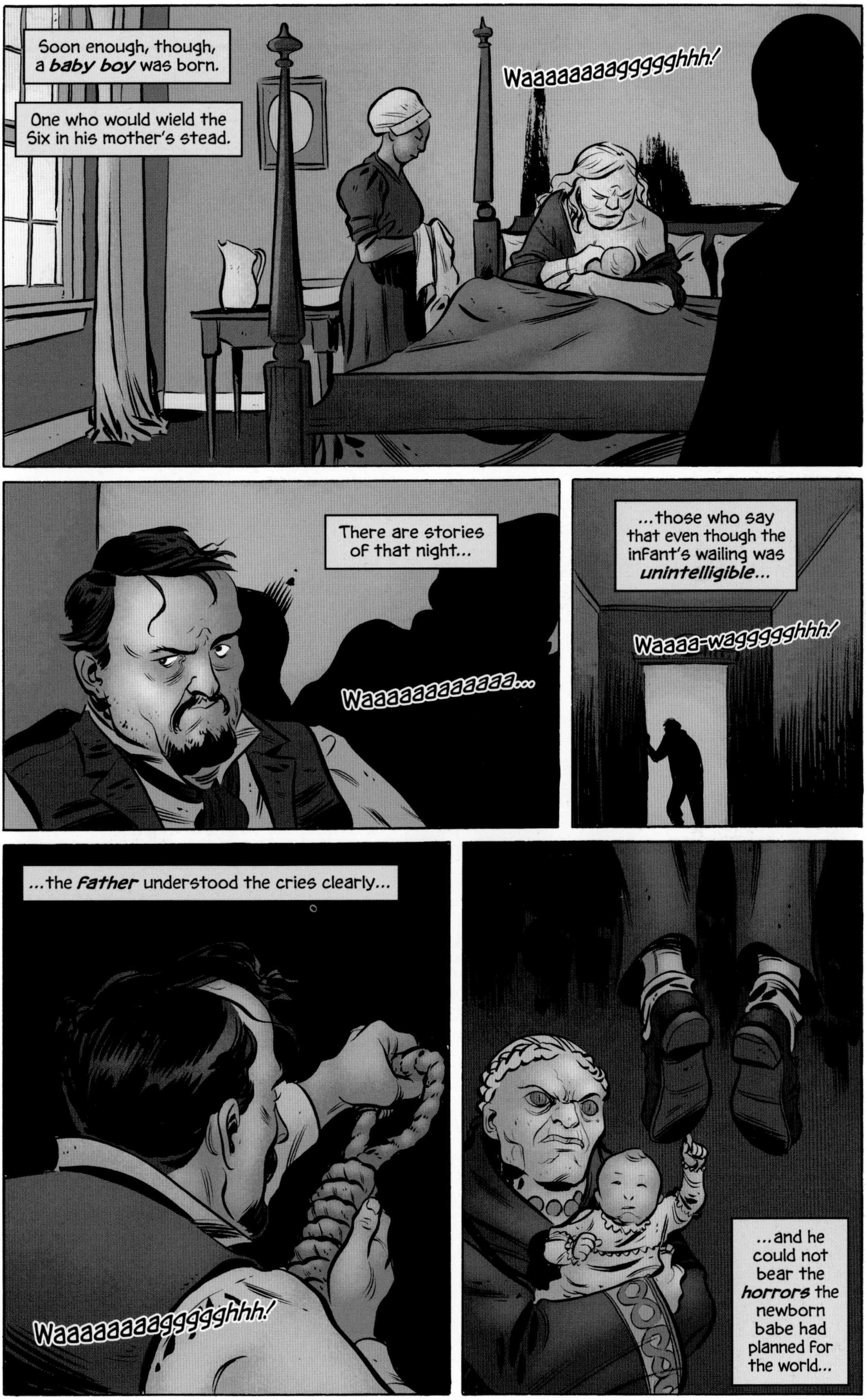
Soon enough, though, a baby boy was born.
One who would wield the Six in his mother's stead.
Waaaaaaaagggggghhh!
There are stories of that night...
Waaaaaaaaaaaa...
...those who say that even though the infant's wailing was unintelligible...
Waaaa-wagggggghhh!
...the Father understood the cries clearly...
Waaaaaaaaggggghhh!
...and he could not bear the horrors the newborn babe had planned for the world...

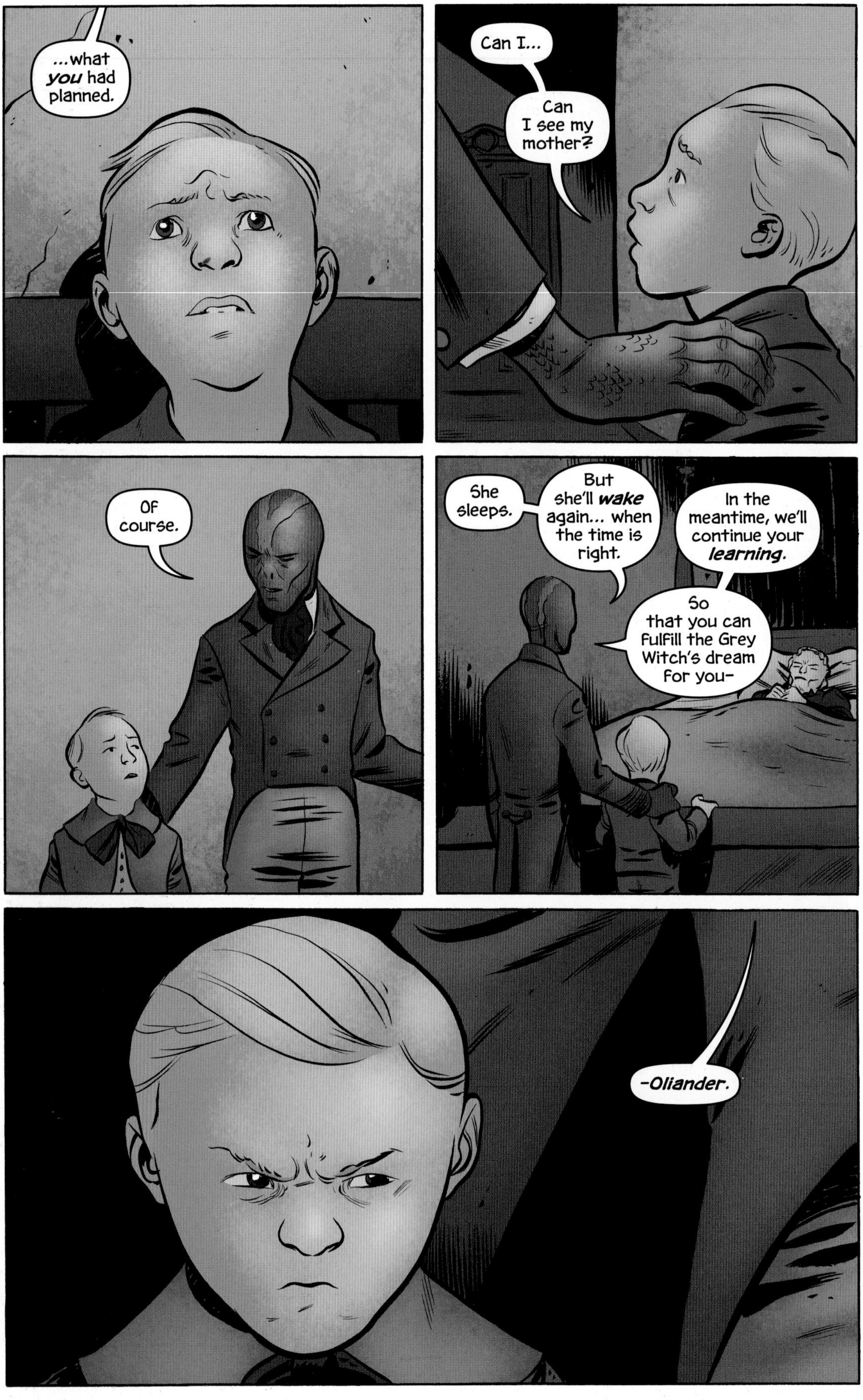
...what *you* had planned.
Can I...
Can I see my mother?
Of course.
She sleeps.
But she'll *wake* again... when the time is right.
In the meantime, we'll continue your *learning*.
So that you can fulfill the Grey Witch's dream for you-
-Oliander.

THE SIXTH GUN

ADVENTURE CONTINUES...

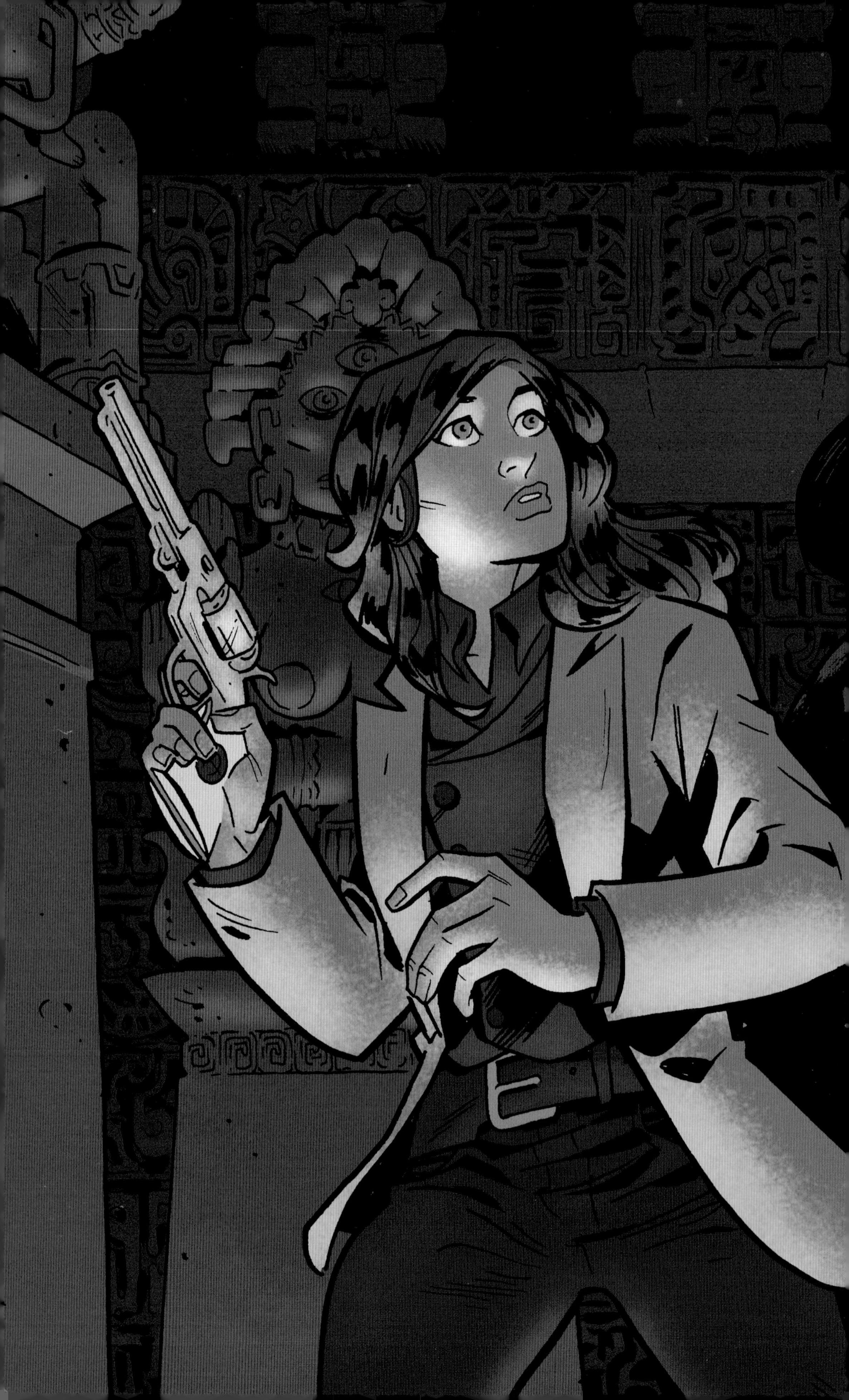

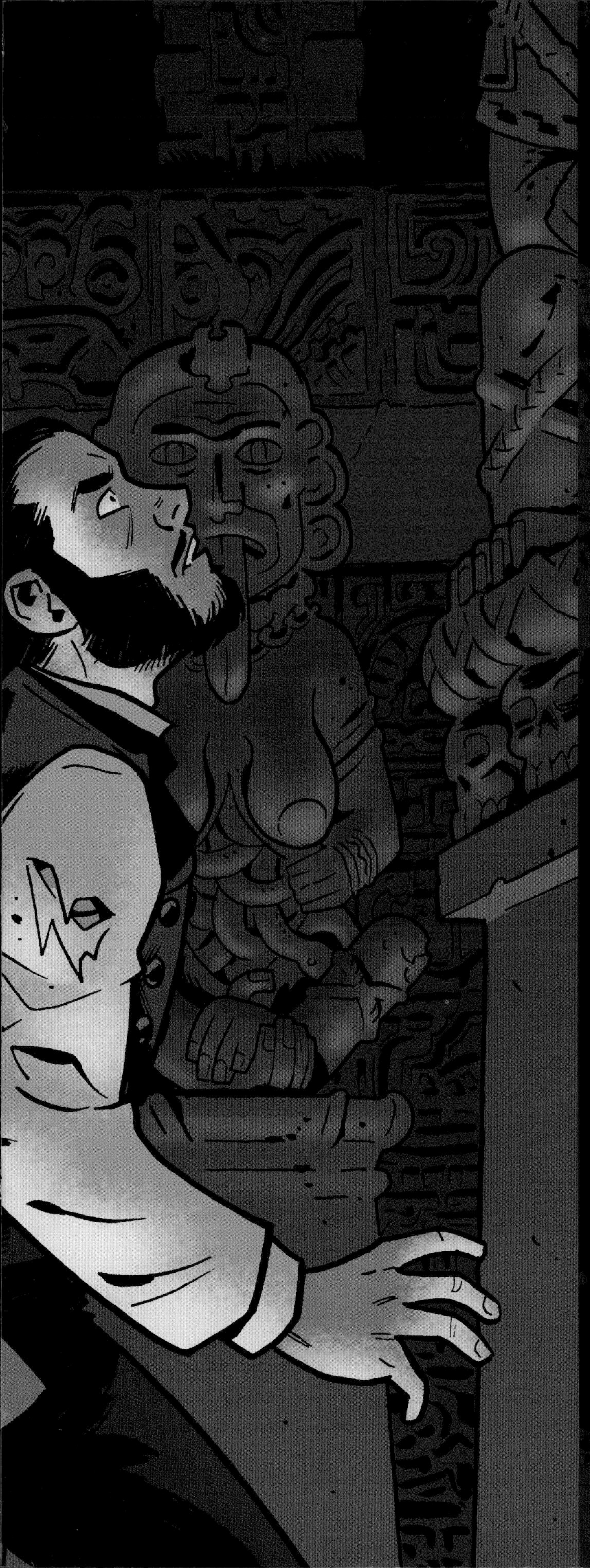

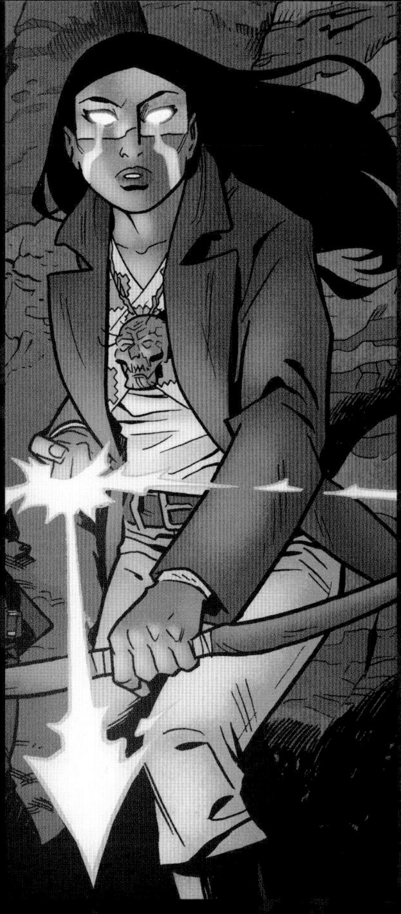

THE ADVENTURE CONTINUES EVERY MONTH!

The Six have fallen into the wrong hands! The Grey Witch prepares to unleash Hell on Earth and remake reality in her own image. To fulfill her ghastly ambitions, she has prepared a terrible sacrifice.

But Becky, Drake, and Screaming Crow stage a desperate final attack in hopes of stopping Griselda. They have lost many friends in the battle to control the Sixth Gun, but their most shocking losses are still ahead of them.

Don't miss a single exciting issue and follow the continuing adventures of Drake Sinclair, Becky Montcrief, and whoever is still alive! Ancient spirits stir, the powers of the Sixth Gun expand, and both the living and the dead grow restless. Available at finer comic book shops everywhere!

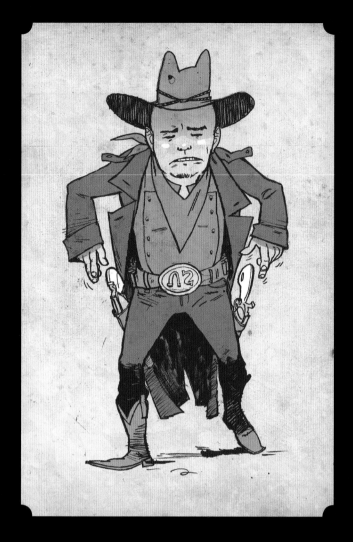

Cullen Bunn is the writer of comic books such as *The Sixth Gun*, *The Damned*, and *The Tooth* for Oni Press. He also writes *Fearless Defenders*, *Venom*, and *Deadpool Killustrated* for Marvel Comics.

In addition, he is the author of the middle reader horror novel, *Crooked Hills*, and the collection of short fiction, *Creeping Stones and Other Stories*.

He has fought for his life against mountain lions and performed on stage as the World's Youngest Hypnotist. Buy him a drink sometime, and he'll tell you all about it.

His website at www.cullenbunn.com.

You can find him on Twitter at @cullenbunn.

Author portrait illustrations by Jason Latour. jasonlatour.com

Brian Hurtt got his start in comics working on Greg Rucka's *Queen & Country*. This was followed by art duties on several projects including *Three Strikes*, *Queen & Country: Declassified*, and Steve Gerber's critically acclaimed series *Hard Time*.

In 2006, Brian teamed with Cullen Bunn to create the Prohibition-era monster-noir sensation *The Damned*. The two found that their unique tastes and storytelling sensibilities were well-suited to one another and were eager to continue that relationship.

The Sixth Gun is their sophomore endeavor together and the next in what looks to be many years of creative collaboration.

Brian lives and works in St. Louis, Missouri.

He is online at brihurtt.com.

Find him on Twitter at @brihurtt.

Illustration by Tyler Crook

Mr. Tyler Crook is an American artist living in the 21st century. For twelve years he lived in an unlit cubicle making art for sports video games. This left him bearded and almost completely translucent. Then in 2011, he struck gold, *comic book gold*, with the release of *Petrograd*, an original graphic novel he illustrated and which was written by Philip Gelatt and published by Oni Press. He is survived by his wife and many pets, but he's not dead... yet. In fact, he is currently very busy working on *B.P.R.D. Hell on Earth* for Dark Horse Comics.

Visit him on the Internet at their home at www.mrtylercrook.com.

Find him on Twitter at @mrtylercrook

Bill Crabtree's career as a colorist began in 2003 with the launch of Image Comic's *Invincible* and *Firebreather*. He was nominated for a Harvey Award for his work on *Invincible*, and he went on to color the first 50 issues of what would become a flagship Image Comics title.

He continues to color *Firebreather*, which was recently made into a feature film on Cartoon Network, *Godland*, and *Jack Staff*.

Perhaps the highlight of his comics career, his role as colorist on Oni Press' *The Sixth Gun* began with issue 6, and has since been described as "like Christmas morning, but with guns."

Find him on Twitter at @crabtree_bill.

ALSO AVAILABLE...

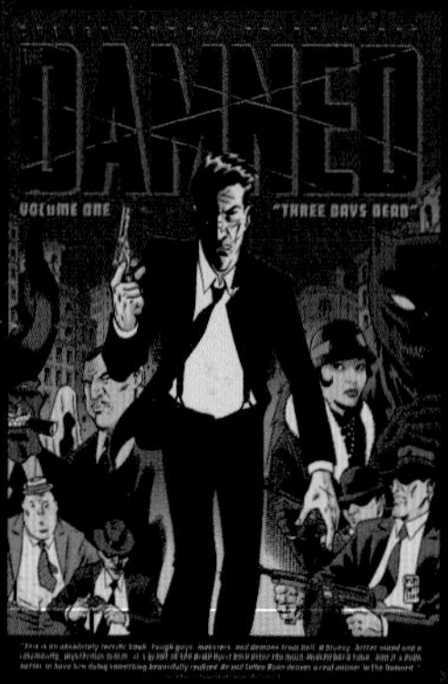
DAMNED
VOLUME ONE
"THREE DAYS DEAD"

THE DAMNED, VOLUME 1:
THREE DAYS DEAD
BY CULLEN BUNN & BRIAN HURTT
160 PAGES • TRADE PAPERBACK
BLACK & WHITE
ISBN 978-1-932664-63-8

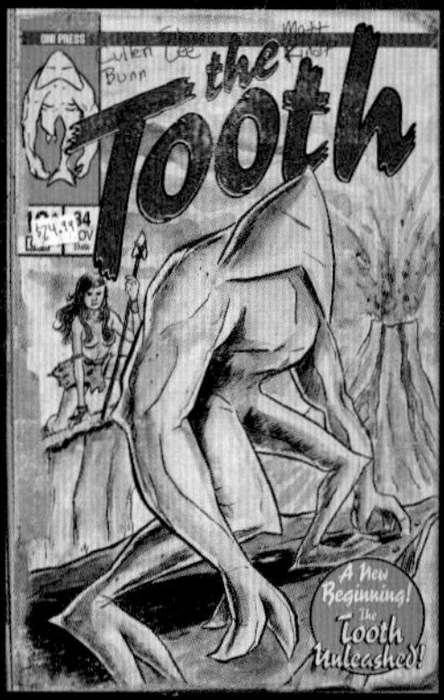
the Tooth
A New Beginning! The Tooth Unleashed!

THE TOOTH
BY CULLEN BUNN, SHAWN LEE
& MATT KINDT
184 PAGES • HARDCOVER
FULL COLOR
ISBN 978-1-934964-52-1

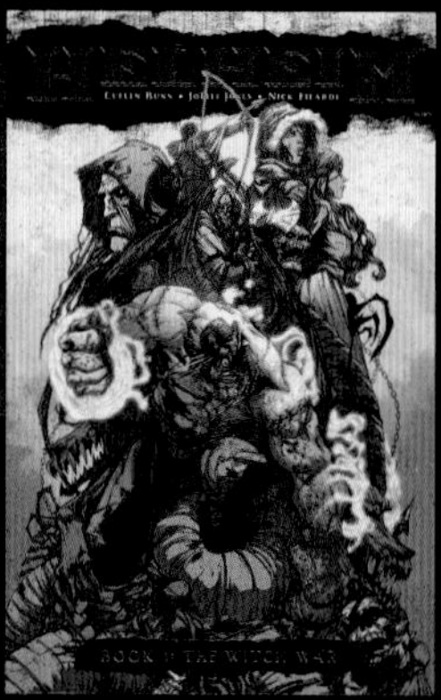

HELHEIM, VOL. 1:
THE WITCH WAR
BY CULLEN BUNN, JOËLLE JONES,
& NICK FILARDI
160 PAGES • TRADE PAPERBACK
FULL COLOR
ISBN 978-1-62010-014-1

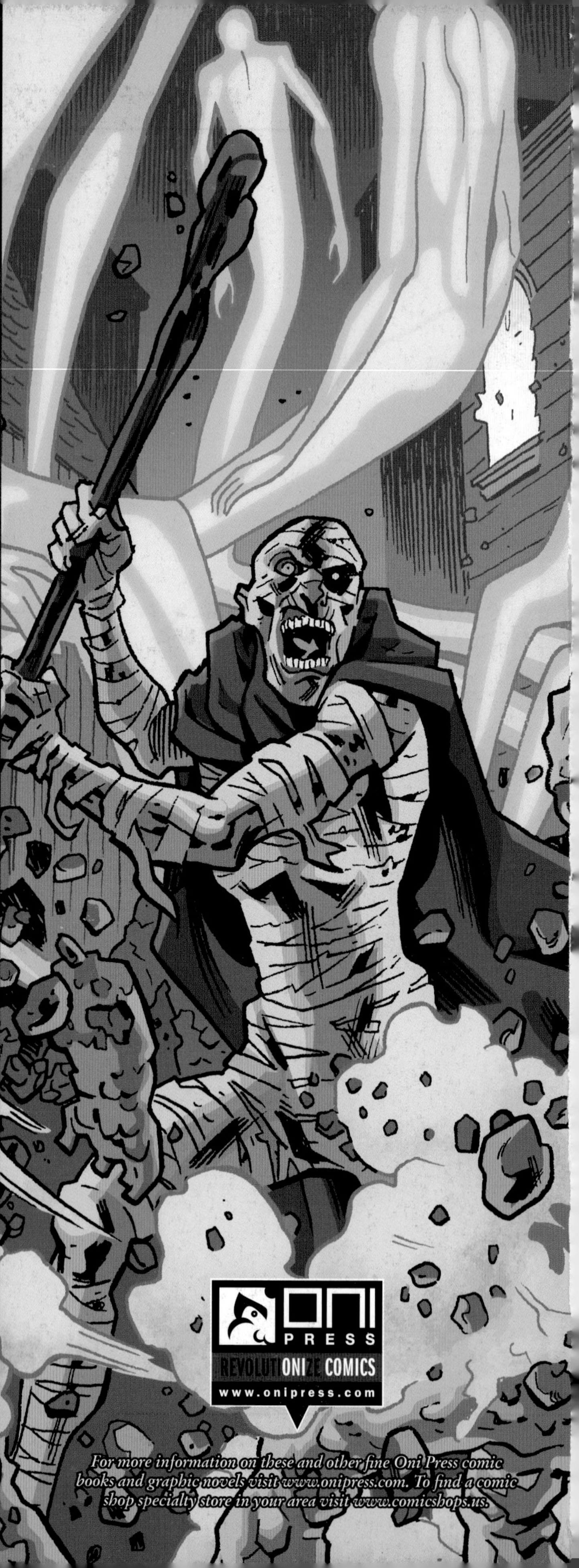
ONI PRESS
REVOLUTIONIZE COMICS
www.onipress.com

For more information on these and other fine Oni Press comic books and graphic novels visit www.onipress.com. To find a comic shop specialty store in your area visit www.comicshops.us.